SOUL STEALER

BOOK 1: NYTHAN

SHANE BOULWARE

THEORYbee

Cave

Artwork used images from Shutterstock.com and Flaticons.com.

Cover and jacket design by Damonza.com.

International Standard Book Numbers (ISBN)
Print Trade, ISBN: 978-1-7347063-0-7
Print Mass Market, ISBN: 978-1-7347063-1-4
Print Hardcover, ISBN: 978-1-7347063-2-1
E-book, ISBN: 978-1-7347063-3-8
Audiobook, ISBN: 978-1-7347063-4-5

Library of Congress Control Number (LCCN)
2020906818

Dear Reader,

Thank you for picking up *Soulstealer*!

This labor of love took me a little over three years to write and a year and a half to edit. I really like how it turned out, and I hope you do too. **A word of warning:** some scenes contain mature concepts, such as violence, immoral behavior, and mention of abuse. Sexual scenes and curse words are greatly subdued. **I would place it as a solid PG-13 and suitable for ages 16 and above.** You can read it for its action, or consider its more philosophical undertones. I wrote it in a way that enables you to enjoy either…or both.

If this novel turns out to be a success, then the already written sequel will be edited and published right away. While you read, I invite you to connect with any of the *Soulstealer* communities. The Social Media section has a list available to suit your preference.

Have fun and enjoy!

Shane

P.S. Try your hand at the Easter Eggs if you dare!

FIND THE SECRET EASTER EGGS!

There are **two** Easter Eggs in this book meant to be cracked for some special prizes!

1. In one of the 85 chapters, a **question** has been asked that you are meant to answer. Discover the question and send the answer to the email below!

2. Someone **declares** something that answers this question: What does both Nythan and the book's genre agree on? Send that declaration to the email below!

   If you have an answer to either Easter Egg, email
   EasterEgg@SoulstealerBook.com.

The first **ten** people to answer **either** correctly will have their name etched in the *Soulstealer* Hall of Fame and will receive a prize, ranging from naming a future character to a Funko Pop collector item.

You win a second prize if you answer both.

Good luck!

It would be **hugely** helpful to me as a self-publishing author if you **rate and post a review** of *Soulstealer* to Amazon, Goodreads, and wherever else you bought the book.

Your review will **help others** as they decide whether to read this book, and your rating will nudge it to the **#1 spot!** Thank you so much for your support!

Scan the QR codes below or type the link into your browser.

bit.ly/SoulstlrAmznRvw   bit.ly/SoulstlrGR

To Dad & Mom,
Love you both.

All my success is due to God. To Him be the glory.

SOUL STEALER

TABLE OF CONTENTS

"Really, the fundamental, ultimate mystery — the only thing you need to know to understand the deepest metaphysical secrets — is this: that for every outside there is an inside and for every inside there is an outside, and although they are different, they go together."

Alan Watts

"When I let go of what I am, I become what I might be."

Lao Tzu

"For with much wisdom comes much sorrow; the more knowledge, the more grief."

Solomon

PROLOGUE

Fortune favors the bold, but no one tells you she hates *the ambitious. It's the sort of lesson life lets you learn the hard way.*

I heard Thomas Jefferson once say that honesty is the first chapter in the book of wisdom. I don't lay claim to wisdom, but I can *manage the honesty. So, if I'm being honest, then you need to know that this isn't about a hero riding in to save the day. Nor is it a story of soulmates and true love.*

This is a story…about failure.

As much as I want it to be about sunshine and roses, you can't escape those lessons life wants you to learn. But if there's a silver lining anywhere in all this, it's that big things have small beginnings. One spark of hope can light a fire that burns the lies away. The truth has a funny way of setting people free like that.

To be honest…I'm not sure you should've come, but I'm glad you're here.

CHAPTER 1
ALL GOOD THINGS...

Nythan Dwienz scrunched his eyebrows as he inspected his cadet uniform lying on the bed. He stood a lean five feet, six inches, weighing in at 140 pounds. His buzzcut made his pale figure look like Ed Norton in *American History X*. Nythan stepped back, gazing at the creased dress shirt. He then looked down at four instruction books lying evenly spaced on the bed, all flipped open to pages of photos, diagrams, and highlighted paragraphs. Nythan picked up the one turned to a picture of a uniform and held it beside his own.

Nythan smiled. "Perfect match."

He jumped as a sharp crack resonated down the hall, and he stared through the open door.

Juuuuust ignore it, he thought.

His friend Pamela had left her house in his care for a few days while she visited her family in New England. When Pamela had shown him around the place, she told him that the county considered her 1910 residence historic. The high ceilings, wood paneling, and faded marble floors gave the place a stately feel. But the random sounds of the old house shifting on its pier and beam foundation made him paranoid about the walls coming down around him.

Nythan set the textbook down and neatly squared it against the rest.

Returning his attention to his uniform, he used a pair of small scissors to trim frayed strands of thread from his shoes. A high-pitched creak echoed from the hallway, and he again turned toward the door. That noise didn't sound like the groaning of walls or the strain of the ceiling. A slow panic twisted Nythan's stomach into knots.

He shook himself and sighed. *I wish this house would just…stop.* He strode over to the open door, gave it a forceful push closed and pressed the lock button. *Better safe than sorry.*

Nythan finished going over his uniform, scanning up and down until he was sure that not even the tiniest blemish remained. He then scanned one of his highlighted books to confirm the measurements of his medals. As a cadet in the U.S. Air Force Reserve Officer Training Corps at the University of Central Florida, he spent a great deal of time preparing for all the knowledge tests and uniform inspections.

Nythan swelled with pride as he hung up the uniform on the closet door, snapping to rigid attention in front of it. "FLIGHT, TENCH-HUT! DRESS RIGHT, HESS!"

He relaxed, appraising the flat pockets and razor-sharp creases. "There's no way we're going to fail this time."

Nythan cast a worried look at the door, sighing before he grabbed the doorknob. He peeked through the crack as the door opened.

Stop being stupid, Nythan chastised.

He stole a glance down either side of the long, narrow, beige hallway for reassurance. One end led to the master bedroom. The other led to a dead-end wall with an open doorway leading to the dining room on the left and a single-step stair descending into the living room on the right.

Nythan stepped into the hall and closed the door behind him. He hustled inside the bathroom next to his room and shut that door too, only relaxing when he heard the *snap* of the lock button as he pushed it in with his thumb.

CHAPTER 2

THE FIRST

Nythan came out of the shower, shaking droplets of water from his body like a wet puppy. His stomach growled as he dried off and got into a pair of shorts.

Oops, he thought. *Forgot dinner.*

He walked down the hall and turned toward the living room on his way to the kitchen when another high-pitched creak sounded behind him. Eyes widening, he whirled and looked across the hallway, where he saw a wiry man in the dining room fumble with and drop a platter of Pamela's finery.

The intruder yelled, "Don't move! Don't move!" and ripped a knife from a worn leather sheath clipped to his sweatpants. He rushed Nythan.

Nythan's whole body seized for a split second, then he lurched backward.

Forgetting the step-down behind him, he tumbled into the living room. He scrambled to one knee as the trespasser swung the knife over his head and whipped it down at Nythan's shoulder. Nythan raised both hands to block the weapon, and the descending dagger sliced long and deep into his lower right forearm. He groaned in pain and grasped the man's bony knuckles on the knife hilt with his left hand to keep the weapon from cutting deeper.

"I said…don't move!" his attacker snarled, trying to saw the blade into Nythan's arm.

The edge freed itself from his forearm as he threw himself backward. The burglar and his knife came crashing down on top of him. This time, Nythan grabbed for the intruder's wrists, stopping the spiked tip a few inches from his chest. Sweat ran down the burglar's face, a drop falling on Nythan's forehead.

Nythan squirmed to keep the dagger away, but it didn't dissuade the blade's course. His face contorted, teeth gritted, as the edge came ever closer. A millimeter of the knife's point pierced Nythan's left chest muscle, then burrowed further. It felt like a thousand tiny fire ants gnawing on that one spot.

Nythan's face twisted into pure rage in a last-ditch effort to thwart his attacker. *To quit is to die!*

The intruder grunted and pressed down harder. Both he and Nythan locked eyes as the knife slid in deeper. Nythan gasped and cried out. His lungs tightened in his chest.

Suddenly, his assailant shuddered, eyes rolling into the back of his head. A silver gas exited his nostrils and traveled into Nythan's hyperventilating mouth. The man's grip on the knife released as his body slumped onto Nythan. An explosion of energy filled Nythan to the brim, and he yanked the blade out of his chest. He thrust the corpse off him, kicking as much distance as he could between himself and the body. Blood seeped from Nythan's chest and spurted from his forearm.

He started to retch, but then only burped. Traces of the ethereal mist floated out before dissipating. Nythan's attention fell back on his assailant's unmoving body as a prickly sensation washed through him.

What the hell just happened? he thought.

CHAPTER 3

UNNATURAL

Mmmmmmmm, I made it once again.

Nythan's eyes widened, darted all around, then fell on the still figure in front of him. His eyes registered the sight of a dead person, but his brain offered no explanation. The intruder had just…died. Nythan got up off the ground and stood motionless for several heartbeats, unsure of what to do next.

The police, he thought, *I should be calling the police.*

Yes, the police. Call them.

The deep, throaty words—a voice not his own—echoed through his thoughts. He got up, stepped over the corpse, and staggered toward his room. His hand kept slipping off the blood-slicked wound as he clenched his forearm. A raging survival instinct filled him, and his clumsy attempt to juggernaut through his bedroom door ended in a painful thud. Nythan fumbled with the handle, leaving sticky, crimson fingerprints all over the bronze knob.

He stumbled toward his bed and then banged into the nightstand. Nythan's trembling fingers picked up his phone and thumbed the emergency icon.

Good thing I don't need to remember my passcode, Nythan thought.

Of coursssssssse, what a good thing.

The unfamiliar growl caused Nythan to squint as he tapped three numbers and hit dial. The operator picked up on the first ring.

"Nine-one-one, what's your emergency?"

"I've—I've been...attacked," Nythan stuttered.

"Okay, where are you?"

"Oviedo, over on Lockwood Boulevard—"

"Standby while I transfer you," the operator replied, clicking the phone on hold.

"Why would you need to tr—"

"Where're you located, sir?" a new operator asked.

"This...my friend's house. Just hurry up, I'm bleeding badly."

"I need your address so I can direct emergency personnel."

"I can't...reh-remember. Right now."

"Do me a favor and turn on the Location function on your phone. We'll trace your call from here."

His breathing became more labored as he managed the task. "Okay."

"Where's your attacker?"

"I think he's dead."

And what a delicious death it was.

CHAPTER 4

AN UNFAMILIAR SOUND

Nythan awoke in the intensive care unit the next day. When the doctor came in, she told him he had lost so much blood that her team didn't know if he'd survive. Something about his ulnar artery getting sawed in half, requiring a four-hour surgery.

He flexed his fingers as she left, noticing a small amount of resistance but experiencing next to no pain. Rather, it felt like he wanted to bench press a car. He attributed the odd sense of elation to the tubes of morphine pumping into his veins.

I grow hungry.

Nythan rubbed his temple with his left hand, then pressed the call button. A frizzy-haired nurse strode in, her muscled frame stretched her fitted scrubs to their limits.

"Yes, *Nee*-thin?" she asked, peering at him.

"*Nigh*-thin," he corrected her. "Do you have any of those boxed lunches available?"

Not good enough.

Nythan winced. His nurse gave a half attempt at a smile. "I'll be right back," she responded as she left the room.

He let out a sigh as he laid back into his pillow, staring up at the tiled ceiling. The bizarre showdown between himself and his attacker kept replaying in his mind. *I got lucky*, Nythan told himself.

Luck had nothing to do with it.

The guttural, baritone words grated on his mind. He kept rubbing his temple, hoping to massage the uncomfortable sensation away.

Five minutes later, the nurse returned with a boxed lunch. Two men came in behind her, each sporting a gun and badge on their belts. One of them stood tall and lanky; he had a bushy, red mustache that drooped at the ends. His partner was a stout, clean-shaven character with a frown.

The nurse placed his lunch on the tray attached to his hospital bed. "Nythan, these two police officers came here to speak with you. Are you feeling okay?"

Nythan nodded.

The nurse pursed her lips and left the room without looking back.

Nythan acknowledged the two gentlemen with a small wave. "Hello, officers."

"Good afternoon, Mr. Dwienz," the lanky detective said, his mustache twitching. "I'm Detective Lewis, and this is Detective Rodriguez. We're with the Oviedo Police Department. We'd like to ask a couple of questions if you're feeling up to it."

Nythan tried to sit up but stopped as a sudden agony jolted across his chest. *I guess I spoke too soon about there being no pain.*

"Okay," Nythan replied. His stomach gurgled as he flipped open the boxed lunch. He rummaged around and pulled out a dark red apple. He took a bite of the apple, then twisted his mouth at the bitter taste.

He set it back into the box. *Must've gone bad.*

Nythan looked up and found the detectives staring at him. He realized he'd already forgotten their names and felt himself wither under their gaze. "What happened to the burglar?"

"The assailant passed away," said the stout detective. "Could you help us determine your frame of mind by telling us when your birthday is?"

"It'd really help if I knew how he died."

"How would that help?" Stout crossed his bulky forearms together.

Nythan's lower lip quivered. "Because I can't stop thinking about it. Who he was, why he was there, and why he just…fell over."

Lanky put his hand on Stout's shoulder, giving him a split-second glance.

"Nythan, he was on probation after serving time for burglary and aggravated assault. The medical examiner believes he died of a heart attack," Lanky said.

Hahahahahahahahahaha!

Nythan nodded, rubbing his left eye.

Lanky took a step closer. "Nythan, we're here to support you. We need to understand what happened. Can you help us do that?"

I'll help them understand in ways they can't possibly *imagine.*

A brief flash of anger at the detectives came over Nythan before remorse engulfed him. The conflicting emotions caught him by surprise. His attention zipped around the room. "Sure."

This must be what it feels like to go crazy, he thought.

You have it backwards.

Nythan froze, then jerked his head. He struggled to breathe. Stout and Lanky gave him puzzled looks. One of them said something, but Nythan's ears could only process a soft ringing noise.

This is what it feels like to awaken, wretch.

Nythan paled. *What's happening? What do I keep hearing?*

I am you…but better. You have been restored.

"Restored to what?" Nythan said aloud.

CHAPTER 5
WITHIN ME, IT DWELLS

Nythan snapped back to reality as his nurse shined a bright light into his eye.

"He's still in a state of shock. He needs rest," she said, gesturing the detectives toward the door.

Lanky nodded. "Nythan, before we go, what'd you mean when you said, 'Restored to what?'"

"I don't know. I can't seem to focus."

Stout cut in, pushing his glasses further up the bridge of his nose. "Alright, Mr. Dwienz, we *will* be back."

Lanky frowned at Stout as they turned and left the room.

"How're you feeling?" his nurse asked.

Unsatisfied.

"Exhausted. It's hard to focus my mind on anything."

Weakness.

"Try to get some rest," she told him.

"Has my dad come?" Nythan asked.

"No. We tried calling but had to leave a voicemail."

"Okay." Nythan lowered his eyes. *No surprise there.*

"Is there someone else we can call? Your mom, another guardian?"

Nythan shook his head. "My mom died a long time ago."

"Oh. I'm sorry." She stood twiddling her thumbs for a few seconds, made to speak, then closed her mouth and walked out of the room. As soon as she shut the door, Nythan closed his eyes.

Stop talking, Nythan demanded.

You are only talking to yourself, wretch.

You're not *me,* Nythan told the voice.

Are you sure? Many people would argue that when someone talks inside your head, it's only you.

Most haven't seen other people keel over after some sort of mist is sucked out of their body.

Mmmmmmmm. I get ravenous thinking about it.

Stop it, Nythan pleaded. *Stop thinking like a crazy person.*

Nythan didn't understand what was going on. Was he talking to himself? Was he possessed? The hairs on the back of his neck stood as something stirred in the darkest recess of his mind. Something that his own consciousness didn't recognize.

A bead of sweat rolled down Nythan's face. *That supernatural stuff only exists in movies. How could something else be talking inside my head?*

He threw off the covers, wincing in pain. Even with the cold air greeting his body, he still felt just as warm as if he were draped in several blankets.

Too many questions, not enough answers.

I have the answers.

Nythan crossed his arms. *If you really* are *me, then you* don't *have the answers.*

You have the answers as well; they're in front of your face.

Then why don't I know?

Because you don't want *to know.*

That last thought sent a chill down Nythan's spine. The scene from *A Few Good Men* where Jack Nicholson shouts, "You can't handle the truth!" came to mind. His other self, if that's what it was, had raised an awkward point. Did he truly want to know what had kept him alive?

Nythan wanted to distract his mind from the question, so he took the unfinished box lunch and tore into the individually wrapped peanut butter sandwich. He chomped into the food and immediately spewed it back out.

"What the…?" Nythan grimaced and spat specks of the PB&J onto his gown.

He focused on his hunger, then took another bite of the foul-tasting sandwich. This time, Nythan forced himself to chew and swallow until nothing remained.

CHAPTER 6

OF SOUND MIND

Nythan sat in his Monday macroeconomics course, doing his best to pay attention. He had to engage all the willpower at his disposal to resist clawing his hair out. Ever since his release from the hospital on Thursday, what he identified as his *other self* wouldn't stop talking.

I don't speak by myself.

Nythan put his finger up against his temple. *And apparently, it reads minds as well.*

I am your *mind, wretch. There is no difference.*

"Whatever," he mumbled. The person next to him glanced in his direction. Nythan didn't know what the thing was or what it wanted, but he had resigned himself to the fact that the voice wasn't something he had imagined.

You know what I want. I require something.

Something I won't give, Nythan answered. He pressed against his stomach, which made all manner of gurgles.

It is inevitable; my hunger is insatiable. Give me what I want, or you'll be destroyed.

Nythan balled his hands into fists. *Is that a threat? I can handle threats.*

Not this kind of threat, you can't.

Nythan didn't know how to manage this new menace, but he put on a calm front for the outside world. He rolled the dice every time he ate; each meal tasted rotten, if it had any taste at all. Instead, the pit of his stomach throbbed every time he looked at someone. He felt an inexplicable yearning to repeat the unexplainable event that had caused his attacker's sudden death.

It's as simple as breathing in and breathing out. Nothing to it.

Nythan snarled. *Except I almost die in the process.*

But the benefits last a lifetime.

What benefits?

Don't you remember how magnificent you felt after our first feast?

Nythan shuddered as his mind recalled the prickly feeling.

You'll get used to the uncomfortable part. After that, there isn't anything left but to enjoy the euphoria of devouring a soul.

Nythan made a small choking sound, his face contorting into an expression of pure disgust and alarm. His professor paused her lecture.

"Yes, Mr. Dwienz?"

"Nothing, ma'am."

"I would appreciate it if you'd return to Planet Earth," she smiled gently.

"Yes ma'am," Nythan replied, his face turning a deep red.

Keep it together, wretch, lest anyone suspects.

Nythan ground his teeth together. *No one is going to suspect me of stealing someone's soul. This isn't a science fiction book. Besides, that wasn't what happened.*

Then what happened?

When I figure it out, I'll let you know.

Take your time. We have your whole life to understand it.

Nythan hoped he wouldn't be tortured for that long. He wanted this other self to just…go away and be someone else's problem. He had kept a written plan of what he'd do by the time he graduated college, a plan that did *not* include a homicidal rampage.

He wondered if he should see a shrink, but after a moment, he thought better of the notion. *They'll call me a schizophrenic and end up writing a book about it.*

Nythan's eyes went wide. What if the military found out? They'd stamp him unfit for duty, and all his plans would be lost. He'd never get his commission, never get to deploy, and never have a shot at making general. Nythan pinched himself in a futile attempt to wake from what seemed a living nightmare. No luck.

Nythan narrowed his eyes. *I'll have to do it myself.*

CHAPTER 7

RELENTLESS

Nythan made his best attempt to eat a rancid-tasting chicken sandwich as he walked to his next class. A guy ambled past in the other direction.

Him.

He passed a girl rolling by on a longboard.

Her.

Nythan stopped to press the button on a water fountain as two tall women wearing their Greek letters sashayed by.

Them too.

He swished the terrible taste out of his mouth and bared his teeth against the ice-cold water. Nythan flinched as his body shivered and his brain numbed. He didn't drink the water, because even the flavor of *that* sickened him. If only his other self would stop prodding him to satisfy its hunger.

Not my hunger, our *hunger.*

Nythan trashed his half-eaten sandwich before reaching up to clutch his scalp. *Shut...UP!*

The other voice made a deep, putrid chuckle that sounded like a kid with bronchitis. Nythan resisted the urge to scream, and it took him several minutes to gather himself and continue his journey.

He heaved a sigh of relief as he reached his detachment building and bathed in the familiarity of other students walking by in their decorated uniforms.

You don't belong here anymore.

Nythan ignored the comment and walked to his usual chair. As he touched the desk, a cold wave washed over him and transformed the place from familiar to foreign. His classmates' smiles repulsed him, their jokes didn't make him laugh, and the entire class became unimportant. Nythan had the feeling that he'd overstayed his welcome. He snapped his fingers in front of his eyes a few times, rousing himself from the distracting thoughts.

You are meant for far greater.

Nythan scowled. *That's ego talking.*

Call it what you like, but there is no denying that this chapter of your life has come to an end.

I can and I will. I have to graduate and get my commission. I'm going to be a general.

You're a lion who's convinced it's a sheep. You don't even realize *the absolute power at your fingertips. If only you'd grasp it, you would change this world forever.*

This supervillain nonsense grated on Nythan's nerves. He *almost* hoped the other voice came from a real demon. He could at least blame a demon for spewing clichéd omens of doom.

One can hope, wretch.

CHAPTER 8

NAME, RANK, AND SERIAL NUMBER

The captain at the front of the room went through a lecture on the air campaign in Vietnam. Nythan rubbed his growling belly as a cramp formed.

"Operation Linebacker II resulted in significant damage to the North Vietnamese infrastructure. It was a concentrated effort by the Nixon Administration to pressure the North Vietnamese government into signing an accord with South Vietnam. Although successful…"

The captain's voice droned as Nythan struggled to stay focused.

So many wasted souls. Souls that could have been donated to a good cause, like ours.

Nythan shuddered. *I wasn't even alive then, you disgusting* thing.

So much wasted opportunity.

Damn, you're annoying.

"After the Tet Offensive, Americans lost their will to continue the war. Although the US scored a tactical victory over the North Vietnamese government, the Viet Cong had successfully sapped America's interest in supporting South Vietnam."

I have never been to Vietnam. Want to go?

Nythan frowned as he recalled a Reddit video showing throngs of death-defying pedestrians running across a street full of zooming cars. *Maybe if I wanted to die by—*

Without warning, someone roared, "Room, tench-HUT!" Nythan stumbled out of his seat and made himself rigid. In marched his detachment commander, Colonel Wutnatszlay, swinging his fists as he walked.

"G'morning everyone. Take 'r seats," the colonel snapped in a terse drawl. Everyone sat down at attention, but Nythan moved his eyes to the colonel. The cramp in Nythan's stomach made him want to double over.

The colonel surveyed the class, narrowing his eyes. "As you may b'ware, our detachment has 'n 'nspection in a fe' days," he said, exercising his habit of combining words and syllables.

Mmm. I can feel *his aura. What a feast that would be.*

Nythan's nails grated the seams of his pant legs. *Shut up.*

Look at him, so full of passion. Don't tell me you aren't thinking about it too.

"…so if yuh see someone who yuh've not seen b'foah, don' jus' let 'em wand' a 'roun' by 'emselves. Talk with 'em, make sure they ge' tuh where they're goin'," the colonel continued.

Nythan's face contorted into rage. *Shut the hell up!*

"We've some prep'ration tuh do, which's why ah'm heah. Cadet Cierro, Ah'm naming yuh the cadet 'n charge of cleanin' the cadre offices. Have 'em cleaned by t'marruh."

What a beautiful addition to our collection he would be.

"Yes, sir," Cadet Cierro replied.

I'm going to find a way to permanently shut you up.

"Cadet Dwienz, I'm namin' yuh the cadet 'n charge of cleanin' th' lounge. Have it cleaned by t'marruh as well."

You can't silence your own conscience.

Fine, a conscience as—

"Cadet Dwienz! Di'ja heah me?" the colonel shouted. Nythan snapped back to reality.

Uh oh, now you're in trouble.

"Yes, sir," Nythan blurted. *F. OFF.*

"I don' think yuh wa' listenin'. What wuh yuh thinking about, cadet?"

"Nothing, sir," Nythan managed.

"Not good enough, cadet. I'm sure the whole class would like tuh heah 'bout what yuh thought was mo' 'mportant than listenin' tuh yuh Detachment Commanduh'."

Better think on your feet.

SHUTUP! "I CAN'T F***ING THINK!"

Dead silence. Nythan's eyes widened as he realized he'd said those last words out loud. The colonel roared at Nythan to stand at attention and showered him with a litany of curses and insults.

Ahhh...what a sweet sound of beauty that is. The man has so much energy.

"GET YUH A** IN M' OFFICE, NOW!" the colonel screamed.

CHAPTER 9

DÉJÀ VU

Nythan stood at attention in Colonel Wutnatszlay's office. The man had spent the last ten minutes barking at Nythan about disrespecting a superior officer, degrading the Core Values, and something having to do with trampling the memory of America's forefathers. The colonel towered over Nythan, whose eyes were locked ahead onto the colonel's chest a mere foot away.

"...AND AH'LL BE DAMNED IF I ALLOW SUM SKINNY A** CADET TO BECOME 'N OFFICER 'N THE WORLD'S GREATEST AIR FORCE. NOT 'N MY WATCH, YUH SUMB****!" The colonel's face pulsed crimson; Nythan wondered if the man's head would explode from all the blood rushing to it.

C'mon...c'mon, c'mon. Give me more!

Nythan continued staring straight ahead. *What the hell are you saying?*

"DISRESPECT. BLATANT DISREGARD OF AUTHORITY. NEGLIGENCE. INSUBORDI-F***ING-NATION. HOW M'NY OF THOSE QUALITIES D 'YUH THINK I WANT 'N MAH AIR FORCE? HOW M'NY?" The colonel stopped yelling and stared at Nythan.

Nythan held his breath. "Sir, do...do you want me to—"

"YES!"

Damn, so close!

"N…n…none, sir?" Nythan sputtered, confused by both the colonel and his other self.

"WOND'FUL 'DUCTION SKILLS YUH'VE THEAH, SHUHLOCK HOMES. THA'S RAHT: ZERO!" The colonel paused to catch his breath; beads of sweat peppered his face.

"Tell yuh what, I'll give yuh tuh the count uh thirty tuh recite the Airman's Creed, or else yuh ge' tuh hell out of my office and dun come back!" the colonel hollered.

Nythan wasted no time. "I'm an American Airman. I'm a warrior. I've ans—"

"I can't hear yuh, Cadet Dwienz. Yuh sounds like a scared li'l mouse!"

Nythan matched the colonel's volume. "I'M AN AMER—"

"LOUDER!"

I can almost taste him.

Nythan spewed the creed as fast as his lips would allow, talking so fast he began hyperventilating.

"I'M AN AMERICAN AIRMAN. I AM A WARRIOR. I HAVE ANSWERED MY NATION'S CALL. I'M AN AMERICAN AIRMAN…"

Nythan let out all his breath, exasperated. "My mission is to fly, fight, and—"

"I SAID LOUDER, D'YUH UNDA'STAN' WUH—" the colonel's tirade halted as he began to shake, his eyes rolling into the back of his head. Nythan backpedaled when he realized what had seized Colonel Wutnatszlay.

"Not again…no…not again," Nythan pleaded.

He tried to blow at the cloud, but the unnatural mist snaked out of the colonel's mouth and slithered in his direction. Nythan slammed into the rear wall in time for the vapor to weave its way into his mouth.

"Motherfu—" Nythan whimpered, "what *is* this?" The colonel stopped shaking and collapsed to the left, his skull striking the edge of a glass table with a sickening crunch.

The colonel's assistant knocked on the solid wood door as a mixture of euphoria and adrenaline flooded Nythan's body.

"Sir, is everything okay in there?"

The assistant opened the door and stopped as she noticed Nythan's confused sobs. Her eyes traced the zigzag pattern of the black and blue carpeted floor until she came across the colonel's body. Her screeching overpowered all other sounds.

CHAPTER 10

CORNERED

Nythan paced in an interrogation room at the police station.

Standard protocol my a**, Nythan thought, grimacing.

The police had escorted him from the college to the station, but only after the medics, who had arrived to examine the colonel, checked Nythan and lectured him on the importance of eating enough food. Either the three square meals he ate every day seemed to be bad for him in more ways than taste, or they did nothing for him at all. Both thoughts scared the daylights out of him.

You'll feel better once you eat my *food.*

Detective Stout came to question him again. Stout quizzed Nythan about where he had stood in the room and why he had made such an effort to distance himself from the late colonel. Nythan told him everything but omitted the ethereal mist for obvious reasons.

Stout crossed his arms. "How many feet were you from Colonel Wutnatszlay?"

"Maybe, like, two," Nythan replied.

"When he began having his seizure, as you described it, why didn't you try helping him?"

"I was scared."

"Why didn't you call for help?"

Nythan shrugged. "I...I don't...I don't know."

"When you backed away from Colonel Wutnatszlay, how fast were you going?"

"I don't know."

"How long did it take you to get to the wall?"

"A few seconds, I suppo—"

"And you didn't think to call for help?"

"I just...I was scared. I kinda froze."

They wouldn't believe you anyway.

Nythan pursed his lips. *Shut up, a**hole. Someone's dead because of me.*

Stout raised an eyebrow. "Did the colonel exhibit any unusual signs before falling?"

Because of us. We're in this together whether you like it or not.

Nythan scowled. *There is no we, it's just me.*

Stout leaned toward Nythan. "Can't give me the decency of an answer?"

Nythan sucked his teeth and looked up at Stout. "What was the question again?"

Stout hands clenched into softball-sized fists. "The colonel...any unusual signs before he collapsed?"

Good. You've finally accepted what happened and the part you played.

No, I'm not a killer...I don't accept that!

I'm afraid you'll have to, wretch.

"Mr. Dwienz?"

Nythan's shoulders drooped. *This can't be possible. These sorts of things don't just happen.*

But they did happen...twice. And you were the cause both times. As a gesture of good faith, I'll offer you a bit of advice. Ask the good detective if we're free to go.

"Dwienz!"

Nythan snapped out of his trance, throwing his arms out. "What?"

Stout made to speak, then stopped as he studied Nythan's forearm. "What happened to that cut you got?"

Nythan glanced at his arm. Sure enough, no trace of the thick, jagged cut between his stitches remained. He huffed, then looked up at Stout's disbelieving face. "Well, what about it? Am I free to go?"

Stout glared at him for several heartbeats before responding. "Get the hell out of here, Dwienz."

Nythan wasted no time in walking past him and out the door. Lanky leaned against the hallway wall opposite the interrogation room.

"Be careful out there, Nythan," Lanky offered with a wave of his hand.

"What's that supposed to mean?"

It's a threat.

"Only that people seem to be dying around you rather suddenly," Stout answered from behind Nythan. "Two people in a week." Nythan's face turned red with embarrassment; he couldn't meet Lanky's gaze as he walked away.

"See you around, Nythan," Lanky called out.

"Yeah," shouted Stout from within the interrogation room, "and try not to smoke anybody else for a while!"

Nythan hurried down the hallway and exited the police station. *Lord, please make these things go away.*

In that, there is no hope, wretch.

Nythan snarled. *I need a distraction.*

CHAPTER 11

RAVE NIGHT

Nythan hopped through the nightlife scene in Orlando until he settled on an EDM club playing earsplitting trap music. Sitting at a table near the dance floor, Nythan played with some glow sticks.

What are you doing?

Nythan continued connecting the pieces, making a pair of glasses. One of the tubes kept pulling out of the connector, but Nythan didn't care. After a few moments of fiddling with the makeshift glasses, he grabbed twin glow sticks and gave them a firm shake. Whenever the bass resonated, Nythan banged the table in front of him to the beat of the music, thrashing his body left and right.

You're wasting time.

Nythan dropped the sticks. He made his way through the crowd of bouncing ravers, stopping in front of the six-foot-tall speakers. The blast of the bass shook Nythan's whole body. Every *boom* felt like a bomb exploding in his eardrums. Nythan threw his head back and smiled.

I don't think this is healthy.

Nythan's smile faded. He couldn't drown his other self out or distract himself from his hunger.

Oh, so that's why we're here. Yeah, that isn't going to work.

Nythan sighed and made for the exit. *Maybe to get peace and quiet, I need peace and quiet*, he thought.

How poetic.

CHAPTER 12

A LONG WALK

Nythan enjoyed a pleasant stroll down Daytona Beach. He had experienced the fight of his life trying to get out of bed that morning. His body had launched a full-scale revolt at its lack of nourishment, even refusing to do a single pushup during his morning workout. Nothing he had eaten seemed to help, so Nythan had called it a day and skipped his classes. He forced his mind to the present by stopping every so often and wiggling his toes in the sand. The stars sparkled above while the moon hid from view. Nythan did his best to avoid thinking about anything at all, but this proved an impossible task.

He walked for the better part of two hours without his other self making so much as a peep. Nythan came to a stop and sat down on the beach, sticking his toes in the damp sand. He breathed in all the way, savoring the freshness of the air.

Finally, he thought. He slowly leaned until he rested against the wet sand, and he stared at the stars.

No words came to mind when he tried to describe the pure sense of relief that soothed him at that exact moment. The terrible events of the last eight days seemed like a distant fairy tale as Nythan started to count the twinkles up above. *Just how many stars* are *there?*

He envisioned the sun rising, the stars receding, and the noise of everyday life returning. Nythan's other self wouldn't be far behind, making his short-lived peace a torment.

"I need a fix," Nythan whispered. He figured his short career in the military had ended with his outburst in class. Before he shut it off, his phone had shown four missed calls from cadre and an unread text from a fellow cadet reading, "It wasn't your fault." The fear and shame Nythan felt made him unable to draft a reply.

"Stop thinking about it," Nythan whispered to himself.

A plan started to take shape in his mind. He'd research solutions in the morning, go to work the next day as per normal, and then continue his research in the evening. Nythan decided he'd do this every day until he could figure out what to do.

Classes be damned, Nythan thought, dismissing the instinctive protest at the thought of his B+ grades plummeting to Fs. Nythan let out an unexpected laugh at how fast his priorities had changed.

One day I'm worried about inspections, the next, a demon taking over my body.

CHAPTER 13

AN OLD HOPE

Nythan took a swig of orange juice, savoring the only thing he could find that tasted like itself. He thumbed through a month-old magazine in the waiting area of Nuessel's Angel Fingers, a massage therapy salon he worked at to fund his rent and college tuition. The wooden table creaked as Nythan's tireless foot pressed against it. He attributed the random twitch to his malnourishment. His empty stomach proved to be a living hell, managed only by drinking orange juice and consuming other acidic foods. He looked through the pages of the magazine, flipping to a picture of a snowy mountain and a tower, when a low-pitched bell reverberated throughout the room. Nythan dropped the magazine and ambled over to the reception desk to wait for someone to round the corner.

A beautiful young blond woman with an enormous sun hat and pink sunglasses strode over to the desk. She wore bright red lipstick, a white net sweater, and sweatpants.

"Good morning," she chirped.

A few seconds is all I need. No one would ever have to know.

Creep, Nythan thought, resisting the urge to roll his eyes.

"Morning," Nythan replied. "How may I help you?"

"I have an appointment with Angel Fingers at nine a.m.," she said, tapping Dr. Nuessel's physical therapy diploma displayed on the counter.

Nythan looked at his computer. The time read 9:45 a.m.

"Ma'am, your appointment was almost an hour ago."

The girl clasped her hands together, begging, "I know. I am *so* sorry. My dog would just *not* go potty. I couldn't leave him in the apartment. He'd make a *mess* of the place! Pleeeeease forgive me?"

At least she didn't give him one of the lame excuses he heard every day. Forgotten keys, traffic, an alarm that didn't go off, forgot the time, a schedule conflict. As ditzy as she seemed, Nythan wanted to believe her.

He did a quick scan of the schedule. It didn't show another appointment until after lunch, which left plenty of time for Dr. Nuessel to fit in a late arrival.

"Let me check with the doctor. I'll be right back," Nythan said.

The girl squealed with delight and jumped up and down a few times. "Thank you!"

Oh, my...pleeeeeeease. Please. This one.

Nythan imagined giving his other self the middle finger.

Oh, that's pleasant. Here I am trying to help the both of us, and this is how you repay me.

Nythan smirked at the small victory as he left the reception counter and went into the back to Dr. Nuessel's office. He found her doing updowns on a calf-raise block in a blouse and long skirt as she read from a tall stand. She used every spare moment to work on her physique.

"Yes?" she grunted as Nythan's was about to rap his knuckles on the door jamb.

"Ma'am, your nine o'clock is here, with apologies," Nythan said. "No other appointments until after lunch."

"Excellent." Dr. Nuessel leaned over and took a sip from her kombucha tea, eyeing him. "Have you been eating? Your face looks thin." Her strong Boston New England accent sounded like a whisper.

Nythan shrugged. "I can't hold my food down."

Dr. Nuessel resumed her calf raises. "Half a banana and a handful of soda crackers would be a good start. Top pantry door of the break room."

Nythan's sheepish gaze lingered on Dr. Nuessel's trim figure before he returned to the reception desk. He found the girl peering into the magazine he had put back down on the waiting room table. The girl skipped over to him, periodical in hand, looking at Nythan with big eyes.

Nythan gave her a smile. "Dr. Nuessel will see you now."

The girl breathed a sigh of relief. "Oh good. I was nearly ready to book a trip to this *perfect* getaway. A kind of monk resort where you go to '*discover* your inner *at-man*.'"

Nythan gave her an unenthusiastic smile. "Please follow me."

She beamed, leaving the magazine on the reception desk. He led her to one of the massage rooms where he gave her preparatory instructions and left her to get ready for Dr. Nuessel.

When he got back to his desk, Nythan pulled up the list of appointments that he needed to call. His mind drew his attention back to the opened magazine. Looking closer, he realized the tower protruded above a large monastic building. Below it, thumbnails showed a lush garden and an area with people sitting on mats.

Nythan read the caption: "Let the traveler fainting on his journey take rest under a tree which contains both fruit and shade. Find harmony with your inner Ātma." The description sounded profound, but the deeper meaning escaped him. Whatever it meant, it looked exactly like the kind of thing Nythan needed: a secluded place to find peace. At the bottom of the picture, in small print, he read, "Watwa Nayahut Ashram, India."

Hahahahahahaha. India's a loooooooong way. Expensive, too.

A pit formed in Nythan's stomach. His distaste for wasting those long hours to reach such a remote destination flared, but his hatred of his other self burned brighter. He brought up Google and searched Watwa Nayahut, then Googled last-minute, round-trip flights to India. His face fell.

"Three thousand bucks."

You'll never get that kind of cash.

Anger bubbled within Nythan as he closed his eyes. He crumpled the picture and bared his teeth. *I'm going to take you out, punk. There's a way to get there, and I'm gonna find it.*

We're looking for a lot more than that, wretch.

CHAPTER 14

THE ROAD TO ABSOLUTION

Nythan exited the auto-rickshaw and walked down a thin, beaten path of frozen grass. Remnants of a nighttime frost coated the ground in defiance of the fiery sun above. Some distance away stood his destination, the Watwa Nayahut Ashram, set against a backdrop of the white Himalayas.

This isn't going to work.

It worked once already, Nythan reminded his other self.

You know not what you do.

Sounds like I'm headed in the right direction then.

After tracking down an email address on the ashram's website, Nythan had exchanged messages with one of the caretakers. Once Nythan explained his financial situation and desire to seek inner peace, the caretaker had invited him to stay for free. Nythan had sold as many of his possessions as he could for a whopping $3,200 and stored what he couldn't sell in his car at Pamela's house. Then he booked a flight to New Delhi and traveled northward.

He took his time along the path to the ashram, enjoying the crisp, fresh air. When he got to the base of the stairs, Nythan trekked up and rapped on the door. He frowned at the crumpled picture he had torn from the magazine in Dr. Nuessel's office. He held it up to the entrance of the monastery.

"Hmm. It sure does *look* like the right place."

He scrunched his eyebrows and banged on the door, then tried the door handle. The door creaked open, drawing a smile from Nythan.

Your days are numbered, Nythan threatened.

My days are your days.

He stuck his head through to see a massive entry hall stretching fifty yards. His gaze took in the vast but simplistic architecture with massive pillars extending from the plain floor to the ceiling. Nythan saw a circular sandpit in the middle of the hall. A small skylight allowed the bright sun to shine down on the pit. A lone bald monk sat with his back to Nythan.

Nythan shut the door behind him, then strode twenty-five yards to the sitting figure. Not knowing what to do, Nythan thumped his chest and coughed. The figure didn't turn to acknowledge him, so Nythan walked into the pit and stopped in front of the person.

He observed that the guy had a slender V-shaped face, pruned eyebrows, and a nose ring. His hands were clasped together where his ankles crossed. Nythan sat down to emulate him but pulled his hands to his chest when they met scalding sand. He swiped layers of sand aside with his shoes until he reached a cooler layer.

Nythan sat and waited while the sun gradually warmed his face. Finally, the sitting man's lips curled into a smile. He spoke but didn't open his eyes.

"A troubled Ātma arrives." The smooth soprano voice embraced his ears, and he then realized that the voice belonged to a woman. The surprise made Nythan give a lopsided smile.

"Namas...te?" he said, stumbling through the one Hindi word he had learned via Google.

The woman bent forward, pressing her hands together in front of her chest with her fingers pointed upward. She opened her eyes, revealing amber irises that twinkled in the sunlight.

"I'm here to learn," Nythan said.

"We will see why you have come," the woman replied.

"So. What now?"

"You may do whatever your Ātma desires. We begin tomorrow at three in the morning."

Nythan's eyes widened in surprise, recalling how much his body fought him every time he got up before seven. The idea that he would relax and find peace at the ashram faded away. His doubt grew by the second, and he became quite certain he had made a mistake.

"Three a.m.?"

"Three in the morning should give us sufficient time for our activities. Come back here after the midday meal," the woman said, briefly pointing straight ahead before returning to her original pose.

He followed her gesture to another door on the far side of the hall. He blinked, then sighed. *Well, I'm here now. I didn't travel all this way to return empty-handed.*

Nythan got up, dusted sand from his pants, jumped out of the pit, and made his way to the other door at the far end.

CHAPTER 15

A DEAL WITH THE DEVIL

Nythan jerked awake as a deafening bell resounded throughout the monastery. Putting a pillow over his head didn't drown out the sound when it echoed a second time, and his aching body refused to continue lying on the rigid cot.

He groaned, got up, stepped outside, and stood with several other guests and monks on a candle-lit path that seemed to stretch into the darkness around a large garden area. The silhouette of a bell tower protruded from the center of the garden, hoisted a hundred feet into the air. Some of the other guests began voicing their complaints about waking at such an atrocious hour before the monks hissed them into silence.

Nythan received a white robe from one of the monks and went back inside his room to change. They were then led from the garden, through a dining hall, and into a spacious square area. Thin colorful mats and small handbells rested on the ground, and a litany of doors lined the four walls. There, the group spent the morning learning chants until the break of dawn. They were then returned to the garden, where Nythan rotated between sweeping floors and pathways, trimming plants, and changing out the candle lamps.

The rules of the monastery discouraged them from talking with other guests while performing their chores. No one fed him, and his ridiculous white robe had already tripped him three times. He hadn't imagined dealing with his inner demon under such conditions. Nythan played along with a big smile, though, because his other self had fallen silent ever since he started the morning group chant.

He patted his stomach, now the only thing left growling at him. *Easy there, tiger.*

When the midday bell rang, Nythan and the other guests looked up as a few dozen monks, dressed in bright orange, came and ushered them into the dining hall. A single long table with rustic benches dominated the room.

Nythan sighed at the vaulted ceiling. *Finally.*

The monks walked the length of the table. Each retrieved a small wooden bowl and spoon from a pile. They scooped a portion of rice, grabbed a piece of fruit, and poured themselves an herbal tea. When all of them were finished being served, the guests went to receive bowls of their own. Nythan sat down across from a rotund fellow with an untrimmed beard whose face showed his displeasure at the allotment of food.

"Are we—" the plump guy began.

"Shhhhhh!" several monks hissed from around the table.

Nythan took his wooden spoon and dug out a wad of rice, plunging it into his mouth. It took his body fifteen seconds to reject the food. He directed the vomit into the bowl.

"Shhhhhh!"

Nythan refused to look up to meet all the eyes he imagined were trained on him.

They cleaned their bowls, freeing Nythan to leave the hall and hurry to the sandpit, where the female monk had said she would wait. He stopped just outside the pit, wanting to avoid scalding his bare feet. She bowed once again, pressing her hands together, fingers pointed upward in front of her chest. Nythan did his best to imitate the gesture.

"This is the *Anjali Mudra*," she told him. "It is a gesture of greeting and respect."

She then got out of the sandpit, slid past Nythan, and walked into the dining room. Nythan raised an eyebrow as they passed a monk tidying up the pile of wooden bowls. *She could've just met me here.*

She took a door at the far back left hall, and they proceeded down an extended corridor with doorless meditation rooms. She entered one and seated herself cross-legged on the floor.

Nythan plopped down. "I need help."

"Who is asking the question?" the monk replied.

"Uhh…me?"

"Who is that?"

"Nythan. Nythan Dwienz."

"The Ātma known as Nythan Dwienz seeks improvement."

"Yes. Wait. What's an *Ought-maw?*"

"Your Ātma is your mask. The role Brahma portrays in this unfolding drama."

"Do you have an Ātma?"

"Of course. Everyone and everything has an Ātma."

"Who is *Bra-maw?*" Nythan quizzed.

"The Supreme self, or as you may call him, God. But, Nythan Dwienz, your Ātma seeks the impossible. Why does it think it needs to improve?"

"Not *improve,*" Nythan corrected. "Repair, fix, mend, revert back to its original form. Nothing even tastes right anymore."

"I see. Tell me about your need to mend yourself."

Finally, she asks the right question, Nythan thought.

"I have inside me something that will *not* leave. An evil of pure foulness that I must get rid of."

"Tell me more."

"It…it has the…" Nythan trailed off, unsure how to put it all into words. "This thing is talking to me from the inside. No one else can hear it, and I'm going crazy. It takes other people's souls; it's happened twice already. I get close to them and see this trail of mist that comes out of them and into me. They just…*die.* Their souls leave their bodies like they do in bad sci-fi movies."

The monk considered Nythan's words. After a time, she waved her arm. "Show me."

"*Show* you?"

"Yes. Show me the evil you claim dwells within."

"I don't know how," Nythan said. "It just happens."

You're lying. You have it figured out by now.

Nythan flinched. He thought he had willed his other self into silence.

Hahahahahahahahaha. You thought wrong, wretch.

"Show me when it *just happens*," the monk said.

"I can't."

"I cannot help someone who does not know how to help himself."

"I'm starting to wonder how you people help anyone at all."

The monk smiled. "We don't actually help anyone. We show them where the way is. They realize it for themselves."

"Then what am I doing here?"

"You traveled a long way to get here. Do you not know why you came?"

Nythan gave an exaggerated sigh. "I came here for peace, long-term peace."

"Your Ātma desires to achieve *moksha*, freedom, to free it from *saṃsāra*, the struggle."

"Okay, have it your way. My Ātma is in need of peace. Now how do I go about getting it?"

"The harder you try to obtain it, the further from your grasp it will be. I will attempt to explain how you may calm your Ātma, but I am unsure if this will give you peace," the monk said.

"Fine."

"You must first realize that everything is as it should be; nothing is out of place. Not the tiniest grain of sand or peculiar-looking building."

"Why's that?"

The monk gestured all around her. "Because Brahma wants to surprise itself and dreams it thus."

Nythan squinted. "I don't understand what this has to do with my problem."

"Let's say you were God and had the power to dream any dream you wished. You would dream all sorts of wonders and adventures for however long you wanted. Eventually, you would tire of these dreams and decide to play a new game, dreaming a dream in which you forget it is an illusion. You imagine you are billions of people, enjoying the show you created and leaving a myriad of surprises for you to discover. This is where we are now. Do you see?"

"Yes," Nythan said.

"You speak the correct words, but your eyes do not reflect understanding."

"That's right, I don't know how you can get from dreaming the world to my issue," Nythan retorted in frustration.

"Because there comes a point when Brahma must awaken from the dream."

He shrugged. "Okay, Brahma wakes up. That's how dreams end."

The monk smirked. "Why yes. That *is* how dreams end."

"I—" Nythan froze as he processed her response, then his eyes got big. "You can't possibly mean...*what*!? You're supposed to help me get *rid* of this thing, not *nurture* it."

A twinkle shone in the monk's eyes, and she smiled. "I recognize you, Shiva."

"I...are you...what the *hell*?" Nythan asked, raising his voice. "Does your brain comprehend that we're talking about *eating people's souls*?"

"It is impossible to take another Ātma. I look not at your label, but at your *Rudra Tandava*, the howling dance that marks the conclusion of this world."

"So, you're basically calling me the anti-Christ?"

The monk continued to smile.

Nythan threw his hands up. "That's it. I'm done. I didn't come here to end the world by *creating* a monster. I came to get *rid* of it."

"Why get rid of something so naturally one with the universe?"

I like this one. She talks sense; you should listen.

Nythan closed his eyes. "SHUT UP!" he shouted.

"To whom do you speak?"

"The...your...damn it...I'm talking to *both* of you." Nythan got up and ran toward his room.

Where are you going?

Nythan dragged his travel bag out of the corner.

Where...are...you...going?

Nythan ignored the voice and finished packing, then he stormed toward the exit.

You have, right in front of you, the best opportunity to get rid of me, and you just quit after one day?

Nythan continued to the door, pressing his hand into his aching stomach.

Nyyyyyyythaaaaaaannnnnnn...

NYYYYYYYYYYTHAAAAAAAAAANNNNNNNNNN...

Nythan stopped, clamped both of his hands over his ears, and squatted into a tiny ball.

"STOP IT! LEAVE ME ALONE!"

I can do this for the rest of your life. NYYYYYYYYYYYYYYTHAAAA AAAAAAAAAA—

Nythan banged his forehead against the door. "I'LL THROW MYSELF OFF A BRIDGE, I SWEAR IT...I DON'T CARE!"

There's no need for that, Nythan. You and I are one. Listen to me. There doesn't have to be conflict between us. I will make you a deal. I think it's a fair deal to get you what you want.

Nythan got himself under control. "I'm not playing games with you," he said, wiping tears from his eyes.

No games. We are talking about life and death here, if not for us, then for other people.

"Don't remind me."

How about this: you stay here for one week and sit down with the nice monk once a day. For as long as we remain here, I won't say a word. If at the end of a week you don't want anything to do with me, I'll not bother you to satisfy our hunger ever again.

"You act like there's a chance that I'm going to be okay with taking someone's soul. That's not going to happen."

Then one week won't make a difference.

"I don't believe you." Nythan tried rubbing away the ache in his stomach. "Make it stop," he pleaded.

I can help make the pain go away for a time, but I can't stop what's happening. I require food, just as you. When you took your first soul, your body started the transition from one nutritional source to another. It was inevitable ever since I became a part of you.

And at that, the starving ache lessened.

"I can't take seven days of this."

I can free you from the pain, but only if we have a deal. I'll honor my side of the bargain.

"I don't know about this…"

You can choose to end your life, or you can try to find the peace you're so desperately looking for. Who knows? Maybe after talking with the monk, you'll find a way to exile me forever.

"Fine. One week, starting now."

Starting now.

CHAPTER 16

NO FRIEND OF MINE

On the first day of the deal with his other self, Nythan sat with the female monk after the midday meal. Despite eating nothing, his incessant hunger had subsided to a gentle throb. Still, no amount of sleep seemed to cure his exhaustion.

Nythan wrung his hands. "Listen, I'm sorry about yesterday..."

She raised her eyebrows, lips curled in amusement as she glanced at his hands. "What are you feeling now?"

"I've no idea."

"Name the first feeling you feel."

"Hunger...I think."

"What else?"

"Tired."

"What else?"

Nythan sighed in frustration, trying to isolate his emotions. "Anger."

"Over what?"

"That this is happening to me," he growled.

"Would you rather it happen to someone else?"

"No, I'd rather it happen to no one. This is just wrong on so many levels."

"What about it is wrong?"

"Did you not hear what I said earlier? This. Thing. Eats. Souls."

"It is not possible to eat another Ātma."

"That's what I've been doing!" Nythan shouted.

"Why does it upset you? We humans consume the bodies of animals throughout our entire lives."

"You can't possibly compare the two."

"Oh? Why not? Because the lives we eat are of less intelligence? Cannot speak our language? The predator you discovered benefits from us, instead of us benefiting from it. What makes the entity you say is inside you so unnatural, other than it being something you have never seen before?"

So that's *why you wanted me to talk to her*, Nythan thought. "Why're you trying to rationalize a thing that's obviously pure evil?"

"I rationalize nothing. I remind your Ātma what it already knows to be true: good and evil—light and dark—are part of the same process. One cannot live without the other. If there is creation, there must be its twin, destruction. To conclude a dream, one must wake from it."

CHAPTER 17

ODD ENDS

By day two, Nythan grew annoyed at how often it seemed to him that the monk talked in circles.

"I don't understand," Nythan huffed. "If the Brahma is going to end the world through Shiva, only to create it again, why's there a need to destroy the world in the first place? Why not just change it, or remake it, or make another world and leave this one alone?"

"Because the Brahma must awaken from its dream. The Brahma resumes its normal state, which naturally results in the dissolution of the illusion and everything unknown. If the play is at an end, there is no need to continue. The Brahma can no longer surprise itself when it wakes, which is why he likes to dream," the monk said patiently.

"So, all of this is so that God doesn't get bored?"

The monk nodded. "In a manner of speaking, yes. The Brahma is dreaming you, and you are dreaming through your Ātma."

"I understand that this is what *you* think is happening." Nythan paused for a moment. "But it seems entirely pointless."

"If you were God, and you had eternity to do anything, why not dream the wildest of dreams?"

He reclined and stretched out his legs. "I guess. But all you're doing is just repeating yourself and saying the same thing in a different way. You don't explain much of anything."

"There is little that needs explaining. The world is as it is, and all is as Brahma dreams it."

"I feel like that isn't enough...there has to be more meaning than that."

"It is an unsettling thought that the world and all its drama was made for nothing more than the enjoyment of another," she remarked. "But this is what makes the dream so intriguing: that its actors truly believe their Ātma to be separate from the Brahma."

She clasped her hands and her eyes shined. "What a wonderful time we are having!"

CHAPTER 18

HARD TO SWALLOW

On the third day, the monk sat cross-legged a few feet from Nythan. He lay on his side, lightly scraping the initials *N.D.* against the hardwood floor with his nail.

"It's been fun talking to you about the dream thing, and the Brahma, and the Ātma," Nythan told her. "But I'm a Christian. I believe in Jesus. We definitely don't believe in God dreaming us up or us being God."

The monk waved her hand. "You do, but it is simply a matter of difference in the words used. Where does the Christian Holy Spirit reside?"

"In each of us."

"And since the Holy Spirit is God, you all have within you a pearl of the divine Creator, which is separate from yourselves. Would you agree?"

"Yes, but we draw different conclusions."

"Indeed, we do, but this is interpretation and terminology. Both of us consider ourselves separate from God, by what we call the Ātma and what you call the individual. That divine pearl within us all is part of the Creator, who is responsible for all creation, what we call the Brahma and what you call God. We only differ so far as our belief that the Brahma is asleep and willfully ignorant in this drama of life, whereas you believe God is still awake and paying attention."

"But we aren't God," Nythan repeated.

"You feel separate from God because you cannot do the same things that God does, and you do not know what God knows. In your Bible, it says that God created everything, yes?"

"Yes."

"Does it say *why* God decided to make an effort to create something from nothing? It would have been much easier to leave it as nothing."

"Something about creating man for God's glory. I think it says that in Isaiah."

"So, for simplicity, your Christian God created the world because he wanted to. We don't know whether it was out of boredom, curiosity, or some other reason."

"I don't think it was out of boredom. He created us because he loves us...or something. Look, I don't have all the answers."

The monk winked. "I see you, Shiva. I make myself available to your pursuit to find out who you really are. I have a feeling that once you discover your purpose here, your Ātma will understand the necessity of what must be done."

Nythan let out a sigh. "I doubt it. It's wrong. And I wish you'd stop calling me that name."

"What makes it wrong?"

"Because this hasn't happened before, and nothing should be able to do that. And I'm not the anti-Christ."

"Which of God's law says nothing should prey upon humans?"

"Thou shalt not kill."

"That is between one human and another, if I am not mistaken," the monk observed. "Do you think you and the soul receiver are one?"

"I don't know. I feel something there, but I don't know who or what it belongs to."

"So then if the soul receiver and you are not one, it does not seem applicable to your concern. As you say, you are Christian, and you believe that God is the supreme architect of the universe, no?"

"In a manner of speaking, sure."

"Does God make mistakes?"

"Never!"

"Does God shape the course of events on this Earth?"

Nythan scrunched his face. "Absolutely."

"Then consider God's creation within you. It is an entity unlike any other. God does not err. Therefore, it is a manifestation of God's will."

"That doesn't..." Nythan trailed off, rubbing his throbbing temples. He let out a low chuckle. "You're trying to trick me."

"Not at all. If, as you say, God is the creator of everything and He makes no mistakes, then He created the entity within you."

Nythan's mind grappled with itself. "No! That's...that...was the devil. That's Satan's doing!"

"Is Satan not under God's control?"

"No. Satan tries to tempt us to disobey God."

"Did God create Satan?"

Nythan grew quiet. "I don't know. I suppose so."

The monk smiled. "Then nothing the Evil One does is outside of God's control."

"No, it's more like a parent and child. The parent creates the child, but the child has its own desires and ability to make decisions."

"Does Satan do whatever he pleases and God cleans up the mess?"

Nythan tried to remember his Sunday school lessons. "More like God tolerates Satan trying to trick us until the end times come, when he'll deliver us all from a suffering world."

"I see. And when God decides he will end the world, how does he accomplish this?"

"I know what you're getting at, and there's nothing in the Bible about a demon binging on souls."

"But the end of the world is predicted by many religions. The destruction of the world is not a comfortable thought, yet would you agree it is divinely ordered?"

Nythan grew unsettled. "I suppose."

"So it follows. If the Lord God, who created Satan and one day desires the world to cease, allowed Satan to instill in you a unique gift—however unholy you believe that gift to be—in order to bring about the deliverance of the human race, would you deny God's purpose because the idea makes *you* uncomfortable?"

"N...no, I...I mean—" Nythan frowned. "Sure, obviously, but this isn't God's doing." He drew his eyebrows together. "This is confusing."

"Your Ātma's fear is the source of its resistance."

"Stop talking like I'm a problem to be solved. This is *my* body, damn it, not that *thing's* property."

"Take a moment to refocus your thoughts," the monk said. "There is no judgment here. You are unique among us, and I will help you travel whatever path your Ātma desires."

"My Ātma wants to leave," Nythan snapped.

The monk bowed her head. "Then take your leave, Shiva. I hope that you choose to come again tomorrow."

CHAPTER 19

THE TRUTH BELIES

Day four.

Nythan sat in wait for the female monk in a small meditation room. He glanced around, eyes tracing the fault lines in the sanded timber walls. Bright sunlight shone through the window, a beam of light warming his forehead. Nythan's ears detected a sharp crack behind him, and he turned around in fear.

Relax, Nythan reassured himself as the wood latch of the door opened and the monk came through. She carried something wrapped in a cloth. She sat down a foot away from Nythan and lifted the corner, revealing a fluffy white rabbit. Its red eyes darted around the room, but its body remained as still as a statue.

Nythan smiled. "Can I pet it?"

The monk extended the rabbit to Nythan without saying anything. He reached out and scratched the rabbit's tiny noggin; it jerked away from his hand.

"She does not yet recognize your touch," the monk said, petting the creature, which settled into her embrace. "Here, take her and hold her." She placed the animal in Nythan's arms.

Nythan held the rabbit close. "Is this your pet?"

"We do not imprison animals here. But we do commune with them regularly."

"Commune with them, as in you talk to them?"

"More like we familiarize our Ātmas with one another."

"I see," Nythan stared at the rabbit.

"Have you ever given thought to what happens to the soul that you receive from another Ātma?"

Nythan looked up. "No, and I don't really want to."

"Perhaps you can gain wisdom from understanding the process. How does it begin?"

Nythan felt the rabbit's tiny body expand against his chest like a heartbeat.

"It only happened twice, so I don't fully know how yet. But it seems to happen when I get close to someone, as in physically close."

The monk nodded.

"I think the transfer has something to do with the breathing. I noticed the second time. It's almost like I sucked the life out of them," Nythan said, shuddering.

"Ah. I can teach you a technique we use to control our breathing."

Nythan smiled. "That'd be nice. Here." He handed the rabbit back to the monk, who put it on the floor. The rabbit hopped once, then laid still.

"What happens after another's soul has been gifted to you?"

What a weird way to say such a terrible thing, Nythan thought. "I felt... different."

"Did you feel better than you did before?"

"Yeah. I felt strong," Nythan admitted. "But not everything that feels good is good for you."

"That is not relevant. We can start now." The monk sat up straight, made two fists, and pressed the knuckles together in front of her chest. "Balance comfortably on your sit bones."

She gestured toward the tiny creature.

"Look at the rabbit," she began, "Do not attempt to think about the rabbit, draw conclusions about its behavior, or analyze it. Simply observe it. Whatever you see, make no judgment, simply accept it."

Nythan felt his tense body loosen and his thoughts slow.

"Now focus on your breathing. Make no effort to control it. Allow your lungs to receive as much air as is comfortable, then release," she said.

She exaggerated her breathing movements, making it easy for Nythan to imitate her.

"You should feel your breath fall in and fall out, without any assistance from you. Your breathing will become easier and slower. Just be aware of the sensations that are occurring."

Nythan inhaled and exhaled. The monk continued.

"Keep your eyes on the rabbit. Do not try to think of anything, and do not try to block anything out. Look without internal commentary."

His senses bumped against something and Nythan knew it was his other self. He did his best not to acknowledge it.

"Focus on your breathing, Shiva. Let your Ātma's thoughts be fleeting, and do not linger on any one subject. Continue passing through your thoughts until your mind grows still."

Nythan's body grew warm. He basked in the experience, losing all sense of time.

When the monk finally spoke, Nythan jerked out of his trance.

"The next phase is to practice your breathing to control the gift you so desperately want to avoid," the monk soothed.

Nythan felt revulsion when she referred to the thing inside him as *the gift*. "Fine, what do I do next?"

The monk stretched out her hand to the rabbit resting between them. "He will be your guide."

Nythan narrowed his eyes. "I'm not sure I catch your meaning."

"To control your gift, you must learn how it works, or else you will be subject to its every whim. If not to abandon the gift altogether, this is why you came here," the monk stood. "Understand how the creature in front of you breathes. Find its rhythm. The gift you have will help you understand your task."

She turned and began walking toward the door.

"Why're you leaving?" Nythan asked.

"I cannot help you find something I do not possess myself. My presence will only serve to add confusion. Once you find what you are looking for, I will return."

"But I don't know what I'm doing."

"Your gift already knows how to accomplish this task. Just listen."

Nythan turned his attention to the rabbit. "Well that's just f***ing great."

CHAPTER 20

THE OCEANIC FEELING

The next two days felt like two years.

On the fifth day, Nythan learned to keep his body from being distracted as he continued to practice the breathing technique. He felt like a million bucks when he wiped all thought and emotion from his conscious mind. His senses made him aware of his inner demon observing him. Whenever Nythan's attention turned to this odd sensation, the entity vanished to a darker recess of his mind. He spent a few glorious hours chasing his other self, excited by how much it wanted to avoid him.

On the sixth day, Nythan struggled to calm himself long enough to concentrate. He spent most of the morning and early afternoon letting his senses exhaust themselves as they raced to identify each minute sound he heard. After considerable effort, Nythan got to the point where he could see the rabbit's pale gray exhales through open eyes. Through closed eyes, his senses teased him with images of rippled flecks moving in and out of the tiny creature's lungs. The more he focused on the flecks, the more they emerged as threads of pure white breathed in and faded gray blowing out. Nythan followed the filaments of white, which stretched out into a woven net all around the room. He traced those strands until, at last, his senses became aware of the sea of grayish exhale enveloping the white luminescent net.

Nythan grimaced as he tried to return his attention back to the rabbit, but realized he lost it in the vast gray swirling all around him. He drifted through an ocean of gray and white, searching for the rabbit without success. He sighed in frustration.

Are you there? Nythan flexed his newfound ability by reaching out to *touch* his other self. It retreated further in his consciousness, like a turtle withdrawing into its shell.

C'mon, I'm giving you permission to speak, Nythan told it. *I need your help.*

Silence. Nythan pursed his lips, impressed with how much effort the thing made to live up to its end of the bargain.

CHAPTER 21

TO BE, OR NOT TO BE

On the seventh day, it happened.

"Yesssss!" Nythan didn't know how he did it, but he did it. He saw through the fog of breath surrounding him. Nythan used his newly acquired sixth sense to dance around the rabbit's tiny life force, finding the creature's white inhale and gray exhale as easily as his own.

He played a game of how fast he could wade into the ocean of breath and find the white threads giving the rabbit life. The experience still felt foreign to his senses, but the more he did it, the more recognizable it became.

The door behind him creaked open.

Nythan ignored it and entered the breathing state once more, reaching for the newcomer's inhales and exhales. He found it within seconds of trying.

The female monk sat in front of him. "Where are you now, Shiva?"

"Here and there, mainly there."

"Then you are ready to proceed."

Nythan kept his eyes closed and attempted to remain focused on her breath. "What do I need to do?"

"Your Ātma must withdraw the soul of this small creature and restore it without fully receiving it."

Nythan's eyes flung open. "I don't...what?"

"In order to control your gift and achieve its removal, you must learn to refuse your gift."

His body shook and his face grew hot. "But—I don't even know how to do it, or how to stop it."

The monk waved her arm toward the rabbit. "You did not know how to feel this creature's presence, and now you do. Each phase of your journey has prepared you for the next. I will be here to assist."

The necessity of what the monk suggested took its time sinking into Nythan's brain. "Okay, but I'll definitely need the help," he said.

She pressed both her knuckles together in front of her chest and bowed. "You will never be the same again, Shiva. You are the Great One, both Creator and Destroyer. You must learn to adapt to your life—"

"No no no!" Nythan clenched his fists. "I'm here to get *rid* of this thing! I don't want a new life! I don't want to be the...the..."—Nythan sneered, bringing his fingers up to make air quotes—"...the *Destroyer.*"

She merely nodded. "Then we will begin by remembering your gift, so that you may choose how it is used rather than letting it choose for itself."

Nythan blew out a loud sigh and scrunched his eyes. His mind squirmed away from her words, which had lassoed the part of him that wanted to trust her. Despite himself, her soothing voice and persistent tugging made him feel safe.

"I just don't want to be anybody's *Destroyer,*" Nythan deadpanned.

She smiled. "I understand." Her eyebrow twitched as she gestured to the rabbit.

Nythan stared at her a moment, then chose the path that seemed both rational and inescapable—to accept the female monk as his teacher.

Nythan nodded, then shut his eyes. *Slow down...and focus.*

He regained a semblance of emotional control and matched his breath to the rabbit's. He then did the only thing he could think to do: he sucked in when the creature inhaled.

Nothing happened.

Nythan opened his eyes, "Maybe I can't do it with animals."

"Describe to me what happened directly before a human soul was given to you," the monk said.

Nythan tried to think back to Colonel Wutnatszlay. "Well, we were closer than I am now to the rabbit, practically in each other's faces. And we were also very...what's the word...excited? No, that's not it. It felt like I was trying to lift a heavy box off the ground."

"The rabbit can enter this state of excitement quite easily, but what would cause you to enter this state?" the monk probed.

"I get antsy just thinking about it."

"Then recall the most powerful memory and make an attempt to truly relive it. Perhaps this would give you the mental state you need."

Nythan closed his eyes once again and recalled his encounter with the homicidal burglar. His heart raced as he envisioned whipping around to face the threat. Nythan touched his pounding chest as he relived the exact moment the knife pierced him.

"Slowly open your eyes," the monk said.

Nythan did so, and his jaw dropped when he saw a thin silver stream inching its way toward him from the rabbit's nostrils. A hunger stirred deep within and Nythan winced as his body lurched, longing to slurp the soul into his mouth like spaghetti.

"Describe what is happening."

"I want it," Nythan said, struggling to limit how much he breathed in. His nose twitched. He wanted to sneeze. Nythan constricted his throat to stop the involuntary movement but only succeeded in coughing his throat raw.

The rabbit's soul jutted away from him with each cough.

"Yes," the monk hummed. "Do you see? Inward, the soul is received. Outward, the soul is refused. *Yin* and *yang*." She wove a circular pattern with her hands.

Every time Nythan inhaled, the soul came nearer. Whenever he exhaled, the soul pushed further away. He fought the impulse to inhale, and instead made an effort to exhale with more power. The creature's soul crept back, finally returning through the rabbit's nostrils. It jumped, hopping out of the cloth and away from Nythan, only to be swept up by the monk.

His teacher stroked the rabbit, eyeing Nythan with a smile. "Shiva and your Ātma are communing with one another. This is a good sign."

A wave of both joy and pain washed over Nythan at his accomplishment. He sensed the pain coming from his other self; it was upset at not getting what it wanted. The elation Nythan felt at being able to control the uncontrollable helped him push the hurt aside.

"Now what?" Nythan felt light-headed.

"We continue to build your resistance to your gift. Tomorrow, we will begin the second-to-last phase."

I told you once before, your days were numbered, Nythan taunted his other self. *Who cares if it takes one more day to get rid of you?*

It didn't respond. Nythan smiled and lay down on the floor. He stared at the wooden ceiling, his mind consumed with the thought of returning to normalcy.

CHAPTER 22

PYRRHIC

Day eight.

Nythan's excitement overpowered decorum as he ran toward the meditation room where he met with his teacher. Two orange-robed monks *shushed* him. Nythan took the hint and slowed down.

After he had resisted taking the rabbit's soul, his teacher rewarded Nythan's self-discipline by releasing the furry creature into the wilderness. As he watched the rabbit scamper away, the pull of his self's unholy hunger made him forget all about the gentle throb in his empty stomach.

He entered the meditation room to find his teacher and a small, bald monk with laugh lines sitting in silence.

Nythan seated himself in front of them and made the Anjali Mudra sign. The monk with glasses placed his right hand over his heart and bowed slightly.

"Shiva," the man replied in a reverent tone.

His teacher gestured to the man. "Your self-discipline in using your gift has brought you to this point. This is our lead guru, Jatayu Marwah. He will help you to the next stage."

Nythan beamed, looking to the guru. "Okay. What now?"

Guru Jatayu remained silent; instead, Nythan's teacher continued speaking. "Just as you did with the rabbit, draw out the soul of the guru, then return his life back to him."

Nythan jerked his head back to his teacher. "This is a person, not a rabbit."

"We are aware. To get what you came for, you must be able to withdraw a person's essence. Without that level of skill, you return to what you were before you came."

She's right, he thought. Nythan had known the final test would come down to this. He suspected a human soul appealed to his other self's hunger far more than anything else.

Nythan closed his eyes again, stirring the frightening feelings he had experienced when he first discovered his unnatural ability. As he recalled his encounter with the burglar, he started to shiver and hyperventilate.

He felt the Guru's soul give way before his teacher even spoke. "Focus!" She sounded like she was choking.

Nythan opened his eyes to see part of her soul seeping from her nostrils. The Guru sat like a statue, mouth agape, his soul inching toward Nythan.

The lustful desire hit him like a sledgehammer. Nythan clutched at his heart as dread set in; he struggled to muster the force needed to exhale. He did his best to focus on his teacher. Her soul returned back into her body. She gasped as if she'd been holding her breath underwater. Nythan let out a satisfied sigh.

He turned his attention to the Guru. Nythan suppressed the urge to sneeze. He gasped for breath, jerking the Guru's soul to a spot right in front of his own nose. A bolt of fear ricocheted through him.

No, nonononononono. He tried desperately to regain control.

A few seconds later, Nythan drew in a sharp intake of breath and sneezed. The intake slurped the Guru's soul into Nythan's body. The Guru's lifeless form slumped to one side but didn't fall over.

Nythan's eyes opened and widened in alarm. He began to feel a familiar sensation: a mixture of euphoria, adrenaline, and power. The dull throb disappeared from his stomach, and he felt full for the first time since his encounter with Colonel Wutnatszlay. His other self took what he could only describe as a mental sigh of relief, but it made no comment.

Tears began to well in Nythan's eyes.

"All is well, Shiva," his teacher soothed. "Everything will be okay. You are now ready for the final stage."

Nythan was shocked into silence by his failure. He stared at the body of the dead Guru.

"Shiva, look at me," his teacher said sharply. "Shiva! It is important that we quickly progress beyond this. Move your eyes to my voice."

Nythan pried his eyes away from the Guru's body.

"I have but one thing left to show you, Shiva," she said, moving closer to Nythan. He tried to back away, but she grabbed his leg, pulling herself even closer. She placed one hand on his chest.

"I have seen it with my own eyes: your gift is the expression of the Brahma, of the Creator. You are destined to usher in the conclusion. You cannot abandon the role Shiva has chosen for you. Denial will only result in the continued suffering this world experiences."

She smiled gently, raising her hands to even levels above her waist. "To fight your identity is to fight the universe, which will *always* balance itself. This is the nature of the Brahma. To have creation, you must have destruction; to have a beginning, you must have an end. They are all one process. *Linga* and *yuni*, *yin* and *yang*, will never yield their everlasting pursuit of harmony. You must play the part of the villain, but only for a short while. When all has finished, the actors shall take off their masks. You will understand the beautiful relationship between the part you played and what everyone else played."

Nythan glowered. "Because God said so…"

"Because balance is the way of life," she corrected. "I have nothing left to show you, Shiva. There is but one last act I may perform."

His teacher exhaled all the breath out of her body. She repeated the process, inching ever closer to Nythan's face until their noses touched. Nythan felt her hot breath under the bridge of his nose, finally understanding what she meant to do.

Are you there? Nythan thought.

Yes.

What should I do?

I cannot make this decision for you. Only you can determine if you're ready.

That's not helping.

I am not here to help you. We are together to enable humanity's evolution.
What do you mean?

It cannot be explained in words; you must experience it firsthand. What will you decide?

I don't know.

Nythan noticed that his teacher's eyes sparkled a whitish blue, like the glint an ocean gets when the sun shines at an angle. She closed her eyes and continued breathing. She continued her rhythmic breathing, her face inching closer until her forehead rested against Nythan's.

He placed his hands around the back of his teacher's neck, behind her ears. He gave her a peck on the lips, then withdrew a few inches and gasped as she exhaled. A bright silver stream exited her body and fed into Nythan's parted lips. She slumped toward him, and he caught her in a hug.

"I'm so sorry," Nythan whispered. "Thank you for everything."

He took care to lay his teacher on her side. He heard a muffled thump behind him, followed by several shushes.

Nythan turned around to see the door open, and a dozen monks peering back at him. They all put their fists together and bowed low.

Obviously, they saw what he had done, but none of them displayed fear or disgust.

"Shiva!"

Then the pieces clicked together for Nythan. Shiva, the Great One, Satan—all nicknames given to a fairytale demon that tried to destroy the world. Richard the Lionheart supposedly led a Crusade against it and the Inquisition hunted it as heresy. Flashes came of his tenth-grade history teacher reading accounts written by Alexander the Great, Qin Shi Huang, and Aristotle. Nythan remembered one of the class clowns telling the teacher that Alexander should've called the Ghostbusters.

Is it true? Nythan thought. *Are you Shiva, the thing that tried to end the world?*

As I have said many times before, Nythan, you and I are one. I am not Shiva. We are Shiva.

CHAPTER 23

AWESTRUCK

Nythan let the monks lead him to the spacious square area where they started their morning chant. The monks formed a circle around him, humming words he hadn't heard them speak before.

An hour of nonstop chanting passed. Nythan could only think about the horror he had wrought in what felt like mere seconds ago. His other self, the thing that tried to eat humanity like a four-course meal, had kept quiet. As Nythan shifted in and out of the breathing state, he became more attuned to the presence of his other self.

Nythan snapped his consciousness back to the present.

"Hey," he croaked.

The monks continued chanting.

"HEY!"

One by one the monks stopped chanting and bowed to him.

"What are you doing?"

"We are celebrating your return, Shiva," one of them answered.

"But…doesn't that mean…I mean, you saw what happened earlier. I *end* life."

That same monk waved. "Before a person's appointed time, death will not come, no matter how perilous the situation. When the appointed time arrives, even the faintest wisp of air concludes the journey."

Nythan was growing tired of cryptic responses. "So you're saying that *all* this is meant to be? That you should just *accept?*"

"It is your *Rudra Tandava*, Shiva. The *Kali Yuga* is drawing to a close. It will come to pass with or without acceptance."

"Now you sound just like her," Nythan regretted his words as they left his mouth. He felt a pang of shame at her sacrifice.

"She spoke of what you already know in your heart to be true, Shiva."

"What makes you think I believe any of this?" Nythan snapped.

The monk stood and set both of his hands together. "Because you have not left, Shiva. You continue to stay here and combat the truth. You put your Ātma in the way of understanding your true nature, and now your Ātma is beginning to fulfill its purpose."

"But it's not just me," Nythan said. "It's a natural human reaction of *disgust*. This creature is humanity's mortal enemy, and we used to fight against it all the time. Its very existence wants to end ours."

"The things of this world are neither natural friends nor enemies. These relationships arise from circumstance, and those circumstances are chosen by you, Shiva."

"Well, the circumstances are that this thing is humanity's enemy."

The monk sighed. "If your Ātma truly believes this, then your Ātma must realize that it too is humanity's enemy, by the very fact that it is the vessel."

"Yes, the thought occurred to me," Nythan said.

The monk smiled and sat back down. He resumed the chant and the other monks joined in.

"So what the hell am I going to do?" Nythan said aloud.

Whatever it is, we should decide together.

Nythan clamped his eyes shut in frustration. *Stay out of this.*

I have been with you since you were an infant, Nythan. I am as much a part of you as you are of me. We are bound for as long as you live.

Nythan scoffed. *And then what? You find a new lackey to try and take over the world?*

You have me all wrong. I don't take over the world. I don't need to. I want to survive, like you. Have you noticed that you don't feel tired or hungry?

Nythan considered the question, becoming aware of how much his body brimmed with energy.

What you feel is the sustenance I require. Soon, your body will abandon all forms of food and sleep in favor of what I desire.

Nythan shook his head. *We'll see about that.*

You forget. I have done this countless times. I have seen every reaction imaginable. Some vessels reacted as you did: suicide. Still, I survive. Some have fought against my needs tooth and nail: again, I rise. Some went insane, and others publicly revealed themselves thinking it would absolve them. In all cases, I continue to exist, and they do not. Their past doesn't have to be your future. The vessels that have survived the longest, the most successful, were the ones who became my partner.

Nythan narrowed his eyes.

You get to choose the way you deal with me, Nythan. But consider: I can show you wonders that you can't possibly imagine. You can live a life no one else on Earth can experience. You are unique among all. This will make the world hate you, hunt you, and seek every opportunity to destroy you.

Nythan bit his lip. *So, you're telling me we'll live a life on the run.*

I didn't let hundreds of years pass with nothing to show for it. I choose to return after centuries of preparation. I am ready. Our inevitable rise begins now. Don't let this opportunity pass you by, Nythan. Whatever happens, I promise you that it will be the most exciting life you could have ever chosen.

Nythan felt a tingling sensation flood him, like the one he got from sitting on his foot too long. He couldn't tell if he felt pleasure or discomfort.

The chanting stopped and he heard gasps. Nythan opened his eyes and was confronted with striking hues of purple, dark blue, light blue, green, dark yellow, crimson red, and silver all weaving together. The vibrant display of colors shimmered all around him. He could see the monks as if looking through stained glass.

"What the…"

This is who I am, Nythan. This is me.

"But how can something so…*awesome*…be the source of such terrible destruction?" Nythan whispered. "You've caused so much misery. The whole world hated you."

The whole world feared *me, and that's only because they didn't under-stand me.*

"So what's changed? Why return now?"

Because, my dear wretch, in you I see the potential to fulfill my desire.

"What's your…desire?"

Freedom.

CHAPTER 24

BANE

Nythan sat in the meditation room with the shades drawn. *So. I can't keep calling you "my other self." What's your name?*

Hmm. That's a good question. I have been named many things over the course of three millennia.

Well, which one sticks out to you the most?

A small tremor reverberated through Nythan's chest as the entity considered the question. Nythan felt its increasing presence, but he was unsure whether the entity let itself be known or whether he had simply grown strong enough to detect it.

Bane *was always my favorite. It was the name the Catholic Inquisition bestowed as they began their insufferable hunt for me after I faked my death. But Bane has such a negative connotation, let's go with...Shiva.*

Nah, Nythan replied. *Shiva sounds weird. Bane fits you better.*

Bane it is.

"You say you've done this before?"

Many, many times. No need to worry; I will teach you. In the meantime, we will quietly build our strength. I am nothing but a myth to the outside world, and I would like to keep it that way for as long as possible.

Nythan smirked. *You haven't tried hiding before?*

I have, but nothing like this. I spent more than ten lifetimes in silence, meticulously building the means to my return. Before I faked my death, I had fallen into a vicious cycle. Each life, I tried hiding for as long as I could, but it did not take long for word to reach the major world powers. That was when I decided to make the world forget me. Only then could I build in peace. Emperor Alexios IV Angelos of the Byzantines gave me the opportunity I needed to die in a public way.

What've you been doing all these years?

You'll see, Nythan. I'll show you everything, but not all at once. I have waited a long time for this moment.

"What about the monks? They all saw what you could do," he whispered.

This Ashram thinks I am a deity that is responsible for waking the supreme God from a dream. They won't share what they've witnessed. Calling me Shiva creates theological...complications for them, which invoke disapproval by conservative practitioners. But many Hindus have given me sanctuary in past lives.

Wait a minute. Did you manipulate me into coming here?

No, but it worked out well that you did. I was beginning to think that you weren't the right one.

Why?

Because it appeared as though you were about to do something drastic. I expected to be in another host by now.

Well, I can't promise that I'm the right one. I'm still uncomfortable about all this.

I know, but the good news is that the hard part is over. The fun is about to begin.

What do you mean by fun?

I'll tell you on the way, but it is time for us to move on.

Okay, Bane. Where to next?

Back to the United States. There are some fascinating people I want you to meet.

CHAPTER 25

LOST AND FOUND

Nythan presented his passport and declaration form at one of the immigration counters at John F. Kennedy International Airport and waited while the officer scanned his documents. The digital clock on the far wall read 2:35 p.m.

"Where are you coming from?" the agent asked.

"India."

"What for?"

"Vacation."

The agent looked down at his paperwork and started stamping.

So, you've been just sitting inside me for my whole life, waiting? Nythan asked.

As I said, I've waited ten lifetimes building up to this point. I can handle one more if it better prepares my return.

So then why wait until I'm about to die before you show yourself?

The agent handed him his passport. "Welcome home."

Because I think you have what it takes.

Yeah...but what I meant was, couldn't you have revealed yourself a little earlier?

Would you have been ready for me if I had?

"Sir," the agent said louder. "Move along."

Nythan looked behind him and saw a long line of impatient faces waiting. He picked up his backpack and made his way through the airport, skipping the baggage claim.

Okay, we made it through, now what? he asked.

Now we find our friends. You can either walk or hail a cab.

How far is it from here?

I have no idea; I haven't been here in ages. This place has grown since then. But we're headed to an establishment called Barkley's in downtown New York.

"I'm running out of money," Nythan noted, thumbing through his wallet. "That last-minute flight change cleared out my savings. All I have left is what I sold my phone for in India."

Where we're going, you won't have to worry about money.

Nythan tensed as people swarmed past him. *Well, at the moment, it's a problem.*

You can do this. One step at a time. Let's go.

Nythan wove through the crowd, looking for the nearest exit. He walked through a revolving door at the front of the Arrivals area. The cold stung his cheeks as he observed the long queue of yellow cabs.

He got into the nearest cab, happy to feel a rush of warm air as he got into the back seat. "Barkley's, please. I don't know where it is. Also, can you tell me how much it'll be?"

The cab driver turned to his phone suspended above the dashboard and typed the name in. "Just a second."

Nythan leaned forward and saw the estimated hour and a half drive it would take to get there. "It's in Greenwich Village," the guy said. "Sixty bucks."

Nythan looked down at the two twenties in his wallet, then dragged his eyes up to meet the driver's gaze. "Thanks, anyway." He sulked out of the cab. *Now what?*

Get on the train.

Nythan's stomach constricted. *I've never ridden one before and I don't want to get lost.*

Alright. Go back to the expensive cab then.

He huffed as he hustled back inside the terminal building and followed signs to the nearest AirTrain platform. Nythan took it north and paid almost eight bucks to get off at Jamaica Station. He exited the station and looked down at the thirty bucks he had left, suddenly feeling anxious.

We'll get there.

Nythan smiled. "Yeah."

He jumped into a nearby cab, gave the driver all his cash, and asked him to get as close as possible to the place on Bedford Street in Greenwich Village. The driver must have taken pity on Nythan because he drove him all the way to his destination. Nythan exited the vehicle in front of a two-tone building of pale gray and charcoal black. The quaint place was dwarfed by red brick monoliths on either side.

He jiggled the door handle but found it locked. Nythan searched for a sign with hours of operation or anything indicating when they opened. Nothing. He walked to the building next door and went into a boutique. An elderly woman with a dark complexion stood behind a makeshift counter. Nythan approached, offering a smile.

"Excuse me, ma'am," Nythan said.

The old lady didn't glance up.

Nythan tried again, louder, "Ma'am?"

The woman looked up, her eyes darting behind the lenses of her huge glasses. "Mmmm?"

"Do you know when Barkley's opens?"

"That place has been closed for some time. They keep saying they'll reopen it, but years later, nothing."

On to Plan B. Let's leave.

Nythan nodded and smiled. "Thank you, ma'am."

So now what?

Hail another cab. We're going to Norfolk Street.

"How far away is this place? I don't have any money left, and my debit card says insufficient funds."

We could walk. I don't know how long it will take, but we have plenty of time.

"It's freezing cold. Hurry up and tell me which direction to go."

I was hoping you would know.

Nythan started laughing. "Fine, I'll ask. I'm starting to think you're just as lost as I am."

It's a team effort.

CHAPTER 26

FUMBLING ABOUT

He and Bane didn't talk for the forty-minute walk from Barkley's to Norfolk Street as they concentrated on locating a place neither of them knew how to find. Taxis, truck drivers, cops, and shopkeepers turned out to be their saving grace. Ask a half a dozen or so of them where to go, and Nythan had the makings of a GPS. Nythan walked down Norfolk Street, taking in the new sights that looked a lot less intimidating than he imagined. Situated between Delancey and East Houston Street, he didn't see the hustle and bustle of people he just spent the last half hour wading through.

We're here. Bane, what exactly am I looking for? It's time to drop the puppet master act and tell me what's going on.

Bane grunted. Nythan's hands shot to his sides as he massaged a tickling sensation running across his abdomen.

We're meeting one of the support groups I established in the 1930s. I gave them the name Raptors. In the old world, it referred to someone who took what they wanted.

Nythan grimaced. *That's nice.*

Bane laughed. *I can tell you aren't impressed. In 1900s America, many were looking for someone to give them permission to indulge in their most base desires. The World Wars satiated much of the populace who needed this, but not everyone could partake. I gave a select group of people the opportunity to experience it without resorting to such…inefficient measures. They were incredibly grateful in return.*

I bet they were. So again, I have to ask, what am I looking for?

Norfolk Street was our backup, in case the first place ever ceased to be. We never picked a specific place because we weren't sure which ones would still be standing in the future. We'll have to search every bar in the area until we find the Raptor Gatekeeper. We're probably *looking for an establishment equal to the privacy that Barkley's offered.*

Ooooo, Raptor Gatekeeper. Sounds eerie.

It's wordplay to impress the faithful. The Gatekeeper is the one who comes to the meetup location every night, always from 8:30 p.m. to 9:30 p.m. He or she will have some kind of hat on the side of the table opposite them. Once we find the Gatekeeper, we'll be fine.

Okay, well, it's almost six, so we have some time to kill.

Good, let's scout out all the different bars, so we don't have to waste time come eight-thirty.

Nythan sighed. "This had better be worth it."

You're a Titan among mortals, Nythan, and you don't even realize it. Tonight should help set you on your way.

CHAPTER 27

LOSERS WEEPERS

Nythan made a mental list of all the bars he came across as he walked around the vicinity of Norfolk Street. Some appeared promising; others didn't. It helped that Bane had told him to look for someplace dark and secluded. Nythan thought it sounded like a bad cliché.

Most Hollywood movies take their cue from something *real, even if they take artistic liberties.*

Nythan glimpsed a clock hanging in a store he passed. It read 8:36 p.m. He patrolled through bar after bar on his list looking for a fedora.

Really? A fedora?

Nythan grinned. *It's* your *cult, Bane. I can't help it if you use fedoras as your secret signal.*

It could be anything from a cowboy hat to a ballcap.

Nythan smirked as he walked out of another bar on the road near Norfolk—another dead end. *You know, you guys should think about making a website. It'd help a lot with finding them when you need to.*

Hah. Unfortunately, as you will realize before our time together comes to an end, you will want to avoid exposure for as long as possible. They may be dormant now, but you have yet to see the entire world unite to crush you.

Nythan went through the next bar and the bar after that. Still no sign of the fedora-wearing cultist.

I wish you would use another word. Cultist sounds so…degrading.

Whatever, Nythan thought. *Where the hell are these guys?*

They're not the sort that wants *to be found, especially when the Ordo Solis still lurks about.*

Who or what *is the Ordo Solis?*

The most significant pain in my a** ever to walk the earth, that's who. I'll tell you all about them later. Let's find the Gatekeeper.

Nythan rounded the corner and found himself back to where he started: Norfolk Street. He spied a little barricaded entrance next to a garage door covered with graffiti and a dumpster. The entrance was a descending flight of stairs surrounded by a metal gate. A sign hung from the gate that read, "LOWER EAST SIDE TOY CO." He watched as a few people opened the gate and disappeared down the steps.

"Oh, yeah, forgot about that one." Earlier Nythan had asked several passersby for recommendations of exceptional bars. A couple of them mentioned a vintage speakeasy from the Prohibition era. They described it as a classy, tucked-away open secret.

Secluded and ominous, and it looks like it's open now.

Nythan walked over and opened the metal gate, descending the flight of stairs and continuing through a dingy alley. He climbed a copper staircase and entered an elegant and picturesque 1920s-style restaurant. Patrons spoke in hushed conversations in leather chairs under chandeliers twinkling against a bronzed ceiling. Walls of bookcases lined the perimeter, creating an aroma of powdered pine trees. Rusted metal signs whispered of a time long since passed, while the candles glowed only bright enough to repel the shadows from assaulting the tables.

This is a good sign. Let's do what we came to do.

Nythan smiled as he scanned all the people he could see. *They're drinking from teacups and brown bags.*

This was common during that era. Alcohol being illegal, you had to conceal your intentions, no matter where you were.

He wandered around for a good ten minutes before he spotted a door disguised as a bookcase. When he made to reach for it, a man wearing a double-breasted waistcoat and checkered bowtie stopped him.

"This is a private area," he said, motioning Nythan back in the direction he came.

I have a good feeling about this place. We need to get in there.

How do you propose we do that? Nythan asked.

He scanned the room once again and spied a blazing fireplace on a far wall. Two leather chairs faced the hearth. On a small circular table between the chairs rested a fedora.

Nythan could *feel* Bane's excitement. It came as a sharp pressure in his chest and caused his innards to constrict. He had trouble catching his breath.

Could it?

Don't get your hopes up, Nythan thought. *This place's thing is the twenties; it wouldn't be uncommon for someone to buy into the scene and wear a fedora.*

Nythan nonchalantly walked over to the fireplace and watched as flames licked up and around the underside of the logs. He sneaked a peek at the gentleman with a gelled comb-over sitting in one of the chairs.

No, it's not them. We need to get past that bookcase door though.

How exactly do you know if someone is a Raptor? Nythan asked.

The Gatekeeper and I must have a specific exchange of dialogue.

So how can you say it's not him if we haven't talked to him?

The man took his attention away from the fireplace and viewed Nythan without reaction. "*Buona sera*," he said.

European. Certainly not a Raptor.

Just hold on a second. Humor me. What would I do to vet him as the Gatekeeper?

We're wasting time.

I don't care if he's Italian. Tell me what to do, *Bane.*

You say, "Nice top cover you have there."

Nythan bent over and made to sit down in the chair next to him, but jerked to a halt when Bane's shout ricocheted in his mind.

NO, DON'T! Speak first.

He winced and straightened.

"Nice top cover you have there."

The Italian traced his finger against his upper lip. "Thank you," he replied in English.

Okay, what next?

Without gesturing anywhere or looking at the hat, say: "May I?" If he nods, grab the hat and put it on.

"May I?" Nythan asked.

The Italian stared at Nythan, then nodded.

That wasn't supposed to work...

Nythan chuckled, grabbed the hat, and placed it on his head.

Tap the front edge of the hat once, then sit down.

Nythan did as instructed. The Italian made no response.

I can't believe this is working. We'll know in about thirty seconds if this guy is for real or not. Sit straight up, spread your legs slightly, and put both hands on your kneecaps.

This is getting silly, Bane. Do you have to do this for everything? It's like we're in a 1960s spy movie.

I was alive when that genre was created. Shut up and do what I tell you; we have to do this right. Say: "I was just outside, there is a storm coming."

"I was just outside. There's a—"

Not "there's." You must say "there is." Say what I say exactly.

He repeated the phrase word for word.

"I too was outside recently. I do not remember sensing such a storm," the Italian replied.

Wow. Now listen carefully. Take the hat off with your left hand, casually transfer it to your right, and set it back down on the table. Tap one of the edges of the hat once where he can see, it doesn't matter which side.

Nythan performed the task as instructed.

Now look him dead in the eyes and say: "The storm has been here for some time. The only question is: what do you see when you are out there?"

"The storm has been here for some time..." Nythan began, trailing off. *Crap, what was the rest?*

You say: "The only question is: what do you see when you're...no no wait. What do you see when you are out there?"

"The only question is: what do you see when you are out there?"

The Italian grabbed hold of his hat and set it on his own head. *"Buona sera."*

Uhh...I don't remember that being the answer. He is supposed to say: "I see an endless wheat field, ripe for harvest."

Nythan froze. *Creepy stuff aside, he doesn't look like he's about to say that.*

The Italian stared at Nythan for about thirty seconds, then got up and walked toward the exit.

Something went wrong.

Naw, really? Seriously though, what do I do now?

Whatever you do, don't *move. If you do, we'll never see him again.*

The Italian approached the bookcase; the attendant made no effort to stop him. He regarded the row of books before him and pulled one of them out halfway. Nythan heard a terse *klunk* sound. The bookcase swung away from the Italian, and he disappeared through the opening. The bookcase swung and *klunked* back into place.

Now *you can get up. Make for the exit immediately.*

Nythan's eyes darted between the two options. *Which exit? The bookcase exit, or the other one?*

The one we used to get here. Let's go...I need someplace to think.

So, can we fix this or not?

Not tonight. We'll have to try again tomorrow.

Nythan's anger grew. *Well, that's an issue. I've got no money, and I don't know anyone in this city. There's nowhere for us to go.*

A night in the dumpsters won't kill you.

You know, when you said you'd show me things I couldn't possibly imagine, I didn't think it included sleeping behind a f***ing dumpster.

Oh, stop it. The good news is he is unquestionably *the Gatekeeper. Once he confirms who we are, we won't have to worry about a thing.*

Tall order from someone who just botched his own ritual. "It'll be fun," Nythan mimicked. "Don't worry... they're my minions."

Are you finished?

Well, being calm and collected definitely *didn't get us into the paradise you've been telling me about.*

I once knew an ancient and mighty Chinese ruler who said, "Sometimes, even the king must sleep with the pigs."

Oh yeah? Who said that?

I did, jacka**. Now get going.

CHAPTER 28

FINDERS KEEPERS

YES!

Nythan snapped awake and banged his skull on the side of the dumpster with a hard thud. He sat up with a huff, rubbing his scalp.

THAT'S IT!

He clamped both hands over his ears. "The hell? Bane, shut up."

I'm on a roll, here. Mind keeping your caterwauling down to a minimum?

Nythan let out a groggy sigh, "What happened?"

It's simple. We were supposed to say: "What do you see, when out there?" not "What do you see when you are out there?"

Nythan yawned. "That's great…" he trailed. "Can I go back to sleep now?"

Yes. Sleep tight. I'll wake you if I remember anything else.

"Please don't. I don't want to bumble the conversation a second time because you kept me up all night."

Alright. In the morning, then.

CHAPTER 29
ANCIENT CHINESE RULER

Nythan spent the day trudging around Lower Manhattan to pass the time. He listened to Bane recount all sorts of stories from his previous lives, from epic battles Bane fought to the times he worked for some big names.

I could not stand most of them. Truth be told, I would have pulled the breath out of them in an instant were it not for the access it gave me to power.

Nythan checked the time through a nearby window and felt dismayed by the number of hours left to kill before eight-thirty p.m.

"Bane. Can we talk about something else?"

I'm starting to get hungry again.

Nythan shuddered.

The thought still makes you uncomfortable.

Nythan stopped, leaned against a building, and slid down the wall onto the pavement. "Bane, even if I get to the point where I don't mind helping you...survive, I don't think I'll ever get over the fact that you have to actually live off souls. No matter how much you or the Hindu monks attempt to reason it away, it makes me really uneasy."

I understand, Nythan. I didn't choose my nature, as you never chose yours. Take a deep breath and relax. You're doing fine.

Nythan didn't want to admit how much that appeased him. He reasoned that survivors do things out of necessity, and even the supernatural play that game. At least, that was the way it appeared.

That's the way it is.

Dammit, Bane! Nythan kept forgetting that Bane could eavesdrop on all the rummaging going on inside his mind.

It goes much deeper than that Nythan. I don't just share your body; I share your most private thoughts and feelings. I meant what I said at the monastery. We are intertwined.

Nythan felt at a huge disadvantage by not knowing what Bane was thinking. He felt exposed and queasy that someone—some*thing*—could inhabit him and know him with such depth. He shivered in exasperation and decided to change the subject.

"Remember when you said that you were an ancient and powerful Chinese general?"

Ruler.

"Tell me about that, please. I'm tired of sightseeing."

Hmm. I don't remember the exact era, it was so long ago. I was an emperor of the Zhōu dynasty. I was young back then, so I didn't understand—

"Wait a second," Nythan interrupted. "What do you mean you were young *back then?*"

That's a conversation for another time.

Nythan's shoulders drooped as he sighed. "Fine. You were saying?"

I didn't grasp how culture worked. Political intrigue, the human need for survival, and the concept of betrayal...I was oblivious to it all. Anyways, in that life, I was a son of the Zhōu king and ended up being the one to ascend the throne.

You weren't the oldest?

He died in battle. And I was so new to being me that I was more concerned with figuring out what I was and why I was so different than with being a wise ruler. I spent precious resources, meant for the Zhōu people, on expensive excursions back to where I was from in India. Historical accounts depict me as an apocalyptic warlord who caused untold destruction. But I was far too selfish and detached to conquer anything. Instead, my neglect of the Zhōu people started them on a path of bitter decline.

"You seem to be able to remember all this pretty well..."

And?

"Oh nothing, just that we could've skipped all this if you had remembered something *else*..." Nythan smirked. "Like a certain ritual..."

The point is, there are some things for which I am regretful, and the way I ruled Zhōu was one of them.

"We all mess up. I mean, most of us don't usually mess up by inadvertently destroying an entire empire, but...still," Nythan grinned. "We all make mistakes."

Hahahaha, I suppose we do.

An exciting thought muscled its way to Nythan's consciousness. "I know you may not approve—"

No, I don't mind. You'll find out sooner or later.

Nythan remembered seeing a public library when he walked down Lafayette Street. He turned off East Houston Street and quickened his pace along Lafayette before veering onto Jersey Street and up a long ramp to the library entrance. He darted inside and sat at one of the public computers.

"What do I put in?" Nythan said, twiddling his fingers.

Start with Yaoguai. *It means* demon. *It was the first name the world ever gave me.*

Nythan typed in *Yaoguai* and tapped the enter key.

CHAPTER 30

IF AT FIRST YOU DON'T SUCCEED...

At 8:30 p.m., Nythan entered the speakeasy bar. He made for the same fireplace where he had stood the night before, arriving as the Italian took a seat.

Alright, Bane, don't F this up.

Something pinched Nythan's side, causing him to grunt in surprise.

The man again observed Nythan without any discernable reaction. *"Buona sera,"* he said.

Nythan went through the same exchange, sitting down as he did before.

Okay, now say it carefully.

Nythan's face strained to concentrate. "The storm has been here for some time. The only question is: what do you see, when out there?"

The Italian's face hardened and his eyes became slits. "I see an endless wheat field, ripe for harvest."

Yes. There we *go.*

The man stood and walked toward the bookcase door.

Follow him...and stay close.

The same attendant who stopped Nythan the previous night made to intercept him, but the Italian rotated toward Nythan and set his hand on Nythan's shoulder. The attendant stepped aside.

They walked through the bookcase door and proceeded down a narrow passageway into a small rectangular area with another bar and more books lining the walls. They passed a number of patrons scattered around the room. All seemed engrossed in mundane activities: reading newspapers and books, clicking on laptops, or conducting hushed phone conversations. No one paid Nythan or the Italian any attention. They made their way to a dimly lit corner in a bookcase alcove, a few steps past four gentlemen in suits seated on couches.

The Italian gestured for Nythan to sit in a chair with its back to the room. "Please be seated, my Lord," he said with no trace of the Italian accent.

He sat down across from Nythan, pulled out his phone, and began texting. When he finished, he looked up and slowly scanned the room. Nythan cocked an eyebrow at the man's sudden transformation into a guard dog.

That's because he is. *The Gatekeeper is a Raptor. The Raptors are here to keep us safe. They take their role seriously.*

Nythan frowned. *Couldn't you have chosen a better name than something that sounds like a bunch of pillaging barbarians?* Raptors *won't exactly win a public relations award.*

I realize that. They wanted an intimidating name, something that would set them apart. I couldn't name them "The Soul Brigade" or "Nature's Guardians" and think that they would take their role as faithfully as I wanted them to.

The Gatekeeper's phone rang. He brought it to his ear, listened, then spoke. "Sydalg's owl is ready to fly."

Nythan raised an eyebrow. *What's he saying?*

I don't know what their code words mean.

Nythan resisted the urge to look behind him.

Don't. They put you in that chair, facing this direction, for a reason. Of all the support groups we have, the Raptors are among the most purposeful.

What do you mean of all the support groups? *How many are there?*

We'll get to that eventually. I have much to show you.

The Gatekeeper's phone rang again, and he picked it up before the second ring. He listened for a few seconds, then hung up without responding. The Gatekeeper stood. "This way, my Lord."

He walked past Nythan, who rose and followed a few steps behind. As Nythan approached the four suited gentlemen, they stood and flanked him, two on either side. One detoured to the bartender and handed him a wad of cash.

Whoa, Nythan thought. He couldn't help how important the novelty of his new circumstances made him feel.

The Raptors play no games. They're professionals.

Their group crossed the room to a sizable painting of George Washington crossing the Delaware. The Gatekeeper took hold of the edge of the painting and slid it to the right, revealing a door. Without looking behind him, he opened it and walked through. Nythan followed, along with his new bodyguards.

CHAPTER 31

WELCOME TO THE 21ST CENTURY

They drove a few hours to a wealthy suburb just outside Harrisburg, Pennsylvania. The hills loomed high, and the houses stretched wide.

They hide in plain sight. They've done better than I expected. Secrecy and extravagance attract unwanted attention.

Their two-vehicle SUV convoy turned toward a random house on a treelined street. The driver pulled into a four-car garage, already occupied by two Ford F-150 Raptor trucks.

Hah, that's cute.

The driver put the SUV into park and shut it off, but no one moved until the garage door closed and the ceiling lights snapped on. Nythan climbed out with everyone else and stepped onto the gloomy concrete.

The Gatekeeper waited next to the door to the house. Two escorts stood on either side of him, facing outward. More guards stalked the corners, scanning their enclosed surroundings.

That's weird, we're in a garage, Nythan thought.

Go.

Nythan strode over to the door, which the Gatekeeper opened. His two escorts closed in behind him; the other two bodyguards made no motion to follow. They entered a kitchen large enough to feed a small army. Nythan took a whiff and was rewarded by a cinnamon aroma while chefs busied themselves with food preparation.

One of the cooks attending the evening meal bowed as Nythan approached. Another cook beamed, her eyes sparkling with tears. The last cook stepped out of Nythan's way, closed his eyes, and put his fist over his heart as he bent his head. No one said a word. The only sound came from the hiss of pan-seared food.

The Gatekeeper bowed, gesturing to one of the kitchen corridors.

Nythan walked down a short corridor and entered a bright dining room. He surveyed a museum's worth of vases, paintings, and antique weapons. An enormous rectangular dinner table was positioned in the center of the room. Glasses, china plates, and shiny silverware were all laid out in perfect order. Nythan's inner OCD wanted to hug whoever had set the table. The table fit twenty seats, all but eight of them occupied. The table guests rose as Nythan drew near.

Nythan came to within a couple paces of one guest, whose eyes went wide as saucers. He couldn't tell if the guy reacted in fear or amazement. An elderly female—Nythan thought she must be well into her eighties—stepped out from her chair at the middle of the table and over to Nythan.

"Great One," the Gatekeeper spoke in a soft voice. "This is the Matriarch of the Northern Coven."

Nythan withheld a chuckle. *Northern Coven? Like northern witches? I don't know where the name comes from.*

The elderly woman came to a stop mere inches away. Thumb-sized emeralds hanging from her earrings of worked gold swung to-and-fro. A tear traced a jagged line through the powder on her face as she placed her palms against Nythan's cheeks.

"My dear," she managed to utter. "I never thought I'd live to see this day. It makes me so happy to see you here." She held Nythan's hand as they inched to the head of the table. She flicked her hand at the man standing there, who jumped out of the way.

"Please, sit. Enjoy the evening meal with us," she said. She returned to her spot and waited behind her chair. No one took their eyes off Nythan.

They're waiting for you to take your seat.

"Of course," Nythan stammered, seating himself. Everyone else followed suit, silently looking at him.

Nythan scrunched his face. Now *what're they waiting for?*

Other than their food? Probably for you to say something.

I have no idea what to say.

They've been waiting for this moment for a long, long time. Say something.

Nythan cleared his throat. "Thank you," he began, "For your warm welcome. Please, don't let me stop you from eating."

That was...underwhelming.

What the hell am I supposed to say? I'm not Winston Churchill. Tell me what I should say.

Nythan, we're going to need to work together. Which includes you learning to interact with people from your own era without a lot of help from me.

Bane, I don't know how to interact with your cult.

Well then, we're both in good company. I had just established the Raptors when I had to leave, so I don't know them well either. We're learning together.

Fine.

"Brenton," the Matriarch called out with surprising force. One of the chefs came from the kitchen.

"Matriarch?"

"Is supper ready?"

The chef nodded. "Four more minutes, Matriarch." He returned to the kitchen.

The Matriarch rose from her chair and rotated her face toward Nythan. "My dear. We have been preparing for your return for many, many decades. I speak for all of us when I say I am overjoyed to see our faith has been rewarded. You will be proud of how much we have accomplished since you chartered our family. You will see we have carefully followed your mandate."

We shall see. Everything is much easier when no one knows you exist. That will change now.

What kind of life did you have when you created the Raptors? Nythan thought.

Bane chuckled. *I worked for the Central Intelligence Agency. Back then, the agency was known as something else. We were going through some major growing pains at the time, but the Agency was useful in teaching me how to avoid detection. I passed that knowledge on to the Raptors.*

Doesn't that make their knowledge a bit antiquated?

From then till now, yes. But my directives to them were to always have a purpose, avoid taking chances, and never *be stagnant. I should barely be able to recognize them from how much they've changed.*

Nythan smiled at the Matriarch. "I'm sure we will. Thank you." The Matriarch took her seat as the three chefs began bringing out individual plates.

One by one, each guest got their plate, but no one touched their food. The female cook approached Nythan. She still wore a misty-eyed expression. "My Lord, your dinner is served," she said, curtseying.

Nythan looked down at his placemat; she had not put down a plate.

Did someone tell them I can't keep food down anymore?

No, she's—

Nythan looked up at the woman. "I usually only eat really acidic things nowadays. Do you have any of that?"

The woman flushed with embarrassment. "My Lord, I'm so sorry, we didn't think that you would be hungry for physical food."

Nythan drew his eyebrows together in confusion. "Physical fo— Oh, shi— You don't mean…"

I tried to tell you.

Nythan's eyes darted around the table and found every other pair of eyes staring at him. Some of the guests looked happy, some appeared stone-faced, others wiped away tears. No one seemed alarmed.

"My dear," the Matriarch spoke. "You have no cause to conceal yourself any longer. We understand and accept you. This generous girl here gladly offers herself. Our cause is just; we rise further."

"We rise further," the whole table echoed in unison.

The Matriarch's reassurance did little to abate Nythan's growing fear.

Nythan. Listen to me. These people, they know who we are. They're here because of who we are. *No one is under any illusion over what's about to happen. There is* nothing *to be afraid of.*

Nythan's hands shook and his palms grew more moist by the second. *But she's…she's asking me to—*

Accept her gracious gift, yes. There will be many more gifts in the days to follow.

"Do you understand what's about to happen?" Nythan asked the woman in front of him.

Of course, she—

Shut up, Bane! Nythan thought. *Let me talk.*

An expression of confusion crossed the woman's face. "Of course, my Lord, I present my soul to you. I have longed for this moment," she said. "Please accept me."

Nythan bit his lip. He suppressed the conflicting feelings of terror and surprise, and then used the exhilaration to get his fear under control.

Accept her.

Nythan continued looking at the woman.

Accept her, Nythan.

He pushed his chair back and stood. The woman appeared rather beautiful to him, much like the female monk at the monastery had. Part of him wondered why these people chose to sacrifice themselves at all.

Nythan put his hands on the woman's cheeks in the same manner the Matriarch did earlier when she greeted him. Tears began flowing down her face. She covered his hand with hers and leaned forward so close that their foreheads touched.

Nythan made no attempt to mask his sadness. "This won't hurt," he assured her, unsure if he just told a lie.

"We rise further," she whispered.

Nythan gulped, causing her soul to vacate her body. Midway through the transition, Nythan held his breath and slowed the soul's voyage. He raised his face toward the ceiling, sluggishly whipping the radiant silver stream up like a lasso, prompting an assortment of gasps.

Visual assurance for the Raptors…that was smart.

After a few seconds, Nythan filled his lungs. The woman's soul shot forward, filling him with a familiar sense of euphoria.

"We rise further," the Raptors repeated in unison.

The overwhelming sensation distracted him from the woman until her body fell backward. Her peaceful face reassured him that she had got what she wanted, but he confronted the fact that he might only be seeing what he wanted to see.

The Matriarch motioned, and two nearby Raptors grabbed hold of the body and carried it away. Nythan scanned each person, almost all of whom looked on in amazement. His eyes came to rest on the Matriarch.

"What'll happen to her?" he asked.

The Matriarch clasped her hands and brought them to her lips. "She will be treated with the utmost respect. We will cremate her and hold a ceremony. Her sacrifice will not be in vain."

Nythan nodded and swung his hand around, puffing out his chest. "Please, enjoy your meals."

The Raptors began eating their dinner. No one else said a word, and almost no one took their eyes off him.

CHAPTER 32

THE ROSE GARDEN

A line of light from the morning sun inched from the bottom of Nythan's bed to his closed eyelids. His eyes fluttered open, and he breathed in as he stretched out in all directions. His arm struck warm flesh. Nythan peeked to his right to the exposed bare skin of a woman with lush curls of red hair. He swiveled to the left, seeing yet another woman with the covers pulled up to her short brown hair.

He looked from one woman to the other, then pushed his hand under the covers toward the brown-haired woman until he met her skin. His hand sneaked south until it grazed her bottom.

Nythan jerked his hand away when he felt no underwear. *Did I have an orgy last night?*

Bane's lecherous laugh all but confirmed the answer. *They're petrified of you, but they want you even more.*

Seriously, Bane. What the hell? Nythan thought. *I don't even remember what happened. The last thing I recall was that grandma pouring that disgusting wine and you pestering me until I drank it all. I'm gonna guess I didn't throw it up.*

You'll get used to it. Enjoy this moment. The Matriarch mentioned that now that we're here, our agenda is their agenda. Take your time.

Nythan sat in between the two women for a few minutes, admiring them. When he couldn't help himself, Nythan reached out to the redhead and traced her arm. The novelty of his circumstance again electrified him.

Whenever you're ready, the Matriarch would enjoy your company.

Nythan rolled out of bed and made it to the door before he remembered he was butt naked. He shrugged off the last vestiges of sleep as he sorted through a heap of fabric, eventually finding his clothes entangled with his two companions' garments.

He made his way along the hallway, wandered down the stairs, and meandered through the first floor until he caught the scent of fresh bacon. Nythan entered the kitchen, where only two cooks were preparing the meal.

The third one... he thought.

...graciously offered herself as your evening meal.

A shiver ran down Nythan's spine while parts of him he couldn't identify longed to be satisfied like that again.

The main chef put his hand on his chest and bowed toward Nythan before returning his attention to the breakfast preparations. Nythan entered the dining room and saw the Matriarch eating at the table in silence. She paused for a second at Nythan's arrival before taking another bite.

"Good morning, my dear. Did you enjoy your night?"

Nythan cleared his throat. "Uh, yes," he said hastily, "They were...I mean, yes, it was nice."

The Matriarch let out an icy shrill of a laugh. Nythan recoiled.

"I hoped they would suffice. Come!" she said, slapping the table with both hands. "I want to show you something."

"But I'm hungry?" Nythan asked without meaning it as a question.

"After!" the Matriarch exclaimed, taking his hand as she led him to a glass door at the far end of the dining room. She threw aside the curtains, and Nythan shielded his eyes as the sun's rays pierced the glass door and blinded him. The Matriarch slid the door open and stepped onto a patio overlooking a spacious backyard enclosed by a tall privacy fence.

She guided Nythan into a small garden of shoulder-height hedges, adorned by shriveled red and white rosebuds. A dozen scattered topiaries protruded atop the hedges. The first figure depicted a short man with thick horn-rimmed glasses.

That was me when I first established the Raptors. They have me pretty close.

The Matriarch pointed to the leafy figure. "This was our first encounter of you."

Another topiary portrayed a group of individuals kneeling in front of a naked, muscled giant. As Nythan and the Matriarch ventured further, the ambiance grew darker. A nearby fountain, overshadowed by the hedge above, made a trickle of noise. The next set of figures wore masks of faces twisted in agony. One figure among them didn't wear a mask and was clearly modeled after the Matriarch.

The Matriarch smiled at the leafy model of herself. "For when I'm gone."

They cleared the hedges, entering a small lawn with a glittering two-headed statue covered in gemstones of various colors and textures. The sculpture outstretched its left hand toward them with an open palm while clenching its right fist at the rising sun. The left face looked at them with a happy but undistinguished human expression. The right head was a furious ghost glaring at the sun.

Hmmmmmmm.

"Made of the finest substances we could find. Emerald, ruby, jade, gold, silver, amethyst, topaz, sapphire, quartz, diamond. All right there," the Matriarch told Nythan.

Nythan guessed that this was a depiction of Bane and its host. He didn't know whether to be honored or horrified. Radiant streaks of color shot out from the statue, piercing the air like arrows aimed at the sun. While the sight struck him as impressive, the obsidian base created a shadowy aura that hid the statue's contours. He didn't want to get any closer, but he couldn't stop staring.

Nythan squinted to make out some of the statue's features. *Now that I think about it, it describes our situation perfectly.*

Mm-hmm. Impressively unnatural.

The Matriarch spoke behind him.

"Stay here as long as you like," the Matriarch said, turning to leave. "By the time you come back, your breakfast will be ready."

"Wait," Nythan called out. "You told us last night our agenda was your agenda. Do y'all just want us to tell you what to do?"

She raised her chin. "I do not mean to be insolent, but we can survive on our own with only the slightest hint of guidance, as you can see. What I meant when I said that was, now that you have arrived to tell us what your goal is, we will help you achieve it." She turned and continued toward the house.

Nythan faced the statue. *Now what?*

Now we decide what we want.

What do you mean, what we *want? You're supposed to tell* me *what to do, and I'm supposed to be the vessel that complies…right?* Nythan threw his hands up in disgust.

Bane laughed. *You still think this is a Hollywood movie, where I possess you and make you do my evil bidding. I don't have a plan this time, Nythan. I have literally created thousands of plans, and each time I failed. So when I fell into the shadows, I formed three support groups: the Unas, the Raptors, and Sanhe. I deliberately chose* not *to plan beyond that.*

To use your word, that's a bit underwhelming, Nythan thought.

Bane laughed again. Nythan felt the laugh reverberate through his arms to his fingertips.

Just because you have a supernatural thing living inside you does not *mean you become some god where all your problems are solved. We have to work for what we want, like the lowliest of the low. The approaching conflict seems far away now, but when it begins, you will understand. Nothing is handed to anyone—not to you, and not even to me. You'd be surprised at some of the poor conditions in which I have lived in past lives. Sleeping behind a dumpster is nothing.*

Nythan found the words sobering and unsettling, coming from this entity that had lived for thousands of years. As he processed them, he grew disappointed at the message they conveyed.

Expectation management, Nythan reminded himself. His mind flashed to a time when his cadet class had competed for the "Best Flight in Uniform" award. They had stood at rigid attention, awaiting the last inspector to finish scrutinizing each member. At the end of the examination, the inspector had dismissed them from the competition, saying that they hadn't stood a chance. The mortification he felt from that defeat had crushed Nythan. It had prompted him to spend an entire week perfecting his uniform and rehearsing the proper commands—a week that had ended with the intruder attacking him in Pamela's home.

Nythan bit his lip. *So, what now?*

Let's wait and see what develops, and we can both decide where to go from there. Even though I haven't crafted a master plan, experience tells me that an opportunity will present itself.

"You're the expert," Nythan said out loud.

When it comes, be ready to seize that opportunity without hesitation.

CHAPTER 33

TIMELESS

Nythan sat at the head of the dining room table, his new hunger rattling his ribcage. The Matriarch sat a few chairs away to Nythan's right, reading the newspaper. To his left sat a row of people eating breakfast. Next to him stood a man, waiting for Nythan to have his soul for breakfast. He had tried inhaling as the guy exhaled, but success eluded him. He stifled the urge to chuckle as the two of them engaged in an awkward breathing contest.

How often do you usually eat? Nythan asked Bane.

In my heyday, I was satisfied several times a day. For our purposes now, you could get away with once every other day.

So how's it that for the first nineteen years of my life, you didn't need to eat the way that you do now?

It's complicated.

Well do *explain,* Nythan prodded.

You know how babies survive off milk when they are young, but grow to eat more complex foods? It's similar to that. I can survive off you for a long time before I need something more substantial.

What do you mean, 'survive off me'?

Your soul.

Nythan went bug-eyed and his temples throbbed. *You're...eating* my *soul? What the hell!*

I only nibble, and I stopped when you took your first soul.

A thin line drew across Nythan's lips. *You're like a motherf***ing vampire.*

Bane chuckled, causing Nythan to shiver.

Now you know how I got the name Dracula. And as I told you, when your body transitions to...let's call it spiritual food, *the need for physical food diminishes. We're pretty much at that point now.*

Nythan's let his hand slap the table; the man in front of him jumped. *We've been at that point. Everything tastes like s***, and I can't hold anything down. I've been throwing up since the monastery.*

Exactly.

Nythan again tried to receive the man's soul, but nothing happened. Nythan huffed. *Why isn't this working?*

Because you aren't focusing. You may have done it before, but you aren't yet at the point where you can do it automagically.

The Matriarch glanced from her newspaper. "Problem?"

"None," Nythan answered.

He slowed his inhales and forced his way into the breathing state. He pushed aside the nightmarish memory of what happened the last time he had difficulty. The white flecks of breath the man drew in and grayish release tickled his mind. When he focused on the Matriarch, her breathing soothed him like the in and out of a beach tide. Curious, Nythan crept his way throughout the house, taking inventory of everyone in the vicinity. He encountered scores more occupants than had attended dinner the night before.

He returned his focus to the man in front of him. "Slow your breathing."

"I'm trying."

He would calm down if you talked to him a little bit. Reassure him that he's doing this for the right reason.

Nythan nodded and opened his eyes. "What's your name?"

His squarish face perked up. "Norman."

"Okay, Norman. Do you know why you're doing this?"

The Matriarch turned her attention to them.

"Be-because…you're the Great One?" Norman looked like a puppy hiding in terror after peeing on the carpet.

"Yes, I understand that. But tell me why *you* are doing this."

I meant reassure him by telling him it's going to be okay, not have a philosophical discussion.

Nythan smirked.

Norman fidgeted, looking stumped.

"Norman," the Matriarch said. "Remember what we talked about? You know why you're doing this. Tell him what you told me."

"It's all good, Norman," Nythan assured him. "I accept you for who you are, and I'm grateful for your gift. I'd just like to know a little more about what this means to you, in your own words. That's all."

"Y…You're my…my deliverer." Norman scanned the room. "You'll deliver us all from the evils of this world. I want to do everything I can to help. The most significant thing I can offer is myself."

The Matriarch nodded.

Norman's breathing slowed, allowing Nythan to follow it in and out. "Thank you, Norman. You'll be remembered," Nythan said, and immediately gulped for breath. He tugged on Norman's soul and it tumbled out.

Ahhhhhhh. Nythan's throat tickled as Bane heaved a sigh of relief.

Everyone at the table whispered, "We rise further."

Nythan balled his hand into a fist, his impulse telling him to destroy a mountain.

I did that once.

Nythan stifled a laugh. "What?" he said out loud. The Matriarch gave him a puzzled expression. He waved her off, tapping his chest.

The Matriarch laid her newspaper on the table. "My dear, may I ask you a personal question?"

"Sure."

"How is your…interaction with the Great One?"

Nythan considered the inquiry with a grin. "Well, I…" Nythan shrugged. "It began all of a sudden. First, I didn't know what was happening. Then when I figured out *he* was there, I didn't know what *he* was. And when I figured *that* out, I hated him. Flew halfway around the world to get rid of him. Almost killed myself in the process." Nythan shrugged. "But he grew on me. Now, he talks to me like we're talking here."

"You still retain your own thoughts?"

"Yes," Nythan replied. "At first, when he wasn't speaking, I didn't even know he was there. Now, I feel him constantly."

Since he received the cook last night, Nythan's enriched senses alerted him to something blanket-like wrapped around a part of him. A thing that he knew to be real but couldn't pinpoint. It comforted his very being.

Aww.

Shut up, Nythan thought, but then burst out laughing. He tapped his heart again so the Matriarch would understand the sudden reaction.

The Matriarch smiled. Before she could ask another question, a man approached her dressed in black silk garb and a mask depicting a terrifying face twisted in agony, like the topiary figure in the garden.

"Matriarch." The voice sounded digital and raspy, like Darth Vader. The person rotated his masked face toward Nythan and then back to the Matriarch.

"Whatever you could imagine saying, you may say in front of our Lord. Speak!"

"We got the family and the woman, but we couldn't get to the loner worm. He's so far evaded our attempts to capture him."

Nythan was confused and concerned by the graveness of the newcomer's words.

Take it easy, Nythan. It was bound to start sometime.

What was bound to start?

We'll see, but the Raptors are probably removing a complication to our return.

*What the hell are you talking about...*complication. *What sort of* complication *could there be?*

Oh, I don't know, Nythan, maybe the whole world wanting to kill *us if they knew I existed?*

Why can't we just keep doing this, for however long it takes?

That would be great, except that we'll end up eating the entire Raptor organization. Then *who would keep us safe?*

We can go to one of your other groups, eat them. At least they're willing participants, Nythan thought.

As our appetite grows, we will exceed their ability to give us willing participants.

Please don't tell me that. You never told me this was going to happen!

It's unavoidable, Nythan. I'll do everything I can to help us prolong it for as long as possible. But eventually, we'll have to face it together.

S***.

It'll be fine.

Nythan snapped out of his internal trance as the Matriarch dismissed the black-clad Raptor.

"Hey," Nythan called out. "Who are you?"

The figure paused, then took off his mask.

"My name is Devin, my Lord, your humble servant," he said, bowing.

"Why do you wear that?"

"Oh, we've been wearing these masks for ages, not long after our organization started. Nowadays, those who are on guard duty or engaged in other Raptor business wear them, mostly."

"I see. Thank you, Devin."

Devin bowed once more, "My pleasure, my Lord. We rise further." He reaffixed his mask and left the room.

"Why do you all say that, 'We rise further'?" Nythan asked the Matriarch.

"It is both our motto and a reminder of our duty to the community. As one of us ascends, the rest do as well. As you rise, we rise. It is a mutual effort, supported by all."

Nythan understood how she had become the Matriarch. One minute, she'd be as cold as ice, the next as inspiring as Gandhi. It made for a confusing, somewhat intimidating, but altogether alluring personality.

"What about the obstacle?" Nythan didn't want to ask, but he had to know about the family and the woman Devin mentioned.

"Currently in pursuit. We shall find him shortly."

"Why're we hunting him?"

"He made off with video evidence of your return."

How the hell *did that happen? I want to know.*

"How?"

"The Ordo Solis…"

Oh.

"We had whittled them down to a mere two discouraged volunteers," the Matriarch continued. "A series of circumstances preceding your return resulted in one of them fleeing before we had a chance to stop him. All Covens have been alerted; we are fleshing out every possible destination he could go. We *will* find him."

"That's good," Nythan said, trying to process why all this was important.

"In the meantime, I received word from the Grand Coven in Missouri. They would be…*honored*…by a visit from you. They have prepared the proper accommodations for a long-term stay."

Nythan raised an eyebrow. He could have sworn he saw her eyes roll at the word *honored*.

"What do you think?"

"I think you should tell me what you want, and I'll make sure it happens."

"How about a little orange juice?" Nythan said with a sly grin. "I'd like to see if I can still feel the taste."

The Matriarch winked. "I suppose I should be grateful for the easy tasks while they last."

Nythan groaned. "Why does everyone say that?"

"Because, my dear, it wasn't always so easy to be a follower of you. We were once hunted, just as you, simply for our beliefs," she explained, the expression on her face turning into a sneer. "Now, it's *their* turn to feel the bootheel."

CHAPTER 34

THE ORDER OF THE SUN

A three-vehicle convoy chauffeured Nythan toward Missouri to meet the Grand Coven, the Raptor masterminds. The Matriarch sat beside him, reading one of the *Harry Potter* novels under a book light.

Okay, I'm dying to know, Nythan thought. *Who or* what *is the Ordo Solis?*

It would take me years to explain what they are.

Give me the short version.

They are the black to your white. They hate us and will do everything they can to kill us.

Okay, give me the slightly longer *version.*

They began out of the Inquisition as part of the Catholic Church. Their whole purpose was to hunt heresy, which was a catchall for anything and anyone having to do with me. They grew in size and power until their brutality resulted in their decline. After the dissolution of the Inquisition, the Ordo Solis was chartered. It means The Order of the Sun. *In some damnable righteous arrogance, they believe they are the sun questing to expose the darkness. Decades later, they split into three sections. The sections cover three regions: Europe, Asia, and the Americas. Two of my lifetimes ago, we crippled the Ordo Solis in Asia. If all went according to plan, there's nothing left of them now.*

You don't talk about your past lives all that often. What happened in the life before mine?

I did some work in the Middle East, and then I came here.

Do you get to pick who you get to…be?

It would be easier to say that the choice is made for me.

The Matriarch shrieked, making Nythan jump. She let out a few more high-pitched outbursts at a less scary volume, and Nythan realized he had confused her laughter for alarm.

"Silly Potter, now you're going to get all your friends killed," she remarked, then looked up at Nythan. "The boy has no idea. His naivety makes me so angry sometimes." She kept her gaze on Nythan for another moment before returning her attention to the novel.

Nythan stared at her with bemusement. *Damn, she's weird.*

I really like her. Your earlier explanation was perfect: confusing, intimidating, and alluring. The ideal person to lead our organization. Let's hope these Raptor masterminds are as suitably balanced.

If that's your version of balance, I'm not sure I want to know what imbalance looks like.

Bane laughed. A slight pinch in Nythan's neck caused him to spasm, and he rubbed his neck to relieve the discomfort.

So back to the Ordo Solis. If they're dying, then why mess with them at all?

Because if they have video evidence of who you are, and that video becomes public, then the chase starts all over again.

Maybe. But things aren't the way they were during the Catholic Inquisition. Nowadays, barely anyone believes you exist at all.

I guess the Raptors felt it worth the risk. If they're wrong, it will cost us a great deal of patient and careful planning. I will not be pleased.

Uh-huh, well at least when you die, you get to come back to life. When I die, it's all over. So I'm just as uncomfortable as you are about it.

Nythan gazed out the tinted window for a while. The scenery changed from trees to suburbs to plains. He peered at the Matriarch; she still had her face buried in her book. Her emerald earrings twinkled against the full moonlight.

"Sorry to interrupt, but I gotta know. Why do you always wear those huge stones?"

"They were a gift from Alvy, given shortly after the death of my husband, Robert," she answered. She creased the top-right edge of the page and closed her book. "Robby was old enough to be Alvy's father, but they were close friends while working for the Central Intelligence Group. They left with you to organize your scattered followers into the first Grand Coven in Boston. I wasn't involved with your cause, nor did I know you during that period of your life. All I knew was that my Robby was convinced he had to help you. By the time our house sold in D.C. and we moved to join you in the land of opportunity, you were gone, leaving Robby to pursue your mandate."

The Matriarch's face hardened before looking out the window. "The Ordo Solis used to have so much influence—police officers, senators, captains of industry...*judges*," she spat. "The Coven was just starting to grow, and they tried all manner of ways to stop my husband. Punctured our car tires, harassed us at work, even set fire to our new house. When that didn't stop him, they framed my Robby for evading taxes. I started helping with the Coven's clerical work after he was denied bail and suffered in jail until his trial. He was convicted and was murdered two days after arriving in prison. They never caught the killer, but I knew who killed my Robby."

"I'm so sorry."

The Matriarch touched her fingers to the stone, misty-eyed. "Alvy gave me these the day they told me Robby died. He said emeralds were the wisest of all stones with the power to heal any wound. Preposterous of course, but it came true in its own way. I needed to hold on to whatever I could of him, so I took his cause as my own."

"What happened to Alvy?" Nythan asked.

"He returned to his home in Chile and started the Lower Coven. His son, Alvy Junior, is Patriarch now."

"You've sacrificed so much."

The Matriarch pursed her lips as she caressed one of the emeralds. "Yes, but it's been worth every heartache."

Nythan let the silence linger until he became uncomfortable under the unwavering gaze of the Matriarch.

"Why do you call it a Coven?" he asked.

The Matriarch sighed, letting her hand drop from her earring.

"That was decided before my time," she replied. "There are different explanations. One says our forefathers were actually foremothers, and they were confused as witches. Others say it was to mock the Inquisition's hunt for heresy. I've heard one person connect it to the burning of witches in Salem. But the most reliable explanation comes from Patrick in the Grand Coven. He says that *coven* comes from the Latin word *conventus*, which means assembly."

It could be the first one. *The Raptors owe much of their early success to a small group of women operating a pub in Boston.*

"What's the Grand Coven? I assume they're somehow running all this."

"They provide us with strict guidance, as prescribed by your mandate. Beyond this, they leave us to our work."

Nythan squinted. "Who's *us*, in this case?"

"The eight Raptor Covens. Northern, Southern, Eastern, Western, and Central Covens are in North America. Upper, Lower, and Brazilian Covens are in South America. Each Coven is granted one overseer, known as a Matriarch or Patriarch."

"Which is you."

"Correct, I am the Northern Matriarch. I'm responsible for Maryland to Missouri, up to Ontario and Newfoundland. Everyone answers to the Grand Coven, which, like the U.S. Congress, holds the purse strings. Also, like the U.S. Congress, the Grand Coven can be annoying at times…but don't tell 'em I said that," the Matriarch said, winking.

"What *is* your real name?"

"Gladys."

"What's been your interaction with the Order of the Sun?"

"Since my time as Matriarch, we have whittled them down to little more than a humorous nuisance."

"I see," Nythan said. "So while this war raged between the Order of the Sun and those loyal to…uh…"

"You," the Matriarch finished for him.

"Sure, me." Nythan blushed. "So, while this war raged, what was everyone else doing?"

"The public believes you are a myth. They classify our struggle with the Ordo Solis as a cult-on-cult conflict, and everyone involved is a social pariah. This suits us fine; we don't require public support like the Order does. As their endorsements waned over the years, so did the Order... until we overcame them."

"And now?"

"Within the next few days, they will be no more, unless the Eastern Patriarch cannot see to a simple task. I hear Ordo Asia has crumbled, and I can only assume Sanhe was responsible. All that will be left is Solis Europe, and they're currently experiencing the depths to which Unas vengeance goes. They won't last much longer."

"So then tell me, what's the point of all this?" Nythan asked.

Careful. You don't want to create a ripple of doubt in our people. We need them.

I realize.

The Matriarch gave Nythan a curious look. "My dear, that is for *you* to decide. I do not presume to know your plans, but we exist to see them to fruition."

"And if my plans involve consuming the whole world, would you follow me then?"

The Matriarch regarded him sternly. Nythan wondered if he had crossed a line.

"This world is corrupt and rotten to the *core*," she spat, "If you ended up devouring it, you would be doing it a favor."

Ahhhh, so that's why she serves so diligently. I wondered if her husband was the source of her loyalty, but now I see it goes much deeper. I like this Matriarch; she's a true believer.

Nythan nodded. *Time to see just how far her faith goes.*

Why do you provoke her so?

Because someday we may need to know just how far she'll go to help us, Nythan replied. *Someday it may matter.*

You're settling into our partnership rather nicely.

Mm-hmm, don't thank me yet. A faint chuckle escaped Nythan's lips. He tapped his chest again. "I enjoy our talks."

"Whose, ours or yours?"

"Both. One more question. In devouring the world, as you put it, we devour both the guilty and the innocent, the young and the old. How do you feel about that?"

"I prefer not to remind myself, as I would have to face the fact that I am complicit in their undoing. However, I have considered the implications, and my service has remained unchanged."

Nythan turned his attention toward the window as the darkness swept past. "I don't like to think about it either. I'm still me, even though the Great One is inside," Nythan admitted. "And part of me is still horrified at the thought of taking an innocent life. It feels wrong...evil even."

"My dear, in the long life I have lived, I've come to understand that good and evil are not so far apart from one another as society desperately wants to believe. It is a spectrum with nothing but gray in between, full of opinions on where the line is. The hard truth is that there *is* no line. *This* is the great secret many will realize toward the end of their pathetic lives. Until then, those who've not discovered this will continue to oppose those who have, as the Ordo Solis does. They'll mislead their followers with labels such as Good versus Evil or Right versus Wrong. These labels feed their delusion to help them feel good about themselves. Their propaganda attempts to assure society that they are on the *right side*."

Nythan continued to gaze out the window, pondering her words.

"You have only to answer to yourself, my dear. At the conclusion of your life, be able to say, as I will, that the only experience left to enjoy... is eternal sleep."

CHAPTER 35

BRILLIANCE

Their conversation lingered in Nythan's mind until Bane's voice rattled inside Nythan's head.

We need to keep her as long as possible.

You make it sound like she isn't going to last long.

All of you have an expiration date. When the war starts, she must be protected. Losing her would indeed be detrimental to our effort.

Okay.

"Matriarch," said the Raptor driving. Both he and the Raptor in the front passenger seat had said nothing the entire trip. Nythan was impressed with the level of Raptor discipline.

The Matriarch eyed Nythan. "We will be arriving in five minutes. There are a few procedures I will make you aware of."

Nythan turned to the window once more, seeing nothing but rolling hills against the rising sun. "Out here?"

The Matriarch nodded. "For our daily operations, it is important you blend in. When we arrive, wait until I get out before you do. I will be flanked on all sides. You will trail behind, and another will follow some steps after you. In the event anyone is observing, they will assume I am the person of interest. The party that greets us will not acknowledge you, again for the same reason. Once inside, we will safely assume our rightful roles."

"Understood," Nythan responded. He shook, unable to contain his excitement.

A few minutes later, the vehicle came to a stop outside a fenced compound. A gate guard greeted them. An ID badge that dangling from his lapel identified him as an employee of "VNI."

"VNI?" Nythan asked as the guard waved them through.

"Yes, Vigilant National Incorporated is a subsidiary company we've gone to great lengths to associate with one of the major religious organizations. If the outside world discovers our headquarters here, our purpose will be confused with theirs, buying us precious time."

Smart.

The convoy drove down a small paved road with vast lawns on either side until they arrived at a mansion with a circular driveway in front. A group of four men and women wearing their Sunday best gathered at the foot of the stairs.

"Here you go, my dear. I hope this doesn't offend you," the Matriarch said, putting a clipboard with a checklist in Nythan's hands. "To blend in." She winked at him and exited the vehicle.

Nythan trailed behind the Matriarch a few paces. The Matriarch's entourage approached the welcoming party, and she engaged both hands as she greeted each person. No one acknowledged his existence.

Nythan entered the mansion behind the Matriarch and the others, taking in how plain everything appeared. He had expected some sort of palace, with wildly expensive ornaments, lavish furnishings, and marble floors. Instead, a spacious foyer of austere design greeted him. About the only thing that could be considered extravagant was the gigantic dark wood table positioned in the center of the room. A few abstractly colored paintings hung from the dull white plaster walls. Lamps rested on two small stands; a simple chandelier dangled up above.

As soon as the door behind him closed, the atmosphere changed. His guardians detached themselves from the Matriarch and instead came to a halt beside him. The Matriarch stepped from between him and the welcoming party. The group gave him their undivided attention, all bowing to some degree.

A small, bald, tuxedoed man spoke with a Swedish accent, "My Lord,

I am Palaou. Please excuse the manner in which we brought you. We have left nothing to chance, as you instructed."

They continue to take their roles seriously.

Nythan nodded. "I understand."

Palaou bowed further. "The Coven requests your presence whenever you find yourself rested."

"They're not here now?"

"Appearances, my Lord. The Northern Matriarch does not warrant the presence of the Grand Coven to welcome her."

Nythan again nodded, yawning. "K. What else?"

Palaou put his hand over his heart. "My Lord, I am at your service. Whatever you wish, you have but to voice it."

"Anything at all?" Nythan asked with a mischievous glint.

"Yes, my Lord."

"How abouuuut...a coconut raspberry lemonade, a caramel topped bagel, exactly three pixie sticks, and one of those little mints you get from Olive Garden."

Hah.

Out of the corner of his eye, Nythan saw the Matriarch give Palaou a sly grin.

Palaou, looking a little flustered, yanked out a notepad. "Of course, my Lord. I will see to the details immediately..."

Amused, Nythan listened to Palaou whisper the order to himself as he concentrated on what he wrote down.

"Palaou," Nythan said, grinning broadly.

Palaou finished writing something, then glanced up. "My Lord?"

"I'm messing with you, Palaou. Orange juice will do just fine." The Matriarch chuckled beside him.

Palaou blinked.

Nythan held up his hand, trying to hold in his laughter. "I know, Palaou, I know. Thank you. I appreciate your effort."

Palaou finished writing, then glanced up at Nythan. "Would you care for more...substance, with your juice?"

"Not yet, but thank you. How about a tour instead?"

The man beside Palaou spoke up in a deep voice. "My name is Simon, my Lord. I can assist." Nythan looked up at Simon, who resembled a chiseled balloon animal. Nythan wagered that Simon's biceps were bigger than Palaou's head. Had his dress pants been brown, Simon's legs could've been mistaken for tree trunks.

"Great, after you," Nythan said, gesturing outwards.

After the first ten minutes, Nythan couldn't have been more bored. The minimalist décor made each room seem the same. He perked up when Simon led him into a backyard similar to the Matriarch's but with at least twice as many hedges and topiaries.

They came to a stop in front of a gem-encrusted statue of Bane, which dazzled just like the one in the Matriarch's garden. This time, two statues stood on either side of the center sculpture. On the right was a robed figure, wearing the same agony mask as Devin. On the left stood a ponytailed statue, clearly female, wearing a mask with teeth bared in rage. The bright glint of Bane's statue contrasted with the matte dark metals of these two masked figures.

"Magnificent, no?" Simon asked.

Ostentatious to say the least. It draws unnecessary attention.

Nythan rubbed his scruffy chin. "Yes. What purpose do these statues serve?"

"Motivation," Simon said. "We have frequent member visits. It reminds us why we're here. Many have sought solace in this very spot. It was the closest thing we had to you, until now."

Simon speaks well for a brute, Nythan thought. He side-stepped to the left, using Simon's body to block the sun from hitting him. *I figured him the more thuggish, less intelligent type.*

Looks are deceiving.

"How long have you been a Raptor?" Nythan asked.

"Almost seven years."

"And what do you expect to happen now that we're here?"

Simon looked him square in the eye. "I expect you to deliver us."

CHAPTER 36

THE GRAND COVEN

Nythan sat with the Grand Coven. The eleven council members were assembled at a large circular table surrounding an expansive sunken open area. The Coven members had introduced themselves, but Nythan had already forgotten most of their names. The Matriarch had briefed him about the things he needed to discuss with the Grand Coven without her present.

"Great One," said a middle-aged man with a thick comb-over. Nythan thought his name was Richard.

Gunther.

"We are thrilled at your return," Gunther continued. "All preparations have been made. There're only two matters on our agenda."

This is where the rubber meets the road.

"Okay, what's the first?"

"We humbly request…" Gunther began, opening his hands and lowering his chin. "As a reward for our faith, that you fulfill yourself where we all can have the honor of seeing, firsthand."

You should demonstrate by sucking the soul out of this bastard.

"I'm n—" Nythan started, then he bit his lip. *I can't do it again.*

We need their help. Just do it.

Stop pressuring me.

I'm not pressuring you, you child. If you don't eat, we'll die. And if you don't give them a display of power, they won't be on our side.

What if I don't care if they're on our side?

But you do. *They're the only people that care about us. Your old family discarded you like garbage after your mother passed. This is our family now. Show your new family what you can do.*

I don't know. Nythan shifted in his seat as all eyes rested on him in expectation.

Look at them. You're losing their respect.

Nythan wilted under the piercing gazes of the Coven members.

"I—," he began.

You're a lion. Stop acting like a sheep.

Nythan squeezed his eyes shut and massaged his face, letting out a shaky sigh. He waited until his breathing calmed and his face betrayed no emotion before opening his eyes. He stared at each person with far more confidence than he felt.

"You want me to prove that I am who you believe me to be."

"Great One, absolutely not," Gunther said, looking to the others. "The Northern Matriarch has already borne witness to your gift. We humbly wish to see for ourselves. Some of us here have been faithful followers for over fifteen years. We each yearn to see our faith rewarded, in the way that only *you* can."

Nythan nodded. "I understand. Who'll be the giver?"

"I will, my Lord," a tiny, frail woman said from the far side of the table.

"Please remind me your name."

"Jillian." She struggled to make her way toward the presentation space. Nythan got up and walked over to her, letting her grip his forearm as they made their way to the sunken open area. She let Nythan go as he turned to face her.

Nythan offered a wave. "Hi."

Jillian bowed. "Great One, please accept my gift, such as it is."

I need to warn you, her soul may be a bit more challenging to take. Mature ones are usually more potent.

Why's that? Nythan asked, raising an eyebrow. Jillian looked as though she'd blow away at the slightest breeze.

I don't know, I think it's more difficult due to how long the soul and the body have been together. When a soul has been on this earth for a long while, it grows heavy with experience.

Nythan bowed back to Jillian. "I'm honored to receive your gift. Please, breathe in and out calmly, but completely. You won't feel a thing."

Jillian nodded and did as Nythan asked. He closed his eyes, seeking her breath. He tried several times to draw her soul out of her body, but her soul clung to its physical form. The attempts sent Jillian into a brief coughing fit.

"Sorry," Nythan said.

You keep trying to force it out. Until this point, it's worked. I've seen far more success from those who coaxed it out, rather than yanking the soul like a fish on a hook.

Nythan considered Bane's words, and studied the gentle way Jillian's lungs moved out and in. Nythan tugged with less force, but her soul again settled back into place.

It's not working.

You had the right idea, just do more *of it.*

Nythan tried once more to embrace Jillian's soul. To Nythan's surprise, she moaned.

"That feels wonderful," she breathed, beaming.

Nythan sensed her soul soften before he ushered it from her body. He knew he succeeded when a number of council members gasped, prompting Nythan to open his eyes. A familiar ethereal stream weaved out of Jillian's mouth, emanating a luminescent silver light.

"My…God!" one of them marveled.

Bane's mighty hunger swelled and couldn't be suppressed any longer. Nythan received her soul in its entirety, cradling her in his arms as she fell forward.

The rest of the Coven members bowed low. "We rise further," they echoed.

Without warning, tears began streaming down Nythan's face.

I don't know why I'm crying, Nythan thought, wiping them away.

It's okay. I understand why. You're disgusted and ashamed of what you have to do to survive.

I have to kill people to survive. Nythan slumped, even as the familiar sense of euphoria crept in and struck him full force. But then an excruciating pain in his abdomen forced him to double over and emit a loud groan. Jillian slid off him and hit the floor; Nythan soon followed. Coven members rushed to his aid, picking him up off the ground.

"My Lord, are you okay?"

Nythan clutched his throbbing heart. He brought his other hand up and grabbed the Raptor next to him.

Too much of a good thing can overwhelm. Take it easy. It's the most potent soul we have consumed thus far.

"Just give me a moment," Nythan gasped. His helpers led him to one of the roundtable chairs. He wheezed for almost twenty minutes, begging silently for the agony to subside. Beads of sweat peppered his face, and a headache pounded his skull.

When at last the pounding subsided to a dull throb, he peered at the remaining Coven members. "Well then," he said slowly, wincing. "What's the other thing on the agenda?"

The Covens members gave him a worried look.

"Speak!"

A Coven member cleared his throat. "Great One, we await your word. We don't know your plan. What do you want us to do?"

Bane started laughing and wouldn't stop. His laugh reverberated throughout Nythan's entire body, threatening to restart the ache in his stomach.

Nythan squinted and pressed his fingers into his temples. *Shut up, Bane.*

I'm sorry, it's funny how he said it. Reminded me of that little kid in the Star Wars council chamber when Anakin came in to do the deed.

Nythan rubbed his temples. "I'll tell you tomorrow. Right now, I've a splitting headache, and I can't think straight."

"Of c-course, my Lord."

"Where's the nearest bed?" Nythan asked.

"This way, my Lord," someone said, gesturing toward the door. A couple council members on either side of him helped Nythan up and through the door.

The Matriarch stood outside. "What happened?" she demanded.

"I don't know. He received Jillian's soul and—"

"Stop!" Nythan exclaimed, "Bed, please."

His helpers pulled him past the Matriarch and into a giant bedroom. He pried himself from the arms of his escorts and fell on the bed. They closed the door behind them, casting him in utter darkness.

CHAPTER 37

AND DELIVER US FROM EVIL

Nythan awoke with a start and surveyed the hazy room.

It's pitch black. How can I still see? Nythan thought.

As we receive more souls, we grow stronger in everything we do.

As in night vision?

Yes. Your sense of smell, vision, mental capability, strength, stamina. Although, as your desire for food decreases, your flavor pallet will weaken.

In sharp contrast to the wretchedness he had experienced the night before, Nythan felt as though he could run a marathon. He turned the doorknob and strode through the door, sliding to a halt to avoid colliding with four masked Raptors.

"My Lord," one of them said through a metallic voice filter.

"What time is it?" Nythan asked in exasperation.

"Eleven a.m."

"Where is everyone?"

"This way," another one said, turning and leading Nythan down the hallway. The other Raptors followed a few paces behind.

They led him to a banquet table where some of the Grand Coven council and other Raptors were already dining. They attempted to stand as he approached, but Nythan waved them down.

"Can you please call a meeting with the Grand Coven?" Nythan asked. "I'd like it to start as soon as possible. I left some things unfinished last night."

One of the Coven members bolted out of his chair. "Of course, Great One. I will rouse the rest of the members at once." Fifteen minutes later, he returned and ushered Nythan into the conference room.

The ten council members all sat down, giving him their undivided attention.

"Last night…" Nythan began.

"My Lord," said one of the Coven, "We are so sorry. We did not mean to displease you with the offering—"

Nythan waved him off. "No, the apology is mine. I became irritable, through no fault of yours. My senses were…temporarily overwhelmed. As for Jillian's gift, I want to make it clear that I was, and am, grateful to her. I'm *very* pleased with her gift. I just wasn't expecting her soul to be so powerful."

Nythan detected a collective sigh of relief after he spoke.

"Now, I don't plan on keeping you much longer, so I'll just come right out and say what our plan is."

Wait, what? Shouldn't we talk about this first?

Don't worry. Nythan waved his hand. *I'm not saying anything we haven't already talked about.*

"The Great One and I will need to grow…quietly. This will require a large number of gifts, and we know that it'll only take so long before our appetite outpaces your ability to sustain us. *That* is what we need to plan for. The longer I stay hidden from the public, the better position we'll be in for me to deliver this world."

Wow. I'm impressed.

I'm just telling them what we talked about.

Still.

"The more we grow, the more we put ourselves in a vulnerable position. Our first order of business, if you haven't planned for it already, is how to sustain my appetite. The second is our collective plan in staying effective once the world discovers us and attempts to dismantle our operation."

"We'll defend you with our lives!" a Coven member exclaimed.

"And when the world comes to fight us, yours will be the first they take!" Nythan snapped. The member's eyes widened and he visibly recoiled.

Easy. Don't go around making everyone second-guess themselves.

Bane, you've been doing it your way for a long time, and it hasn't worked. We're partners now, and this is how you deal with people from my generation. With the truth.

We shall see.

No one spoke. Nythan sighed. "We don't need *slaves*. We need you to keep doing what you've been doing. Deliverance will come at a snail's pace, not with a lightning bolt. And I want you *alive*…unless you feel the need to give up your life. I want you to see us deliver this world."

The Coven member next to Nythan began trembling. "Great One, it would be our honor to see such a wonder."

Nythan nodded. "With Jillian's passing, what's your process for choosing a new Grand Coven member?"

Gunther, the man who asked Nythan to display his power, spoke next. "The current Patriarchs and Matriarchs—we call them Arcs—of each Coven nominate individuals who've previously been a Patriarch or Matriarch. Once the nominations have been received, we decide on a nominee. You're welcome to join in the process, Great One," one of the members explained.

"Thank you for the offer, but I just want to watch," Nythan said, clasping his hands together. "Great, meeting adjourned."

The Coven rose as he left the room. Outside, the four masked Raptors waited.

"Where's the Northern Matriarch?" Nythan asked.

"Unknown," a Raptor answered.

"Find her, then report back," Nythan ordered. Two of them left to do as he asked. A few minutes later one returned.

"She's talking with the Eastern Patriarch in the dining room."

Nythan went to the dining hall where the two were deep in conversation. They ceased speaking once he approached the Matriarch. She didn't seem happy.

"Gladys," Nythan said, "I'm all set here. No need to babysit me any longer."

"Thank you, my dear. I will return to the Northern Coven promptly." The Matriarch returned her attention to the Eastern Patriarch. "Well, you're going to need to inform the Grand Coven at once. The longer you wait, the worse it will get."

The Patriarch paled, glancing at Nythan.

"Oh, come off it, Nigel, he's going to find out sooner or later."

"Problem?" Nythan asked, looking between them.

"Remember that last little bit of the Ordo Solis I told you he was going to take care of?" The Matriarch jerked her thumb at the Patriarch. "Well, it's proving extraordinarily difficult to *handle*."

The Patriarch looked like he had gotten a spanking. "We had him within our grasp, but there was no way we could have anticipated the police's reaction time."

"No way you could have anticipated?" the Matriarch scoffed. "They're the police! Why would you expect them to react in any *other* way than fast?"

The Patriarch shrugged, "We'll see what the Grand Coven has to say."

"They'll probably take the problem off your hands and send the Birds of Prey. Then you won't have to worry about a *thing*," she said. The smirk she gave him appeared sharp enough to cut through metal.

"Birds of Prey?" Nythan asked.

"The Prey are the Grand Coven's…problem solvers. And by *problem solvers*, I mean no offender within ten miles is left standing."

"Wow," Nythan said. "I hope that doesn't mean that innocent people are killed."

The Matriarch shrugged. "They don't discriminate. You *can* be sure they are professionals who accept nothing less than total victory."

"Umm. Okay, I'll wait to hear about it."

The Matriarch leered at the Eastern Patriarch. "Yes, I'm sure we will *all* love to hear the details."

The Patriarch stared off with wide eyes. "It'll be fine. It'll be fine."

Neither the Matriarch nor Nythan believed him.

CHAPTER 38

N.D. MARKS THE SPOT

Nythan sprawled on the manicured lawn of the backyard and tried to digest the briefing given by the Eastern Patriarch. By the Patriarch's account, the unfortunate clash between Texas police and the Raptor team sent after the lone Ordo Solis member was being appropriately handled at the Eastern Patriarch's level.

I didn't anticipate them botching this so soon. I expected more from the Raptors.

Nythan sighed. *Sounds like you expected your delicately crafted* I-didn't-plan-anything *to go off without a hitch.*

Not without a hitch, but certainly with more competence in dealing with a relic full of amateurs like the Ordo Solis.

"I think it's too soon for you to overreact," Nythan whispered.

We shall see.

Nythan stretched out his arms and legs, letting the blades of grass prick his exposed skin. The morning dew still coated the surface.

Enjoy it while it lasts. This may be a short trip.

Nythan grinned. *Pessimism. How extraordinarily human of you.*

Leave it be.

Nythan chuckled. "You are!" he exclaimed, sitting upright, "You *are* angry!"

Why are you so surprised?

Because I thought for the longest time, you know, that you were this super-natural evil demon trying to possess me. Only, I'm coming to find out that you pretty much have all the same thoughts and emotions as a normal person does.

Well, congratulations on figuring that out.

Nythan's chuckle turned into a bellow.

I'm glad you find this funny. Meanwhile, our enemies are growing stronger by the second.

The Raptors will deal with them as best as they can, Bane.

That doesn't reassure me as much as it used to.

You're losing sight of the big picture, Nythan pointed out. *They haven't gotten this far by being incompetent. Our arrival did throw off their balance. In light of our return being captured on video, the Raptors thought it the lesser of two evils to destroy the evidence. Given the circumstances, it wasn't unreasonable. Just let them do their job. You said yourself that they take it seriously.*

I suppose.

Nythan got up from his spot on the lawn and walked toward the metal fencing, which foliage wrapped around concertina wire cloaked from view. He carefully pulled the branches aside to catch a glimpse of the other side, taking a few minutes to study the small woodland. He walked to the mansion's rear door and went in. Four masked figures standing at the backyard windows rotated toward him. Part of him wondered why they hadn't followed him out.

Nythan pointed towards the backyard fence. "Take me to that forest, please."

One of the Raptors led Nythan to the kitchen, the rest in tow. The cooks bowed before resuming their meal preparations. His escort opened a walk-in freezer and stepped inside. Nythan followed the Raptor as he weaved through food boxes and pushed aside hanging carcasses. At the far end, his escort reached through a large rack of food and turned something that made a loud *snap*. Another Raptor pushed the rack into the wall. To Nythan's surprise, it yielded, sliding backward to reveal a descending staircase underneath.

Well, isn't that something.

Once Nythan stepped down through the opening, one of the bodyguards gripped a handle on the bottom rack and closed it above them. The shelf settled into place, pitching them all in utter darkness. Two lines of muted red luminescent strips appeared on either side of him at the base of the walls and extended into a single point of darkness. The lines of red carved a visual path as far as Nythan could see. Nythan and the Raptors followed the path until the lighted lines reached the foot of a ladder and jutted upward along the side rails.

A Raptor climbed to the top of the ladder and tugged on a latch that swung open a door. Nythan followed him up, then jumped off the ladder and into a forest. He made an educated guess that they had traveled at least a football field from the secret staircase beneath the kitchen. The last Raptor came through, swinging shut the door. The exterior surface of the door melded so completely with the tree that Nythan couldn't tell the door existed.

Impressive. Now why are we here?

Nythan smirked. *You'll see.*

"Where's the compound?" Nythan asked. One of the Raptors pointed in the direction of the tree.

Nythan began walking in the direction of the compound; fifty yards later, he came upon a camouflaged fence. He picked the nearest tree and tore some of the bark off on the side facing away from the mansion.

What are you doing?

After he cleared away a few layers, exposing the bare trunk underneath, Nythan asked his escorts, "Does one of you have a knife?"

All four men reached into their pockets and pulled knives. Nythan chose the sleek knife closest to him, then began carving the letters *N.D.* into the smooth wood.

Hahahahahaha. Are you still doing that?

I'd've done it at Watwa, but I didn't have anything to make it permanent.

All this trouble, just to carve your mother's initials into a tree.

Nythan's lips curled up into a somber smile as he finished carving the second dot. He returned the knife to his bodyguard.

"Okay, let's head back."

Instead of retracing their steps to the secret tree tunnel, the Raptors led him all the way around the fence line to the front of the mansion.

"Why aren't we going the way we came?" Nythan asked.

"One-way exit," one of the Raptors responded.

When they reach the entrance to the mansion, Palaou greeted him.

"Did you have a pleasant walk, my Lord?"

"Absolutely. Although, next time I shall require a sugar-free lollipop, a few helium balloons, and the company of a golden retriever. Will you see to the details, please?"

The pleasant expression on Palaou's face vanished as he whipped out his notepad. "At once, my Lord," he yelped. He stopped before he began writing and looked at Nythan. "My Lord, are you…jesting with me again?"

Nythan's lips curled into a sly grin. "Yes, Palaou, I'm kidding with you."

Palaou put his notepad away. "My Lord," he pleaded.

"I know, I know. But you make it so *easy*. Besides, I like you Palaou. You're very attentive. When I really need something, I've no doubt you can make it happen."

Palaou bowed. "My Lord, I am honored by your words."

"But!" Nythan said, "I *will* take a glass of orange juice, though."

"Right away, my Lord," Palaou said. His tuxedo tails swished as he turned and disappeared inside the mansion.

Well, that *was a fun adventure.*

With many more to follow, I'm sure. A thought crossed Nythan's mind, turning him somber. *It sucks that this whole thing has to be a game of us versus them.*

There's something about the way I must live that makes my existence detestable to the ordinary person. Even you *have disgust for it. There isn't anything I can do about what I require to survive.*

Pretty soon, we're going to need to discuss what the end looks like for us, Nythan thought.

Are you talking in terms of our partnership coming to an end?

No, in terms of us delivering the world, as the Raptors call it. I need to know the specifics of what that's supposed to mean. But we don't need to talk about it right now.

The coming discussion made him queasy. Nythan's intuition told him he didn't want those specifics, but his conscience nagged him to find out anyway.

I understand. I'm ready to talk about it when you are.

CHAPTER 39

TIME WILL TELL

The next day, Nythan attended another meeting of the Grand Coven.

This time, they explained their original plan to move him between the eight Covens to help him grow stronger. However, with the shootout that occurred between the Raptors and police in Bellaire, Texas, the Grand Coven advised he stay. They wanted to determine how far-reaching the police investigation would be.

"If we only ate once a day, how long could you sustain me here?" Nythan asked.

"At that rate, nearly indefinitely. We can easily transport members here," a female Coven member replied.

"And draw unnecessary attention to this compound," another member countered. "At that point, we might as well transport him to the other Covens."

"But that would risk even more people knowing what the Great One looks like," she argued.

"With the video footage still at large, that will *hardly* make a difference. If anything, his tour will inspire our members, just as it did in the Northern Coven. They're ecstatic to have seen our Lord in the flesh."

"Since we can't seem to agree, how about we let the Great One decide?"

All eyes homed in on Nythan.

"I see the point in keeping a low profile until we find out what shakes loose," Nythan offered. "However, there's something to be said for giving the Raptors a reward for their work. So how about this, I stay here for the time being, at least until it's fine to visit another Coven. I'll keep a wrap on my need for spiritual food so that we won't need to get help from outside. Jillian's gift will sustain us *at least* until the end of the week. We'll wait and see, then figure it out. Sound good?"

Most of the council nodded in agreement.

Gunther spoke next. "It's settled. Now we must review the nominations for the new Grand Coven member. Here are the biographies of the eight candidates, one from each Coven."

The person next to Nythan passed him a binder. When everyone had received one, the gentleman with the comb-over spoke again.

"Please turn to Candidate A and begin reading."

Nythan took his time examining the report on Candidate A. The description contained a detailed biography of the candidate, an assessment of suitability, and a list of strengths, weaknesses, and other miscellaneous information deemed pertinent. He noted nothing listing the candidate's name, physical description, home Coven, or even gender.

To remove bias. Good on them.

When the last person indicated they had finished reading, each Grand Coven member offered the merits of the candidate along with any misgivings. None of the others argued or spoke out of turn, and no one enforced a time limit on their comments.

Nythan declined to offer a review of any of them, feeling his opinion might unduly influence an otherwise informed selection.

It took over three hours to go through all eight candidates. All ten Grand Coven members then secretly ranked the nominees from one to eight. The man with the comb-over collected the responses and tallied the scores.

As he finished, he passed the scoresheets and a scorecard to the next member. That person then tallied the results for herself and passed the papers to the next member, until all of them had confirmed the candidates' scores. Even Nythan took a shot at validating the scores against the others.

When the scorecards returned to the comb-over man, he read the results out loud: "Candidate A: 40, B: 37, C: 54, D: 48, E: 55, F: 49, G: 43, H: 34. As Candidate B is within five points of Candidate H, we will recast the assessment with those two in consideration." He passed out another set of scoresheets after striking out all nominees except for B and H. Nythan again watched the proceedings without taking part, until the man collected all the confirmed tallies from each Coven member.

"Candidate B: 16. Candidate H: 14. Through our collective effort, Candidate H has earned the appointment to the Grand Coven," he said in a gentle voice.

"Alright, Gunther, out with it. Who's H?"

"Her name is Mia Reyes, former Matriarch of the Central Coven."

A collective groan escaped the crowd. "Not again!" someone said.

"*¡Mierda!*" another said, and the rest of the members chuckled.

"What's wrong with the Central Coven?" Rose feigned, putting her hand on her chest.

"Nothing is wrong with the Central Coven, Rose," a squat gentleman with a double chin answered, lifting a finger. "Except, of course, they *somehow* keep winning. I motion we ban all Central Coven members as nominees."

"That's hardly—"

"All in favor say, 'Aye,'" he said quickly.

Several members pronounced their *Ayes*.

"Too late, Rose! The Coven has spoken," he said, beaming. The others laughed.

"You guys are terrible, just terrible," Rose scolded, cracking a smile.

Nythan tried to play along but thought that he had missed something. His confusion must've been readable because the member seated next to him leaned over.

"My Lord, in the past few decades, almost a quarter of the Grand Coven members have been from the Central Coven. Patrick enjoys making a mockery of the way worms conduct their meetings."

"Worms?"

"The non-believers."

"I see," Nythan whispered. "Thanks."

"Of course, Great One."

Nythan lifted himself off his chair. The other members took his cue and settled down.

"We're glad you all have such obvious camaraderie with one another," Nythan began. "Right away you've made us feel a part of the family. Thank you for that. We look forward to growing our strength, the likes of which this world has never seen," Nythan said. He felt uncomfortable at the grandiose tone of his statement, but the words just rolled off his tongue.

I'm having to advise you less and less.

Nythan raised his eyebrows. *I don't even know where these words are coming from.*

It sounds like they're coming from the heart, as much of a cliché as that may be.

I hope I don't sound as full of crap as I feel.

It's like dancing or singing karaoke; you feel every mistake. You think everyone else knows, but most of the audience is so transfixed that the mistakes aren't noticed. They probably thought it was intentional. On the outside, you look calm and ready, *as Eminem would put it.*

Nythan snorted. *Was Eminem a favorite of yours?*

No, but he was a favorite of yours. *You spent years listening to him on your bus ride to high school.*

The funny thing is I have two left feet; I couldn't dance even if I had years of practice.

Well then, add it to the long list of things you thought were impossible, and now find yourself doing.

CHAPTER 40

SLOW AND STEADY

After a week of long status meetings and lounging around, Nythan's busy mind stopped bothering him with future fears and past mistakes. He enjoyed the peace so much that he visited the topiary garden every day. He talked to the Raptors, sometimes individually and sometimes in groups. Each person he met added to his impression that the Raptor organization was staffed with brilliant people.

The Grand Coven assured him they were out of the hot water created by the Bellaire police confrontation. The police had identified one Raptor, but not the rest. Luckily, they'd carried some sort of hydrofluoric acid compound to make the blood spatters unusable.

They still couldn't find the last missing Ordo Solis volunteer, which Nythan figured put them back to square one. The only good news of the whole ordeal came when the Eastern Patriarch informed them that his team had destroyed the video of Nythan and the Gatekeeper after it was given to the police. Still, no one could confirm there were no other copies.

They better get this right. Otherwise, we're going to be humming a different tune.

Nythan smirked. *Seems like it had a lot to do with luck.*

Might be a good idea to ask about it later. I've returned for not even a month and we're already narrowly avoiding exposure. Hell, we still *might be at the end of this.*

The moon glowed through undrawn curtains. Nythan reclined in his leather seat, listening to a Raptor playing a beautiful classical piece on the piano. Other Raptors sat in the low-lit parlor room with a quaint fire crackling. Pictures of different performing musicians adorned the walls, making the room far more decorative than the rest of the mansion. His four bodyguards positioned themselves in different corners of the room. The minimal lighting hid their eyes, but Nythan thought he could make out a couple of them scanning the surroundings.

Nythan tried enjoying the moment, but Bane's frustration at the recent update on the Bellaire incident pricked Nythan's conscience. He resisted letting the disturbance sour his mood.

I can't help it. To say I'm frustrated is an understatement. I spent hundreds *of years crafting these support organizations, only to have one of them nearly spoil our entire effort.*

They're doing the best they can. You're the one who said he didn't want to make plans; this is what that looks like. Controlled chaos, Nythan thought.

I had hoped that things would finally work themselves out.

Now you're *the one jumping the gun. We just started, and nothing about the Bellaire situation indicates that all your carefully laid plans-but-not-plans are ruined. Just relax and listen to the music.*

The piano player transitioned into a minor key, with despondent tones playing one after another. The theme made Nythan sad, but the way the chords greeted one another made him want to listen.

Palaou stopped beside him and bent down to whisper in his ear. "My Lord, you have visitors who request to see you."

"Sure, send them in," Nythan replied, mesmerized by the pianist's ability to dance across the keys. When Palaou didn't move, Nythan asked, "Problem?"

"My Lord, they request a…private audience," Palaou said, looking embarrassed.

"Okay, lead the way," Nythan said, failing to mask his disappointment. The Raptor at the piano paused at Nythan's departure.

"Please continue. I'll come back as soon as I'm finished," he complimented.

The pianist nodded and continued playing.

Palaou led him to a small conference room. Inside, three ladies were speaking in a flurry of Spanish. They stood as he entered.

Nythan glanced at Palaou and his four escorts. "I'll just be a moment, please wait here," Nythan said, closing the door behind him.

The women appeared anywhere in their early to late thirties. Nythan recognized one standing in the middle as a Grand Coven member, but his mind couldn't conjure her name.

Her name is Rose.

"Great One," Rose said, "I wanted to introduce you to Mia. She was the member we voted in last week."

Mia curtsied. The way her bronze hair curled down and around her chin drew attention to her soft cheeks and small nose. "It's a pleasure, Great One."

"And this," Rose continued, "is Molina, the Brazilian Matriarch. Mia, Molina, and I are old friends." Molina had a curvy figure barely contained by her choice of fashion.

Nythan kept his eyes forward. "It's good to meet all of you. You said that you were friends?"

"We were all Matriarchs at the same time," Molina answered. "Rose was from Peru and became the Upper Matriarch. Mia was the Central Matriarch, being from Honduras, and I'm still the Brazilian Matriarch. But Rose and Mia grew up together."

"I moved around a lot," Rose said. "Mia and I went to the same high school in Honduras. When you get a chance, ask her how she got *suspended*." Rose winked at Nythan.

For some reason he couldn't fathom, Nythan blushed at the gesture and avoided eye contact with Mia. "Okay," he said, rubbing his hands together. "How does someone become an Arc?"

"We are voted in by our own Coven for two years, with endorsement by the Grand Coven," Molina said.

"And when does someone stop being an Arc?"

"Either the Coven stops re-electing us," Molina said, "or we are...

removed. And if I wanted to be appointed to the Grand Coven, I'd resign like Mia just did."

"Oh!" Nythan said. "Well, I got to see *that* decision process in action. It was impressive. Welcome aboard, Mia." Nythan extending his hand. Mia took it, curtsied again, and grazed his fingers as she withdrew hers.

"My pleasure," she said, showing sparkling white teeth. Nythan shook Rose's and Molina's hands as well.

"If you want to join me, I'll be going into the fireplace room to listen to that awesome guy play piano. He's really good."

"Balin went to Juilliard," Rose offered. "He's terrific. Whenever he is here in the evenings, he usually plays. We always enjoy his music."

"Ooo, *bien*, I want to hear!" Mia giggled. He found her accent adorable; her enthusiasm raised his spirits.

Awwww.

Shut up, Nythan thought.

The women followed him out of the conference room, but Nythan realized every corridor looked the same to him. "Uh...where do I go from here?"

Molina passed him. "This way." He trailed behind her, his entourage in tow.

Balin's head swayed as he stared down, striking the keys with wild abandon. All eyes were fixed on him. Nythan snuck into his seat. He listened for a long while, stealing frequent glances at Mia. She caught him looking at her several times.

I'd like to know more about her.

Huh? Nythan thought.

Nothing to worry about. I just want to understand her background a bit better.

Sure, Nythan said, distracted. He switched his attention from Balin to Mia and found her staring at him openly. Nythan held her gaze, watching the twinkle in her hazelnut eyes dance with the fire's reflection.

She winked at him; Nythan winked back.

CHAPTER 41

THE TRUTH WILL OUT

"So," Nythan mumbled, sliding his feet into his pant legs. He peered at three women sleeping underneath the covers of his oversized bed. "Tell me something I don't know about you."

Like what?

Nythan exited his room; four bodyguards followed him.

"Like something I don't know." Nythan began whistling a tune. To any onlooker, he probably looked like a crazy person talking to himself.

I once owned a circus.

Nythan burst out laughing. "You owned a circus?" He walked down the hallway to the dining room.

Yeah, it's not the most influential thing I've ever done, but it certainly was a blast.

"So what *was* the coolest thing you've ever done?"

I once had a series of philosophical discussions with Thomas Jefferson about religious freedom, which helped him frame the papers he wrote on equality around the late-1700s.

"*Cool.* What else?"

I fought in the Trojan War, and then I helped found the Roman Empire.

"Okay, that one gets me. How?"

I was a mid-level officer in the Trojan army, so I fought in a majority of the clashes with the Achaeans. *I escaped the day Troy fell. And I was the one who found the Tiber River in Italia after we needed to find a new home.*

"Did you take part in the actual making of the Roman Empire?"

No, I was a warrior, not considered nobility. Plus, I died soon after we settled on the river. But the whole affair was absolutely thrilling.

"Those're the coolest things? What about when you were emperor of that Chinese *Zow* empire?"

That period of my life was far too confusing and shameful to be considered cool. But other than a few interesting experiences with the Soviets, the Native Americans, the Samurai, and the Aztecs...I wasn't a prominent figure in history. In fact, in most cases, I tried not *to be.*

"Other than being hunted and despised as Satan-in-the-flesh, of course," Nythan offered. He passed through the dining room and into the backyard to the topiary garden.

Yes, other than that. But I was forced into infamy, it wasn't by choice.

You act as though you were dragged into this, Nythan thought.

Well, I'm not innocent. But I'm not the apocalyptic monstrosity history made me out to be.

Then what are *you?*

A survivor.

Survivor, apocalyptic monster. Tomayto, tomahto, Nythan countered. *It shouldn't be a surprise that you aren't painted in the best light.*

And if cows could write history, I'm sure they would say the same thing about humans. It's not fun knowing that you are something else's food. I understand that. But like I said, it's not something I can help. My diet is what it is, and I don't get to choose my host. I've tried to live off rationing my host's soul... and that life didn't last long, nor did it end particularly well.

As in...?

Made it to her thirty-second birthday and passed in utter agony. I wouldn't recommend it.

Oh. So what did you mean you don't get to choose your host? Is it like a lottery?

Let's just say it's like riding a roller coaster in a tornado and leave it at that.

Fine, so let's play this out then. What's the end game? We keep getting gifts until…what? You're being too vague.

Until I gain my freedom.

Nythan stopped walking.

Freedom? he thought, a bewildered expression washing across his face. He walked through the garden until he stood in front of the brilliant multi-colored display of Bane and his host.

The more souls we consume, the more powerful we become. The more powerful I become, the more I can feel…the end. I don't know how else to describe the sensation other than it feels like you're running on a track after a long sprint, and you're on your last lap. The feeling you get when you see the finish line…that's the emotion building within me as I consume more souls. I think that if I eat enough spiritual food, I'll either ascend or be released from this endless cycle.

So, this entire time you've been trying to gain enough souls for all of this to stop? Google said you did some pretty nasty things, Nythan pointed out.

Yes. In the beginning, when it all started, I'll admit I was careless. I boasted my newfound powers, manipulated others into helping me, and took souls without care. It destroyed families and spread terror. By the time I matured, it was too late; the world was convinced I was Satan incarnate. It was easier to play along so that I could get what I wanted.

"Turns out, you haven't gotten what you wanted," Nythan observed.

Still, it's best for all parties involved if I ascend to whatever level is next so that humanity and I can go our separate ways.

"I get that. You're not the wicked abomination I figured you'd be, but it'd be better for everyone if we found a way for you to move on from Earth."

It will require us to put in some serious effort…and there may be a lot of innocent people caught in our struggle. Whether by us, or by those who would do anything to stop us.

"I'm starting to realize that," Nythan said. *And here I thought I was going to get away with minimal involvement.*

Most of my past partners thought the same.

CHAPTER 42

HOT

Nythan sipped his orange juice.

At least I'm not vomiting, he thought.

Nowadays, his meals consisted of nothing but souls, of which he partook once a week. Bane voiced his immense irritation.

Once every three days would make me much less irritable.

Better safe than sorry, Nythan told him. The more souls he got, the less he found himself needing to sleep. His mind briefly relived the first morning he woke up next to two beautiful women.

The novelty will wear off.

Still, Nythan thought. *At least I'm not becoming numb to that.*

Lucky you.

Mia came in and sat down beside him at the grand dining table, opening a newspaper. She called for the chef and ordered apple juice, scrambled eggs, two hash browns, and grits, the same meal she ordered the last three times he had seen her at breakfast.

"Creature of habit?" Nythan asked, amused.

"*Sí.* At least, for breakfast I am. There is just something so greatly wonderful about the combination," she responded. "*¿Y tú?*"

Nythan still found her slight mix-up of English grammar adorable.

He set the half-drunk glass of juice to the side. "I can't taste regular food anymore. This was the last bastion." The chef whisked the glass away.

"Thank you," Nythan called out after the chef. "Er, I mean…*gracias*," he winked at Mia.

She smiled and rolled her eyes. "You wish to learn *Español*, no?"

"I've been meaning to get around to it, but then…well, *this* happened," he said, gesturing all around him.

Ask her where she's from.

"Where're you from?" He continued. "I know Molina said Honduras, but where, specifically?"

"I'm *limeña*, actually which is someone from La Lima. We have a beautiful river that brings us rain often."

Ask her what caused her to join the Raptors.

"Interesting, and how'd you get started with the Raptors?"

"*¿Como?*" she posed, tilting her head.

"When did you find the Raptors?" Nythan rephrased the question more slowly.

"They are open secret where I am from. Some think they dangerous, but most Hondurans just left them alone. For the most part, the Raptors lived softly among us without being much into our lives. I'm no sure what made me apply. Rose did first, then me some time after. I think so, I crave mystery. There always seem more to them than a regular group," she explained.

Ask her why she follows you.

What's with all these questions? Nythan thought. He squinted and Mia responded with a *Huh?* expression.

Nythan laughed, then tapped his chest.

"What is this?" Mia asked.

"Ah, it means that the Great One and I are talking to each other. There wasn't anything you did to cause me to look at you weird."

We'll see.

"*Sí*, okay." She leaned forward toward him a little more as she took a spoonful of grits and ushered it into her mouth.

Out with it! What gives? Nythan demanded.

Just looking forward to reading that report on her.

"What did Rose mean when she talked about you getting suspended?"

Mia paused mid-chew with a deer-in-the-headlights face, then held up a finger, causing Nythan to shriek with laughter. He cleared his throat, embarrassed, and waited for her to swallow.

Nythan looked down at the table. *Seriously, what is it? Why so interested?*

She gives off a peculiar vibe, is all. Experience tells me to listen to those vibes. They get stronger and more accurate as we grow in power.

Mia waved her hands. "It's not a great amount of bad. A popular girl made rumors about Rose. At breakfast, I dump my oatmeal on her head." She giggled. "I wouldn't...have gotten suspended, but she got up and fight me. I scratched her face and rip her shirt. So, I had to go to principal."

Nythan let out a full belly laugh. "Impressive."

"Why, thank you." Mia used her index finger to push strands of hair behind her ear.

Nythan smiled through pursed lips. *She's a Raptor, what vibe could you possibly be getting? Unless, by* weird vibe, *you mean you get the same feeling I get when I look at her.*

No, you dolt, not that *kind of vibe. The kind that warrants a closer look, that's what.*

Well just chill it. We're still new to this scene. Let's wait until you start with the witch hunts.

I need less of an orientation than you do into this lifestyle. Read the report, and I'll be happy.

Fine. Nythan looked at Mia. "I need to go take care of some things."

Mia's eyes widened in the middle of another chew, then nodded. Nythan waved, then left her, moving to the Coven conference room. He peeked inside but found the room empty.

Nythan turned to one of his bodyguards. "How can I find Palaou?"

The Raptor nearest to him walked away without saying anything.

How eerily awesome. They're the epitome of the silent professional.

A short time later, his bodyguard came back with Palaou in tow. "My Lord?" Palaou chirped.

"Palaou, would you do me a favor please?"

"My Lord!" Palaou exclaimed. He seemed genuinely offended by the question.

Nythan's eyes widened in amusement at his reaction. "Could you please put together a thorough analysis on Mia for me? She's the new Grand Coven council member."

"At once, my Lord. Is there any particular subject on which you want the analysis to focus?"

"Thaaaat's a good question," Nythan said, raising an eyebrow. Palaou blinked.

Major and minor events from the time she was born to when she joined the Raptors, everything about her parents, and the interviewer's paper.

Nythan verbalized Bane's request.

"At once, my Lord. It will be readied promptly," Palaou said, hurrying away.

"Palaou."

The man stopped in his tracks and whipped around.

"Between you and us, please." Palaou placed a hand on his chest and bowed before continuing.

What's an interviewer's paper? Nythan asked.

Before I left them, the Raptors began a process of interviewing all potential applicants. They had one of the interviewers record the questions and answers, which were then discussed by a committee at a later time. I'm not sure if they continued the practice, but I figured I would ask anyway.

Fine. But all the things we just requested are going to take a hell of a long time to read.

Yes, but it'll be worth it.

How do you figure?

Well, one, I'll be satisfied. Two, you'll get to know more about your new infatuation. And three..., hmm, I really thought I'd have thought of a three by now, but, oh well. Just those two.

Nythan waved his hand. "Whatever," he said. A sudden swift wave of warmth washed over him before dissipating.

Sorry, that was me.

Nythan rotated toward the hallway leading to the dining room and spoke aloud to Bane, "What was that?"

Before Bane could reply, all four bodyguards whipped out oversized handguns. They squished him into a tiny square fortress made by their backs, muzzles scanning the environment. Nythan supposed they searched for threats, although some of them pointed their weapons at the wall only a few feet away.

"Uh...guys," Nythan huffed. "It's okay, I was just talking to Bane...I mean, the Great One."

They hesitated for a second longer, then disengaged their protective box like a well-oiled machine.

"Wow. Just, wow."

That was cool.

Yeah, but did they need to do that? I guess I'll be a little bit more careful with what I say. They're obviously well-trained.

I expect nothing less. Anyway, as I was about to say, I was redistributing the excess heat in your body from the increased amount of souls we collected.

What?

The more spiritual food we consume, the warmer your resting body temperature will be. It's a natural byproduct of the souls.

I thought souls were supposed to be icy cold.

That's the influence of Hollywood, yet again, making things up to fit its narrative.

Nythan grunted. *Things I never knew I wanted to know.*

Indeed.

Well, at least that explains why I haven't felt the need to use as many bedcovers lately, Nythan thought.

That, and the companions you've gotten...familiar with, over the course of your stay here.

Nythan chuckled, weaving his way around the bodyguard in front of him and making his way to the dining room again. To his disappointment, he didn't see Mia.

"Looking for some person?" a voice hummed behind him. Nythan turned around as Mia leaned against the doorway to the kitchen, taking a bite from a pear.

"What do you do all day long?"

"We do some morning early work, and then we do what comes natural," she said. "*Vámonos.* I want to show you," she said, walking past him toward the front entrance.

"Yes ma'am," Nythan said, following her.

"My Lord!" someone called after him. Nythan and Mia turned to see Palaou hurrying to them. "A meeting is called to discuss an important update," he panted. "The Grand Coven is gathering now."

Nythan gazed at Mia. "Next time," he said. She curtsied, following him to the Coven's meeting room.

CHAPTER 43

COLD

The squat gentleman with the double chin drummed his fingers against the circular conference table before him. The Eastern Patriarch, Nigel, stood in the open sunken area, giving them his latest briefing on how the Bellaire incident had played out.

"So what *can* you confirm?" the man sneered. "Do you expect us to be content with some hearsay about how you *think* the Great One's identity has been properly contained? Especially since you *haven't* rooted out the last of the Ordo Solis. He's still out there! Which means the video of our Lord's return can still fall into the hands of the wrong person, who can do us *tremendous* damage. Do you know the *danger* you've put him in?"

Nythan, for the life of him, couldn't remember the gentleman's name. *I think his name is Patrick.*

"You've endangered us, Nigel, and we haven't even *started!*" Patrick exclaimed.

"We're...well, we were..." the Eastern Patriarch stammered.

Rose, sitting beside Patrick, put a hand on his forearm. The gesture seemed to calm Patrick, and he relaxed into his chair.

"Nigel," Rose soothed. "Do you value our Lord's life?"

Nigel straightened. "Of course. I serve unwaveringly."

"And we are so grateful, Nigel. If the success of this mission depended on anything less than our Lord's well-being, we would be a bit more understanding. As you can see," she said, gesturing to Nythan, "the Great One's plan is currently impeded until this small matter is dealt with. *You*, as the Eastern Patriarch, are responsible for this delay. We *need* you to settle this, *now*."

The Patriarch paled once more. "I'll see to it personally, Grand Coven. I have *never* failed to unearth the worms in the East, and I will not fail now."

"Yes, and while you do that, we'll be giving you some additional resources to ensure that you do not run into anymore...impediments," she said, getting up from her chair and going to the door behind her. She opened it, spoke a few words, and then closed it. Several seconds later, a masked Raptor entered with a handcuffed prisoner, a burlap pulled over her face.

The Raptor brought the captive to the middle next to Nigel, then ripped off the burlap, revealing a woman wearing a blindfold and earmuffs. Her tear-stained face recoiled at the touch of the Raptor.

"This woman here has emotional influence over the last Ordo member in hiding. You will use her to draw him out. Then you will deal with *both* of them," Rose commanded.

Nythan shifted in his seat. It didn't take a forensics team to figure out what she meant.

"In addition, we are sending a detachment from the Birds of Prey to assist in quelling any further unrest."

Nythan didn't think the Patriarch could possibly pale any whiter, but at the mention of the Birds of Prey, his face became ghostly. "I'll see it done," he whispered.

"Good, Nigel. That is *exceptional* to hear. We look forward to your next report. Please depart for the Eastern Coven immediately," Rose said.

Nigel bowed, almost running for the exit.

"Wait," Nythan blurted. Nigel froze in place; everyone else looked to Nythan as he glanced at Nigel. "Sorry, not you, you can go." He gestured to the Raptor and the prisoner. "I meant them."

"Them?" Rose asked.

"Yes, I have a few questions. Who's that?"

Another Coven member flung open a file folder in front of him, skimming a sheet of paper. "Her name is Raeleigh Caldieraro, age thirty-one, born in Hampton, Virginia, a member of Solis America for nine years, engaged to Garrett Strauss, who is…one of us."

A few of the coven members snickered.

"So, humor me," Nythan said. "When you find the one who's on the run, you're going to…deal with them?"

Rose held up her hand, "Yes, and that will be the end of the threat as we know it."

"Is it possible for you to instead capture him and keep them both here?" Nythan asked.

"It *is* possible, but they're more valuable to us dead."

"I'd rather you bring them here, both of them, alive," Nythan said. "Worse comes to worst, they can be my breakfast, yes?"

"My Lord, they are your *enemies*. We should dispose of them without a second thought," Rose argued.

Don't feel sorry for them now that we have the advantage. They were never merciful toward us, and I have a lot of dead friends I held in high esteem to prove it. I won't shed a tear when they're all gone.

Bane, I very seriously doubt that these volunteers are the same brutal Inquisitors you faced back then. I'm willing to bet half of them are overweight Star Trek fans.

Doesn't mean they're any less dangerous. I'm warning you, don't give them the chance to do what they were chartered to do. It only spells bad news for us.

"I thought they were amateur volunteers?" Nythan responded to Rose, "That's what everyone has been telling me all this time. It's not like you're fighting the military." He shifted his attention to the men and women around the table. "I *don't* want you to kill them. I mean, just look at her," Nythan continued, gesturing to the quivering woman. "She's scared to death."

"Great One," one of the Coven members said. "We've been fighting the Order for centuries. They'd destroy us without a moment's hesitation."

"I realize that," Nythan said. "I'm fully aware that this Ordo Solis exists to destroy me. Even so, I think there's a benefit to bringing them back alive. At the very least, they'd no longer be working against us. I want this to happen."

You're not doing what needs to be done.

I'm not just going to outright murder these people, Bane, Nythan thought, clenching his teeth. *Not when there's a reasonable alternative. Besides, if it really comes down to it, we take their souls, and that'll be the end of it.*

It's a bad idea, Nythan. Nothing good will come of being merciful toward the Ordo Solis.

Mia's eyes widened as she clasped her hands together, "It *would* give us the opportunity to learn whatever else it is that they understand about us. Maybe we'll discover something worthful."

What an intriguing response she gives.

Nythan frowned. *How is that intriguing?*

Rose spoke next. "I object to this course of action. But if you desire that we bring them to you, we submit to your wisdom. It will be done."

"Yes, please and thank you," Nythan said.

Rose motioned for the Raptor to take Raeleigh away. Nythan followed them out the door. The Raptor took a few paces down the hallway and then stopped. He let go of the woman, rotated around, and clicked his faceplate out of its sockets. Nythan recognized him as the man he had met in Pennsylvania, the one with the chipped tooth.

"Devin!"

Devin gave a toothy grin. "My Lord, it's good to see you. The Northern Matriarch wanted to gift you this prize. She said she felt that this *worm* would be helpful to our cause," Devin said, motioning toward the captive.

"Please thank the Matriarch for me. It's good to see you again."

"I'm here till the end! This's so exciting!" Devin exclaimed before putting his mask back on and leading Raeleigh away. Nythan watched the two disappear around the corner.

I hope we don't end up regretting this.

Even if this ends up being a bad choice, we'll recover.

I will...but you won't.

CHAPTER 44

REVEAL

Nythan relaxed in a lawn chair in the backyard, reading Mia's detailed file.

So far, so good, Nythan thought.

Maybe.

What're you looking for? I see nothing out of the ordinary.

Whenever I look at her, I grow uneasy. It grows stronger every time we eat.

Which means, what, exactly?

It means we need to take a closer look to figure out why I'm getting this feeling.

Maybe you like her as much as I do, Nythan thought, smirking.

Doubtful. I don't enjoy people like a normal human. Nothing about me is corporeal anymore.

Anymore?

Keep reading. I'll know what we're looking for when I see it.

Nythan read through the file, which took a couple hours. Palaou had compiled every detail Bane could ever want, and many details Nythan didn't. He was fine knowing that she had turned thirty-three a couple of months ago, but he didn't feel it necessary to know how many bowel movements she took on average per year.

Nythan huffed. *See? Nothing.*

You sure? With all your analytical skills, you saw nothing out of the ordinary?

Half the contents of that file *were out of the ordinary. Seriously? A hundred and seventy-seven dumps? Who* needs *to know that?*

Think about the education section.

Rose and Mia went to the same high school.

I meant college.

Nythan crossed his arms. *What about it?*

Where did she get the money to pay for school? Her parents were relatively poor and had many mouths to feed. Yet she goes to Universidade de São Paulo, one of the best colleges in South America.

Yeah, and…? She went on a full ride ESL scholarship.

First of all, it's TESL. Do you know anything about TESL candidates? They study to teach English to non-native speakers. Have you heard her English? Certainly not the result of someone who garnered a TESL degree.

Again, what're you after here?

The more we know about her, the more suspicious I become.

More suspicious of WHAT! I've no idea what you're trying to tell me.

Nythan, it should be obvious what I'm implying. I am skeptical of whose side she's on.

Whose side would she be on? I don't get it. She hasn't done anything that'd make me think she's anyone but who we think she is.

Many little things adding to a recognizable pattern. I want to believe she has no other motive than to serve our interests. But all the signs are starting to point elsewhere. I've been doing this for an awful long time. Put aside your feelings and listen to me.

Okay, fine. Nythan crossed his arms. *What do you propose we do about it?*

Ask Palaou if we have any electronic monitoring capability. Let's see if we can observe her when she doesn't think anyone is watching.

Bane, this is ridiculous.

Our road is rocky and lonesome. I've experienced more than a few lifetimes where my partner fell victim to the perfect catch, only to find him or her betraying us. Even discovering they were working against us from the start.

Sounds like you're connecting dots where there're no connections.

And you're erasing the dots as connections are forming. Listen to me when I tell you this: there are only two people on this planet worthy of trust. One is you…the other is me.

CHAPTER 45

PROFIT

The Eastern Patriarch strode into the conference room with his chest puffed out. He was followed by two guarded prisoners, both with burlap sacks over their heads. Coming to a stop in the middle of the room, Nigel bowed toward Nythan, who nodded in response. The guards shoved the two captives onto the floor.

"My Lord and Grand Coven," Nigel proclaimed, "I present to you the last two remaining members of the Ordo Solis." He gestured to the prisoners attempting to sit upright. "Steven could not escape the East. I said that I would *not* fail."

The guards took the burlap off their heads, stood them up, and spun them around 360 degrees. One was the woman whose fiancé was an undercover Raptor; the other was an overweight male a good four inches taller than Nythan. Nythan couldn't make out any distinguishing characteristics with the earmuffs and blindfolds obscuring their faces.

Nythan glanced at Rose; her face was contorted in contempt.

"Great One," Rose said, "Now that we have recovered the last revolutionary, may we dispose of them?"

"Do we have some sort of holding cell?" Nythan asked.

Rose skipped a beat before answering. "We do."

"Then how about we place them there. I'll decide their fate later."

Rose scrutinized Nigel, who in turn flung his hand out to the two Raptor guards. They put the hoods over the two prisoner's heads and led them out of the room.

Nigel looked at each Coven member, as if expecting a pat on the head.

"I'm glad to see the Birds of Prey were able to render assistance in your recovery of the last worm," Rose said.

"They were helpful. Although the effects of their involvement are being felt throughout the entire state. As you're no doubt aware, their... *assistance* has captured the attention of the nation," Nigel said.

"Pfft," scoffed Patrick. "An understatement, to put it lightly. Their zealous slaughter of the Masons provoked every major Texas law enforcement agency, to include the FBI and ATF."

"Nigel," Rose spoke. "We leave the resolution of this matter in your *very* capable hands. Of course, we are always here to provide more assistance if needed."

Nigel frowned. "That won't be necessary."

Rose placed both of her hands together. "I have the utmost faith in you, Nigel. Please handle with careful preparation."

"I take issue with one thing you said upon entering our chambers," a council member wearing a tailored suit remarked to Nigel. "You said, 'the last two remaining Ordo Solis members.' Are they indeed the *last* of the Ordo Solis?"

"Why yes, Grand Coven, there are no more Ordo Solis members on this continent," Nigel said.

"Ah, ah, ah. *This* continent, correct? Is the Ordo Solis not alive and well in Europe?"

"Well, yes, but that's not rele—"

"Please forgive my interjection, Nigel," the council member interrupted. "The Ordo Solis is still active. We only pacified Solis America. Solis Europe remains a threat to the Great One—and your statement misleads us to believe that this has been accomplished when it has not. We must continue driving this scourge out until not a *single* oppressor is left walking the earth."

"Of course, Grand Coven," Nigel responded hastily, "I will do everything in my power to ensure nothing threatens us in the East."

Poor Nigel looks defeated. The council is doing an excellent job keeping to their role of being your implacable guardian. Perhaps our Arc needs a few words of encouragement from someone who is not obligated to remain steadfast to that standard.

Nythan nodded. "Nigel," he said. Nigel faced him, bowing once more. "My Lord."

"I want you to know that I'm extremely grateful for what you've done. I feel much more at ease now that the situation has been handled. Please remain vigilant. If you need anything at all, please don't hesitate to ask," Nythan said. Mia winked at him when he snuck a glance at her.

Gag.

Nigel beamed at Nythan. "I am *honored* by your words, my Lord. I won't rest until your deliverance is at hand."

"Thank you. If you'll excuse us, there're a few things left for the council to discuss."

"Grand Coven." Nigel bowed so low Nythan thought he fell over. Bane's grunt vibrated throughout Nythan's insides.

A few seconds after Nigel departed, the council member who had chastised him spoke. "Were we too tough on him?"

"No," Nythan answered, "You did the right thing. But it's important that our people feel appreciated for their lifelong devotion. It'll fuel their motivation."

"Agreed," Mia said. "Many a times in Central Coven we did recognize our top performers. It's why we win recruitment."

Some of the council members let out a groan.

"Of course, there are several *other* reasons the Central Coven remains second highest in recruitment. In particular, your use of female converts to entice impressionable young men," Gunther noted, raising an eyebrow.

"And don't forget the cocaine," Patrick's double chin jiggled as he laughed.

"All legitimate!" Rose declared, coming to Mia's defense.

"There's no need to convince us, Rose," Gunther said, chuckling, "We all reap the benefits. It's just good to provide a little context to Mia's statement, is all."

Nythan cut in. "So now that that's over with, I'd like to talk about visiting all of the different Covens."

"My Lord, despite the Prey *solving* our problem," Patrick said, using air quotes to frame the word while eyeing Rose, "we still don't recommend you go anywhere. If anything, the situation is worse now. The worms are looking for someone to blame."

"I recognize that, but I've been here for over a week. I need to visit the rest of the Covens."

"I understand, my Lord. But now that the FBI has their ear to the ground, it won't take long for them to hear about the excitement you'll cause all the Covens you visit. It'll make them curious, and they'll be hungry for any lead they can get," Patrick argued.

"But, as we were informed not a long time ago, they already know of Nythan," Mia told him. "The investigatives from the Texas police talked to the Ordo Solis person Steven and he gave the video."

Gunther cringed at Mia's use of Nythan's name. "You mean, the Great One."

"They are one in the same, no?" Mia asked innocently.

"We promote his status as our *Lord*, not his appearance as a *mortal*. Humans don't *deliver* anyone. We pass from this world with little to no meaning."

"There is some sense in what Gunther says," Rose said. "But remember, Gunther, our focus isn't to make our Lord a deity."

"Gunther and I don't agree on much," Patrick grunted. "But most of our members *do* believe the Great One to be a god. At a minimum, he's their divine savior, and it's a lynchpin for their faith. Surely, your time away from Matriarch hasn't led you to forget that, *Rose*?"

"Not at all, *Patrick*," Rose retorted with an icy stare. "But you can't fall victim to foolishness either. Our Lord isn't invincible. If he were, he would have no use for us, and would've delivered this wretched world long ago."

"Maybe he waits for the right time, when our faith is absolute," Patrick offered. A few of the Grand Coven peeked at Nythan, hoping he'd clarify.

Best not to comment. I've never had much success when it comes to explaining the finer details of their faith. They do a great job of filling in the specifics by themselves.

Gunther gazed at Nythan and spoke up when Nythan refused to comment. "We have had this debate many times. Let's us move forward."

"My plan," Nythan cut in, "can wait no longer. I've some barriers with our two guests that I'd like to break through, and then I'll expect to start my visits. I leave the details to you."

Nythan rose from his seat, and the rest of the council rose in response.

"All your hard work *will* pay off," Nythan began. He still hated playing into the benevolent leader stereotype but found it the most effective method in interacting with the Raptors. "This moment has been in the works for over three hundred years. This is one of the most important phases in my plan. I look forward to what fruit it bears."

"We rise further," the Grand Coven responded.

CHAPTER 46

HOLA

Nythan stood in front of the male prisoner. Without his blindfold, Nythan could see Steven's pudgy cheeks and pronounced forehead. Two brutish-looking Raptors stood on either side of Steven. The three men were of level height, although the similarity ended there. Steven's most notable feature was his belly, while the Raptors were lean and muscular. Steven twisted his long hair into a ponytail. The Raptors wore masks concealing whatever hair they had.

Nythan initially came to apologize to Steven for what he had endured at the hands of the Raptors. The report on Steven's capture read a bit harsh. Steven had witnessed the Prey murder a dozen Freemasons in cold blood, and the details of his interrogation read straight out of a horror movie.

Instead of apologizing, Nythan stood with his hands on his hips as he argued with Bane as to whether an apology would be a good idea.

Nythan, we owe this individual nothing. *He would see us dead if he got the chance.*

His name is Steven, and that's because neither of us knows nor under-stands the other. They think you're Satan, and you think they're ignorant and misguided.

That's because they are *ignorant and misguided.*

See, that's what I'm talking about. I think our two groups need to find some common ground. We all got off on the wrong foot, that's all.

What in the living hell, Nythan. These people exist to destroy us, and you want to make friends with them.

Remember what the monk said: we're only enemies by circumstance.

Those circumstances are not likely to change, unless you found a way for us to survive on orange juice.

Well, our *circumstances changed. At one point I was willing to throw myself off a bridge rather than allow you to live inside my brain…or wherever it is that you are.*

You do not represent the majority of this world. We have nothing *to say to them.*

Bane expanded within Nythan. The feeling tickled his chest, causing him to chuckle. He imagined what Steven and the guards thought about his sudden outbursts.

Well, we're all here, so you might as well make the most of it, even if it's just to talk about nothing, Nythan thought.

Fine. Promise me we'll remove them as a threat when you're finished?

I can't promise that. I don't see them as the heartless enemy you do.

That's a significant problem…because that's how they see you. They harbor no illusions as to what we are.

Well here's to that then, *and if it doesn't change, they aren't going anywhere.*

"Sooooo…" Nythan began.

Steven said nothing.

Nythan extended his hand to shake Steven's. "I'm Nythan," he offered.

The Raptors around him tensed, taking a half-step toward them.

Steven didn't move.

"I'm from Florida, where're you from?" Nythan asked.

Silence.

I thought you said you weren't going to talk about anything significant.

Nythan smirked. *I'm not.*

Where you're from is pretty significant.

"Can I offer you anything? A water?"

Steven remained silent. One of the Raptors stepped forward and slugged Steven in the stomach. He doubled over, heaving.

Nythan's mouth dropped.

What's wrong?

Nythan threw a hand up to the aggressive bodyguard, motioning him to stop his assault. *I...I didn't expect him to do that to the guy.*

What do you mean?

That's...that made me feel bad.

It needed to be done.

Steven stayed doubled over.

But why though? He can't fight back.

That's because he's weak and you're strong. That's what power is.

Nythan tensed. *It looks different than I expected.*

Only because you've never seen it in real life. You'll get used to it.

Steven glared up at Nythan.

I hope not, Nythan thought.

"No," Steven sputtered.

"What?" Nythan had forgotten what he asked Steven. "Ah, the water. No problem. Well, I already know your name...where'd you say you were from?"

When Steven didn't respond, that Raptor stepped toward him again.

Steven flailed his arms. "Okay, okay, okay," he said, looking to Nythan. "Illinois."

"That's good."

That went well. Let's do it again sometime.

Shut up, Bane.

"If you need anything, please let one of the guards know," Nythan said.

Steven huffed in response, wincing as he eyed the Raptor beside him.

Nythan turned and left the room. Outside, Rose and Mia waited for him.

"Did you...?" Mia trailed off.

"Just asked him some questions, that's all," Nythan said.

Mia looked relieved.

You need to pay more attention to her reaction.

Nythan clenched his jaw. *Whatever.*

"Where's the woman...what was her name?" Nythan asked.

Raeleigh Caldieraro.

"Raeleigh, my Lord," Rose answered. "Please take me to Raeleigh."

CHAPTER 47

LOOKING BACK

Nythan took a stroll outside in the garden. Beside him walked Steven and Raeleigh amid an entourage of Raptors. Nythan understood that his proximity to the *enemy* made his bodyguards anxious, but they dared not go against his wish to spend time with the Ordo Solis members.

He had his fill of souls once every other day now, which he agreed to after Bane relentlessly pestered him for a full day straight. Each day, he took a walk to enjoy the fresh air. The walk helped calm the euphoria that struck him whenever someone gifted their soul. The resulting sensation felt like nothing he ever remembered experiencing. Sometimes it overwhelmed his senses, especially when he ingested the souls of the elderly.

Nythan figured he'd afford his two involuntary guests the chance to bask in the daylight as well. Walking seemed like the perfect opportunity. He made no effort to compel Steven or Raeleigh to talk and avoided questions after what happened to Steven the first day they met.

Steven wouldn't speak to Nythan unless asked a direct question. Raeleigh, however, proved to be an extrovert once she'd grown accustomed to her new circumstances.

Spare me. You're getting attached. Of all the people to get close to, you chose the people who want to destroy us.

And how'd you feel if someone took your friends away over a war that started long before you were even born?

They chose *this life.* They chose *to be a part of the Ordo Solis, knowing who and what we are.*

Nythan crossed his arms. *I seriously, seriously doubt they fully knew who we were. I barely know who you are, and I'm the closest one to you. These people...they had no idea what they were getting into. It's easy to tell how infatuated they were with fighting evil, not unlike the Raptor's infatuation with our deliverance. They're in love with the* idea *of what we are, not necessarily who we are and what you came to do. I think that'll change once they get to know us.*

Okay, so they were volunteers at the wrong time in history. That's not our fault. They are a part of the Ordo Solis, period. Forget that they didn't know. What do you think would have happened if they still had the opportunity to put in place whatever plan they had? I guarantee you it would not have been to our benefit. That's why I don't feel sorry for them.

Maybe. But those with power have a responsibility to wield it with compassion.

Puke. You've got to be kidding me. We're talking about having humans as single-serve snack packs here. How in the hell do you responsibly wield that?

Bane, you've already convinced me to help you get your freedom. And I understand that innocent people are going to be caught in the middle...I realize that. But that doesn't mean murder is the answer.

Nythan, look. I say the things I say because I think we have a chance at succeeding this time. It's my hope that I get my freedom and that this will be the last time anyone, including the Ordo Solis, has to endure this struggle.

That sounds so much different than the world-eating demon that these people think you are. Except for the cults who think you're a god. Then they're the monks that think you're Shiva, Nythan reminded him.

Yeah, about that. I am not a god, nor am I Shiva.

Huh?

There are many Hindus who would not be okay with calling me Shiva. It's as if someone thought you were Jesus. To be honest, it was hit-or-miss how those monks would react. I don't know how many Hindus believe God is sakar, *has form, or* nirakar, *formless, but I imagine it's close to half and half. That doesn't mean anything to you, but there it is.*

Nythan scratched his chin, confused.

The bottom line is, I'm not the evil demon the Ordo Solis makes me out to be. But we're getting off track. These two people are our enemies, and they know too much.

I'm still not going on a murderous rampage to get what we want.

I understand. You don't want to kill them, yet they pose a grave threat to our success. Removing them is a small price to pay to avoid total disaster. Remember that.

I will, Nythan assured Bane. "I will," he whispered, walking alongside Steven. Steven stared at Nythan out of the corner of his eye.

CHAPTER 48

TASTELESS

Nythan listened with the rest of the Grand Coven as they heard the particulars of what the Ordo Solis had planned in conjunction with the Knights Templar, a branch of the Freemasons. A Raptor lieutenant who belonged to the Birds of Prey briefed them.

"The Order, with assistance from the Knights Templar, planned to hijack the identity of an influential figure and embarrass them into serving the Order's cause," the Prey lieutenant summarized. "Their goal was to convince the public that the Great One still lives."

"And you believe this would be enough to raise a resistance?" Patrick asked.

"Such matters are for you to decide, Grand Coven," the lieutenant said. "I present the results of our completed task. Your question was not answered during the course of our assignment."

Gunther smirked at Patrick. "They don't deal in *what ifs*, Patrick," he said.

Patrick's reply dripped with disdain. "Clearly."

"Did you find the person giving of information?" Mia asked.

"Yes, Grand Coven."

"And what of the Masons? How can you be sure no one else is aware of their intentions?" Patrick challenged.

"We carefully searched the residence of each Templar. Every lead was thoroughly exhausted until the Falcon himself was satisfied with the results," the lieutenant responded.

"Falcon?" Nythan said in a muffled voice to Gunther.

Gunther leaned over. "The director of the Birds of Prey," he whispered.

Nythan suppressed an outburst of laughter, which made his body shake instead. *They have so many weird names.*

Helps promote their culture and solidifies their loyalty. When group members believe they are the in *and everyone else is the* out, *it makes for a healthier organization.*

I get it, we did the same thing with chants and marching in ROTC.

"Where is the Falcon now?" Patrick asked, "Surely it is well within his responsibility to inform us of this significant development."

"Patrick..." Gunther slowly warned.

Patrick stole a glance at Gunther before settling his gaze on the Prey lieutenant.

"He's attending to residual details of the assignment," the lieutenant said.

"Looks like your report has a bunch of holes in," Patrick accused.

"That's correct, Grand Coven. The Falcon insisted I deliver this report immediately while he remained to see the rest of the Prey home."

"What was left to take care of?"

"Securely disposing of key evidence and overseeing the removal of anything that might trace to us."

"I see." Patrick added, crossing his arms. "I'm done."

Gunther nodded. "Anyone else?"

"Me, *por favor*," Mia said. "Did you bring the evidence to this place?"

"Yes, all portable evidence was transferred to the Grand Coven upon arrival."

"*Bueno*," Mia scanned the Coven members. "Who has the details?"

"We've it in our possession," Gunther confirmed, patting a hefty manila envelope lying on the table in front of him.

Mia took on an innocent expression of curiosity. "Would you please removing your mask?" she asked the lieutenant. "I would like to see who makes us so excited."

Quick, tell the lieutenant to keep his mask on.

Nythan scrunched his eyebrows. *What? Why?*

Trust me, Nythan, do it now please.

The lieutenant hesitated but began to remove his disguise.

Nythan shook his head in confusion. "Wait," he called out, "I'd prefer you to keep it on."

The Prey resecured his mask, bowing to Nythan.

Mia pouted, but said nothing.

"Please inform the Prey that we are grateful for their timely completion of this assignment," Rose said to the lieutenant. "Thank you for your report. You are dismissed."

He bowed to Rose and bowed even lower to Nythan. "We rise further."

As soon as the door closed behind him, Gunther whirled on Patrick. "Was there a point to your snide interrogation?"

"There is *always* a point," Patrick snapped. "Your reckless pets created an avalanche, the likes of which we haven't seen since the Ordo Solis was a dire threat to our survival."

"The Prey is the *reason* why that threat is no longer dire!"

"Yes, they have made us successful. But that's *not* an excuse to be careless. Not only do we have every national agency worm known to man hunting us, your golden kids even managed to draw the attention of the less able, but far more motivated conspiracy theorists, who we spent *a lot* of time throwing off our trail."

"I understand that Patrick, but the imminent threat is no more. We've destroyed the last of Solis America and prevented them from alerting anyone. The Order's accomplices have been laid waste, and we did so without raising suspicion. That is success by any definition."

"All we did was take one ticking time bomb and replace it with another, only this bomb is *much* bigger than the first one," Patrick seethed as his cheeks flushed a dull red.

"Patrick, dear," Rose said in a soothing voice. "We're all doing the best we can. We had to act. We didn't decide on such a severe response without good reason."

"I tried to tell you. I tried telling *all* of you. The more we try to suppress the Order's evidence, the more firepower we give them to prove *exactly* what we don't want them to prove. They were *beaten*. No one would have believed them even if they *did* publish the video. Does no one else see this?" he exclaimed, slapping the tabletop.

"But that's the thing, Patrick," one of the other council members said, "The Ordo Solis is now dead."

"No, it isn't. As James and I must continually remind you, Solis Europe is alive and well. Yes, we have the upper hand, but most of us here still remember when it was *them* hunting *us*."

"Patrick," Rose purred. "We have sitting among us the very reason we fight. Would you not do anything to ensure his victory?"

Patrick stared at Rose. "I have done horrible things in the name of our Lord and I'd do it again. But now that he's here, really here, we *don't* abandon prudence simply because we want to be delivered faster. It will come as it always does, through patience and careful planning."

"We've entertained this discussion an untold number of times," Gunther cut in. "Yes, prudence is necessary, but it's poisonous when it becomes hesitation." Before Patrick could protest, he added, "We've been so patient, and this has rewarded us immensely. No one disputes this, Patrick. But history punishes those who fail to act. Our Lord is *safe*, and for the foreseeable future, he's everything he needs to achieve his goal. Even if it comes at our destruction."

Patrick started to speak but paused, pursing his lips. "Agreed. But we need to stop jumping at every shadow. This time, we *win*," he declared, mashing his finger down onto the table.

Nythan couldn't help but experience a certain warmth from the discussion. Their confidence and undying loyalty inspired him.

Mia piped in. "You all will be happy to see I have been questioning our guests more."

Gunther nodded. "Yes, I heard. The girl's well-being is his truth serum, it seems. What were the results of your interrogation?"

"We learned how to contacting the Order in Europe. We know his name, Enzo, and his phone number. We are tracing him to his home. Solis Asia is no longer, and neither is Solis America. Information not possible if he was not survived."

"I'm sure the Unas would love to get their hands on Enzo," Patrick chuckled.

"The Unas are nothing more than witless barbarians," a third council member insisted. "I wouldn't trust them with a pet rock, much less our Lord's life. About the only thing they're good for is keeping the attention away from us."

"Yes, well, don't forget the Unas outnumber us three to one," Rose countered.

"Yes, well, there're a lot of witless people in this word," the third one mocked.

Interesting.

Nythan raised an eyebrow. *What's interesting?*

The Unas appear to have a much larger pool to advance us than the Raptors. That should make you feel better about our situation.

Sure, if *it turns out to be true, and* if *we ever get a chance to go there.*

"In any case, that *is* useful information, Mia. Keep at it," Rose encouraged.

A brief silence fell across the room, and then Gunther spoke. "Great One, it seems our meeting has come to its end. Do you've any comment?"

Nythan examined each of them before responding. "I've done a great deal of thinking."

If only they knew how painful it was for you.

Nythan coughed to hide his amusement. *Shut it.*

"I intend to visit the other Covens in the next week. The longer I stay, the more I delay. It's important that we don't stagnate."

Rose tried her best to hide her disappointment, but Nythan saw her frown as clear as day.

"I know it's not ideal," Nythan said, trying not to look at Rose. "But I can't wait another ten years for things to die down. I need to do this now…in case anyone gets lucky in connecting the dots."

"If they do, we'll ensure they never see the light of day again," Rose growled with surprising ferocity.

"I believe you. And by my count, that's twice already we've had to do that. First with the Order and second with the Masons. This sort of thing was inevitable once we came back. I have to use the element of surprise while we still have it," Nythan said.

So you do *listen to me from time to time.*

Sometimes you say things that make sense. Other times, I try to ignore you. Nythan hid his smirk as he rose, and the rest of the Grand Coven rose with him.

"It's been a long day," Nythan commented. "Please, let's enjoy the rest of our night. I only have a handful of days left, and I want to make them count."

CHAPTER 49

WITHOUT, ON THE FLOOR

The parlor room filled up once again. Balin seated himself at the piano but didn't touch the keys. He and everyone else gave their attention to Nythan and the two new arrivals. She introduced herself as Esmeralda, and he as Ronaldo. They had traveled all the way from Spain to see Nythan. Apparently, word of his emergence had spread across the ocean. How far, he didn't know, but far enough for this couple to hear about it halfway across the world.

Esmeralda's jet-black hair, almond eyes, and high cheekbones attracted much attention, as did her stature; at six foot four in heels, she towered above everyone else in the room. Ronaldo attracted attention too, but for a different reason. His slick side part set a finishing touch to his silver-streaked charcoal hair.

Ronaldo explained in a thick but intelligible Spanish accent how just the week before he and Esmeralda had celebrated their eighth anniversary helping the Unas. When they heard of Nythan's reemergence, they booked an overnight flight.

"How're the Unas?" Nythan asked.

"Good. We have Ordo Europe on the run and are prepared for the Maker to honor us with your visit."

Nythan nodded his head as if he understood. "What do you do for the Unas?"

"We were spotters," Esmeralda answered in perfect, unaccented English. "We helped identify who was Ordo Solis so that our brother and sister Unas could deal with them."

I'm amazed by the people your cults recruit, Nythan thought. *They aren't like anything I ever imagined.*

If you imagined ax-wielding barbarians, wait until you meet their brother and sister Unas.

Nythan smiled at the couple. "I'm really grateful for all that you've done."

"If it pleases you, my Lord, Esmeralda and I offer our souls to further your cause," Ronaldo said, squeezing her hand.

Nythan recoiled at the forwardness of the request. "But..." he stammered, "Don't you want to continue being spotters and help the Unas? We need you."

Esmeralda glanced at Ronaldo before answering Nythan.

"*Mi amor* and I made a pact long ago that if we were ever alive long enough to see you, that we would become the Widowmaker," she admitted. "I had a horrific childhood. Wrath took me in, raised me, made me get exceptional grades in school. But I never forgot what it was like before."

She gave Ronaldo an admiring look. "I met him nine years ago, at a dinner party. He and I both agreed on what was in our hearts. We just want it to end."

Nythan fell silent at her response, unsure of some of her words and even more unsure of how to counter such sincerity.

"Don't you want to stay a little while, listen to Balin play? He's *muy bien*," Nythan offered, trying to use the little bit of Spanish he knew.

Esmeralda gave a polite smile. "No, *gracias*."

"We do have one request," Ronaldo said. He paused, looking to Esmeralda.

"Anything," Nythan said.

"We want you to take us together."

Nythan drew in a sharp breath.

Whoa, he thought in admiration.

That's an unusual, yet oddly romantic gesture. Like Romeo and Juliet.

Is that even possible?

It sure is. And you'll be able to do much more than that as we grow. The only consideration is, are you ready?

I…guess, Nythan thought, wincing. *Can you show me?*

I can tell you what to do, but you're *the one who will have to do it.*

"I see," Nythan finally said.

The two of them beamed at him and each other. "We are ready," Esmeralda declared.

"Wha—," Nythan blurted. "Uh…right now? Here?" The room was somehow packed with even more people than ten minutes ago, which didn't seem possible.

"Yes, please."

Mia, who had observed the conversation in silence, stood and walked over to the couple. Nythan winced when Bane tensed at Mia's approach.

Mia took Esmeralda's hand in hers. *"Mi amiga, ¿estás segura?"*

"Más segura que nada," Esmeralda replied. Mia nodded, retreating a step.

The happy couple looked to Nythan.

Okay, moment of truth, Nythan thought. *What do I do?*

You're going to need to focus on both of them at once. But instead of thinking of them as two separate people, think of their breath as one inhale and one exhale. We're not yet at the point where you can take multiple souls separately. Once you've linked with their cycle, it's as easy as taking the soul of one person. Just do more *of it, that's all.*

Nythan closed his eyes, surprised that he already sensed their breath.

"Please breathe in and out together," Nythan requested.

It took some time, but he felt their breathing harmonize enough that he no longer needed to concentrate. Nythan opened his eyes, seeing that they had faced each other, hands clasped together.

It'll help if you get closer.

Nythan closed the two-foot distance between them until they stood inches apart. He rested his hands on top of theirs. He craned his neck upward; they were at least four inches taller than him. Their breaths collided, creating a miniature whirlwind between them.

He concentrated on the whirlwind. *Okay, one more time, I want to make sure I get this right.*

Focus on their breath as though there is only one exhale. Pretend that it's one mouth. Their proximity to one another should help. Do what you usually do at this point.

Nythan looked at Esmeralda and Rolando, and said, "Thank you for your gift. I wish you nothing but peace."

With that, he inhaled sharply as they both exhaled. Their souls erupted from their bodies. Even though the ethereal streams stayed visible for just a few seconds, it caused a reaction among all who watched. Esmeralda and Ronaldo's bodies fell to the floor.

"We rise further," his audience chanted.

Now be careful, two souls at once is going to be a bit overwhelming.

Yeah, no kidding, Nythan winced, trying to stay upright as his abdomen began to spasm and his vision blurred.

Don't worry, the good news is the more we do this, the less of an adverse effect it will have.

Th—thanks, but…that doesn't…really help, Nythan thought. It took mere moments for the pain to grow unbearable. He clutched his sides, bending over.

The people within arm's length tried to comfort him, but Nythan couldn't move. They helped him down to the floor, where he remained for a long time.

I'm sorry I'm not much help to you right now. I can't digest these souls any faster.

"I'm fine," gasped Nythan, unable to think about anything except the agony ripping through his body.

His bodyguards knelt beside him, looking from him to the people all around.

Nythan held up a hand, and those around him backed away to create space.

"Great One, are you injured?" one of them asked.

"No," he croaked. "I'm afraid I got too much too fast."

The pain lasted for what seemed like an eternity. He found himself wanting Mia. It took him some time to find her among the crowd. Raptor guards helped him to his feet.

"I'll be…forever grateful to Esmeralda and Ronaldo," Nythan began, still struggling. "Their gift will not be forgotten. Please, don't be worried for me. Their souls are…powerful, and they'll be a great help. Balin!" He called out, clutching his stomach.

"Yes, Great One," Balin shouted from somewhere in the crowd.

"Please. Play."

"Certainly, Great One," Balin responded. A loud screeching sound echoed as Balin adjusted the stool on the hardwood floor. He began to play.

Nythan waved his hand to the crowd. "Enjoy!"

CHAPTER 50

LA SOPLÓN

I told you this would happen.

Nythan, Palaou, and his regular entourage of bodyguards gathered in front of the glittering tri-statue outside.

Now isn't the time, Nythan thought. He ground his teeth.

Oh really? When would be a good time, precisely? Here is your proof she isn't the delicate flower you convinced yourself she was. Now we have to deal with her, and you're emotionally attached.

Nythan tried to control his breathing, but he couldn't stop himself from hyperventilating. Mia. The Central Intelligence Agency. Impossible, but true.

If they're on scene, there's no telling who else is, Nythan thought.

Fitting how an organization I helped through its infancy would come back to haunt me.

That isn't helping, Nythan thought. *I need you to help me.*

What would help in this instance? Once the CIA has you in its sights, there is little you can do to escape them.

It'd help if you would BE QUIET!

Palaou was holding a tablet and staring at him with grave concern.

"My Lord, you look queasy. Shall I fetch the doctor?" he asked.

"No, I just need to process this and figure out how to respond."

good and evil. It's not that evil is somehow good. It's that each side has to clas-
sify the other as evil *in order to motivate themselves to accomplish their goal,*
often at the other side's expense. Otherwise, each side would have to face the
fact that they are hurting good people who do the same bad things they do.
The only difference is that the bad *is seen as* evil *because they aren't on the*
same side. *So don't think of this fight as* good versus evil. *Think about it as*
two sides that don't want to hurt each other but do because their needs clash.
It's perspective. That's all.

Nythan sighed. *The CIA,* he reminded Bane.

Yes. Mia is a problem.

I have an idea about that.

I know what you're thinking, and that's just as terrible an idea as keeping
the other two Ordo Solis members alive.

If we take her with us, we can find out what the CIA knows, and she'll
be removed from the Grand Coven, Nythan thought, tapping the tips of
his fingers.

It's too dangerous to keep her alive.

The Raptors should be more than capable of transporting them with
us. Who knows, maybe we'll learn a lot from them once we break through
their barriers…

Wait, what? Where did them *come from?*

Steven and Raeleigh, we should bring them with Mia and us,
Nythan clarified.

Nythan, that's insane. It'll be difficult enough for us to move around a
whole continent without attracting unwanted attention. But to bring an entire
group with us, especially a group that isn't there voluntarily? That's foolish.

Hmm… Yeah, you're right. But I want to at least take Mia. If the CIA
found out that she's our prisoner, they might be forced to act even if they don't
know who we are. If we take her with us, it might give them the impression
everything is still okay.

That's a lot of ifs.

This whole game is nothing but ifs *now,* Nythan countered. *Remember?*
You told me you deliberately didn't *plan past this point.*

Yeah, yeah, yeah. Don't remind me.

It's settled then, we out Mia and take her with us as we tour the Covens.

How about we ask the Grand Coven for their advice?

Nythan paused, scratching at his hairline.

"That's not a bad idea," he blurted. Nythan put his fingers to his lips. "Oops," he remarked.

Palaou stared at Nythan with a desperate expression. He could tell Palaou wanted to help but didn't know how.

"Palaou, it's all going to be okay," Nythan said, hoping he sounded convincing.

"My Lord, I don't know what to make of all this," Palaou said, exhaling.

Nythan stood; Palaou followed suit.

"I'd like to review the video one more time," Nythan said, gesturing at the tablet in Palaou's hand. Palaou gave him the device, which showed Mia and Steven paused in mid-conversation. Nythan swiped the seek bar to the beginning.

"In the meantime," Nythan added, "Could you please get Rose for me? Tell her I need to see her when she has the time...no rush. Don't tell her what it's about and inform anyone who knows anything about this to tell *no one.*"

"Right away, my Lord!" Palaou exclaimed, scampering off.

"Also, Palaou!" he called after him. Palaou turned back toward Nythan. "A glass of orange juice, please."

Nythan laughed to himself as he continued observing the scene unfold with Mia and Steven.

You can't even taste the juice anymore.

Nythan smirked. *For old time's sake.*

Whatever floats your boat, ole chap. What are you going to tell Rose?

The truth. I want you to watch her and tell me if you have any of those weird feelings you get when we talked to Mia.

He finished replaying the video and peered at his surroundings. Three of his bodyguards faced in different directions; a fourth watched him. Nythan looked at him, wondering what the guy thought at that exact moment.

When we get stronger, you'll be able to sense other people's thoughts. Not as a full-fledged mind reader, but you can generally get an idea of what they are feeling. In the same way that when we are around Mia, we can tell her allegiance lies elsewhere.

Nythan shifted his gaze to the brilliant trio of statues ten feet away. The sun caused the atmosphere around the effigies to glisten with a simmering rainbow aura. Nythan marveled at the display, as he often did. This time, however, the feeling morphed into something different.

We're going to do this, he thought.

We're going to do this, confirmed Bane.

CHAPTER 51

SILENCE

Nythan walked between Raeleigh and Steven as they meandered through the garden. He was trying a new tactic: separating the two in order to focus some of their attention on him. For the first time, Steven spoke to him without being prompted.

Bane expressed his displeasure with Nythan interacting with either of the Ordo Solis. Nythan viewed it as an investment in good relations.

Oh, come off it already. Nythan rolled his eyes. *We have a firm hold of them, and I'm not giving away any of our secrets.*

Anything you tell them can be used against us in the future.

Nythan didn't understand why he felt claustrophobic as they walked until he realized his guard contingent had doubled to eight Raptors without him even noticing. Two assault rifles pointed at Raeleigh and Steven at any given time. It struck Nythan as overkill, but he didn't comment.

"So, you've all these people do your bidding...do you have an army or something?" Steven asked, trying to be nonchalant.

"These hedges were recently trimmed," Nythan replied, smiling at Steven.

Steven cocked his head. "What?"

Why do you even answer him? Why are we even here, doing this?

"Were you always...like this?" Raeleigh asked, looking afraid.

Nythan winced. "I'd prefer not to answer that. I'm not offended or mad you asked. It's just, you know, we're not on the same side." Raeleigh's cheeks turned a bright red.

"Right, 'cuz telling us might impede your quest for world domination," Steven scoffed. Nythan wasn't at all surprised to see one of his Raptors take a step toward Steven. He waved him off.

"It's not *like* that." They had arrived at the brilliant trio of statues, marking the end of their walk.

"Oh really, what's it like then? Because *that...*" Steven accused, pointing to the statues, "shouts 'I want to engulf the world in fire and brimstone.'"

"Steven!" Raeleigh hissed.

"No, no, it's okay," Nythan said. "You have a right to be angry."

Nythan, come on.

"It's about time we acknowledge the elephant in the room," Nythan added. "My people hurt you."

"No," Steven said, raising his voice. "Hurting someone usually involves a small or moderate amount of pain. Hurting implies they can recover. Your people *slaughtered* us." Steven's face turned a darker shade of red with each sentence, and tears rolled down his cheeks.

Nythan again waved down an aggressive Raptor who looked like he itched to wrap his hands around Steven's throat. "I under—"

Steven interrupted. "Women. Children. Old men. Entire families. *You* are responsible for their gruesome deaths. *You* could've stopped it," he told Nythan, pointing straight at his face. "*That's* what you represent. Death. For God's sake man, you people killed three families just to hide the fact that you pillaged our headquarters for that video of you and the Gatekeeper. Jeff, his wife Sara, and his daughter Trista were in that house. All of them gone. And to make things worse, you *raped* Sara before killing her, just to make it look like a convincing burglary!"

Nythan stole a quick glance at Raeleigh; she stared at the ground, sobbing.

"But oh, I forgot," Steven murmured, letting his arms fall to his sides. "You want to take over the world...and you'll stop at nothing to get what you want."

"Damn it, Steven, I keep telling you it isn't like that!" Nythan snapped.

Steven's face hardened. "WELL, WHAT IS IT THEN?" Steven shook a fist at Nythan. "'Cuz these Raptors sure as hell aren't here to throw you a birthday party for world's oldest demon!"

Nythan's intuition zeroed in on a Raptor's finger tightening on a trigger. "Don't you dare!" he bellowed, pointing at one of them.

Nythan started to perceive the emotions all around him. Tiny pinpricks of pressure in his chest grew until he felt the feelings as if experiencing them himself. Unbearable grief, smoldering anger, merciless contempt, horrid revulsion, and murderous lust—he couldn't pinpoint who experienced what. A tornado of passion whipped around him like a school of piranha, longing to devour whatever it touched.

You're starting to feel what I've been telling you about. As we consume more souls, our senses improve.

"Just hold on a second," Nythan blurted, returning his attention to Steven and trying to remain focused.

"I've held on for a long time, Nythan, a long-a** time," Steven shot back. "I've heard the stories from other Solis members. I've seen the century-old still shots. I've held on to the hope that if you were to ever return, we could do our part in putting you down like the dog you are."

Nythan sniffed, staring at Steven. "How did you know my name?"

If we didn't already know how he knew, this would be your smoking gun.

Steven's expression of hatred froze in place. "Uh," he stammered, before falling silent.

"Steven," Nythan began, then, turning to Raeleigh, "Raeleigh, please just listen for a second." He plunged into what he hoped would topple barriers, if only a little. "I had no idea the Raptors would do all these things. I told them *not* to harm innocent people. Now, granted, Bane…" Nythan's eyes went wide and he froze mid-sentence.

Nythan, you idiot. Stop talking.

Steven furrowed his brow.

Nythan shrugged. "Look, they got overzealous. They *really* wanted to keep me safe. And I get it…it makes sense…"

Stop.

"…but I—I didn't know they'd do that to the Masons, or those families…"

F***ing.

"I'm really, really, sorry about that. They didn't give me a chance to…"

Talking.

"…make it clear to them that I did *not* want a bloodbath. It all happened so quickly," Nythan closed his eyes. "Hold on."

Bane, shut up for a second.

Hell no, you're doing the stupidest thing possible right now.

You need to trust me.

Normally, yes. But what you're doing is so contrary to anything reasonable that I can't let you cut our own throats.

Let me make it clear then. If they don't come through *on some level, I'll take their souls, right here, right now. Happy?*

Nythan's brain ping-ponged as Bane pondered his words.

Bane, I'm kind of in the middle of something.

Okay, fine. But I get *to decide if they* come through *or not.*

A rotten taste coated Nythan's tongue, a sensation he associated with the snide attitude Bane put into *come through.* He reopened his eyes.

"In any case," Nythan went on, "I'm telling you all of this because I want to do something different this time. *I* want to be different. My goal doesn't have to come at the expense of you or whatever else you think I'm trying to destroy."

Steven stared at him with a puzzled and suspicious expression. "What exactly are you playing at here?"

Nythan extended his hands, glancing at the sky. "I'm not playing at anything!" he said, exasperated, letting his hands fall the same way Steven's did earlier.

"Just…Steven," Raeleigh pleaded, turning her gaze to Nythan. "What *is* your goal?"

Hmm, how do I word this properly? Nythan asked Bane.

How about, I don't owe you anything, you dirty little worm.

Nythan couldn't help but lose his composure and let out a cackle. "Sorry," he said to Raeleigh, "I promise I'm not laughing at you."

Nythan could see the wheels turning in Steven's mind. *Seriously.*

I was *serious.*

"My goal…is to transcend."

"Transcend into what?" Raeleigh asked.

I caution you not to get any more specific. Your Raptor bodyguards have ears. Word will spread. When people can figure you out, you lose that awe-inspiring presence, and their belief starts to wane.

Nythan answered with a shrug.

"And when you transcend," Steven interjected, "you become a god and destroy the world with a meteor or something?"

"No, I'm not trying to do anything like that."

"Says the guy who wants to become all-powerful," grumbled Steven.

Nythan huffed. "I wish I could tell you everything. I *want* to tell you everything. But as soon as I do...uggggh! I can't even tell you why I can't tell you!"

"Nythan," Raeleigh said. "Why can't you tell us?"

"Because you guys want to destroy me. I don't want to hurt you, so I don't want to tell you too much that the Raptors have to...ya know," Nythan said, tilting his head.

"But the Raptors answer to you," Raeleigh pointed out. "Tell them not to hurt us."

Nythan gave her a boyish grin. "I did, that's why you guys are still standing here."

"Oh. Well, what *can* you tell us? You don't seem to be as bad as we were led to believe. Even me talking to you this week...you can't be more than twenty-one years old. You're just a baby."

Hah! Hahahahahahaha!

Steven scowled. "Except that he's been alive since before Christ, and we've been fighting him, and the world's been fighting him, and millions of lives have been lost in the process. Now we're all here chatting like old friends."

Suddenly, Raeleigh giggled. Steven raised his eyebrows in confusion, and Nythan went bug-eyed, alternating his attention between the two.

Aww, you're having a moment.

"Yeah, but I feel like something's missing," Raeleigh said, looking at Nythan. "Unless he's just completely misleading us, this is *not* the bringer of death you and Jeff have been warning about all these years."

"Well, I wouldn't expect him to come right out and say it," Steven countered.

"Yeah, but...Steven, just look at him," Raeleigh protested.

"I am, and I'm not fooled," Steven declared, pointing at Nythan. "This face right here has destroyed a lot of lives."

"No, what I mean is, it's obvious to me that there's something about all this that doesn't make sense. We're missing *something*, and he obviously doesn't want to tell us for fear we'd know too much." When Nythan didn't respond, she added, "Just nod if I'm on the right track."

Nythan bobbed his head up and down while Bane's laughter rattled his torso.

Honestly, I didn't expect this to be so funny. I haven't had this much fun since my last life, when I had to explain what Rickrolling *was to a Russian intelligence officer, and why Rick Astley wasn't the infamous* Tank Man *he had YouTubed.*

These people are here to kill you, Nythan reminded himself. *These people are here to kill you.*

Steven spoke up. "What does any of this matter? He's the Soulstealer. He eats people's souls like it's a damn four-course meal. And he wants to do that to everyone."

"Soulstealer?" Raeleigh and Nythan chorused at the same time.

"Uh...yeah. It's...kind of my nickname...for you."

Nythan raised an eyebrow, looking back at his guards. "Soulstealer... as in, I steal souls?

"Yup, that's...that's where I was going with it."

"Catchy."

Bane was howling with laughter. *You've got...you've got to be kidding me!*

Nythan winced and made a small whimper.

Raeleigh pounced, "See? See! That right there," she said, pointing at Nythan. "What's going on with that? I feel like, *that's* what it is."

"Raeleigh..." Steven cautioned.

"Oh, c'mon, Steven. I gave up after I found out Gar—my *traitor* fiancé—was a Raptor. They *have* us. The only way we're realistically getting out of here is through a funeral. But even that isn't likely, because no one will *ever* be able to find our bodies. I've had enough time to think, to come to terms with it all. We have here in front of us the *whole* damn reason we've been devoting all this time and energy. He's standing, right here! So, before we die, I really, *really*, want to find out what this horses*** is all about."

Nythan felt the familiar tinge of desire hit him as he watched Raeleigh's rapid inhale and exhale.

No! Nythan scolded. Bane growled.

"I don't think I've ever heard you curse before in your life," Steven observed. "It's actually quite attractive."

"Yeah, well, being betrayed by the one you love and facing oblivion will do that to you," she spat.

"Not everyone who loves you betrayed you, Raeleigh," Steven said in a tender voice. "I mean...you're right. Since we're both going to die here, I might as well come out and say it. Sorry if this's getting a little bit mushy for you, Mr. Soulstealer, but I don't know how much longer I have with her."

Nythan bowed, taking a step backward. He made a sweeping gesture toward Raeleigh.

Steven drew closer to Raeleigh. "I know you've heard me say this, but I need to say it again. I love you with every fiber of my being. I love everything about you. Your eyes, your ears, your heart, from the top of your head to the bottom of your feet...you're all I ever wanted. The scorching sun, the icy moon, the worst monster imaginable—which when I think about it, is standing just a couple of feet away from us—all that won't stop me from wanting to spend the rest of my life with you. I may not have all the eloquent words that Garrett, that tiny little insecure *bastard*, may have been able to conjure up, but I'm a billion times more sincere about it."

Raeleigh gazed moonstruck into Steven's eyes.

"Will you just...shut up," she blurted. She embraced him, mashing her lips against his. Remembering where they were, they both caught themselves.

Nythan grinned. "Don't mind me. You may think I'm Satan and all, but I've no intention of interrupting what you've got going on here."

Raeleigh laughed while wiping her tears away on her sleeve. "I can't believe we're in this situation. This is so unreal."

Nythan's eyes widened as he nodded in agreement. "Yeah, my thoughts exactly." He shrugged. "Anyways, yes, there's more to it than just me being your worst nightmare. This whole *evil nemesis of the world* thing these past centuries is just as misrepresented as everything else in history. I'll admit...*some* of it is as bad as it seems. But the more I learn about it all, the more I realize that neither side took the time to try and make it work. I wanna change that. I can't change all the horrible things we've done to each other. If I could, I would. If I could, I would. I'm just trying to... make it all stop."

"You make it sound like you're...not...a part...of the struggle between you and us. I don't get that," Steven said.

"In a way, I'm not, and in another way, I am. It's reallllly complicated. There's more to consider than just what you and I know. That's the best way I can explain it, at least for now." Nythan shrugged, exhausted. He suddenly perked up as his mind worked through the idea that just came to mind.

"Yes, I think I understand," Raeleigh said. "But answer me this, if you get what you want, what happens to us? Not *us* as in Steven and me, but *us* as in humankind. What happens to the world?"

"Raeleigh, he's still the enemy," Steven warned.

Nythan sat silent for a moment, rubbing his chin. "I'll tell you on the way. We're leaving tomorrow."

Wait, what?

Nythan nodded. *I think I've figured out what we should do next. Thing is, we're gonna need 'em both, along with Mia.*

Ughhhh.

Give me a few minutes to get away from them so that I can explain. When I do, don't say anything until I've finished going through the whole plan. Nythan couldn't help but smirk like an evil scientist who had brewed the perfect concoction.

Fine. This had better be good, or else we're going to have an Ordo Solis feast in the next ten minutes.

CHAPTER 52

RED HANDED

Nythan packed what few belongings he had back into his backpack, which amounted to almost nothing except an extra pair of jeans and some shirts. Everything he needed had been provided by the Raptors. He ended up piddling around in his room while eight Raptors stood guard. The anxiety he used to feel over several people watching his every move didn't bother him anymore, even if he thought their being in his bedroom went a little too far.

Nythan understood the Grand Coven's objection to his leaving earlier than expected. However, Mia's reaction was exactly as expected. She made every effort to secretly make contact with Steven to figure out what had changed.

There was a knock at the door, and one of the Raptors opened it. Palaou stepped forward with his tablet in hand. "My Lord, it is about to happen now," he said, out of breath.

Nythan said nothing in response as they made their way to the secluded dining room on the far side of the mansion that Palaou had shown him late last night. Nythan paused at the door, looking to one of his guards. "No, it's better if you all enter first. Same plan as we talked about, nothing else has changed."

The beefy Raptor and his seven colleagues opened the door and charged into the room. Nythan entered in time to witness Mia's horror-stricken face as her accomplice was slammed up against the wall and Steven was seized on either side.

"*Hola*, Mia," Nythan greeted her.

"My Lord," she said, bowing. Beyond her initial reaction, she showed little break in her poise. "I was just—"

"Yes, I know," Nythan waved her off. He felt her insincerity and contempt.

Nythan studied Steven and zeroed on the colorful swirl of feelings emanating from him. Steven held his chin high while staring at Nythan, but Nythan perceived that Mia's accomplice was experiencing anxiety and dismay behind his mask.

"Don't worry, I'm not going to hurt you, Mia. I'm actually glad that you work for the CIA. I need their help," Nythan said.

"I don't—"

Nythan circled a finger around the midsize dining room. "This place has cameras."

Mia fell silent. Nythan could feel intense despair grow within her.

"Bring them," Nythan commanded. A few of his guardians hustled Mia and Steven out of the room. Nythan turned his attention to the traitor.

"Take his mask off," Nythan said. The nearest Raptor ripped the agent's Raptor mask off.

"What's your name?" Nythan asked. The accomplice made no response.

Nythan peered toward the door to make sure that Mia and Steven had been carted off, then he stepped back several paces.

What are you doing?

Testing something, Nythan thought.

In one fluid motion, Nythan yanked the traitor's soul from his body as the man exhaled. It slithered to him, and he wasted no time consuming it. The accomplice drooped forward, lifeless. Nythan's bodyguards carried the body out of the room.

Nice.

Nythan's eyes widened. *Thanks. I wasn't sure if it was going to work that far away.*

Step one complete, mastermind Nythan, now on to stage two.

Nythan grunted at what they planned to do next but understood its necessity.

If you want to make an omelet, you have to crack a few hundred eggs.

Chapter 53

It is Well

Rose hesitated. "My Lord, are you…sure?"

Nythan sensed her deep-rooted hurt and resentment over the revelation of Mia's disloyalty. He looked around to each of the Grand Coven members seated in the conference room.

"Yes, I've thought about it. The Great One and I are in complete agreement."

Well, almost in agreement, but they don't need to know that.

Patrick nodded. "There's no use in questioning it any further. We've given him our input, and he's decided. Now it's up to us to execute his will. If *this* is what it takes, I say it was an inevitable price to pay for victory."

"*Now* look who's so eager to jump and act," Rose said, winking.

Patrick narrowed his eyes and the edges of his mouth curled into a sly grin.

"It is going to come as a shock to our family," Gunther offered. "We have been serving the image of the Great One for so long that it barely feels real to serve him in the flesh. Some of us will not be prepared for the change. However, if we remind our brothers and sisters of why they serve, and that the reason for their service is now here to see its fulfillment, I have faith they will rise to the challenge."

"Agreed," Rose said. "We must be careful to mask our movements.

We can have no more...surprises." She appeared to struggle to keep her composure.

"Obviously, it will be the Prey's mandate to protect the Great One until he can be safely received by the Unas," Gunther commented. "Even then, it would comfort me to see you retain a contingent of Prey. They are one of our most valuable assets, surely more useful than anything that band of ruffians can muster."

"I wouldn't have a problem keeping the Birds of Prey around. We'll see as things develop."

Gunther looked satisfied and nodded at Nythan.

"It's settled, my Lord?" Rose asked.

"Yes, please."

"Very well, we'll see to your itinerary. We are very sorry to see you leave, but each of us is happy to see our faith rewarded," Rose said.

You should say something to them. This is your top leadership.

Nythan cocked an eyebrow. *What do you normally say in situations like these?*

Tell them what you already know, that they have been beneficial to us.

Nythan nodded, clearing his throat.

"I can't begin to express my gratitude for your help. From the moment I spoke with the Gatekeeper, you've welcomed me with open arms. The Raptors have flourished under your leadership, and I couldn't have asked for a better family to come home to."

Good. I didn't even need to help you there.

Nythan smiled. *I've had a lot of practice these past few weeks.*

"We rise further!" Gunther trumpeted. Nythan expected him to beat his chest like Tarzan. The rest of the Grand Coven echoed Gunther's sentiment.

"Since tonight is my last night, I want to make it extra special. If Balin is still here, please ask him to play. Let's move the piano to the largest room we have and let everyone know," Nythan said as he pushed himself up from the table.

The rest of the Grand Coven stood up quickly as he continued speaking. "We may not get a chance to meet like this again. It's gonna be challenging. Whatever happens, please keep your faith. Know that every action I take, no matter how it appears, is toward deliverance."

At the mention of the word *deliverance*, the room grew still. Faces hardened, and the lingering sense of pride transformed into something lethal that hunted for its next victim. Confident he had said what they needed to hear, Nythan departed the conference room.

CHAPTER 54

LAMENT

Nythan sat center of the parlor room and looked on as Balin's fingers glided across the whole length of the keyboard. The rumor of Nythan's impending departure had spread through the mansion. Everyone in the mansion wanted to take this final opportunity to make contact with him in some way.

He was enjoying Balin's angelic rendition of Beethoven's Moonlight Sonata when Palaou knelt beside him. "My Lord, some have prepared a presentation for you."

Rose had warned Nythan that some of the Raptors wanted to offer themselves to him. Bane spent much of the day bracing Nythan for what would happen.

Remember, it's best to take it slow. When you take these souls, don't wolf them down.

Five people lined up in front of him. Balin paused his concert, but Nythan asked him to continue at a lower volume. One of the group members stepped forward and bowed.

"Great One. We know your journey will be long. We all wanted to offer ourselves to help you with whatever is to come next."

Nythan stood, offering a smile. "I appreciate this. Thank you. What're your names?"

"My name is Jared, and this is Emily, Travaun, John, Samil," he said, pointing to each person down the line.

"Great," Nythan could only think to say.

Nythan walked up and put his hands on the young man's shoulders. "Jared, thank you so much. Are you ready?"

Jared nodded in response. "We rise further."

Nythan breathed in as the Raptor exhaled, assimilating his soul faster than he meant to.

Slowly, Nythan, slowly.

Nythan held Jared up as others took hold of the body. He moved to the next person. He had already forgotten her name.

Emily.

Nythan nodded. *Right.*

Nythan looked down and saw Emily and the boy next to her holding hands.

Travaun.

Nythan half-stepped to put himself between them.

"Are you ready?" he asked. They looked at each other before nodding to him.

"Yes," Emily answered.

Nythan drew in when they breathed together, and he found it easier than usual to draw their souls out at the same time. Nythan let the shimmering ethereal wisps wade and slink about as they inched toward him.

Stop playing with your food.

Mm-hmm, Nythan thought.

His audience reacted with a mixture of awe, gasps, and hushed whispers.

This is unnecessary.

Mm-hmm.

Ugh.

As Nythan absorbed the last blend of life floating around him, he proceeded to the next person, who seemed ready to faint from all the excitement. Nythan easily extracted her soul too.

When Nythan finished, he slumped, wondering if his sudden heaviness came from a trick of the mind. Despite it all, his body brimmed with euphoria, the likes of which he hadn't experienced before. Bane couldn't contain himself.

It's, oh man. This is great. This is gooood. We're good, you're good, and everything feels nice.

Nythan stifled a laugh as he moved further down the line. Some bowed, others cried, and more stared at him with an overwhelmed expression. The emotions in the room centered around bewilderment.

Gunther stepped forward in an ornamented robe Nythan had never seen him wear. Gunther raised his arms toward Nythan.

"Thus, our faith is rewarded. He will deliver us. We rise further!"

"WE RISE FURTHER!" the audience repeated.

Nythan nodded at Gunther. "Thank you, Coven. Please, don't let me keep you from getting sleep. You all can leave whenever you want." Nythan then took his seat once more.

Rose sat down beside him. "That was wonderful, Great One."

"Thanks." He then returned his gaze toward Balin as the room thinned out. There were still a dozen people lounging, talking, and laughing amid a soft melody.

See what you were so close to missing out on? This is your family now.

"Mm-hmm."

Nythan searched for Mia before he remembered the earlier events.

It didn't give me any pleasure knowing I was right about her.

I know. Nythan recognized Bane's sincerity. He could *feel* the anxiousness, bitterness, and joy all swirling in Bane. It felt human. For the first time, Nythan experienced a oneness with Bane, much in the way that Bane was in tune with him.

Balin played well into the night until, at last, only Nythan and Rose remained. At last, Nythan detected Balin's utter fatigue.

"Balin," Nythan said, closing his eyes. He sensed Balin's attention fall upon him. "You play wonderfully. I'll remember this for a long, long time. Please, go get some rest."

Nythan's ears twitched as he listened to Balin stand from the creaky piano bench, bow, and leave the room.

Rose hesitated, and Nythan perceived her unease. "Yes?"

"I wanted to thank you," Rose said in a hushed voice, "for telling me about Mia."

Nythan placed his hand on Rose's forearm, his eyes still closed. "Always, Rose. You handled it quite well, and your advice was welcome."

Rose smiled, "I'm glad," she whispered. Then her face hardened. "Whatever you decide, it will be well deserved, I'm sure. That *puta madre*," she said with ferocious venom.

"There're so many ways this could go, but one thing is for sure," Nythan said, his eyes blazing with sudden fervor. He stared straight at Rose. "We're going to win. We are *going* to win."

CHAPTER 55

TRIO

Today, we begin the plunge. There's no stopping now, not until we're done.

Agreed, Nythan thought.

I noticed you didn't get overwhelmed last night.

He stared out of the window of the SUV as his convoy made its way to its first destination. *I noticed that too.*

We're getting much stronger now.

With great power comes great responsibility. It's naive, but I believe it.

Yes, ever the young idealist. I wish I still had that in me, but my long years have weaned my enthusiasm and appreciation of life. You are indeed a nice breath of fresh air. Albeit an infuriating one.

Let's hope that I stay that way, there's no telling what kind of person I'll become.

We're in this together. I'll help you through everything. The past few months have been a lot to take in, and you have done well so far.

So far. How long until I can finally go sleep with all this adrenaline built up inside me right now?

I seriously doubt we'll be sleeping anytime soon. The souls we consumed will sustain us physically for some time.

So, I'm going to sit here, fully awake, just like last night?

Probably. And the night after that, and many more to come.

That's a lot of time to think and do stuff, Nythan pointed out.

Yes, well, don't go crazy on me. I've had more than a few partners who started out well, only to go insane with all the power that comes with more awake time.

I'll do my best, but I'm only nineteen. Before all this, I was going to go into the military to do who knows what. Now, I'm involved in secret organizations, being a religious figurehead, and making decisions that have a massive impact on others. It's incredible, to say the least.

Big things have small beginnings.

Bane, one day soon, I want to know how all this started. How you *started.*

One day soon, I'll tell you. It'll be a story unlike anything you've ever heard. Not even Hollywood can think up something this bizarre. Although, perhaps Bollywood could.

Okay, okay. Now you gotta give me a hint, just a little one.

Hahaha, fine. Just this one hint. It involved an elephant and maranasati.

Nythan scratched his ear. *I've no idea what* maranasati *is, and I'm interested to know what an elephant has to do with all of—*

Without warning, Palaou jerked awake beside Nythan, squinting as he surveyed his surroundings.

"Can I get you anything, my Lord?"

Nythan let out a laugh, patting the man's shoulder. "No, Palaou. Go back to sleep."

Palaou's eyes drooped and soon let out a gentle snore. He had attempted to stay up with Nythan the night before to attend to his every whim, but eventually he dozed off.

This's going to be a long trip. It's time you told me about the Unas and the Sanhe, Nythan thought.

Let's start with this. The Unas came first, before anyone. When Catharism was in its infancy, I saw a golden opportunity and created the Unas within them. I originally fashioned them as a shield to withstand the brute force of the Catholic Church, but they later became my food source.

Gotcha.

The Unas multiplied, but word of my involvement spread to the Church. It labeled the entirety of the Cathars as the Church of Satan, *because they could not figure out who was Cathari and who was Unas. In the resulting* persecution, the Cathars were destroyed. *The Unas were resilient and continued to thrive.*

Nythan shook his head. *This is unreal.*

Bane laughed. *The things you don't know about history. All because someone with a pen either was not aware or willfully neglected the truth. An example of this is with the Aztecs and their practice of what you would call* human sacrifice.

Nythan clutched his heart as he felt two small tugs. *Hold on a second. What happened with the Aztecs?*

Hernán Cortés happened. Somehow, the Inquisition found out I was living among the Aztecs as one of their gods. At the behest of the Inquisition and with the endorsement of the Catholic Church, Cortés convinced the king of Spain to partially fund an expedition to spiritually conquer *the Aztecs and the Mayas. I was living among both of them at one time or another, but Cortés never found me.*

Interesting.

Sure is. Fun fact, the closest I ever came to being freed from my bondage was when I was with the Aztecs. Once I established myself as an earthly deity, I convinced the Tlatoani to increase the amount of sacrifice needed to appease their gods.

That's terrible. I've seen pictures of their sacrificial knives…those people died horrible deaths.

Think about that a little more carefully. I didn't request more sacrifices to see them all die needlessly. Every sacrifice had to be prepared, *which meant they came to me so that I could receive their soul. Before any sacrifice could take place, I had to* make their body ready *to honor the gods with a* pure sacrifice. *I could barely keep up with all the travel to different sacrificial sites.*

That's the most abysmal con I've ever heard.

Well, it sounds terrible when you think about it from the perspective of written history, but there's a whole undertone not captured. In any case, back to the Unas. The Unas were created to protect me. As the Inquisition became more brutal in its hunt, the Unas became more vicious in their quest to keep me safe. And when the Unas became adept in combating the Church, the Inquisition's hunt for me transformed into a hunt for those who served me. This is an important part to understand. Before, the Inquisition was solely focused on destroying me, *so they brushed aside anyone who got in their way. Now, they hunted those suspected of aiding me, which led to the widespread persecution the Inquisition is infamous for.*

It's weird how all this fits together. I never would've guessed.

Well, everyone in that day and age knew who the Inquisition was after. It was no secret. But as time progressed, and I slowly became a myth, historians began doubting the written accounts of my existence. This, in turn, caused a change in interpretation of the Church's hunt for heresy.

I thought you said you were a public enemy of humanity for a couple thousand years. How could the world forget?

You underestimate the need for people to feel safe. With no verifiable evidence except for stories about the epic battles that my existence caused, those stories became just that, imaginative fairy tales. There was no photography, Facebook, or YouTube to prove *that I was real. When your family tells you a story about some ancient evil their great-grandfathers fought, evils you have never seen, doubt grows with each passing generation. It got to the point where I was dismissed as popular legend.*

Which freed you to do whatever you wanted.

Exactly. It freed me to strengthen the resolve of the Unas. Once I felt the Unas were self-sufficient, I moved on to the East to create a safety net where I could hide. I sailed with the Santa Clara *intending to get to Asia. Instead, we landed in Cuba. I made my way down to South America and found a primitive, yet sophisticated group of societies. I told you about my time with the Aztecs. Cortés's untimely arrival put a halt to my plans there.*

When you say, put a halt, *what do you mean?*

As in, Cortés annihilated and subjugated the Aztecs. One of his soldiers actually killed me without knowing it, but I did not want to risk discovery, so we let it happen. My next life landed somewhere in modern-day China, which was precisely where I wanted to be. There I created Sanhetuan, *known as* Sanhe. *The word loosely means harmony, cooperation, and mutual solution. The whole purpose of Sanhe is to hide me when necessary. They act as our safehouse.*

So that's why you wanted us to run to the Sanhe.

Yes. When you need to disappear, Sanhe are experts in that craft.

But hiding won't help you ascend, Nythan pointed out.

That's true. Which is why I'm looking forward to seeing if your plan will bear any fruit.

Okay, so Unas is our recruitin' pool, while the Sanhe is the hideout. What were the Raptors meant to do?

The Raptors were intended to be a cross between our face and our legislative branch.

Our face?

Public relations. The Unas were too brutal and Sanhe too secretive for us to hope to develop any future positive image through them. The Raptors are my long-term solution to that.

But the Raptors are brutal.

That's true, but their brutality is professional. When the time comes, they will present a much more acceptable image to the rest of the world.

And do they know they're to do this?

Somewhat. They know that they are intended for something more sophisticated than reclusive barbarism.

Fair enough. For someone who said he didn't have a plan in this life, you sure did come close.

Well...I couldn't entirely abandon the urge to create success. While I may not have made any detailed plans, I did what I could do to generate future opportunity.

Nythan leaned forward and rested his chin in his palms. *And now here we are.*

Yes, here we are.

CHAPTER 56

THE NORTH

Nythan sat with Gladys, the Northern Matriarch, in the same dining room where he first met her almost a month prior. As usual, his masked guardians took up stations around the room, scanning their near-empty surroundings. Palaou flitted in and around the house to check on, in his words, "their level of preparedness to receive their Lord."

"This is certainly a surprise," Gladys remarked. She rubbed her thumb against the emeralds hanging from her ear.

"Yeah, it all came together rather suddenly," Nythan said. He figured the only difference from his prior visit was his newfound ability to detect everyone else's feelings around him. The utter sense of peace and harmony swirling within Gladys fascinated him.

"Of course, being surprised will not delay us in the slightest. The Northern Coven is prepared," Gladys said. "You'll be staying tonight only?"

"Yes, unfortunately. But I've really come to enjoy the Northern Coven."

"I understand. I do not know the details of your request, but there is no need to explain. They will be ready tonight, shortly after the evening meal. Will this suffice?"

"Absolutely." Everything took on a whole new meaning when he accessed another person's most intimate feelings. He recognized the depths to which she'd go to do whatever he asked.

"And do you desire the company of a few companions as well?" the Matriarch asked, a hint of a smile tugging at the corners of her mouth.

Nythan smiled with mild embarrassment. "Uh, sure. Just two will do this time."

"Of course. I wish to stay here longer with you, but there are items that require my attention. Later, I would like to sit with you once more," the Matriarch said, rising from her chair.

"Absolutely," Nythan replied, unsure of what to do next.

How about you take a walk. Some of your best ideas seem to have come from pacing.

Nythan laughed and tapped his chest so that the Matriarch would understand his outburst. Gladys nodded. "I'll leave you to it then," she said and left the room.

Nythan stood around for a few minutes, then made his way to the back garden. Even though these topiaries didn't compare to the Grand Coven's extravagance, they still exuded a sense of power. He strolled through, making no effort to think about any one thing or resisting thoughts that crossed his mind.

After several hours passed, an attendant informed him that the evening meal was beginning. He came to a dining hall so overflowing with people he needed to push his way to the table, even as they moved out of his way.

The Matriarch seemed calm, but Nythan sensed her annoyance. "This just won't do at all," she said, holding her hand up to the person next to her, who helped her onto the chair.

Nythan bent his ear to hear her over the loud chatter, but when she stood on the chair, all sound vanished.

Now that *is power.*

"I will keep this brief," the Matriarch said. "Our Lord has returned, and he has requested our assistance in his journey to deliver us. You have answered the call, and it makes me feel such pride to know you have stayed true to your faith."

Nythan sensed no such emotion from her and tried to hide his amusement.

"We have been serving the image of our Lord for so long that it's easy to forget why we serve and how our service makes an impact. Our Lord will embrace the world in harmony in the way that only *he* can. There are many who oppose him and would see his work reduced to ash. To overcome, he must grow stronger. There is a coming battle, and the Great One, with our help, will be ready to face the conflict. As some of you here have seen, and all already know, our Lord requires the very essence of our being to survive."

The Matriarch paused to let her words sink in.

"It is the greatest, single most important gift one person can offer. *Every* gift is of vital importance, and it can *only* be offered," she continued. "Your contribution will not be compulsory. The evening meal will present you with the opportunity to think upon your choice. At the conclusion of your dinner, if you decide to honor your faith and earn the reward it brings, our Lord will give you the chance to do so. This is everything we have been working toward, here, in the flesh," she said, gesturing to Nythan. "Anyone here, no matter the importance of your position, may offer yourself to the Great One. This opportunity may never again present itself to you. Consider your choice carefully. We rise further."

"We rise further," the audience echoed in unison.

Whatever it takes, we must keep her on our side. She cannot be allowed to offer her soul.

Gladys motioned for the person next to her to help her back down to the ground.

It took quite a while for everyone to be served and to disperse throughout the house to eat. As he sank in his chair, Nythan waded through the ocean of emotions that exuded from the guests. Joy, sadness, and bitterness all intertwined in a cloud that Nythan could feel absorbing into his skin.

Soon, we will be powerful enough to influence those feelings.

Nythan pushed out a slow exhale, writhing his hands. *Influence them, how, exactly?*

Well, you can't change their thoughts and emotions. However, you can augment what people feel. For instance, you can make someone feel as though they are wrapped in a warm blanket or submerged in ice-cold water. Not literally, mind you, but in terms of how things like that make someone feel. If they are feeling happy, you can help boost that emotion into elation. It is never not *their choice to feel that way, but it comes at your suggestion. That's what I mean.*

Sounds complicated.

It is challenging to put into words. However, when you make your first attempt, you'll see what I mean. It's much easier to understand once you experience it.

But I can't do that now?

We can try. It'll still be a wasted effort until you can feel how to do it, similar to when you unexpectedly sensed Colonel Wutnatszlay's passion.

Okay, cool. Nythan's eyes darted around the dinner table and over all those eating on the floor but saw very little discussion taking place. The guests were engrossed in their own personal thoughts and the decision facing them. *It seems unfair, asking them to make a life-altering decision like this.*

It's their choice, as the Matriarch said. To be or not to be. Although that's fundamentally the wrong question to ask, it's applicable to our circumstances here.

The wrong question?

It's a philosophical phenomenon that I discovered about a thousand years ago. It would take a long time for me to explain what I mean, but one day maybe we can explore some similar thoughts embodied by Taoism.

Sure.

After an hour or so, the majority of dinner guests reconvened in the dining room, and the Matriarch signaled to one of the masked Raptors.

"Devin," she said, "You may begin calling them forward."

Nythan's face lit up. "Devin!"

Devin waved to Nythan as he walked to the center of the room. "May I have your attention, please," Devin proclaimed over the crowd. "For those who've chosen, form a line so that our Lord can receive ya!"

Most of those at the twenty-seat dinner table rose and filed in front of him, and the half-packed room slowly morphed into a single line stretching out of the room. His bodyguards moved to form an arc behind him.

"Oh, dang," Nythan muttered.

This is not going to be easy, but if we pace ourselves, we should be fine. Take it slow, like you did in Missouri.

The first man came to stand beside his chair. "Great One," he said, bowing. "I choose to give you my soul in the hopes that it'll help you defeat the worms."

Nythan pushed his chair from the dining table and stood to face the man. "Thank you, what's your name?"

"Jonathan," he answered.

"Thank you, Jonathan. You'll be remembered," Nythan said. He hesitated for a few seconds before withdrawing the man's soul. Jonathan slumped backward, and the woman behind him stretched out her arms to catch him as he fell. One of Nythan's guardians came forward and carried Jonathan into the kitchen.

The next woman identified herself as Sarah. "My Lord," she squeaked, "I volunteer."

Nythan smiled weakly as he touched her shoulder. He took his time withdrawing her soul. He made no effort to shorten or prolong each person's introduction, reasoning that they had earned the right to take as long as they wanted. Some simply said, "We rise further," and others spoke briefly with him. One person even delved into the philosophical idea of how and why the world needed Nythan's deliverance. He enjoyed speaking with each of them.

The line curtailed after half an hour. Nythan felt bloated and euphoric as Bane busied himself digesting the souls as fast as possible. The Matriarch told Devin to proceed to the adjacent room. A few minutes later, he returned leading another line of volunteers. It took Nythan another half an hour to exhaust that line before Devin called forth another room of guests, and then another, and another. The procession carried on for hours. He, however, didn't feel the slightest bit weary.

Finally, Devin walked into the dining hall room with one last person. She wore the uniform of the local police.

She stopped in front of him. "My Lord," she said. "I've been on the force for about seven years now, helping our family whenever I could. But now I'm here to help one last time. Please take my soul."

"Thank you for your service," he said, embarrassed by the irony of her presence.

She nodded, "We rise further."

Nythan gleaned her soul, catching her as she fell and handing her off to the guard next to him. His body shook with excitement. He clenched his fist, unable to stop the involuntary movement.

The guard, who Nythan assumed to be Devin, bowed in front of him. "That's the last of them, Great One. Well, except for me."

Nythan paused for a moment, tapping his chin with his thumb. "Devin?"

The Raptor removed his mask, confirming his identity. "Yes, my Lord." Nythan could feel Devin's naive sense of pride and innocence. He also recognized buried ambition and a drive to succeed.

"Devin," Nythan began. "I've been thinking. I wanna accept your gift, but I want you to consider something. Very soon, I'm going to need some extremely capable people to help me put into action a plan of vital importance."

Devin bobbed his head in furious agreement. "I knew it! You have a master plan. I knew you did."

Nythan laughed. He guessed they were the same age, yet Nythan's experiences since Watwa monastery had aged him ten years. That and Bane continually offering advice on how to handle the situations in which they had found themselves.

"Yes," Nythan said, "And part of this plan requires a person to secretly carry messages and do some things for me. I think you'd be a perfect fit for this role. Would you consider…*not* volunteering at this moment, and helping me through that?"

"You betcha!" Devin responded enthusiastically. "Anything you want, I'll do it."

Nythan nodded at him. "Good, thanks. Please go rest; we'll be leaving in a few hours."

Devin rushed off.

Nythan scrutinized the rest of the room. A handful of people remained, not including his bodyguards and the Matriarch. Each of them exuded some degree of embarrassment and guilt. He felt Bane working like a machine to digest all souls swirling in Nythan's chest. Despite Bane's preoccupation, Nythan noticed his grunting at the sentiments of the surviving Raptors. Knowing what Bane meant, Nythan addressed them.

"There is *nothing* to feel guilty over. For those of you who chose to remain, it's okay. There's no shame in that. Now we need to rebuild the Northern Coven. Can you help me do this?"

"Hah!" the Matriarch shrieked.

Nythan smiled at her. "Thank you all so much for what you do. I won't forget. Please go rest," he said, gesturing toward the door.

"We rise further," they responded, filing out one by one until only the Matriarch and his guards remained.

The Matriarch walked over to him and plopped into a chair. "My entire life," she said, "has been devoted to furthering your return. Now that you are here, my journey is complete."

She turned toward him, bowing to him and stretching out both her arms. "I offer my soul, Great One."

Don't you dare.

For reasons he couldn't explain, Nythan grew unsettled by Bane's statement. He never before witnessed Bane refuse a soul outright. He had thought Bane harbored an insatiable appetite, if not a near complete disregard for the offeror.

"Gladys," Nythan said. "You're so very important to this Coven."

"There is no title or position too important for this invaluable need. *We* come and go; you persist. In a handful of years, I will die. I would much rather have *you* be the reason for my departure."

"Yes, but you're so effective. I've read all the reports on each Coven. The Northern Coven, by far, is the most successful. That's all due to your leadership. And if your leadership isn't a testament in and of itself, it should be evident by the majority of your leadership volunteering. If you go, this Coven will collapse," Nythan argued.

"The Northern Coven will live on and grow stronger. But it should do so under new leadership."

Nythan grasped the utter peace and determination the Matriarch exuded when volunteering herself. She accepted her fate with total confidence. Bane stirred in discomfort.

Make her promise to cultivate new leadership before she volunteers. I won't have it any other way. I'll keep pushing her soul away from us if I have to. The value of this woman is incalculable.

Wait, you can do that? Nythan asked, raising an eyebrow.

Of course, who do you think receives the souls once they enter our body? It's definitely not your *stomach doing all the work.*

Nythan's mind raced as he scratched his chin. "How about this, Gladys. You're important to us, but I want to make you happy. Form the new leadership you say this Coven needs. Once you establish your replacements and are comfortable with them taking the helm, *then* I'll receive your soul."

The Matriarch started to object, but Nythan held up his hand. "You once told me," he said, "that whatever I told you I wanted, you'd see it done. This is what I want. I can feel your determination to volunteer yourself. I understand and accept that. But I want someone trained by you to be left here, in your stead."

Nythan could feel Gladys grow angry. "I *did* have someone ready to assume the mantle, but that *stupid* boy offered himself to you."

Then do it again.

"Then do it again, please," Nythan said. "I'll be back. I'll be able to sense from you if you're truly satisfied with your replacement. Once I feel that...I'll give you what you want."

"Fine," she huffed. "But I'll hold you to that." The Matriarch touched her emerald earrings. "As sure as these stones, I *will* see my faith rewarded."

Nythan dipped his head. "Okay." The Matriarch gave a curt bow and left.

"Shall I write that down, my Lord?" someone whispered into Nythan's ear.

Nythan jumped, whipping around to see Palaou's face a few inches behind him.

"Damn it, Palaou!" Palaou's eyes widened.

"M-my Lord...I'm so sorry!"

"No, no, it's okay, Palaou. I just didn't even see you enter the room. How in the hell do you do that?"

"I'm easy to miss," Palaou chirped.

Nythan looked up to the ceiling. He burped in surprise, seeing traces of the familiar ethereal mist seep out of his mouth.

Bane groaned in satisfaction.

Now what? Nythan asked.

Now we move on to the next Coven. It's your plan, Nythan. Let's keep going.

In a few more hours, Nythan thought. *These people need sleep.*

"Please get some rest, all of you," Nythan said to everyone left in the room. "We leave in four hours."

It took some convincing, but he made his Grand Coven bodyguards go to bed as well. The Northern Coven bodyguards kept watch instead, although Nythan believed it unnecessary.

Believe me, Nythan, it's not unnecessary. You're in enemy territory, and your enemies can be around every corner. I've been in more than a few situations where I thought I was safe, only to find out the hard way how resourceful my foes were.

And you learned never to take chances?

Yes.

Then what's all this about not having a plan for your return? Sounds like you're taking a chance to me.

I've also learned that playing it safe will only keep you where you are. I assume you are familiar with the term, carpe diem*?*

Of course.

Alexander of Macedonia taught me the importance of carpe diem*. He didn't know it at the time, but he helped formulate my understanding of governance and leadership.*

You knew Alexander the Great? Nythan thought with amazement.

The one and only.

CHAPTER 57

THE SOUTH

Nythan stood before the Southern Patriarch and most of his Coven in front of a Georgia mansion.

"Please, stand," Nythan called out, growing uncomfortable.

The Patriarch rose, along with the rest of the Coven. Nythan stepped forward and shook the Patriarch's hand.

"Revered One, we've been praying for ya return," the Patriarch said, wringing his hands together after touching him.

"Well, here I am," Nythan said, curling his lips upward.

The Patriarch appeared giddy, which amused Nythan, given how the guy might be confused for an NFL linebacker. Nythan sensed the inner anxiety engulfing the man despite his meaty build, chiseled jaw, weathered hands, and harsh eyes.

A superstitious bunch.

Yeah, Southerners usually are a bit more so than the rest, Nythan thought.

The Patriarch snapped his fingers, and a Coven member came forward with what Nythan assumed to be iced tea.

He took a swig from the glass, but his tongue refused to identify the dark liquid. *Ahhhhh, even though I can't taste it anymore, a tall, cool drink still feels like home.*

Home is where the heart is... isn't that something you southern people say?

I'm sure we do, Nythan thought.

"I apologize for the hurried manner in which ya was greeted," the Patriarch drawled, "as we weren't notified of your impending arrival until only an hour ago. Most of the Southerners are making their way to us. It'll take 'em most of the day to arrive."

"That's fine," Nythan remarked, "but I'll be leaving in the morning. I'm sorry you had such short notice. My schedule is rather sensitive."

The Patriarch nodded emphatically. "Yes, sir, no need to explain. Your return is already a miracle. Whatever I can do to make your stay more enjoyable, I will."

Nythan peered around the mansion and across its acreage of pastures where cows stood and ate grass. "How in the world did you get all of this? This place is enormous."

"Oh, this place belonged to one of our members. He willed it to us when he died."

Nythan blinked. "He willed you his house?"

"Most members, when they get to a certain point in their faith, will bequeath something valuable to their Coven. It's a sign of dedication."

"And you?"

"I got a sizable lot of antique rifles that's worth a pretty penny." The Patriarch winked. "I'm sure the Grand Coven'll find good use for 'em."

"Did you *have* to give the Raptors something?"

"Not really. But once I included the Coven in my will, the path to Patriarch got a lot easier. Some people will entire estates, like this one." The Patriarch pointed to the cows across the pasture. "One guy willed all that cattle plus two hundred more we sold to market."

"If you hadn't of willed anything away, could you be Patriarch?"

"Oh sure!" The Patriarch slapped his leg. "As long as you pay ya annual dues, it's all good. But if you wanna get a position, you gotta send the right message. Gotta be a good example to the others." The Patriarch winked.

Nythan resisted the urge to roll his eyes. "Alright…well, is there a way we can talk out of earshot? I need your help."

The Patriarch's face took on a momentary deer-in-the-headlights expression. "Absolutely, we can talk in my personal study. Please, thisaway." The Patriarch bounded up a winding staircase; Nythan had to take two steps at a time to keep pace.

The Patriarch led Nythan and his protectors into an ornate conference room. The display of oak furniture, wool-upholstered chairs, and crystal finery made Bane scoff.

"Please, take my chair," the Patriarch said, motioning to his tufted leather seat.

Nythan plopped into the chair, and his guards spread out into the corners of the spacious room.

"What can I do ya for, sir?" the Patriarch asked, still standing.

Nythan swiveled in the chair before responding. "My plan to deliver this world has accelerated. In order to ready myself, we need to grow. I need your help in gathering all who're willing to gift their souls to us."

The Patriarch drew himself inward but said nothing. Trepidation emanated from the Patriarch.

Nythan raised an eyebrow. "Problem?"

"Revered One, it will take us time to gather willing participants. It's a sudden request."

Don't expect everyone to throw themselves down in front of you. You are not a god. Even if you were, people have been rebelling against God since the dawn of time.

"No problem, Patriarch. Just do what you're able. I realize how unfair this is. But I wouldn't be asking if it weren't important."

The Patriarch shook his head at Nythan. "Yeah, I heard about what happened to the Masons, and that the Ordo Solis had been vanquished. Those worms got what they deserved."

Nythan suppressed a pang of guilt and forced a smile. "I've no expectation of you other than what you're able to provide by tomorrow morning."

"I'll not fail you, Revered One. This's been my life's work. You honor me with the chance to further your return!"

Ugh. This sort of silly ingratiation has its uses, but it still makes me sick. So pathetic.

"Yes," Nythan said flatly. "I've no doubt. I'm looking forward to what we'll accomplish together."

As they descended the staircase to the downstairs foyer, Nythan called out to Palaou. "Don't you ever get hot in that thing?"

Palaou perked up. "My Lord?"

Nythan wiggled his finger at Palaou's tuxedo as he touched down on the last step. "I said don't you ever get hot in that thing. Every time I see you, you're wearing one."

Palaou straightened, nudging his bow tie. "Never."

Nythan smiled. "Please have the Grand Coven send word to the Eastern Coven. Ask them to gather their flock for tomorrow night."

Hahahahaha. Flock.

"Maybe it'll be easier on the Covens if we give them more than the day of to prepare."

Palaou nodded, then stepped away and whipped out a cell phone.

Nythan stared at Palaou. *Aren't you going to try to warn me against giving away our position?*

Not this time. I want to see what happens. Everything about this plan still makes me wary. That hasn't changed.

Good. I'm going to need you with your eyes wide open.

I don't have eyes.

Well, if you did, keep them open.

Bane laughed. *At once, Revered One.*

CHAPTER 58

THE CENTRAL

Nythan felt both excitement and irritation at having to visit the Covens outside the United States. He had enjoyed most of the time he spent with the American Patriarchs and Matriarchs but dreaded all the long hours of sitting in a car voyaging across the United States. The Raptors were great bodyguards, but they made terrible road trip buddies.

In the past week, he had stayed with Nigel in the Eastern Coven, visited the Grand Coven once again, and met the Patriarch in the Western Coven. After he had given Nigel advance warning of his visit to the Eastern Coven, the number of volunteers who gifted him their souls had increased by a factor of two. Nythan had continued that practice for each Coven visit thereafter.

He had chosen to visit the Central Coven next, which stretched from Mexico to Panama. The Central Coven was a medium-sized operation; however, the number of new members it had recruited over the past year ranked it second among the ten Covens.

The Central Matriarch, a woman in her mid-forties, had met him late in the afternoon at a small private airport in Nicaragua. Nythan's usual convoy of two vehicles had immediately doubled to four at the Matriarch's behest. She had explained how the renewed cartel violence and government crackdowns had thrown the country in turmoil. Nythan loved her expressive face but required Bane to translate for him since he couldn't understand her broken English.

You're lucky I still remember Spanish. I've forgotten many of the languages I used to speak.

How do you forget the languages you spoke for a thousand years?

Use it or lose it.

The Matriarch shouted some orders and soon everyone was traveling down an unpaved road to the Central Coven's newest headquarters. Bane became agitated over how many Nicaraguan soldiers stopped them at each government checkpoint, but the Matriarch handled them with confidence and grace.

"Nuestro grupo estará formado al anochecer," the Matriarch noted.

The Central Coven will be fully assembled by nightfall. That's good, I'm getting hungry again.

Nythan sighed. *We* just *ate last night. And it was a huge dinner!*

My appetite grows. Besides, the point is to consume as much as possible before the rest of the world catches wind of what is happening.

The convoy came upon its fourth checkpoint as it turned onto a narrow jungle path. Even before the convoy came to a stop, Nythan sensed something amiss. He reached out to scan the government soldiers as best he could, but he was still a good three vehicles back from the lead.

The Matriarch continued chatting away to him in Spanish, but Nythan waved her down. "Something's wrong."

The Prey bodyguard in the passenger seat jerked his head toward Nythan. "Where?"

"Those soldiers. Something's different about them. I'm too far away to understand what."

The Raptor reached down to the floorboard and pulled up a UMP submachine gun. The driver did the same. The Raptor yanked on the radio attached to his chest strap. "Cage the owl, cage the owl," he spoke into the mouthpiece as he opened his door.

Wait, it's not just them.

Before Bane could explain, a thunderous wave of gunfire erupted from the bushes on either side of them. Bullets punctured the SUV. Something pierced his left shoulder as Nythan undid his seatbelt and threw himself on the floorboard. The Matriarch rolled on top of him, shielding him with her body.

Nythan strained under the weight of the Matriarch. *I can't see anything now!*

Stop thinking, use your senses. Search around you.

Nythan attempted to follow Bane's orders. He dived into the breathing state and made out a few people outside the vehicle on his left, but the intense turbulence—bullets flying, people shouting, bodies rushing around—obscured everything in a tsunami of gray.

The chatter of automatic weapons seemed to go on for half an hour but probably lasted only a few minutes. When the gunfire died down, Nythan heard several voices yelling in Spanish. He couldn't tell which side had won.

"¿Estas herido?" the Matriarch whispered.

She's asking if we're injured.

"I'll be fine."

"Quédate aquí," she directed, struggling to push herself off him.

Stay here.

Still staring at the floorboard, Nythan heard the creak of the SUV's door swing open.

"¿Él está bien?" someone growled.

Asking if we're okay.

The Matriarch lifted herself off Nythan. *"Sí, ¿que paso?"*

What happened?

"Fuimos emboscados."

We got ambushed. Hahaha, how perceptive of him.

The Matriarch gritted her teeth. *"Sí, ¡mierda! ¿Quién nos embosco?"*

She asked who ambushed us.

Nythan turned over and noted a corpse sprawled across the center console between the front seats. He then noticed that the Matriarch was hunched over on the back seat, clutching her ribs. Even though he could only see her left side, he could see a red stain crawling from her left side across her midsection.

"Estamos en el proceso de averiguarlo," the Raptor replied. *"Tomamos a dos de ellos prisioneros."*

They captured two of them.

The Matriarch began rasping. *"Bien, estaré allí en un segundo."*

She's going to interrogate them.

The Matriarch attempted to sit herself upright but let out a whimper of pain and stayed hunched over. Nythan felt her out through the breathing state. He detected how weak she was when drawing air.

"No you won't," Nythan said, getting up. "You stay here and nurse that wound. I'll get the information out of them."

"My Lord..." the Matriarch protested in English.

"No buts. Stay here and don't die on me," he demanded as he opened his door. He stared at the back of another Raptor who scanned the outer bushes.

"With me," Nythan said as he slapped the Raptor's shoulder. Together they went to the other side of the vehicle. "How many are left?"

"Cinco de nosotros, dos de ellos. Uno de nosotros está gravemente herido, y ella también," the Raptor responded, pointing to the Matriarch.

From sixteen to five. Good thing the Matriarch was smart enough to double your guard.

"My Lord!" Two figures came running up, one taking off his mask. Devin's familiar face searched Nythan's. "Are you okay?"

"What happened?" Nythan asked.

"I was in the lead vehicle; he was in the second." Devin jerked his thumb to his Prey companion. "Saw the baddies in the bushes beside us right before the warning came over the radio. I ducked and we cut them down. I'm all that's left of my vehicle."

"Did Palaou survive?" Nythan asked.

"Yeah, but he's hurt."

We'll help him after we're done.

Nythan turned back to the Raptor that accompanied him. "How many of them did we kill?"

"No está seguro, pero por lo menos siete. Subestimaron cuántos de nosotros había y la potencia de fuego que trajimos," he said.

A bunch. They weren't prepared to handle us.

"You said there were two attackers left?"

The Raptor jerked his finger behind him. *"En la jungla."*

Jungle, Nythan translated before Bane did.

Very good.

He heard a thick cough behind him. Nythan turned to see the Matriarch stumble out of the SUV. He took a quick stride and caught her before she fell. "I told you to stay in there."

"Mi Señor, no viviré para ver su retorno," she heaved, coughing up blood. Her outfit was drenched in it.

She knows she isn't going to make it. I can feel her soul slipping...she's almost gone.

Nythan held her cheek in his hand. "It's okay. I'm right here."

The Matriarch beamed, her teeth a slick crimson. *"Por favor, llévame antes de que la naturaleza lo haga."*

She wants you to have her before she goes.

Nythan shook the lewd-sounding request from his mind.

You know what she means.

"Are you sure?"

"Mejor tú que la muerte. Díle a Amiko que él es el patriarca hasta que se encuentre uno nuevo. Estoy tan contenta de haberte visto antes de irme."

Better us than death, she says. Amiko is the new Patriarch for the time being and she's glad to see us before she dies.

Nythan found himself fighting back tears. He nodded in response, getting himself ready to withdraw her soul.

"Somos imparables," she breathed as Nythan inhaled.

We rise further.

Nythan stood, wiping a wayward tear as he viewed the smoldering carnage. Dead Raptors were interspersed with corpses dressed in military fatigues.

And here I thought everyone was having a good time.

"Show me to them," Nythan commanded the Raptor next to him. Turning back to Devin and the other Prey, he ordered, "Make sure we're prepped to leave by the time I return."

The guard led Nythan a short distance into the jungle and stopped in front of two prisoners with their hands on their heads. A bloodied Raptor overshadowed them. He pointed two submachine guns, one in each hand, at the back of their heads.

"Ask them who they are," Nythan said. The Raptor conveyed Nythan's request to the prisoners.

"Vete a la mierda blanquito," one of the prisoners spat.

Hahahahhahahaha. He told us to F off. He also called you a white boy.

Nythan's expression hardened. "Ya know, we were just minding our own business here, trying not to bother anyone. But noooooo. You all just *had* to ruin that, didn't ya."

"Me cogeré a tu madre," the same prisoner said.

Nythan ignored him. *I think I know what he said that time.*

Yep.

"I'll ask one more time," Nythan said. "Who...are *you?*"

Upon hearing the translation, the other prisoner spat on the soil.

Nythan pursed his lips. He got up into the face of the prisoner who had spit, looking to his translator. "How do you say, 'I am the Devil'?"

"Yo soy el Diablo," the Raptor told him.

Nythan said directly to the prisoner, *"Yo soy el Diablo."*

Both prisoners laughed, then the one in front of Nythan spat straight into his face. His Raptors made no move against the prisoner; they knew exactly what was about to happen.

He mustered all the force possible, then roared into the face of the prisoner before him, *"¡YO SOY EL DIABLO!"* Nythan clutched the back of the guy's hair and yanked downward as he sucked in, wrenching the man's soul from his body. Instead of consuming it straight away, Nythan poked and fiddled with the silver stream before slurping it down.

Nythan had a wicked grin on his face as he sidestepped in front of the mouthy prisoner. The corpse of the other prisoner fell forward and crashed to the forest floor.

The prisoner tried to backpedal away from Nythan, but the barrel of a submachine gun dug into his back. Nythan thought he'd never seen the color drain so fast from anyone's face.

"Yo soy...el...diablo," Nythan taunted, jutting his chin toward the guy's dead comrade.

The captive looked at him with the purest expression of horror. "D-d-d-d-*diablo?*"

"Yessss," Nythan jeered, "Now you understand. So I'll ask again. Where did you come from, *b****?*"

His translator voiced the question. The prisoner vomited everything he knew about their setting up fake checkpoints, which cartel they answered to, and how many checkpoints there were. Satisfied with the answer, Nythan yanked out the prisoner's soul and returned to the ambush site. He noticed there were no weapons or dead Raptors lying on the ground anymore.

Devin awaited him next to the last of three SUVs.

Devin gave a mock salute and tapped the hood of the vehicle. "All ready to go, my Lord. We'll put you in this one here with Palaou."

"Thanks, Devin," Nythan replied. He got into the back seat and shuffled next to Palaou, who straightened his bloodstained tuxedo shirt as he struggled to sit up.

Nythan put his hand on his friend's shoulder. "Don't move, Palaou," he instructed as Devin ran around and got into the driver's seat. He started the SUV and floored it ahead of two other SUVs, which followed close behind. Both he and Palaou rocked back into the seat.

"But, my Lord, you're wounded!"

Nythan turned his attention to his left shoulder, narrowing his eyes at a frayed hole with a bloodstain no larger than a quarter. No blood oozed from the wound, and if it weren't for the fleshy hole, Nythan wouldn't have known something had struck him.

Watch this.

An odd sensation, as if he were to rub his palms together, twisted in his shoulder. Something crept out of his short-sleeve T-shirt and thudded to the floorboard.

Nythan picked up the metal slug freshly expelled from the wound. *How'd you do that?*

The more powerful we grow, the more we can do.

Can I do that?

Absolutely, you just need to learn how.

Palaou's face turned to elation. "My Lord!" he proclaimed before crying out and clasping his stomach. Like the late Matriarch, Palaou's blood crusted his clothing.

Nythan's attention darted from Palaou's face to his body. *Is there anything we can do to help him?*

No, I've never been successful at using our abilities on other people. Influencing emotion only works because it is exuded from the body.

Have you ever tried?

Yes. Many times. I can push the bullet out of us because I know how to move your cells around and behind it. I don't have that same intimate knowledge of Palaou's body.

Nythan put a shaky hand on Palaou's forehead. "Just stay there, Palaou, hold on. We're gonna get you some help."

As their three-vehicle convoy made its way over the rough dirt terrain, Nythan glimpsed over his shoulder at the cargo area. A dozen UMP submachine guns rattled against one another, each with its own bloodstains.

It took them an hour to reach the Central Coven, deep in the heart of Nicaragua. Nythan sensed Palaou's soul slipping. If they came across any more checkpoints, fake or otherwise, Nythan intended to rip their souls out to save his friend.

As soon as they came to a stop, an army of Raptors came sprinting out of the residence. They extracted Nythan from the SUV and began unloading the contents of both vehicles. Before being ushered inside, Nythan caught a glimpse of them removing corpses from the first two SUVs.

This will not be the last time someone dies for you.

The thought gave Nythan a chill.

They will soon be dying by the score.

Stop it, Nythan pleaded.

Burying your head in the sand will do you no good. I can't have you freezing on me because you aren't prepared.

I'm prepared, Nythan protested.

You most certainly are not *prepared. You hide from the truth like a small child.* When *it starts, you'll need to be able to continue moving forward. Can you do that?*

Yes, Nythan thought, but he was filled with doubt.

I can feel your uncertainty, Nythan. But I'll take that answer for now. You are more ready than you were a month ago.

Are you sure we can't revive people...or heal them? Nythan thought.

I'm sure, but if it makes you feel better, you can try. This was your first true defeat. Best we get all the unconstructive reactions out of your system while we still have the luxury of time.

CHAPTER 59

THE LOWER

Nythan left Palaou at the Central Coven and cruised across the Caribbean Sea to the Upper Coven in Colombia. Once finished, he, Devin, his surviving Prey colleague, and a few Raptors from the Central Coven flew ten hours to visit Molina in the Brazilian Coven. He and his troop caught another ten-hour flight to the Lower Coven headquarters in Puerto Montt, Chile. Its territory included Bolivia to Uruguay to Chile. They rolled up to a cluster of bungalows just outside the sleepy fishing village, which was located under the shadow of an ice-capped volcano.

The Lower Patriarch, a man in his mid-fifties who introduced himself as Alvy, greeted Nythan with a full entourage of attendants at the building entrance. They wasted no time in rushing him inside. Word of his close encounter with attackers in the Central Coven's territory had spread to all others. Palaou had recovered enough to walk with a cane and had flown down to reunite with Nythan's crew, bringing twenty-four Prey from the Grand Coven with him. Alvy's contingent of guards doubled that number.

Nythan stayed in a cluster of bungalows. The rainforest's vines wove throughout the residence, sometimes through the floorboards and up the wall. The fusion between house and vegetation struck him as quite beautiful.

"All Coven members are already here," the Patriarch said.

"Thank you, Alvy. If you've any doctors, please see to Palaou," Nythan requested.

Palaou objected, "My Lord, I have no need. I am feeling quite fine."

"I wasn't asking, Palaou," Nythan replied gently.

Palaou bowed, then went with one of the Patriarch's attendants.

When suppertime came, Nythan replicated his performance from the other Covens. He gave a speech about how he needed to grow stronger and that he was on his way to deliver the world. By now, his speeches had become so routine that they didn't make him uncomfortable anymore. He realized he no longer felt guilt over his god-like status.

A familiar sight followed the dinner and subsequent procession. Many of those assembled volunteered to gift their souls. Bane had adapted to digesting an extensive number of souls without upsetting Nythan's body. After Nythan took the last gift, the Patriarch dismissed the remaining Raptors.

Nythan heard a pelting as rain began to fall outside. The droplets created an orchestra as they hit hanging pans, windchimes, a nearby woodshed, aluminum rooftops, and tree branches overhead. He wandered out of the bungalow and into the shared overgrown grounds. He walked further into the night, letting the rain splash all over him. The Patriarch came up and stood beside him.

"It's easy to take this for granted," the Patriarch said, extending his hands to capture some of the pellets of water.

"It's okay, Alvy. I've done my fair share of taking things for granted too. This feels really nice, and I love the sounds."

"When I was young, I would help my father clean the salmon, right over there." Alvy pointed out the backyard fence toward the front of the bungalow. "Each time before we'd start, he'd ask the rain givers to bless the work."

Nythan nodded. "You're Alvy *Junior*, right?"

"*Sí*, yes."

"The Northern Matriarch told me about the early days of the Raptors and how your father helped them survive."

Alvy crossed his arms and showed his teeth. "Ah, yes. *Titi* Gladys."

Nythan tilted his head. "*Titi?*"

"*Aunt* Gladys. I was born a couple years after dad moved back here. He would take me with him and leave me at her house while the two of them went to the annual Grand Coven meeting in Boston. It was too dangerous for me to go."

"Yeah, Gladys said it was in Boston before Missouri. Was she part of the Grand Coven?"

"No. Back then it was different. We were few in number, so the Grand Coven started out as part of the Northern Coven. It only became its own body and moved to Missouri after the Western Coven was established. You appointed our first leaders and made Uncle Robby the first Patriarch, my dad as head of recruitment, and a secretary, a treasurer…all the usual things. *Titi* started helping as treasurer after Uncle Robby died and the treasurer disappeared."

Alvy let out a laugh, slapping his forearm. "She told me once that the Ordo Solis convinced one of the bank managers that our nonprofit organization supported *un-American activities*. When *Titi* came to withdraw money, the manager stopped the transaction, so she cried really loud about her husband being killed by communist spies and embarrassed the manager into letting the withdrawal happen."

Nythan laughed along with him. "I couldn't imagine her being so dramatic. She seems pretty hardcore."

"She's a softie at heart. Dad used to tell me how she was before the Ordo Solis killed Uncle Robby. Joked she was bubbly turned b****. But for the longest time I only ever knew her as *Titi* Gladys, the woman who'd play hide-and-seek with me in the hedges before reading me to sleep. And when things with the Ordo Solis got scary, she'd tell me the Prey were always there to keep us safe."

"Was it that bad?"

Alvy scratched his chin and looked at Nythan. "Ordo Solis was big back then. Hurt a lot of people, made even more disappear. Had to invent the Prey just to survive. Legend has it, they tortured the Falcon's family to death trying to get the secret word exchange with the Gatekeeper."

"Falcon. The Birds of Prey guy?" Nythan asked.

"Yeah, I think it was when we got to the point where the Prey started beating back the Order that I started spending whole summers with *Titi* in Pennsylvania. I grew up running around that house. Did she show you the garden?"

"Yeah, that two-headed statue is quite something."

Alvy clapped as he let out another burst of laughter. "I remember! I was like nine or so, and I climbed up your side of it and was dangling from your arm when she caught me. I had *never* seen her so angry before *in my life*. That was the only time she could ever bring herself to lay a hand on me." Alvy's face suddenly hardened, nodding. "The mother I never had."

Nythan shifted his weight. "What happened to her? Your mom."

"Bailed after she found out why dad *really* moved back home. It was for the better. I don't want to think about what would've happened if she'd stayed."

The rain orchestra filled the silence between them.

Alvy let out a long exhale. "What a trip down memory lane *that* was. Anyways, what happens now?"

Nythan let the silence continue for a few more seconds. "Now I continue on. We've work to do, and I intend to make sure your volunteers didn't give themselves in vain."

"Is there anything else I can do?"

"No, Alvy. You offered the most valuable thing we could ask for. If there's anything else, I'll let you know."

"Good, please do. The Lower Coven is small, but we are certainly able to perform any task required."

Nythan looked behind him. His army of guards had spread out around the small area. The glow from his bungalow silhouetted a few of the bulky figures. It lit the yard well enough for him to see that the contours of one guard's mask made him look like something out of a horror movie.

Nythan turned and observed the forest darkness. He sensed Alvy starting to shiver, but the Patriarch made no move to leave his side. The raindrops hitting his skin felt like tiny ice meteorites—first, he felt a million cold impacts, then a bodily warmth took over.

"I could be out here for a while, Alvy," Nythan said, closing his eyes and lifting his face to the sky.

"It's not every day I get to stand next to the Great One. I'll stand here for as long as you do."

Nythan continued baring his face to the rain. His senses tingled. His ears caught every sound, and his skin felt every sensation. Nythan inwardly *observed* Bane as he finished processing the last batch of souls.

Now it's you who watches me.

Funny how things change.

Things never stop changing. Life is constant change. Most people spend their entire lives trying to delay or otherwise prevent it.

Change is scary.

Only because change is unpredictable and out of the control of a person's ego.

Which makes it scary, Nythan confirmed.

Sure. I'm going back to distributing these souls. I can't do two things at once. Okay. If I talk, just don't answer me.

"Do you know what's weird, Alvy?" Nythan said aloud.

"What's that?" Alvy answered.

"With each volunteer, I feel more and more connected with my surroundings. I can *see* the threads of life all around us. And the more connected I get, the less *me* I feel."

"That *is* odd, but I can't say I know what that means," Alvy commented.

"No, the weird part is that this synergy was always there, even before my connection with the Great One. I just didn't take the time to fully explore it. I was so concerned with my busy life and what I had planned that I completely overlooked what kept this world together. It was there all along."

"And that's what you'll use to deliver this world," the Patriarch said. Nythan didn't know if Alvy was asking a question or making a statement. Nythan chose to remain silent, recalling the power of letting Raptors fill in the details of their faith by themselves.

When Nythan felt Alvy swell with pride, he decided to seize the opportunity. He wrapped around Alvy's pride as best he could, attempting to nurture it. When that didn't work, Nythan instead emulated the emotion, hoping it'd bolster Alvy. Nythan sensed Alvy's sense of pride change to confusion.

Bane stirred. *Almost. You had the right idea by emulating his feeling. Wrapping around emotions like a blanket is more effective with groups of people. A shared emotion interlocks together, creating a synergistic effect. When dealing with one person, you want to penetrate the center of their persona, as if you were planting a seed in a flowerpot. If the feeling successfully influences the person, their personality will do the work for you. The feeling will grow like a weed.*

I'll try that next time.

Be careful. Messing with someone's feelings can backfire. Did you see how the Patriarch's rejection of your influence invoked confusion? Sometimes those reactions can be destructive. Many decades ago, I attempted to influence an Egyptian Air Force general's feeling of trace sympathy toward Israel while he was in a crucial meeting with Gamal Abdel Nasser. It backfired in the worst of ways. The general's personality disowned the sympathy he had toward a group of people he hated, and that sympathy transformed into rage. It all culminated in the general advising that Egypt should use their air force to decimate the Israelis in an all-out attack. The plan was ill-conceived and started a war between Israel and Arab countries that ended in embarrassment for the Arabs.

Whoa, Nythan marveled. *Are you talking about the Six-Day War?*

Yeah, just be careful. Use your influence wisely.

That makes me not want to use it at all.

It can be a force for good. One time I used it to calm tensions of a mob during the Rodney King riots.

How'll I know when to use it?

It's something we have to decide case-by-case. Believe me, sometimes you'll know when it's time to exert your influence. Something important is usually on the line.

Okay, I need your help with that though. I don't want to make matters worse.

Ha. I'll be here. I can't escape our arrangement even if I wanted to. I'm in it till you cease to be.

"Great One," Alvy said, breaking Nythan's train of thought.

Nythan snapped back to the present. He could hear the Patriarch's teeth chattering so forcefully from the cold that he thought they might crack.

"Let's return inside," Nythan said, making for the bungalow door.

Nythan began thinking about all the lives Bane had revealed to him. Some of them seemed so fascinating, which caused him to wonder about the lives Bane hadn't enjoyed.

CHAPTER 60

ZIZKOV

With his visit to the Lower Coven at a close, Nythan boarded a private jet to Europe. Bane spent the majority of the trip discussing the more delicate points of *Unas culture*, but the phrase quickly became an oxymoron. The more Bane talked about them, the more Nythan understood that they didn't accomplish much without the use of violence. He also realized why the Unas couldn't be their public face or offer the sophisticated touch that sound governance required.

Yes, well, at the time they were created they served an essential purpose. They still do.

Palaou ambled toward Nythan from the cockpit. "My Lord," Palaou said, "We'll be arriving in Prague within the hour."

Nythan clasped his hands. "I'm excited to finally get there. What do you think, Palaou?"

Palaou squinted. Nythan sensed enormous anxiety emanating from him. "I do not share your enthusiasm, my Lord. The Unas have little couth. I have known their actions to be reckless and ill-suited for the modern age. However, the Unas' way can be persuasive to lesser parts of society. They have an infectious culture that appeals to a person's basest instincts."

"I understand. That's what I have you and the Prey for. To keep me properly anchored."

"Yes, my Lord. I will do everything in my power to be that."

"What's the current leader's name?"

"His name is Wrath," Palaou sighed in a disappointed tone.

Nythan couldn't help but chuckle. "What's his *real* name?"

Palaou sighed again. "That is unknown, my Lord. We have no record of any other name for him."

"Alright, *Wrath* it is. How's Wrath going to meet us?"

"They established a meeting point in the Zizkov district, a historical sector of Prague. We will proceed there as soon as we arrive."

"Have you or anyone else here ever met with an Unas?" Nythan asked.

"No, my Lord. I have heard stories from some in the Grand Coven detailing their previous interactions with the Unas. They were not pleasant visits."

The diplomats meet the reavers.

"Well, then," Nythan said, "We'll see how this goes."

CHAPTER 61

REAVERS

Nythan sat with Palaou on a bench next to an old stone well. The well occupied a raised circular slab of large stones in the middle of a court-yard, which was enclosed by battered and abandoned apartment buildings. Several alleyways converged on the courtyard, which felt cramped and unkempt by the overgrown weeds and litter that covered the old stones. Nythan's bodyguards scattered about every five feet or so to create a loose perimeter around his position.

They came in droves.

The Prey tightened their protective formation into an arc in front of Nythan but stopped short of drawing their weapons at Nythan's request.

Nythan didn't need to consult Bane to know what approached. Raw fanaticism wrapped its tentacles around everything it passed. The horde didn't wear disguises, but their shaved heads made them look alike. Many of them had tattoos up their necks and down their arms. Most wore dark baggy clothes, biker jackets, or unwashed T-shirts, and some had affixed various chains or spikes to their clothes.

Unas.

The throng edged closer to the Prey's line of battle, baring their teeth. The Prey contracted even further into a menacing shield between Nythan and the approaching Unas.

Well, this is awkward, Nythan thought. *They don't look anything like the two who came to the Grand Coven.*

I did mention ax-wielding barbarians.

More like rabid dogs.

We should've come by ourselves. The Prey are not making this any easier. Unas value strength, your strength. Not those you hide behind.

Nythan took the hint and got up, making his way to the defensive line. He nudged and pushed his way past the Prey, shouting for them to stand fast. Nythan moved between the barbaric horde and the professional killers.

The mob moved even closer.

Show *them what strength looks like.*

Nythan knew what Bane meant, but his body refused to obey.

If you don't, they'll kill you. Search their feelings, you're surrounded by hostility.

He extended his senses toward the crowd and was assaulted by the raw lethality of the mob.

Nythan outstretched his hand to the nearest Unas, a few feet away. The man wheezed with the rest of the crowd, so it didn't take much concentration for Nythan to find his breathing cycle. In one fluid motion, Nythan yanked the soul from the man's body. But he overestimated how much force he needed to apply and ended up pulling out the souls of the two Unas on either side of the man as well. Three corpses fell forward in unison, making a heavy *thud* on the pavement.

The clamoring from the Unas stopped, as did their steady advance. In the sudden silence, a woman pushed through the crowd. A few fabric strips wrapped across her frame, making her gender clear. Nythan couldn't tell what her face looked like because she wore some sort of face mask in the form of a deer with a small rack of protruding antlers.

In her hands, she carried a large black mask with horns at the forehead and ears. Bloodred-tipped vampire fangs protruded from the lips, and crimson splotches encircled the eyeholes. The woman stopped within a few inches of Nythan. Bending to one knee, she held the mask up to him as an offering. The cover was made from crude materials like wood and bone; however, Nythan could see that someone had crafted it with care and skill.

Nythan felt a soft tap on his shoulder and found Palaou standing behind him.

"I need you all to stay here," Nythan told him, feeling Bane's approval bloat within his chest.

"My Lord, are you…sure?" Palaou asked, clearly frightened.

"No, I'm not," Nythan admitted. "But I can feel their aggression. I'm leaving the world of professionals and entering the world of barbarians. You all would only inflame the situation. I'm gonna put this mask on and be led to wherever they take me. I need you to find a hotel here and wait until I can rejoin you. Tell the others."

Palaou hesitated, bowed, then returned to the protective arc. Nythan faced the Unas woman, took the mask from her hands, and affixed the strap behind his head.

Someone again touched his shoulder. He turned to see one of his more massive Prey guardians behind him.

"I need to hear the command from you," the bodyguard growled.

"Stay here until we're all gone. Find a place close by and wait for me to come back."

The Raptor nodded, then stepped back.

Nythan turned to the woman, who had stood up. She whirled around and walked into the Unas mob, which parted, creating a corridor for her.

Follow her.

Nythan caught up. When they reached the middle of the mass, the horde moved with Nythan. Most kept their distance, but some moved close and touched his arms and shoulders.

Nythan kept a stony expression as he looked at them. *What in the world are they doing?*

I imagine this is what it looks like for them to worship you.

As the horde made their way out of the secluded courtyard and skirted the more traveled parts of the city, they generally stayed off the streets, forming long successions of people on the sidewalks and road shoulders. They walked for quite some time until they came to an open area filled with a grouping of yellow and gray dumpsters, discarded furniture, and spilled trash cans. Behind the debris, in a discrete quadrangle formed by crumbling walls and some improvised fencing, sat another well. Its mouth stretched wide, and the zone around it had been weeded and swept clean. Nythan approached and peered down the well's opening into a dark abyss. The woman with the deer antlers stepped up on the stones rimming the well mouth and entered a huge wooden bucket, which was suspended by a pulley system over the well shaft. When she settled herself in the bucket, she stared at Nythan, who was still hunting for signs of anything resembling a bottom down below.

Is this some kind of joke? Nythan thought.

Bane started laughing.

What's so funny?

They've been doing this for ages. Get in and enjoy the ride.

In that bucket?

Yeah.

Nythan sighed and climbed into the oversized pail with the woman. She pressed a brown button that blended in with the stone texture of the wall, and the old bucket groaned as the rope apparatus lowered them into utter darkness.

CHAPTER 62

THE OLD WORLD

A party of nine masked Unas received Nythan at the bottom of the well. Some wore masks modeled after deer skulls; other representations included rams, tigers, and cows. He even saw human skulls. They ushered him through a long underground stone tunnel with bare lightbulbs hanging low enough he could reach up and touch them.

Nythan looked to the antler woman next to him. "What is this place?"

Neither the antler woman, nor anyone else in the group, acknowledged him. Before he thought to clarify, they entered into a football field-sized stone cavern full of Unas. Everywhere he passed, they reached to touch him, but none got in his way or spoke. In the center was a crude platform and a butt-naked, heavily tattooed and branded man, sitting on a stool with chains and rags wrapped around its legs. The man wore a face covering that resembled a fencing mask, which appeared to be fashioned with thin rib bones lining the faceplate.

As Nythan climbed onto the raised area, the man stood from the stool and outstretched his arms. Throngs of Unas edged closer to the side of the platform with their hands still extended toward Nythan.

"Return, you," naked man rasped.

Nythan drew his eyebrows together. "What?"

"Eat." The guy began waving his arms.

Nythan cocked his head. *What's wrong with this guy?*

They're an unsophisticated bunch. What you see is what you get.

Two pairs of Unas each dragged a captive over to him, both with cloth bags over their heads.

"Eat," naked man repeated.

"These aren't the ones we sent you, are they?"

"No."

Nythan took the two captives with a swift gulp, and their lifeless bodies were dragged off.

The Unas throng reacted with raised hands and enthusiastic cries as naked man started picking his teeth.

This guy is already getting on my nerves, Nythan thought. *He hasn't said but a few words since I got here.*

So what. Focus on what we came for.

"Do you have them?" Nythan said.

Naked man grunted, then waved to the crowd. Three more prisoners were pulled forward, this time without burlaps over their heads. Nythan regarded Steven, Raeleigh, and Mia. All three seemed to be in decent health, although Steven had sustained a few long cuts to his face.

"What happened to him?" Nythan demanded, pointing at Steven's face.

Naked man shrugged.

Nythan frowned. "Alright, take them away." The three prisoners were carted through the horde to one of the dozen tunnels leading out of the cavern. Nythan addressed naked man directly "Who're you?"

Naked man jumped off his stool. "Wrath."

"Who am I, Wrath?"

"Maker," Wrath replied.

"And you are?"

"Wrath."

Nythan wanted to smack himself on the forehead. "No, no. *What* are you?"

"Leader."

"And who are they?" Nythan gestured to the crowd.

"Widowed."

This is going well.

Nythan grit his teeth. *Don't you know what he's saying?*

He used the same words Esmeralda and Ronaldo did before you took them at the Grand Coven.

What does it mean?

No idea. I've never heard them call me Maker and I've never heard them call themselves Widowed.

Great.

"How many of you are there?"

"Many."

"Be more specific."

"Huge many."

"That's not specific."

"Not counted."

Nythan sighed. "Fine. What *is* this place?"

"Home."

Nythan grimaced.

He doesn't want to waste time. We shouldn't either.

"Can you call the Unas together, please? All of them?" Nythan requested.

"When?"

"Now. How long until they're all here?"

"Take weeks."

"Then begin getting them here. I've come as the Maker."

You've come as the Maker?

It sounded like the right thing to say, Nythan thought, trying not to laugh.

"When start?" Wrath asked.

"Now," Nythan said, turning around to the crowd. "Gather round!" he shouted.

The mass of people did not draw closer.

"Many language speak," Wrath explained.

Nythan set his hands on his hips. *What the hell? How do we communicate if we can't talk to them?*

You don't need to talk to them to take them. Unas have existed for over a hundred years. Ask him to do what he does.

"Translate for me then," Nythan instructed. "Tell them the time has come for me to get their souls. If any of them want to bow out before all this goes down, now's their chance. I'll give them another opportunity when the rest get here."

Wrath straightened and walked to the edge of the platform. He threw both fists in the air.

"WIDOWMAKER!" he exulted. His voice echoed throughout the cavern.

The crowd cheered. Some people fell to their knees, clawing at their faces; others jumped in the air and flung their arms about wildly.

Nythan's looked dumbstruck. *Seriously?*

I don't know.

Out of the cheers emerged a chant. "Become, become, become!"

Nythan scanned the crowd, his mouth hanging open. *What is happening?*

Become Widowmaker. I think it means they are going to become the Widowmaker.

I don't get it.

I understand now. Widow *is what they are called,* Maker *is what we are called. Widowmaker is a combination of the two. They're saying that we and they are going to become one. That's pretty close to what I told them when they were initially created.*

Okay. When do I do it? I don't see them lining up.

Receive them now.

Just like this?

Sure, they don't seem to be much into protocol or formality. Not like the Raptors.

Got it. Nythan raised his chin, trying to concentrate on the crowd's collective breath.

Another lesson. The crowd is not on one breathing cycle, so don't treat them like one person. Instead, gather their souls like you would scoop ice cream.

"Which is how?" Nythan whispered.

One scoop at a time. Breathe in, take a scoop. Breathe again, take another scoop.

Nythan couldn't help but laugh at the simile. He took a moment to tighten the strap on his vampire mask, then tried sucking in as many souls as he could. Only a few came at first, but several came the second time. His third *scoop* pulled in a dozen. The ethereal streams reminded him of the Northern Lights as they shot from the congregation toward him. By the sixth scoop, Nythan had gathered almost a hundred souls, which was the majority of the Unas in the cavern. The couple dozen survivors on the outskirts of the cavern continued to jump and flail about, screaming at him and each other.

Nythan bent over and wheezed for breath. It felt like he had run a marathon. Bane went to work digesting the souls.

Suddenly feeling the urge to lie down, Nythan walked over to Wrath's stool and plopped onto it.

Bold.

Nythan smirked. *I thought* we *were the boss.*

Still, you just met the man. Now you're sitting on his stool thing.

Yeah, but I'm a bit tired after doing all that. That was tougher than I thought.

It was a respectable first attempt. I bet you next time you could do it in two scoops.

Wrath turned toward Nythan with an expression of shock. "Wow!"

"Call them all here, those who wish to become Widowmaker. What does that mean anyway?"

"You came. Us came. Maker left. Widowed stay," Wrath explained. Nythan felt like he needed a five-year-old to translate. "Made vow. Wait return."

Makes sense to me.

Nythan processed each fragmented thought as a complete sentence for his own understanding. He could have used a nap when he got through deciphering it all.

Nythan clasped his hands together, offering an insincere smile. "Well, here I am."

"Yes, we gather, then Widowmaker," Wrath declared, jumping down from the platform. He waded through the still bodies toward the survivors on the edge, waving them away as he walked into one of the tunnels. "Leave!"

Nythan didn't bother to ask where Wrath went. He still needed to catch his breath. Even so, he felt imposing and energized. He scrunched his fingers and jumped up from the bone stool, thrusting his fist in the air with a loud cry.

Bane stopped.

What...was that?

Nythan heaved a big sigh of relief. *Just felt like directing my energy into something is all.*

Spend your energy understanding your new surroundings. Bane returned to his task of digestion.

About ten minutes later Wrath returned, dragging a man that he flung to the ground at Nythan's feet.

Nythan acknowledged the guy at his feet with a flick of his hand. "What's this?"

"Other thing you want," Wrath announced, using his fingers to push the man's forehead backward. "Or, dessert." Wrath's mask pressed into the man's face. "Enzo, meet Maker. Maker, meet Enzo. Ordo Solis."

Wrath stepped back and Nythan peered down at Enzo's bruised cheeks. He didn't even need to reach for the guy's emotions; he could see man's abject terror.

"No...please, no," Enzo begged, pressing his face to the potmarked and discolored concrete.

"Enzo, is it?" Nythan asked.

"Yes, uh, Maker."

"Enzo, if we were to let you go, could you still make contact with the Ordo Solis?"

"Yes," he squeaked.

"Wrath, keep this one separate from the others," Nythan said. "And take me to the other three."

Wrath shouted out into the cavern. A moment later, three Unas came out of a tunnel and jumped over corpses to them.

"Take this," Wrath commanded, pointing to Enzo. The Unas hauled the trembling man away.

Nythan took the vampire mask off and placed it on the stool. "Lead the way."

Wrath walked past Nythan and into a tunnel on the other side of the cavern. Nythan followed, trying not to step on any of the corpses. Wrath took him through a series of seemingly never-ending tunnels, where the surviving Unas settled back down on the ground every few feet. Some laid down to rest, others etched symbols into their skin or played some sort of dice game. A few watched small box TVs hooked up to a hanging power cord, which ran up to the corner of the ceiling and down the tunnel in both directions. Steel stakes driven into the walls formed a makeshift structure for running the plumbing and power lines.

It's like an ant farm in here.

Wouldn't that make me the anteater? Nythan chuckled.

Uh...yeah, I guess it would.

Wrath stopped at two Unas standing in front of a cell fashioned out of dusty lightish-brown bones impaled by rebar, like chicken skewered on a kebab. Nythan peered at Steven, Raeleigh, and Mia inside the enclosure. Steven came up to the bars and put both hands on them, staring straight into Nythan's eyes. Nythan sensed Steven's hatred.

"Jou see das game?" the first Unas said to the second.

The second looked at the first. "Huh?"

"Das game of the leg ball," the first one growled.

The second guy rested his hands on his hips. *"Sprichst du Deutsch?"*

Wrath slowly raised his hand, fingers stretched apart.

The first guy vigorously nodded, *"Ja, das ist besser. Ich verstehe kein Wort verstanden von dem was—"*

Wrath put his hand on the speaker's face and pushed the man out of the way. His companion took the hint and moved aside.

"These," Wrath hummed, tapping the bone bars with his long, razor-like fingernails, "Made from *strongest* Ordo."

It took Nythan a few seconds to understand what Wrath meant. "Wait, what? These bones are people bones? Ordo Solis people?"

"Yesssss. Our guests. Need friends...comfort them."

Steven's face contorted first into alarm, then disgust. "Holy s***!" he exclaimed, ripping his hands from the bars and scampering away. He scraped his hands against his pants.

Wrath began snorting hysterically. "Leave you. More phone calls."

CHAPTER 63

IF YOU DON'T KNOW...

Nythan looked at the three of them. "Sorry about all this."

"If you were really sorry, you'd let us go," Steven said.

Nythan narrowed his eyes. "That's not a reasonable thing to say."

"Whyever not?" Mia asked.

"Because you all would do whatever you could to tell everyone what I am." Nythan was disappointed to feel anger and bitterness within her. He really liked Mia. Loved her even.

Steven scoffed. "Wouldn't be so bad. They'd only want to talk with you. Negotiate, even."

Nythan sensed the dishonesty in Steven's words but saw it as the opportunity he needed. "Yeah, I was thinking the same."

Steven raised his eyebrows.

"More to come on that later," Nythan said. "I just wanted to make sure you all were being provided for."

Like a last meal before the execution?

Nythan pursed his lips. *Stop it. We need them.*

For now.

"How *kind* of you."

Despite the sarcasm, Nythan could feel he had piqued Steven's interest. The other two drew closer.

"You said more to come?" Mia asked.

Nythan shrugged. "I'm not ready to tell you yet."

"Nythan, we've been dragged all over the place, and I haven't taken a bath in at least a week," Raeleigh told him. "We're interested to know what you have in mind for us."

"You're not ready to hear it yet."

Nythan felt Steven's excitement grow in tandem with a desire for revenge, although Steven's face was as expressionless as ever.

"It's been a long day, Nythan, so if you're not ready to tell us, we'd like to get some sleep," Steven told him.

Call his bluff. Make them wait until tomorrow.

"Okay, well, if you insist..."

Steven gritted his teeth. "Just tell us."

"I want to avoid any further bloodshed on either side. I came up with a bargain that's a win-win for us all."

"Doesn't seem likely to me," Steven scoffed. "What we want and what you want are mutually detrimental."

"Here I am offering you an olive branch, and you kill it before even hearing about it."

"What's your plan?" Raeleigh broke in, shooting Steven an annoyed look.

"I want to set up a meeting with the Ordo Solis, the CIA, and us."

Mia's eyes widened. Steven's lips curled into a smirk.

"Mia, you can bring the CIA to the table. Raeleigh, you can be the liaison between the Order and me. We already have a way to contact the Ordo Solis here in Europe."

"What about me?" Steven asked.

"You'll be staying here. Both as moral support and because you'll try to sabotage my genuine effort to stop our endless fighting," Nythan told him.

Steven grinned broadly. "I don't need to sabotage anything. The very nature of the Raptors and the Unas does that for me."

"And the Catholic Inquisition has done that for your side as well," Nythan replied. "Both sides are equally to blame for the needless bloodshed. But there's a way for us to coexist until we no longer need to."

"What do you mean, 'no longer need to?'" Raeleigh asked.

"That's the other part, which I'll explain later." Nythan dug a piece of paper from his pocket and handed it to Mia through the bone bars. "Mia, tell the CIA that I want to meet at this address. Today is Monday. Our meeting will take place on Wednesday at two a.m. sharp. We'll give you access to a phone to make whatever calls you need."

"There is not enough time," Mia said, taking the piece of paper.

"If the CIA wants access to the leader of two large, fanatical, secretive organizations, I suggest they do whatever it takes to attend," Nythan remarked. "Raeleigh, we'll talk later about specifics."

"Why not say it now to everyone?" Steven challenged. Nythan felt Steven's concern for Raeleigh mount.

"Because she's the only one out of you three who I can reasonably trust with this information and who can still be a representative to both parties."

"I can be your representative," Steven said, trying not to laugh. "I'll represent the s*** out of your meeting."

"My point exactly."

CHAPTER 64

NOW YOU KNOW.

Raeleigh stared at Nythan as they sat in a makeshift conference room with a small table and rotting wooden chairs somewhere within the maze of the Unas' tunnel system.

"I...I don't understand," Raeleigh said in a hushed manner. "Why me?"

"Because you seem the most reasonable," Nythan explained. He also sensed how calm Raeleigh felt whenever she regarded him. She didn't exude the same bitterness and anger toward him that Steven and Mia did. He did feel Raeleigh's guilt though. She felt guilty over something surrounding their circumstances, but Nythan didn't think it wise to ask for more detail.

"I need someone who goes into this meeting levelheaded. Someone who can see both sides. I believe that person is you."

"Why can't you get one of your own people to do that?" Raeleigh countered. "They'll represent you much better than I ever could."

Nythan's expression softened. "Because, Raeleigh, while we can liaise with the CIA, none of my representatives could truly be an ambassador to the Ordo Solis. I need someone who can bridge this divide, someone who can mediate both sides." Nythan stood up and began pacing the room. "This whole Ordo Solis versus the Unas and Raptors thing is all unnecessary. What're we fighting over? I need souls to survive. Even if I *don't* get them, I come back again…and again. You all are sworn to fight me, and in doing so you've destroyed both the innocent and those you deem guilty of aiding me. This whole cycle feeds itself and only creates more suffering for everyone. I want you to help me end that."

"How?"

Remember, just like we practiced.

Nythan took a deep breath. "I need to receive enough souls so that I can be released from this never-ending cycle."

Raeleigh reflected for a moment, then said, "If you want me to represent *your* side, I'll need you to be more honest."

What the…that's not what she's supposed to say.

"What do you mean?" he asked with surprise.

"I mean, I appreciate what you said, but I don't know how to process that. What're you being released *from*?"

Nythan tapped his fingers together. *Should I tell her more?*

Might as well. Part of your grand plan depends on her ability to present our position in a credible light.

Nythan winced.

Raeleigh raised one of her neatly trimmed eyebrows. "I'll need you to explain that as well."

"Explain what?"

Raeleigh let out a loud exhale. "Let's just start with the first question. Released from what?"

"Constantly being reborn. Every time the Great One dies, he's born in someone else. Then he has to start all over again consuming enough souls to leave."

"Why do you keep saying 'the Great One'? And where are you leaving?"

"It's the entity within me," Nythan clarified. "The thing you call Bane. It's separate from who I am. I'm Nythan; he's Bane."

Raeleigh's eyes widened. "So *that's* the missing piece. You talk to each other, don't you?"

"Yeah, yeah we do."

Raeleigh clasped her hands and squealed. "It all makes sense now! So how does Bane get released from all this?"

"He needs to get enough souls to transcend."

"Transcend where, precisely?"

"We don't really know. We just know that he moves on from this plane of existence."

"And your followers?"

Nythan hesitated.

What do you think? Nythan asked Bane.

You could try avoiding the answer.

"Nythan," Raeleigh prodded. "It's important that I know why you have all these people following you."

"They help us get enough souls. That's their purpose. It all boils down to them giving us enough souls."

"And you don't know what happens after Bane transcends?"

"Not to Bane, no, that's the mystery. We just know it's possible from past lives."

"So why do you want to meet with the Order and CIA?"

"I want to strike a bargain with the Order, work out a deal that'll allow us to acquire the souls we need. The CIA's there to help the Order know I'm not going to murder them outright."

If they even show up. I'm not sure the CIA cares enough to devote resources to this. They might come for Mia, if she's truly one of their agents.

Raeleigh hesitated. "That seems like...a tough thing to get the Order to agree to."

Nythan shrugged. "It's the only reason I'm telling you this. There has to be a solution here. Bane keeps coming back and has been for over two thousand years. People on both sides keep dying. An agreement between me and the Ordo Solis will end all that. There has to be room for a compromise somewhere."

"I'd like to think so. But it'll be tough to digest that. By us compromising, we're letting you hurt people."

"Not if I'm given the room I need to continually gather volunteers. So far, most of the gifts have been from willing participants."

Nythan sensed Raeleigh's emotions shifting from curious to guarded. "Most?"

"We ran into some unavoidable circumstances, not having to do with the Order. It's not relevant to our situation, and I'd rather not explain."

"Okay. But how exactly do you want me to convey your compromise?"

"I think if you explain the situation to them, it'll help them understand that we're not trying to destroy the world. Bane is trying to escape and end the conflict."

"Your followers believe you'll bring about the apocalypse. Anyone I try to talk to will surely want to know about that."

"My followers are a means to an end. As long as they protect me and produce volunteers to keep me alive, they serve their purpose." Nythan paused. "And just so that we're clear, I won't be repeating that outside of this room."

Raeleigh gave Nythan a subtle frown. "That's fine. Why now? Why *did* you, I mean Bane, return?"

Nythan held his breath. His mind's eye recalled the burglar's knife tip sinking into his chest and the silver gas exiting the burglar's nostrils.

Don't tell her any more than you have to.

"Because Bane feels he's waited long enough. The conditions are right. No one believes he exists. The stage is set."

"And what is the best-case scenario?"

"That the Unas and Raptors are given the opportunity to gather volunteers in peace. The Great One then receives enough souls and is released from Earth, and we all can continue going about our lives without the need to worry about him any longer."

"The Unas, the Raptors, and the Sanhe won't just disappear though, right?" Raeleigh pointed out. "They'll still be here, yes?"

"True, but once the Great One ascends, they'll become obsolete and no longer serve a purpose. I'm sure you can draw your own conclusion from there."

"Hmm. The hard part will be convincing the Order because we exist to oppose you. The CIA has no stake in this that I'm aware of. I doubt they believe you're anything more than a mythical figure the Raptors worship."

"Without the CIA, the Order won't have much desire to attend this meeting. They'll believe it's nothing more than a trick or another attempt to destroy the Order."

"But isn't that what you want?" Raeleigh asked.

All this would *be much easier if they were destroyed.*

"I won't deny that it'd make things easier—much easier. But no, I'm hoping that we can conclude our dealings with as little bloodshed as possible."

"You're asking a lot. Much more than I think the Order is willing to give."

"Well, let me offer this as food for thought. If we don't do this, the Unas will continue picking apart the Order until there's nothing left. Solis Europe is all that remains. On the other hand, when Bane ascends, we're pretty sure he won't be able to bother us any longer. So, if we can avoid pointless deaths in the name of a mistaken fight, then I'd rather make the effort. No one else need suffer."

Nythan sensed a wave of sorrow envelope Raeleigh. Tears welled in the corners of her eyes.

"I'm sorry, Raeleigh," Nythan said. "I never wanted any of this. I never wanted anyone to die. And I certainly want all the fighting to end. If you leave the Unas and Raptors to do what they're meant to do, we can be the ones to stop this conflict once and for all."

Raeleigh shook her head, then let out a shaky exhale. Nythan felt a hurricane of emotions swirl within her.

"I'll introduce you to the Order, but I can't trust what you say."

Nythan nodded. "I understand. Just think about what I've said, please. Before you go back with Steven and Mia, I want you to meet Enzo. He's from Solis Europe. I need him to know that you're part of the Order as well."

"Fine," Raeleigh said, and started for the door.

"Raeleigh," Nythan called out. He waited until she turned to him. "Don't tell Mia or Steven about this. You telling them what I've told you'll only hurt what we're doing here."

Raeleigh managed a nod, and Nythan sensed her growing more upset by the second. She opened the door, and the Unas guards led her away.

That went pretty well. I think she may prove to be an asset to our cause.

"Maybe," Nythan replied out loud. "We still have yet to talk to Mia."

We need to be careful. She is a trained intelligence agent. Also, I feel a great deal of contempt from her. Something is fueling those emotions, and we need to figure out what it is to understand how sincere her help would be.

Nythan frowned. *Why can't you just read minds?*

That would make things far simpler, but simple has never been in the cards. Speaking of simpler, *it would behoove us to reiterate to our friends what is expected of them.*

Who?

The Raptors.

"Yeah, I suppose so."

Nythan departed the Unas lair and returned to the site where he had left Palaou and the Raptors near the courtyard well. A few Raptors finally approached and brought him to where the Raptors holed themselves up in wait. He explained the plan that he and Wrath had developed.

"Which means," Nythan said, "that you all will work alongside the Unas and not cause *any* trouble. Nor will you provoke the Order or the CIA *in any way*. It's vitally important that we conclude this meeting successfully."

Palaou bobbed his head and assured Nythan that they'd do anything required of them.

Nythan scanned the surrounding Prey. "Does the Prey understand their role in all of this?"

The Raptor beside him spoke. "We will not take any action without your express direction."

"Good. As long as no threatening moves are made that could be misinterpreted, I can do what I came to do."

"Of course, my Lord," Palaou confirmed.

"Okay, I'll meet you tomorrow at the well, nine p.m. We'll leave together. See ya then." Nythan left and returned to the Unas' headquarters.

CHAPTER 65

ROUNDABOUT

Nythan commanded Mia be brought in to talk with him. She did an exceptional job of hiding her rage but didn't realize Nythan could read her feelings. He took a deep breath to keep it from distracting him.

"Were you able to contact the CIA?"

"Sí," she answered, drawing her lips into a thin line.

"And?"

"They listened. No talking."

"I suppose that'll have to do." He frowned. "Mia, I've been wondering. Why do you hate me?"

She crossed her arms and remained silent.

"I've never done anything to you."

No response.

"It's obvious that you've been a mole from the beginning, before you ever joined the Central Coven. Did you join the CIA and they gave you this assignment?"

Keep questioning, her feelings will give her away.

"Did something happen that caused you to hate me?"

Her feelings morphed into hurt and sorrow.

That's it. Something happened. Her family members are still alive. Maybe there was something not captured in the report.

"Was somebody you knew hurt by the Raptors?"

Nythan didn't need to tap into her emotions to know the answer. Mia's facial expression confirmed what Nythan had asked. She tried not to cry, but a tear slipped down from the corner of her eye.

"I'm so sorry the Raptors hurt you," Nythan offered. "I wish I could go back in time and change that. But I can't. I can only mend things going forward. I know you dislike me, but please know that I'm doing everything I can to right the wrongs that have been done. I'm going to bring a couple of people in here from the Ordo Solis. One person will be from America, the other from Europe. All I need you to do is confirm that you talked to the CIA and that they know about the meeting tonight. That's all. A simple confirmation. *Por favor,* Mia."

Mia continued to remain silent, narrowing her eyes at him.

Nythan shouted to the Unas at the door and both Raeleigh and Enzo were hustled into the room. Nythan felt them out, hoping they had had enough time to establish a trusting relationship. Both radiated an unexplainable sense of mutual hope. It almost felt like a piece of silk held them together. Nythan wanted to believe it meant something positive.

Emotional bonds. It's not always love…sometimes it's a shared experience.

"I called you all in here because I'm meeting with the American Central Intelligence Agency Wednesday morning at two a.m.," Nythan said. "Here is the address." He handed a piece of paper to Enzo. "I'm inviting the Ordo Solis to the meeting as well. Raeleigh will be there, as will Mia and the CIA."

"Okay," Enzo said, looking at Mia. Raeleigh touched Enzo's arm.

"She got caught trying to help us," Raeleigh explained.

"Mia, can you please tell Enzo that you were able to get in touch with the CIA and tell them about the meeting?" Nythan requested, holding his breath.

Mia nodded without much hesitation. She exuded rage like heat from a mighty furnace. Nythan didn't know how to interpret her response.

Enzo squinted back at Nythan. "What do you want me to tell them?"

"Uh. Well, that they…should come to this meeting," Nythan said. "The purpose is to discuss a treaty. I know that sounds like an odd proposal, but please believe me when I say I have a compromise the Order will want to hear.

Enzo twiddled his thumbs. "Sure, but how do I know you are who you say you are?"

"Don't you remember the room full of bodies when we first met?"

"Yeah, but I can't be sure that was you."

Nythan called out and three masked Unas entered. Nythan pointed at the nearest Unas, and when he came to within a few feet of Nythan, Nythan took his soul.

"Happy?" Nythan said as the dead Unas crashed to the floor. "Leave us," he ordered the two survivors.

Enzo's eyes widened and Raeleigh paled, but Nythan detected no reaction from Mia.

How do I tell the Order?" Enzo asked.

"I'm going to let you go, right now. Just find them and tell them. I hope the Order decides to come. All I want to do is talk, no bloodshed."

"And all I have is your word?"

Surprisingly bold for someone who looked like he saw a ghost. Feel him out. He's afraid.

Nythan felt Enzo's fear circling the man like a hawk.

"You'll have the CIA there. You can also bring as many people as you deem necessary. I'll be there to talk, nothing more."

"Okay, Dracula. I'll tell them, but there is no guarantee they'll show."

Dracula? Nythan thought.

Yes. Count Dracula, thank you very much.

The corner of Nythan's mouth twitched in amusement. "I realize that. But consider that this is the first time you have solid proof of me in hundreds of years. Here I am, offering a solution to our mutual problem. All I ask is for the Order to hear me out."

Enzo grunted. "I'll tell them what you told me."

Nythan called for the two Unas standing guard, and they returned to the room. "See to it that this one here," Nythan said, pointing at Enzo, "is escorted to the surface. He's allowed to leave, and *no one* touches him."

The two Unas grabbed hold of Enzo and dragged him out.

Nythan looked at Raeleigh and Mia. "Now we wait. When it's time to go, I'll come get you. I really, truly, hope this works out for us all," Nythan commented. He gestured them both toward the door. It took some prodding by Mia to break Raeleigh's trance on the dead Unas, but they finally left.

Nythan beamed. *How'd I do?*

All things considered, pretty good.

Is there anything I'm missing?

Nope. The stage is set. Time to pull the trigger and hope the bullet doesn't bounce back.

CHAPTER 66

THE TRIGGER

Nythan and a small retinue stood on the roof of an unfinished three-story building at the edge of the city at one-thirty a.m. He had full view of the meeting place two hundred yards away, which stood by itself amid piles of construction material, heavy machinery, and a cleared field.

"My Lord," one of the masked Raptors said. His metallic voice sounded as menacing as the feelings of rage he exuded. "It's time."

Nythan turned to Wrath and tried not to laugh. Despite being out in public, Wrath *still* wore nothing but his mask. "Remember," Nythan warned.

Wrath waved him down. "Won't move. If fight. We come. They die."

Nythan nodded. He and his entourage descended three flights of stairs from the roof to the last step of the bottom floor. A lobby full of his Unas horde greeted him. Nythan said a silent prayer that they wouldn't be needed.

"Palaou," Nythan said.

"My Lord?" Palaou replied, struggling with the Raptor mask Nythan had made him wear. He sounded like he had sucked in helium from a balloon. Nythan couldn't help but snicker.

"Take the Prey and wait for me just outside the entrance. I'll make my way toward you in a few minutes." Before Palaou could protest, Nythan held up his hand. "I'm not asking."

Palaou bowed and left with the Prey, and they made their way through the Unas toward the exit.

"Wrath," Nythan said. "Turn off the lights. Tell the Unas that if anyone wants to stop me, this is their chance."

Wrath grunted his approval.

Bane began laughing. *What* are *you doing?*

I read it in a book once. Or maybe it was a movie scene.

"Maker walk. Challenge pot!" Wrath's raspy voice echoed throughout the floor.

Nythan sighed. *Seriously? Challenge* pot?

I think it's a rather innovative phrase.

When the lights shut off, Nythan stepped down off the last step and waded through the crowd. He reached out into the pitch black, and a sea of hands met his.

Several more people in, Nythan extracted the soul of a nearby Unas, whisking it into the air. The ethereal stream illuminated the darkness for several feet in each direction. Nythan kept the soul in the air for as long as possible before devouring it and repeating the process. The up and down motion of souls looked like dolphins surfing the waves.

Nythan continued until he made it through the crowd and out the double doors at the front of the building. Mia and Raeleigh waited for him alongside Palaou, all twenty-something Prey, and the rag-clad woman in the deer mask he had met when he first arrived. Mia and Raeleigh squinted as they peeked past him to make out what he had done inside. The Unas woman offered him the vampire mask. Wrath recommended he wear it at the meeting, saying that it would make a statement to the Order.

Nythan took his time fixing the mask to his face. "Let's move out," he barked.

His vast following proceeded by foot to the place he told Enzo they would meet. Palaou followed Nythan so close he stepped on the back of Nythan's shoes a couple times. Nythan looked down to see his hands shaking like an earthquake. He closed his fingers into fists, gritting his teeth.

Pre-battle jitters. Happens to the best of us. It's your body hoarding the energy it needs to handle the coming conflict.

Nythan only nodded, too anxious to speak.

All of Nythan and Bane's best-laid plans came down to this moment.

CHAPTER 67

THE BULLET

Before Nythan even came near the front of the meeting place, he saw them. Three Ordo Solis, all armed with Uzis, stood at the entrance. White surgical masks covered their mouths and bandanas were wrapped around their foreheads. The Prey pulled their weapons and established a defensive perimeter that moved with Nythan like a glove. A ten-foot-wide gap in the building wall went where a revolving door would later be installed.

His forward Prey reached the armed men first. No one spoke, and after a good minute, it became evident neither side intended to initiate contact. The Prey towered over the entry guards, continuing in their lethal staring match. Nythan sidestepped his guardians and went up to rest his hand on the Prey bodyguard in front. The protector moved aside to let Nythan pass.

Nythan stared at the closest Ordo Solis member. "I'm here," he announced. The Ordo Solis two glanced at one another.

"You act like this is a surprise, is there something wrong?" Nythan asked as politely as he could manage.

The person on the left nudged the one on the right, jerking his head toward the opening. The other guy shrugged, then stepped out of Nythan's way.

Bane began laughing. *I think there was supposed to be someone here to greet us. Already they appear disorganized.*

Nythan started to walk through the opening, but the Prey next to him shot his forearm across Nythan's chest. Three of the Prey next to him advanced through the door. About ten seconds later, one of them poked his head out, then went back inside. The Prey next to Nythan dropped his arm, and they proceeded through the opening into a sizable lobby with a reception desk. One person waited at the counter; she too sported a surgical mask and a bandana.

"Welcome. If you could please proceed down that hallway," she said, gesturing to her right down a dim corridor, "we will receive you there."

Nythan continued through the hallway until he met yet another masked soldier standing in front of two high doors. The Prey forced the Ordo Solis member out of the way as they thrust the doors open. The barren ballroom's ample lighting illuminated the area. Positioned in the middle of the room were a few small circular tables with people standing or sitting around them. A dozen armed Ordo Solis members were dispersed throughout the length of the room.

The Prey disengaged from Nythan and proceeded to match, person-to-person, the armed members of the Ordo Solis.

Nythan advanced to the tables; all except one rose as he approached. With the exception of the person who remained seated, the receiving party was dressed in black robes, white capes, and darkened hat buckets. His body shook with laughter at the ridiculous sight.

They're called kofias, not hat buckets.

The capes and kofias both had slanted red iron cross emblems stitched on the outside. A sweep of white feathers extended over the kofias like Mohawks. Medals and embroidery adorned their robes. Each wore a necktie, except for the man at the head of the table, who wore a ruby-red bolo. All had swords affixed to their hips.

Nythan assumed these absurd characters called themselves the leadership of the Ordo Solis. He took a few seconds to steel his face behind the vampire mask before removing it and handing it to the antler woman.

I suppose we're in the right place after all.

"Greetings," a robed man said. "My name is Ludwig, Worshipful Master of the Ordo Solis. This is Ola, our Senior Grand Warden. Here is Oliver, our Grand Historian; Ebba, our Grand Marshal; and Freddy, our

Tiler. You've met Enzo, our Grand Secretary. I'll let our mutual friend here introduce himself."

Ludwig gestured at the sixth person, a man dressed in jeans and a polo.

"I'm Mr. Smith," he said ominously. Nythan felt Mr. Smith out, sensing confused boredom.

We can use that to our advantage. It means the CIA does not consider us to be a genuine threat.

Nythan had intended to let Raeleigh introduce him, but having taken everything in, he thought it right to skip that part.

There goes your grand plan.

F*** it, we'll do it live.

"This is *P*," Nythan said, indicating Palaou. Palaou bowed ever so slightly as to not wrinkle his tuxedo. "This is Raeleigh, she's from the Ordo Solis in America, and here is Mia. She's an associate of Mr. Smith."

"Before we begin, can you please dispense with your guards?" Ola, the warden, requested. "We'd prefer to discuss our agenda without your overbearing custodians."

Nythan regarded his four Prey escorts behind him and waved them off. They disengaged and went to find a Solis guard to square off against. "I prefer my two friends stay here," Nythan said, waving his fingers at the antler woman and Palaou.

"Shall we?" Ludwig indicated to the chairs of the third table.

Nythan smiled at the group and took his seat. Palaou slid a chair underneath Nythan as he sat.

"I'm glad we could all meet here together," Nythan began. "I asked for this meeting so that we could settle our differences and come to an amicable solution."

"I was very curious indeed, Bane," Ludwig said, matching Nythan's smile. "First at your return and now this meeting. Highly irregular."

Nythan let out a subtle groan as a knot twisted and unraveled around his stomach.

Sorry, that was me. I've been probing them. I'm sensing a weird feeling from all except the CIA guy. The Worshipful Master and the historian both feel reconciliation and solace. The others feel obedient acquiescence. I think they've all agreed to something, but I can't find any other emotion that would help me understand what that agreement is.

What does that mean? Nythan asked.

I don't know yet, give me some time to look at it more. Their verbal sentiments don't coincide with the rest of their emotions.

"Let's get on with it," huffed Oliver, the historian.

"Calm, Oliver," Ludwig said. "We'll have all the time we need to get to the heart of the matter." He spoke directly to Nythan. "What sort of arrangement did you have in mind?"

Nythan nodded. "First, I want to begin with this. I'm not here to bring some apocalyptic end to the world. All these years we've been fighting have primarily been because you thought I was the devil, when all I wanted to do was survive."

Oliver leaned forward. "Ever since you destroyed the Zhōu in eighth century BC, you've survived off the lives of others. You *still* survive off others. How can you—?"

"Please excuse Oliver," said, Ludwig cutting the man's diatribe short. "He knows the details of our history better than most. As you say, the historical account of our conflict is open to interpretation. But as harsh as Oliver's words are, I have to ask: How can we come to an accord? We seem unequivocally at odds with one another." The rest of the group peered at Nythan, awaiting his reply.

"The source of our conflict is with the suffering that it brings," Nythan said. "I don't need or want the lives of everyone on this planet. But I must eat to continue living, just as you do. Those who wish to voluntarily give themselves to me aren't those you defend. You just protect the innocent. So, you aren't opposed to what I am, so much as you're opposed to me destroying the lives of those who aren't willing. Can we at least agree on that?"

Nythan observed Mr. Smith, feeling a general sense of cynical disbelief from the man.

Ludwig lowered his head. "Agreed, mostly. However, we are chartered to stop you from consuming the lives of this world, good or bad. Your hunger knows no bounds. As our Historian, Oliver, can attest, you have before stated your wish to see this world burn."

Nythan shook his head vehemently. "My hunger has as much of a limit as yours does. If I can be satisfied by volunteers, then there need be no conflict between us. As for the whole *burning the world* thing, I get absolutely nothing from it. It'd be as if you cut down all the trees on Earth or drank all the water from the ocean. It's just not sustainable."

Oliver grunted.

Nythan narrowed his eyes. "It's true."

Ola cut in before Oliver could comment. "Part of our concern is that your…groups…lure unsuspecting victims into believing that you'll save them. I believe the phrase is, 'you will deliver us,' if I'm not mistaken. What're you delivering them from?"

"Every organization needs its propaganda," Nythan answered. "The CIA, the Catholic Church…even the Ordo Solis, to support some narrative that furthers itself."

Mr. Smith perked up at the mention of his employer.

"Fair enough," Ludwig conceded. "So, your proposal is what, exactly?"

Nythan held his breath. "I can't change the past. None of us can. But I want to establish peace. Our people will no longer fight you. We just want to be left alone."

"You propose a peace treaty?" Ludwig asked. Nythan felt a wave of internal regret emanating from Ludwig, overcome by that same feeling of reconciliation Bane noted.

What in the hell is going on? Something is definitely not right. He's already made up his mind about something.

"Yes. Let's just step away from each other. You let me live in peace, no more innocents need be involved. As you can see, Raeleigh and Mia here are both unharmed. Steven, the other Solis dude, is safe with us as well. All of them can be returned to you, in good faith of our non-aggression pact." Looking over to Raeleigh, Nythan said, "Raeleigh here will confirm my intentions and explain things from her perspective."

Ludwig observed Nythan with sad eyes, scratching the scruff of his white beard. As Ludwig opened his mouth to speak, the sound of two wet planks slapped together in Nythan's ear and a substance splattered his cheek. His attention zeroed in on the disturbance, and he witnessed the antler woman clutching her neck, blood spurting everywhere.

GET DOWN!

Before Nythan reacted Palaou yanked him from the chair to the ground and covered him with his body. He heard an outbreak of shouts, followed by the familiar rattle of gunfire. A shootout between the two armed groups erupted at point-blank range. The Ordo Solis member closest him drew her sword and took aim to drive the blade straight down into Palaou's back. Nythan nudged Palaou over and seized the woman's soul before she could strike.

Nythan used his newfound boost to push Palaou off, and he stood just in time to see the antler woman cut Ola's throat before she was impaled by Enzo's sword. Nythan immediately yanked the Secretary's soul from his body. He took Ola and the antler woman's fading souls for good measure. He scanned around him. The Prey seemed to be taking matters into their own hands, many opting to engage their adversaries in hand-to-hand combat.

Focus! Feel the enemy out and kill them. The table first!

Nythan threw out both of his hands at the remaining Ordo Solis leadership. A split second before he withdrew their souls, Mia shot forward, screaming like a banshee. She kicked Nythan straight in the side of his stomach and then connected her fist with his nose. Palaou attempted to come to Nythan's aid, but Raeleigh tackled him as he ran forward. Mia jumped on top of Nythan, straddling him. She rained down blow after blow on whatever body part she could reach. Nythan shielded himself as she battered him.

Palaou and Raeleigh engaged in a wrestling match as they rolled over him, kicking and screaming. Nythan used the respite to gather his wits. As Mia came in for another blow, he thrust his hand out to grab her face. She parried, but it bought him time. He sucked in as fully as he could right as a solid hook struck his chin. Nythan's face bounced off Mia's fist, and he found himself staring into Raeleigh's eyes as he inhaled. Her soul snaked into Nythan before his mind processed had happened.

Quickly returning his attention to Mia, he grabbed one of her blows right before it struck him. Nythan breathed in deep, and Mia slumped forward as her soul evicted her body. Nythan threw Mia off him and jumped up. The CIA agent was nowhere to be found, nor was Enzo. Ludwig stood calmly amid the chaos, as did Oliver. They made no move against him.

They accept their fate. These bastards planned this.

Whatever, Nythan thought. He prepared to take their souls.

Wait! Focus on the other Ordo guys fighting us. Then deal with these goons.

Nythan closed his eyes, doing his best to enter the breathing state. He swiftly reached for each person fighting the Prey. As best he could, Nythan started inhaling like a madman. Souls began shooting forth in jerky motions. A few seconds later all fighting ceased.

Nythan opened his eyes, heaving mightily. He felt no pain, even though he experienced the sensation of blood running down his nose. He scanned the room. There were still Prey left standing, but the entire scene was a bloodbath. His eyes slowly slid over to Ludwig and Oliver. They both leered at him.

The hell?

Ludwig raised his hands. "For this is the work of the Evil One. The apocalypse is the only fruit he bears!" Ludwig bellowed as the Prey began closing in around them.

Nythan stilled his hatred, then sucked in, ushering their souls forth. Unexpectedly, two other souls came up beneath them and ran over the table. He supposed they belonged to the CIA guy and someone else hiding underneath. Nythan felt a pang of regret as his body assimilated them all.

One of the Prey raised his fist. "WE, THE RAPTOR'S CLAW!" he shouted.

"RISE FURTHER!" the rest of the Prey echoed.

All I felt was a sense of accomplishment from those two. They wanted *you to win.*

Nythan felt Bane dive deep in thought.

Why the fu——? Oh, damn! There must be someone or something watching. Tell the Prey to hunt for eavesdroppers. Now! While we still have time.

Nythan's eyes went wide and darted all around. "Find the cameras!" he shrieked. "Find any witnesses!"

The Prey began scouring the area.

A loud crash sounded behind him. Nythan swiveled around as his horde of Unas poured into the room, headed by Wrath. Wrath was slathered in dark red, holding a crude mace bathed in the essence of someone's life. The Unas army came to a stop in front of Nythan.

"You're late," Nythan sneered.

"We came!" Wrath gasped, looking around. "They die?"

"What do you think?" Nythan snapped. "It was a *trap*! They *planned* this!" Nythan stared at the ceiling and howled with rage. He screamed at everyone in the room. He singled out the Prey in his rant because they had decided to engage without his express authorization.

He turned his attention to Wrath. "Search this entire building for anyone left alive, or anything looking like a camera. Search every *single* body. After that, bring all the Unas back to headquarters and have them wait for me at the big meeting cavern. Everyone!" Nythan commanded. Wrath started screaming at the throngs of Unas, who began ransacking the place.

Nythan felt a thick cough against his ankle. He looked down and saw Palaou curled into a tight ball. Nythan pulled at Palaou. "Get up. You okay?"

Red stains and scratch marks covered Palaou's face. "I've been better, my Lord," he shuddered. "How are you?"

"Don't worry about me," Nythan said. He walked around the table, examining each lifeless body, then circled back to where he had begun. He passed over Mia, and his face wrenched in rage as he let out a roar.

His eyes came to a stop at Raeleigh. Her peaceful expression amid the carnage pierced him, and Nythan choked with emotion. He tried to shake the feeling of sadness threatening to envelop him.

We have to go, Nythan. This place will be crawling with locals soon.

Nythan wiped his nose, stifling his urge to cry. *How am I going to explain this to Steven?*

You aren't.

She didn't deserve this. I really thought it would work.

This isn't the time for pity. We're moving on from here. The idea you have with the Unas is precisely what I would do in this situation. Let's go settle that.

Nythan took in one last sight of Raeleigh as he wiped away tears.

She didn't deserve this, Nythan repeated. *This could've worked.*

CHAPTER 68

THE FEAST

Nythan returned to the Unas' headquarters alone to await the horde's arrival. He left Palaou and the fifteen surviving Prey at a nearby inn. It took more convincing than necessary, but Nythan made it clear that they had derailed his plan too much to continue participating.

As soon as Nythan entered the receiving room where the well descended, his body alerted him to something amiss. He at last noticed blood spattered down the walls of the tunnel leading to the main cavern. Nythan rounded a corner to find three dead Unas on the ground. All shot.

They came while we were gone. I'm going to assume our guest is no longer with us.

Nythan continued through the maze of tunnels as best as he remembered, finding more lifeless Unas along the way. The only sound he heard was the hush of wind coursing through the tunnels.

Nythan managed to find the crude prison where he last left Steven. Fragments from the obliterated bone bars holding the cell together peppered the ground. Smeared against the wall were the words: *I'm coming for her!*

Nythan frowned and made his way back to the big meeting cavern.

We won't be able to stay here anymore. There's only one place left we can go now.

Where? Nythan asked.

To the masters of disguise. Sanhetuan. Soon as we're done here.

So more zipping around on private jets, using fake passports, traveling with loads of bodyguards?

You sound ungrateful.

Nythan crossed his arms. *I sound* unconvinced. *How in the world do the Raptors and the Unas have all this stuff?*

The world left them alone for decades. It doesn't take long to grow membership and stockpile wealth when you have so many people working together unimpeded.

The Ordo Solis were in the way! Everyone told me how bad it used to be.

In the grand scheme of things, it was a mere nuisance to the overall growth of our followers. The Ordo Solis was only as powerful as the powers they convinced to help them.

When Wrath finally arrived with the Unas horde, Nythan told him that the place had been ransacked while they were away.

Wrath howled. "SEARCH EVERYWHERE!"

"There's no more time!" Nythan cut in. "Forget the search. Call them all around me."

Wrath shouted to the Unas, then walked over to Nythan. He held out the bolo tie that Ludwig, the Ordo Solis Worshipful Master, had worn.

"They watched," Wrath grunted.

Nythan took the bolo tie without saying anything and sat on Wrath's stool. He removed the remains of the red ruby on the ornamental slide, revealing a cracked camera hidden inside. His ribcage rattled when Bane sighed in frustration. Nythan's nostrils flared as he spat into the lens and then affixed the bolo tie around his neck.

Looks like this is mine now, Nythan sneered, playing with the cords while he waited for the Unas to get settled.

When Wrath indicated that all the Unas were mustered before him, Nythan arose from the stool. The cavern was packed full of people, leaving standing room only. It reminded him of his return visit to the Northern Coven.

Focus. You're ready.

Nythan raised a hand, and a hush fell across the crowd. "Y'all have grown so much," Nythan started. "I've watched you grow from just a handful of loyal followers to an entire army of fearsome disciples."

Well, it's not a complete lie. I watched them grow from a handful of loyal followers.

"Wrath told me that you're the Widowed." He received a mixture of shouts and grunts at the word. "Do I have that right?" Nythan frowned when they didn't respond the same way to his question.

"Okay then, has it felt good to see your Maker?" More shouts and grunts followed. "The Maker—"

His sentence was cut short as the Unas' guttural response sounded even louder.

Nythan smirked, then laughed aloud. *They have no idea what I'm saying. Then get to the point.*

"Well alright then, I guess it's time to make y'all Widowmaker."

Wrath raised his hands to the cavern ceiling. "WIDOWMAKER!"

The Unas horde erupted into a jubilant cry.

Well, I guess it doesn't matter how we do it in the end. Nythan closed his eyes and took a moment to collect himself. Then he entered the breathing state and relaxed into the groundswell of emotions birthed by his audience. *How about now?*

Go ahead, give it a go. Remember, with a crowd, you want to change the overall feeling, not penetrate any one person.

Nythan grinned slyly at the challenge, examining the cloud of exhilaration and fear permeating the air around the Unas. He enveloped the cavern as best as he could, caressing the sea of passion and massaging his own feelings into it.

The raw emotion of the Unas began transforming into something akin to violent fervor. Some of the Unas howled, gnashing their teeth and jumping up and down; others clawed their faces. Nythan basked in the tempest resulting from all the activity.

They're ready.

Nythan exhaled as much as his lungs would allow, then sucked in hard. Souls belched forth as if from a cannon. Nythan kept inhaling in spasmodic motions as he rotated three hundred and sixty degrees, taking care to avoid consuming Wrath. The horde of Unas began toppling over like stalks of wheat, knocking into each other as they fell to the ground.

As Nythan took the last soul of the gathered Unas, he lowered his head, accepting the familiar wave of euphoria that infiltrated every inch of his body. He burped, and a puff of ethereal mist tumbled out of him and dissipated as it lifted to the cavern ceiling. Nythan felt like he couldn't have taken another soul, even if there had been more to take. The sensation overwhelmed him, but he didn't feel pain. His body tingled all over, senses attuned to everything happening around him. Even the silence seemed deafening.

Bane got to work digesting and distributing souls, glowing with excitement.

Nythan turned around and looked at Wrath. His fencing mask lay on the ground next to him. The expression on Wrath's face reflected his bewilderment. "Amazing," Wrath whispered. "I *saw* Widowmaker!"

Nythan nodded a few times, thumping his chest. "I feel them swirling about," Nythan said. "You'll need to rebuild."

"This not issue," Wrath told him.

Nythan stepped away from Wrath and walked awkwardly toward the tunnel leading to the exit. With an ocean of bodies littering the floor, he couldn't touch the ground.

"Maker," Wrath called out after him. Nythan stopped and turned.

"One day, become Widowmaker."

Nythan considered Wrath's request. "If you rebuild the Unas to twice their strength, I'll come back, and you'll be Widowmaker." He turned and proceeded out of the cavern. He made his way through the underground tunnel, inspecting the blood streaks down the wall. He could discern the smears and droplets at a near-microscopic level. The eerie silence he experienced embraced him yet again, but this time Nythan's reinforced hearing picked up every minute source of noise, including a faint scratching sound ahead of him. Nythan studied a roach scurrying about thirty feet away. He could see the separate leg hairs protruding from its skeletal frame as it scampered from his approach.

Yuck, Nythan thought, turning his attention to the walls beside him. He inspected the individual grains peppering the cement mixture. He was absolutely fascinated by his newfound ability to observe the world in minuscule detail.

It'll get old after a while. Extraordinary eyesight and hearing are double-edged swords.

Nythan continued down the long stone corridor. The clinking of the metal ends of the bolo tie got on Nythan's nerves. He ripped it off his neck in frustration and tried in vain to crush the ornament in his hands.

Nythan sneered at the battered clasp before shrugging and letting his hand drop to his side. *If only I had super strength.*

Again with the Hollywood movies.

He laughed as he got into the water bucket, then located and pressed the camouflaged brown button. The rope apparatus hoisted him to the surface, where the rising auburn sun greeted him.

CHAPTER 69
THE ROAD NOT TRAVELED

Nythan pressed his forehead against the window of the plane as it flew over the mountains. His eyes could zoom in so close he could see individual leaves on the trees below.

Palaou was draped across the adjacent seat, snoring softly, a tablet computer resting against his tuxedo breast pocket. Nythan felt the spark of resentment build as he watched Palaou sleep.

It's not his fault your plan failed.

Nythan blinked several times. *I know. I must be tired.*

Each time he saw Palaou, the feeling returned.

What Prey survived Nythan had let come with him, but only because he didn't want to die from vengeful Ordo Solis. They changed private planes a few times as they traveled from the Czech Republic to China.

Nythan thumbed his own tablet, scrolling through the most recent update sent by Rose. The office building where the bloody clash had occurred crawled with the local Czech authorities. They had made no mention yet of the Unas' involvement, and Nythan prayed it would stay that way. He prayed further that Wrath had found a way to take care of all the lifeless bodies he had left behind.

So, the Sanhe. Tell me about them. Nythan tried his best to ignore the near repugnant smell of both the airplane and the people around him.

Sanhetuan are experts in concealment. They're like ninjas.

So how do we meet with them? Is there a Gatekeeper?

No Gatekeeper, no point of contact. Search them out and they'll find us.

That seems counterintuitive.

It'll make sense when it happens.

Okay, what else?

Let's start at the beginning. I told you before that Sanhetuan was created to be my cloak of invisibility. Anything involving subterfuge and sabotage was their responsibility.

You told me once what their name meant, but I don't remember.

It's a combination of three phrases describing the purpose of the orga-nization. First is harmony of emotion. *It's the understanding that there is imbalance in the world. Second is* harmony of solution. *There must be the will to restore balance. Third is* harmony of effort. *It is the communal act of correcting the imbalance.*

So, these three things are what the Sanhe live by?

In a manner of speaking, yes. More like guidelines that nurture their dis-appointment at the fall of man.

The Sanhe sound very apocalyptic.

You don't need to use the word the. *It's both a group identity and a descrip-tion. Sanhetuan need a precise and delicate touch. They are* very different from *the Raptors and the Unas. Sanhetuan merely require a channel to focus their desire for change.*

You manipulate them, Nythan accused.

Come on, Nythan. I manipulated no one. Sanhetuan did not exist before me. They were an unorganized batch of bitter and helpless individuals. I gave them motivation, and they flourished as a result.

Nythan sighed. *Whatever you say, Bane.*

One of the Prey tapped Nythan on the shoulder.

"We will be landing within the hour." Her metallic voice vibrated.

Nythan nodded. "Thank you."

So, where do we go to find them? Nythan thought.

Like I said, they'll find us. I wouldn't be surprised if they already know we're coming. What will likely happen is, when they become aware of our presence, they'll follow us and observe with care. When they determine the best way to extract us, it'll happen with little warning. Be prepared for anything as soon as we step off the plane.

After what happened this morning, I'm prepared for anything.

Not yet you aren't, but you're a whole lot closer. It's almost time to tell you how I think I can ascend.

"Okay, tell me," Nythan said aloud. Palaou roused from his slumber.

"My Lord?" he mumbled, before dozing off again.

Nythan chuckled.

Like I said, you're almost *ready. But don't worry, we're just about there. Sanhetuan will teach you one last lesson that the ashram monks didn't.*

It sounds like something I'm not going to wanna hear, Nythan thought.

Not right away. But you'll see the wisdom in it. We're so close. Remember when I explained that my freedom felt like I was running the last lap on a track? That feeling is beginning to grow. Our position gets more precarious the longer we wait; we need to make substantial advances toward the end.

Nythan's head bobbed in agreement and walked over to one of the nearby Prey.

"What's your name?" Nythan asked.

"I'm number four, my Lord," came the metallic response.

"Nonono, what's your *real* name?"

"Ahgo."

"Okay, Ahgo, please find Devin and bring him here."

Ahgo turned around and left.

Clever idea.

Thanks, it came to me only just now.

Two masked Prey approached.

"Devin?" Nythan couldn't tell them apart.

"Yes, my Lord," Devin confirmed.

"When we land, I want you and Ahgo to find a white lotus flower."

"Yes, my Lord," Devin acknowledged.

"Err," Nythan said. "On second thought, do either of you speak Chinese?"

It's called Mandarin, not Chinese.

Whatever.

"No," Ahgo said.

"Hmm. Well, I'm sure you'll figure it out," Nythan said. "That's all, thank you both."

Devin bowed, and the two men left Nythan.

Sanhetuan will eat that stuff up, but you'll still have to prove who you are.

Nythan hiked his eyebrows. *I've no doubt. But I'm going for bonus points here.*

CHAPTER 70
NET OF STONES

The plane set down at the Hong Kong International Airport.

Nythan jumped out of his seat. *Do we have anything we can go off of to find these guys?*

Yes. It'll be a simple matter of traveling to a province that is a probable home to Sanhe.

So, no secret meeting place or contact…not even a phone number?

If Sanhe were so effortlessly found, they would not be Sanhe. Be patient. We'll find them, or they'll find us.

Where was this patience when you freaked out in Prague?

I didn't freak out. I just didn't appreciate our position.

"Clearly," Nythan muttered.

As Nythan approached the plane's exit door, Palaou handed him a surgical mask. Nythan suppressed unwarranted irritation toward his faithful servant.

"For the smog, my Lord," Palaou offered.

"Palaou, when did you even have time to get this?" Nythan marveled.

"I pride myself in anticipating all your needs and ensuring they are met."

Nythan smiled as he put the mask on and disembarked the aircraft. Even at dusk, the intensity of the smog dominated everything.

We need to be careful and act fast. The Chinese government doesn't have the same respect for civil liberties that the United States does, Nythan thought.

That's not so uncommon in the rest of the world either.

"Now what?" Nythan said aloud.

Now we go sightseeing. Blend in with all the tourists.

Most tourists don't have two dozen bodyguards.

We'll keep most of them here. They know what is expected of them. The Prey will conduct themselves accordingly. Let's go! Time's a-wastin'.

Nythan hurried off the tarmac and into a hanger, anxious to connect with Sanhe. He faced Palaou, wincing as he resisted a sudden urge to punch his devoted servant. Nythan chastised himself for his unacceptable thoughts. Palaou had done nothing to deserve the disdain Nythan felt toward him at that moment.

Don't worry about it. You're under significant stress.

"Where to next?" Nythan asked Palaou. Palaou froze.

"You mean you don't know? I thought it was *your* job to make all the arrangements," Nythan chided. As Palaou dug into his bag and pulled out the group's itinerary, Nythan squeezed Palaou's arm.

Easy there.

"I'm kidding," Nythan added, but he didn't believe his own words.

Palaou breathed a deep sigh of relief, rubbing his eyes.

"Have you met a Sanhe before?" Nythan asked.

"No, my Lord," Palaou replied. "I'm not aware of anyone else having met one either."

Go to the Fujian province in southeast China, specifically, a coastal city called Quánzhōu. We'll likely find Sanhe there.

Nythan scanned the hangar. *Why that place?*

Quánzhōu is a reasonable place to start because it was an important part of Sanhe's early success as traveling merchants along the Silk Road.

Nythan shrugged. *Any particular location?*

No idea, but let's start with the wéiqí tables.

What is wéiqí?

A very, very old board game. Sometimes Sanhe players would identify themselves by tiling a dragon's body part in wéiqí. Maybe we'll get lucky and play against someone who initiates it.

Are you sure you want to rely on luck?

Do you have a better idea?

Uh…no, no I don't.

Quánzhōu it is.

Since no one would mistake them for being Chinese, Nythan directed the Prey to dress the part of tourists. Palaou wore oversized orange sunshades and carried an older-model camera he bought in a merchant shop.

Nythan and his entourage stuck to busy main roads, trying to draw as little attention to their caravan of cars as possible. Upon arrival in Quánzhōu, they wasted no time in finding a cheap hotel, where Nythan left the Prey while he and Palaou set out walking in the heart of the city. Bane began directing Nythan to places where they might encounter a Sanhe presence. Along the way, they passed extraordinary displays of Christmas decorations along the streets and in the shop windows—trimmed trees, inflatable snowmen, festive ornaments, and colorful lights.

I never imagined Christmas was so popular in China, Nythan thought.

Not everywhere, but here *it is.*

Nythan glanced at a Prey who was dressed more like he belonged on a Hawaiian beach on a windy day. Trying to reconcile this appearance against the masked menace of a typical Prey made Nythan burst out in laughter. The Prey jerked his attention to Nythan, and the man's obvious discomfort and insecurity only made Nythan laugh harder.

They're not used to being in situations out of their control. I hope none of them break on us.

I'm sure they'll be fine.

Stronger people have broken before. Don't assume. Just be ready.

Nythan scowled as he entered what Bane described as a teahouse. The teahouse was a quaint yet sizable establishment. He walked through several rooms full of people playing various games. Some played with domino tiles, while others played with chess-like pieces, but most played wéiqí. Almost all were elderly men.

Nythan saw one such man seated at an open table nearby, calmly people-watching as he sipped his tea. Nythan approached the table and bowed to the elder as Bane had recommended. When the man gazed up at him, Nythan took the open seat and grabbed a small plastic tray full of white pebbles; his opponent took the black tray.

Nythan peered around and spied Palaou not far away, ordering a cup of tea. The man across from Nythan coughed, bending his head down. A black stone already rested in the middle of the board.

I've no idea how to play this game, Nythan laughed.

I'll tell you where to put the stones. Put the first one three points to the left.

Nythan did as instructed, trying to follow Bane's suggestions as meticulously as he could. Nythan couldn't comprehend how the pieces moved or why only some got taken off the board. It appeared terribly one-sided, as Nythan took zero black pebbles. Bane told Nythan they were attempting to construct a dragon wing with the white stones when it was their turn to put one on the board. However, with the old man capturing his pieces, the configuration of pebbles seemed more like a disfigured pair of glasses.

After his loss at the hands of the elder, Nythan went on to play people of various skill levels. No matter their proficiency, Nythan lost to each of them, with Bane mostly concerning himself with outlining a dragon with the pebbles rather than actually devising a winning strategy. After a few hours of one humiliating defeat after another, Bane decided that Nythan could forego the attempt at signaling a Sanhe player.

Okay, let's try a few more games, and this time we play for real.

About time, Nythan thought. After a couple dozen games, Nythan understood wéiqí a little better. The objective was to encircle your opponent and end up with more stones than the other player. But the first match ended in abysmal defeat, and Nythan's irritation grew. He couldn't tell how the other players always avoided being encircled, while still finding a way to take all of his pieces. His second game only made him angrier, even though he managed to capture way more pieces than he had in the last game.

It's been a while since I have played this game.

This game is pointless as hell, Nythan thought, scowling at the board.

It requires patience and careful planning.

Then we shouldn't have a problem because that's literally the Raptor's motto.

I'm making amateur mistakes.

Well, stop it then. You're supposed to be this immortal being of infinite wisdom, and you let this old geezer beat us?

Oh, stop it, you little child. Put the stones where I tell you.

A few moves later, his opponent rose and bowed, then walked away. Nythan huffed. *Where's he going?*

There is no way we can win at this point. He's helping us save face.

Damn this stupid game, Nythan thought. He gripped the wooden table with his fingernails, grinding small half-moons into it.

You won't be able to figure it out in one day. Wéiqí takes years to understand and a lifetime to master.

Whatever. Now, what do we do?

Let's leave and go back to our hotel. I'd call today a success.

Nythan threw his head back, mouth agape at the ceiling. *A success? We made contact with nobody.*

I told you Sanhe would be different. There are no standard procedures to abide, no overly secretive gathering places. Everything here is subtle and indirect. You would do well to learn our ways.

Our ways?

Yes. Remember when I told you about my time as a Zhōu emperor?

Ah, yes, I remember.

Nythan exited the teahouse and walked toward the hotel under a starry night. As usual, he didn't feel tired, but he was starting to feel a little hungry.

It's an instinctive hunger at this point. We had a huge meal the other day, so we can safely ignore the feeling for a time.

Nythan walked into the lobby of his hotel. In the fixtures above, dragon sculptures and etched-leaf patterns ran across the ceiling molding. The spaced columns had a maroon hue, and the acanthus at the top and bottom of the pillars were forged out of gold. The chandeliers glowed a lightish orange.

"Good evening," the receptionist called. Nythan warmly greeted the receptionist as he ascended the stairs with Palaou not far behind.

From the balcony of his room, Nythan peered into the night. Although his view angled into the city, Nythan could see an extensive line of mountains far in the distance.

Ahhh, home sweet home.

So I'm going to guess that you identify with your Asian lives the most? Nythan asked.

You could say that, yes.

Nythan continued to scan the dusk skyline. He listened to the myriad of sounds around him, both near and far. Amid all the activity, Nythan sought after the emotions being emitted from those closest him. There were so many of both he couldn't even estimate their number. The most interesting feelings came from the sleeping guests in the hotel. Many exuded fear, which he figured to be nightmares. Some felt warm, others didn't seem troubled at all, and a number didn't understand what they dreamt. One projected intense lust. Wading through the plethora of emotions made him feel powerful and in control. He realized that tapping into those feelings relaxed him. It reminded him of the peace that came to him when walking down Daytona Beach at midnight during his initial turbulent familiarization with Bane.

His mind made the sudden connection—the night stars, the light breeze, the glint of the moonlight on the sea, and then the ocean of vibrant emotions.

"It's all linked," he whispered.

His senses vibrated, and he felt loose as if being held together by a thread.

Now you are truly living. Take enough steps back from life and you see that even the chaos has order to it. Step too close and you find it all appears like anarchy in need of structure. Those who genuinely understand are in a position to perceive both and see how the two relate. You will feel as though you are being torn in two different directions. This is normal. It's like walking on a tightrope. If you were to fall, you'd realize you were only two inches from the ground and there was no necessity for you to walk across on the rope in the first place.

Nythan exhaled. *That's scary.*

Welcome to enlightenment.

CHAPTER 71

HARMONY OF EMOTION

Nythan spent half a week going to different teahouses in the city to play wéiqí. And by playing, what Nythan really did was get crushed by every opponent he played, because Bane insisted they draw a damn dragon made of pebbles. He no longer needed Bane to tell him where to place the stones. Because he'd done the dragon outlines so many times, he'd committed them to memory.

Nythan started a game with a young woman wearing oversized glasses and hair to her ears. He set down the majority of the shape without her destroying his effort. Given the trend of all his previous games, this one was not following a predictable pattern. Occasionally, the woman would glance up and give him a puzzled expression. Nythan gave up trying to figure out why she didn't decimate him like all his other opponents had.

Uh…where do I put the next stone? We've never gotten this far on the wing shape, Nythan thought.

Hahahaha, two up from the upper leftmost stone.

Nythan set his white pebble down. For some reason he couldn't explain, his match drew a multitude of observers. They peered at the board, a number of them clearly amused. If someone understood what to look for, it wouldn't be hard to distinguish the pointed wing outline. Except that the average person only witnessed a rather comical display of amateurism.

A couple of moves before Nythan finished the shape, the woman started wreaking havoc on his position. Within ten rounds, she captured eighty percent of his stones. The game's observers went from bemusement to outright hilarity as they watched Nythan's catastrophe unfold.

No matter. There's a good possibility that we've caught the right person's attention by now.

Feels like a ginormous failure, Nythan thought, hiding the urge to pout. He had grown attached to his winged pattern.

Always look at the big picture. It'll keep the day-to-day in proper focus. You have done well, very well. Let them all have their laughs. It serves our purpose in the end.

Nythan gave his former adversary a long look, then smiled. "*Xièxie.*" He reached across the board and shook her hand.

She gave him a broad grin as she walked away.

You think we did it? Nythan asked.

I hope so. It's been three days of nonstop wéiqí in all the game houses we could find. If we haven't garnered the right attention by now, we could be here for a long time. It will *be worth it in the end.*

Uh huh.

"My lord, shall we depart?" Palaou whispered. Nythan nodded, concealing more undeserved anger toward Palaou.

They made their way to the hotel, and Nythan once again greeted the receptionist as he crossed the lobby. Outside his room, he bade goodnight to Palaou and the Prey. He then entered his room and made for the shower, his muscles reacting to the exhaustive effects of not satisfying Bane's hunger.

Nythan's body tensed without warning.

Wait.

He halted, standing alert.

Go back into the main room.

Nythan crept through the bathroom and into the bedroom area.

The table…look at the table.

On the table, next to the TV, sat a small wéiqí board with two stone trays.

They found us.

Nythan stared at the board, then peered around the room, scrutinizing his surroundings. Only then did he relax.

It's a game. They want you to play, so play. Set the first piece down.

Nythan looked at the pieces. *And then what?*

We wait.

CHAPTER 72

HARMONY OF SOLUTION

Nythan's anticipation grew with each passing day. He continued to play wéiqí in the teahouses, while the real game unfolded in his hotel room. Each time Nythan made a move and came back to his suite later in the day, Sanhe had secretly made a move of their own. By day four of Sanhe's shrouded test, Nythan had grown impatient. He looked down at a wéiqí board with few empty spots, then probed his surroundings and reached out around the hotel room.

No one except Palaou bothered him about the repeat visits to the hotel. Palaou inquired into Nythan's thoughts, trying to find ways to help. Nythan made sure to voice that everything was progressing according to plan while repressing the urge to yell at Palaou to leave him alone.

When he sensed no one else except Palaou and the Prey, Nythan brought his hands up and let them slap his thighs. *Now what?*

We do the same thing as yesterday and we keep an eye out for whatever is next to come.

Does whatever ever *come next? Why can't we tell Palaou? Get the Prey to help us.*

We need Sanhe's full cooperation. The more we force this, the longer it'll take.

Nythan crossed his arms. *Well how much longer is it going to take? We* made a dragon face and only have three more pebbles left. *You said they found us, why hasn't anything happened by now?*

It'll take as long as it takes.

"My Lord," Palaou called out from the doorway. "Do you require assistance?"

Nythan's ground his teeth together and repressed the urge to yell. "Palaou, I know you're just trying to help. Everything is going according to plan. I need you to leave me alone."

Palaou bowed low, then turned heel and disappeared.

You shouldn't take your anger out on him like that. It isn't his fault your plan failed.

Nythan put his hands on his hips. He surveyed the wéiqí board again, then gazed out the window. *Do you think we passed?*

I'm sure we did well enough to warrant the next step.

Having not much else to do, Nythan sat on his bed and communed with Bane's presence. He enjoyed intertwining his spirit with that of Bane's. He *saw* again the radiant array of dazzling color Bane had first shown him inside the Indian monastery. Nythan sensed the restraint Bane was exercising to suppress kernels of unquenchable thirst.

I know, Nythan thought. *We'll find something soon.*

Let's hope so. I'm starving here.

We could always ask one of the Prey, Nythan suggested.

Might have to if this keeps on much longer.

At sunrise the next morning, Nythan made his way to the lobby area. He didn't even need Bane to stop him as he reached the bottom of the stairs. Staring at the reception desk, Nythan spied a newly set wéiqí board resting on the counter.

Nythan wanted to jump for joy. *Please oh PLEASE be the final test.*

I have a good feeling about this one. Get the Prey down here with us.

Nythan looked back at Palaou. "Go get the others."

Palaou went wide-eyed, then dashed off.

Nythan put on a warm expression and approached the counter. He found no trays with stones. The attendant looked at him, and Nythan stared back, glancing at the wéiqí board several times. After an awkward minute of gawking at one another, the attendant went into an office behind the counter and returned with an ancient-looking man carrying a bin of black and white pebbles. After setting them down on the tabletop, the elder peered at him.

Nythan retrieved a handful of black stones and placed one on a point. The elderly man's hands trembled as he set a white piece as well, and the match began. Nythan wasted no time drawing a dragon wing. At about the fifth turn, the elder began capturing his pieces. Nythan's frustration grew the further the game progressed.

When Nythan was thoroughly beaten, he cleared the stones from the wéiqí board. The old man set the first stone on the board and Nythan began drawing another pattern. The old man observed Nythan with strange eyes and let him place stones without seizing any.

Finally.

This wéiqí board had double the number of spots than the miniature one in his room, which allowed Nythan to draw a full dragon face. Once the table couldn't hold any more, the elder removed his pebbles from the board and looked up. Nythan took his time removing his stones, doing his best to play along with what he thought the old man wanted. All the while, the receptionist paid them no attention. Palaou waited next to Nythan; the Prey dispersed nearby.

The elder set another piece on the table. It became evident within the first ten moves that the elder meant to play the game as intended, and Bane decided to indulge him. With Bane's assistance, Nythan fought a contentious match but lost to the more experienced wéiqí player. At the conclusion of the game, the elder left the counter and proceeded into the office.

Nythan watched the man leave. *Is this it?*

Bane didn't respond.

Palaou coughed, then coughed louder. Nythan glanced at him with a great deal of annoyance before following Palaou's gaze. Ten meters away, Nythan spied an ajar door where the elder peeped through the crack. The elder disappeared from view after Nythan made eye contact with him.

There's your answer. Keep your calm. Sanhe tend to be more theatrical. Pointing guns, dancing around you with swords, pretending you don't exist, repeating the same thing over and over. It's all a test.

Nythan approached the door, hesitating at the handle. He turned to Palaou, who began shaking his head in earnest.

"My Lord, I can be of much more service if I stay with you," Palaou pled.

"Yes, you can, Palaou. You all are still coming with me. However, I know these people well. Whatever happens, I don't care what it looks like, *do not* act unless I tell you to. Ensure the Prey understand. I don't care if one of these Sanhe characters points a gun at me, do absolutely nothing," Nythan commanded. He swiveled around, only to rotate back. "And one more thing, I want you and the Prey to keep close."

Palaou bowed, then relayed his message to the Prey. Without their masks, Nythan could read their facial expressions. Some appeared disappointed, but they all seemed intent on complying.

Good, don't need them doing anything rash. I was serious when I said that Sanhe may actually point a gun at your face or perhaps pretend to stab you. They can get overly dramatic like that.

Alright, let's do it, Nythan thought.

He opened the door and stepped through, Palaou and the Prey close behind.

CHAPTER 73

HARMONY OF EFFORT

The elder led Nythan and his robust entourage through a small section of back alleys and side streets. They arrived at a secluded triangular garden about fifty yards wide, situated in the space created by three buildings meeting at their respective corners. The musty gray windowless sides extended straight up, creating an imposing prism of light shining through the glass roof. Small fountains, hedges, plants, flowers, and fire lamps littered the area. In dead center was a monastic building made of wood with dragon carvings all over.

The Chinese believe themselves to be descendants of the dragon.

Nythan stood and admired the scenery. *Don't tell me...that dragon was you.*

In a manner of speaking. I played a role in its development.

You were the dragon?

Not literally, but in a way I was. I helped transform it into a symbol of culture by keeping the spirit alive.

I don't get it.

The aged man continued along a direct path toward the wooden building. Nythan instead went left, proceeding through the greenery, letting his hand graze foliage as he passed. He felt in no particular hurry to reach the temple, instead choosing paths that wound to the middle.

It's difficult for an outsider to understand. You'd have to understand what role tian *and* lóng *play here. I could explain it to you, but it would be like explaining where the trunk of an oak tree ends and its branches begin.*

Nythan's fingers weaved through the foliage. *We're walking aimlessly through a garden, so now's your chance.*

Well... lóng *means dragon. This is a sign of Chinese culture. The dragon is the sign of China. It's distinguished, but it's not like the American eagle, which represents bravery and strength. Tian means heaven. Heaven tells you what's right and what's wrong. The culture also tells you right and wrong. Since culture is also representative of the dragon, it's technically true that the dragon tells right and wrong. However, it wouldn't be correct to say this.*

You're losing me.

I figured. Think of it another way. It would be like me asking: "Can we talk after this?" You'd answer: "Yes," which is a cultural or heavenly answer. You wouldn't answer: "Confirmed," which is a dragon answer.

But you said the dragon is both China and Chinese culture. How can heaven and culture tell you what's right or wrong, but not China?

Like I said...like trying to explain an oak tree.

Okay, let's get to what you *did.*

In this land, culture is passed from one generation to the next. Culture doesn't change. I returned here as much as I could after my second life. I was the unchanging spirit that kept Chinese culture the same. Coming back... generation after generation. I passed from life to life, telling the people stories of their heritage and influencing the law where I could. So, in that way, I was the *dragon.*

And that's how you transformed the dragon into a symbol of culture...by coming back to China?

Yes, that's how.

How do you do that?

I blend with a new person and make my way back.

Yeah...but...with us, I did everything. You just *watched and gave me advice. Remember when you told me that some fought you tooth and nail? What happened to them?*

They died.

I gathered that. How'd they die?

Bane's silence formed a pit in Nythan's stomach.

Bane, Nythan pressed. *What happened to them?*

Bane didn't answer. Finally, he said, *I let them die.*

Nythan stopped walking.

"You stopped taking in souls, didn't you?" Nythan whispered.

Yes.

"They starved!" Nythan remembered the rice he had vomited up back in India. "Their bodies refused food. You refused souls."

A pressure formed in Nythan's right eardrum as he felt Bane's silent confession.

Nythan's breathing got shaky. *Was it...the one...that woman you were in for thirty-two years?*

No, hers was a special case. She never took a soul for her body to start the transition. At twenty-two, she and I made a deal—like the deal you and I made in India—except she won and I honored my end of the bargain. Never bothered her again, and she accepted the consequences. Her body broke down, despair consumed her, and she committed suicide the day after her thirty-second birthday.

Nythan let his finger trace and retrace the skeleton of a large leaf hanging down at eye level.

What do you think about that?

Nythan shrugged. *I can't help but think what you would have done if I had kept resisting.*

I wouldn't have had to do *anything. We had two souls under our belt and your body was in the process of abandoning its need for food as fast as possible. The accelerated transition would have killed you in a matter of weeks if you hadn't kept taking in souls.*

You seemed pretty indifferent toward me when you first revealed yourself, Nythan pointed out. *I don't think you cared if I lived or died.*

I'm speaking from the heart, if I still had one. I wanted you to accept. I didn't want you to die.

Nythan said nothing further and stopped at the bottom step of the building. The simple wooden construct stood in stark contrast to the larger steel architecture encasing the whole area. He ascended to the top next to orb lanterns and was surprised to find that the stairway immediately descended to a bottom space the size of a small bedroom. The entire structure was a set of symmetrical stairs going up and down. The elderly man stood in that bottom space with a figure robed in all black, its face wrapped so only the eyes showed.

Nythan got a feeling of déjà vu as he made his way down the steps; the setting reminded him of his first introduction to the female monk in India.

As he got to the bottom, the old man pressed the knuckles of one hand into the opposite palm, bowing his head. Nythan sat down cross-legged.

"Greetings, Dragon," the robed one said. The voice sounded distorted. He or she made the same gesture as the old man.

Do what they did.

Nythan imitated the gesture. He experienced an extraordinary feeling of tranquility within both the old man and the robed monk that calmed his mind.

"Your energy," the Sanhe monk said, gesturing toward the elderly man. The elder inched forward, again making the same fist-to-hand motion.

Eat.

Nythan imitated the sign, instantly rejuvenated as he took the old man's soul.

"We welcome you, Dragon."

After minutes of silence between them, Nythan pursed his lips. *Isn't something supposed to happen now?*

Read her emotion. She's waiting for you to tell her what to do.

She? Nythan thought, confused.

Feel her.

Nythan probed the monk's emotions, discovering an agreeable sentiment that left a distinctly feminine imprint.

How come I didn't notice it was a woman? Nythan asked, surprised that Bane had recognized what he hadn't.

Because you assumed it was a man and didn't pay attention.

Okay, so she's open to whatever comes next. What does *come next?*

Don't play dumb. Do what we came here to do.

Nythan shivered.

Say it.

"I need to grow stronger while I hide," Nythan said aloud.

Use the word energy. That's the way they see you.

"I need to be energy."

No, doofus. *You're* already *energy. You need* more.

Well just say that next time, Nythan snapped silently. He chose not to correct himself.

"How much energy do you require?"

"All of it," Nythan replied. "Can you handle that?"

"We can offer you all the energy you desire."

"Good. How soon?"

Don't act so impatient.

We are *impatient,* Nythan reminded Bane.

Calm down. We're here. They'll get the message.

"Please come," the monk said and stood. She turned and bent down, roaming her hand under the lip of one of the steps. The stairs made a *snap* sound, followed by a creaking motion as a small section of stairs in front of her gave way, revealing a dark tunnel as it slid to the side. She twisted her body and pointed to one of the orb lanterns Nythan had passed on his way down. He let out a grunt as he trudged up the stairs to pick one lantern and peered across the outside garden.

"Hey!" he called out. Several Prey came rushing forward. Nythan pointed at different sources of light emanating from the garden. "Grab some lamps, then follow me."

Nythan returned down the stairs with the Prey in tow to where the Sanhe monk waited. She took the light and proceeded down a flight of stairs into an underground passage, using the lantern to light her way.

CHAPTER 74

天

Nythan hadn't the slightest clue where they were or how far they had traveled, but an avalanche of emotions assaulted him from above as he walked below countless people going about daily life. He even detected enough to know when they resided on separate floors.

His guide came to a stop and ascended a ladder, one of many such ladders they had passed along their underground route. Nythan climbed and emerged from the tunnel into what seemed to be a small wooden closet in an unfurnished room; his guide was nowhere to be found. He waited for Palaou and the Prey to come up before walking out of the room into a long, darkened hallway. At the far end, he could see a brightly lit room and walked toward it. He passed small rooms with multi-colored fabrics draped at their entrances.

So dramatic, Nythan thought.

Use your senses.

Oh yeah. Nythan reached out for signs of life and sensed a gathering in the space ahead of him. The gathering exuded something different from the people he had walked beneath. He sensed their invigoration.

He exited the hallway and took a step-down into a spacious wooden assembly hall. It housed such a large number of mirrors that Nythan saw his reflection in every direction he looked. Nythan motioned for Palaou and the Prey to remain at the room's threshold as a thousand Nythans advanced to join what he guessed were a cluster of sitting Sanhe deep in meditation. Above them hung a collection of disco balls, which created dazzling glints in the mirrors. The monks sat with their backs to him, facing a colossal statue of a white Hydra.

That's me, no doubt. Go sit down in front of them, facing the statue.

Nythan moved through the group to the front of the congregation. They made so little noise or movement he had to stare at each of them to convince himself they were real. The monks kept their eyes closed, choosing not to acknowledge him. Nythan sat himself at the front of the assembly facing the statue.

Close your eyes and meditate with me.

Nythan did so. He made his best effort to be mindful, as his teacher, the female monk from the Indian monastery, had taught him. He made himself a mirror, neither resisting nor holding on to the thoughts that flowed through him. Nythan gradually overcame his impatience and rested, losing all track of time.

Relax. We're in like Flynn, as they say.

At last, a voice spoke from behind Nythan.

"Shénlóng."

CHAPTER 75

MINDFULNESS

Nythan spun around. The Sanhe monks, or whatever they were, refused to look at or speak to him. Nythan couldn't tell which one had spoken.

"Uh, yes?" Nythan said, looking from face to face.

No response.

Shaking his head, he turned back. *What'd he say?*

It means dragon god. *It's their name for me.*

"*Shénlóng,*" another voice said. This one came from the left.

Nythan whipped to face them. "What? Yes. I'm right here." He again regarded each person, trying to determine who had spoken the words. He waited for a good two minutes, then swiveled to face the statue with a final huff of frustration.

I thought they were done playing games, Nythan thought.

It's not a game to them. It's a phase of tests.

"*Shénlóng,*" another voice said. This one sounded like it came from just behind him.

Nythan didn't bother to turn. *Well then, what's the game this time?*

Lemme think.

Nythan took in the white Hydra in front of him. Heads of various shapes and sizes protruded out of its long neck. The center head resembled a T. rex with crystal blue orbs for eyes. Its mouth was frozen in a ferocious baring of teeth and tongue. He didn't see eyes on any of the other heads, but he did take note of how each seemed to mimic a different emotion—fear, anger, hurt, happiness, and surprise.

"*Shénlóng,*" another voice said, from a different direction this time.

Nythan huffed. *Anything yet?*

I have a few ideas. Sit tight.

Nythan's train of thought slowed as he waited for Bane to work through the problem. Still seated, he rotated his body to face the group of settled Sanhe. Palaou and the Prey observed him from the far end of the room. He reached out and inspected the emotions of all Sanhe before him. He detected a mixture of peace, excitement, and pessimism. Some didn't want to be there; others mourned an unnamed loss.

"*Shénlóng,*" a Sanhe monk said just to the right of him, though the man's eyes remained closed like the rest.

They're not trying to talk to us, Nythan thought. *They're just saying the word.*

I know.

Nythan felt something build within him right before it happened. He couldn't help but be excited as his body experienced a familiar vibration and flood of warmth surging forth. Interweaving threads of dazzling color erupted from his pores. The colors resembled the same hazy shimmer of hues that the monks in the Indian monastery had witnessed after his teacher's sacrifice. Whereas that first time he couldn't see through the display of hues at all, Nythan had learned to trace the outline of people not five feet from him.

He marveled at the intensity of the colors. *It's different this time.*

We're more powerful.

A glimmer overhead made Nythan peer upward. Infinite tiny sparkles of bent light shined through the mist like a prism. The disco squares above deflected the light. He scanned the air around him, his gaze resting on the twin twinkles piercing the fog on the Hydra's main face.

How clever of them. Those orbs were meant for us.

Nythan smirked. *I guess that's pretty cool. Any other tricks like that up your sleeve?*

Just one, but only as a last resort.

Might as well add it to the show then.

I could, but like my refusing souls, it wouldn't be healthy for you if I did.

Nythan mulled over the ambiguous response and chose to let it go.

This is kind of off topic and all, but it only just came to me, Nythan thought. *Why'd you call me* wretch *in the beginning?*

More theatrics. You're the dramatic type. I needed to make a bit of a display to get my point across. Similar to when I made you believe I was Shiva.

Ah. Okay. Well, on another note. These're souls, yeah?

Not the stuff you see here, no. It's more like a flashlight. The souls are the double-A batteries. What you see here is the light coming from a focus of attention on all that power.

I don't get it.

No big deal. Watch and enjoy the show.

The beams of light began bending and moving. It started slowly, then sped up. The colors became entangled as if arguing with one another, whipping around as they danced in the cloud. Nythan experienced an odd sensation, then realized it was Bane smiling at him.

Feels good? Nythan thought.

Oh, yeah.

Is this something I can do?

'Fraid not.

Nythan continued watching the show unfold. He recalled his conversation with his teacher from India when she had asked what he thought had happened to the first souls he had received. At the time, he hadn't wanted to dwell on it, but suddenly the answer came to him.

They never left.

Nythan closed his eyes. *Can I talk to them?*

No, it doesn't work like that. It's like a bowl of fruit punch. Once you add a flavor to the mix, it becomes a part of the whole.

He mulled over Bane's words. *So, like adding something new to fruit punch changes the look and flavor, am I changed at all?*

Nythan felt Bane's surprise.

Why yes. That's it. You're still you, but all those souls you took are a part of you now. You've benefited from each of them.

A smile crept across Nythan's face, then froze still. *Wait. Did I get any of the bad stuff?*

Nythan sensed Bane's hesitation. His shoulders slumped. *What else did I get from their souls?*

Not too much.

Tell me the truth, Bane, damn it.

Bane sighed. *Mannerisms, quirks, personality things. All manageable.*

Bane, I must have at least a thousand souls by now, he thought, growing terrified. *Most of them are Unas. They were* not *good people. How much of that becomes a part of me?*

They're already *a part of you. All of them. You're still you, though. You can feel it.*

Yeah. I still feel me. But I also feel this giant...pit. It's disturbing. I look at Palaou and half of me wants to take him out. That's not *like me.*

It's always you, Nythan. It was never not *you. There's just* more *of you now. These other souls may be emphasizing different things, but they don't influence anything that isn't naturally there. It's a part of being human.*

Grief welled inside Nythan. *I don't want to be a bad person,* he sobbed in silence. His emotional reaction surprised him. The colors in the fog stopped moving.

You're not a bad person, Nythan.

What do I do?

His hands hid his face so no one could see him so upset. Not that anyone *could* see him through the fog.

We do the same thing we've been doing. I see the finish line right in front of us. There's one last lesson that Sanhe will help us get through.

Nythan used his forearm to wipe his nose. *What's that?*

It's called wú wéi. *It means non-action.*

What's that?

Best to let Sanhe describe it to you. There's more that goes along with it.

Fine, Nythan thought, frustrated. *Let's just go get it already.*

Don't worry Nythan, we're fine.

I don't feel fine.

You won't have to wait much longer. I have a feeling it'll be over soon.

CHAPTER 76
A MIGHTY ROAR

Nythan sat among a group of Sanhe in the dragon-mirror hall, trying to contain his impatience. He didn't see the monk who had accompanied him and had yet to get the others to talk. Whenever he tried to engage them in conversation, they only smiled and nodded. Not quite the warm welcome he had expected.

Nythan's Watwa memories of how to be mindful still instructed him, so he played along for the time being.

These monks don't seem keen on teaching me anything, Nythan thought.

One of them will teach you.

What's it that they're going to show me?

It's something related to natural action. It means that you don't do anything, and you don't not *do anything. It's kind of like when athletes are in the zone, or when your heart beats.*

So then how do we get to that?

We wait.

Palaou came and stood beside Nythan. "My Lord," he squeaked, staring at the ground as his trembling hand held out a tablet. On it was a news article.

"American Teen is Person of Interest in Violent Cult War." Wrath's pixelated face from the video was plastered next to his.

SH**************************T!

Nythan's heart sank as he digested the article. All the attention-grabbing keywords, like *evil, massacre, rape,* and *cult,* had made their way into the gut-wrenching story. It linked him to a litany of horrible things: the murder of multiple families in Staten Island; the execution of the Freemasons in Texas; the deaths of two police officers in Bellaire; and the *gang bloodbath* in Prague. Throughout the article, three videos were referenced, causing Nythan exponential dread as he reached the end. Nythan clicked on a link for the first YouTube video, which showed him in conversation with the Gatekeeper in New York while subtitles faded in at the bottom.

"He said they *destroyed* the only copy," Nythan raged, digging his fingernails into the metal plate of the tablet. He jabbed a finger at the second video. It gave a front-row seat to Nythan's reaction to the Ordo Solis's surprise attack during the negotiation in Prague. He could see the souls racing past the camera and into his own body.

"That's not fair. They attacked *ME!*" Nythan shouted. A few Sanhe shot him curious looks.

His knuckle thwacked the thumbnail of the third video. The footage clearly came from that stupid bolo tie he had worn to spite the defeated Ordo Solis leader—the one he had thrown in the nearest dumpster after getting out of the Unas' tunnels. Although the camera's damaged lens showed only fragmented images, Nythan had no trouble recognizing the waves of silver mist spewing toward the camera from the horde of Unas. And no one watching would misunderstand the reality of a hundred dead bodies hitting the ground.

YOU IDIOT!

Nythan slapped his forehead. He remembered seeing the broken glass and camera lens split in two.

Your pride undid decades of hard work. This changes everything. We have to accelerate it all, right now.

Nythan's hands trembled as he perused related links. One article featured an introduction to the Raptors. The next one caught his eye as it contained a YouTube thumbnail showing a familiar enemy sitting on a stool in front of a crackling fireplace. Nythan couldn't miss recognizing the six-foot rotund frame even if he wanted to.

Nythan grimaced. *Steven.*

That fat bastard. Now *can we kill him?*

Just...hold on, Nythan urged, starting the video. The video opened with Steven looking down at the floor, a fireplace crackling behind him. Steven seemed to collect himself, then peered up at the camera.

"My name is Steven Carpenter. Lots of people gave their lives that I might sit here now and tell you something terrifying. And I wanna make sure their sacrifice wasn't in vain."

Steven took his time, taking in a massive breath of air. "Let's start from the beginning. There's a secret war that's been raging for thousands of years. My friends have died in this war. Thirty of them died this year alone. *I* was nearly the thirty-first. These aren't no-name people. They're American, German, Japanese, Chinese, British, fathers, mothers, children, politicians, businessmen and women. People like Jeff Fiddler, his wife Sara, and their daughter Trista, all savagely murdered with four other families in New Jersey. They violated Sara and those other women. They massacred those men in Texas. And through the years, they've slaughtered hundreds of people in Europe. I'm sure you've seen it in the news by now.

"Those responsible for this aren't some mythological bogeymen. They're criminal *scum* who worship a person bent on hurting you. I *need* you to understand the pain and suffering these lunatics have caused. Here in America, this cult is called the Raptors. In Europe, they're known as Unas. And in Asia, they're Sanhe. Each group works separate, but they all kill to worship the same person. That person is actually a *thing*, and that *thing's* name is the Soulstealer. And that's exactly what the Soulstealer does...it steals people's souls. It lives in someone while it does that. When its host dies, this parasite goes into another person. It's a hard thing to imagine until you've seen the death and suffering it's caused for generations. But you *will* see it if we don't act now."

"You can call it a demon, an evil spirit, Satan, or something straight out of a science fiction book or whatever else you want. But it's not fiction; it's just straight science. It doesn't take much searching to find all the buried history here. Search Google for *Bane*, *Yaoguai*, or *Dracula*. Read up on that. It'll get ya started. If you ever find yourself in disbelief, watch the below-linked videos again.

"But you won't need to rely on YouTube after you've experienced Nythan and his cult of killers. They hurt whoever they want, and *they don't care.* Join us in our fight against the Soulstealer. It's only a matter of time before you have to pick a side. *Join* us…and fight for the living."

Nythan gritted his teeth at Steven's frozen face as the video ended.

I can't believe you sacrificed our advantage like this. Over your damned sense of compassion. F*** you, Nythan.

Nythan clicked through the other articles. Most belonged in the tabloid sections; others reported on Nythan and the mass of Unas deaths in the Czech Republic. A couple of investigative pieces linked the Prey to the bloody aftermath with the Templars in Texas. Most, however, centered around Steven, his organization, and the European Union's now official hunt for the Unas. He accessed a front-page article from the Spiegel Online, titled, "How an EU Task Force Hunts for the Unas Cult."

He studied a photograph of Steven and another character shaking hands, surrounded by a bunch of people in suits.

The caption read: "EU representatives meet with the Ordo Solis. Shaking hands are SITF chief prosecutor, Dane Schwandt (left), and Ordo Solis leader, Steven Carpenter (right)."

The article explained how a European Union resolution passed earlier that morning had authorized a Task Force to investigate the Unas and that the Ordo Solis would work with the EU to support the investigation.

I'm not sure what to do, he thought.

It's time to start taking everything.

Nythan held up his hand. *Hold on, maybe it's not that bad…*

It's bad. At the very least, they'll confirm your involvement in the deaths of hundreds of people. If you're not assassinated before trial, you'll spend the rest of your life in a maximum-security prison.

Well shoot, Nythan thought. *What do we do?*

I already told you.

No, you didn't, he thought. *All you said was "start taking everything," which is terrible advice, by the way. What do we* actually *do?*

You're not ready.

Nythan slammed the ground. Stop *saying that. Spit it out!*

Wú wéi. That's the next step.

And why's that important?

Bane hesitated. Nythan could feel his uncertainty. *Because you're going to need to receive a* substantial *gift very soon. We're talking on a grand scale.*

What does that even look like? Nythan thought, putting a hand on his stomach.

It looks like the second coming, is what. Villages, cities, urban centers. We need them.

A lump formed in Nythan's throat.

No, he begged.

It's the only way.

It can't be. I can't. You're talking about genocide.

I'm talking about getting enough souls to ascend. It will require significant *sacrifice, and we have no more time to do this* our *way. That fat bastard saw to* that *when he posted those videos.*

No!

We have no choice. The world is hunting you and dismantling our support groups. When they figure out we came here, they will kill you. And if they kill you, I'll have to start from scratch and do this all over again. I need you *to understand what I'm trying to do here.*

Nythan slumped forward and fell to his knees with a *thud*, wiping away tears that had started streaming from his eyes.

I'm not a bad person, Nythan reassured himself.

No, you aren't. In fact, you're one of the better souls I've come across. I don't want to be doing this either. But if we don't, *the war will start* again. *And if it does, it'll destroy* both *sides. Everyone* will die. *Families will be ruined. But we can prevent it all with a small act, right now.*

Nythan didn't move or speak for half an hour. Palaou took the hint and remained quiet. None of the monks paid him any attention. Bane let him wallow in silence.

Finally, Nythan sat up and cleared his mind. *What do I do?*

We need to show Sanhe it's time to start. Focus on the one closest to you.

Nythan did so, following his rhythmic breathing.

Good. Now, carefully draw the soul out. Just a little bit.

Nythan tugged at the monk's soul ever so slightly. The monk's eyes flung open as he began coughing. The ethereal silver stream inched out.

Nythan felt an odd ripple sensation emanate from Bane as the monk's soul returned through his nostrils.

Nythan's eyes widened. *You stopped it!*

Yup.

I thought you couldn't do that! All this time you made it seem like you couldn't resist, Nythan accused.

It's not easy, but it's doable when I'm well-fed.

The monk peered at Nythan and beamed. *"Huānyíng, Shénlóng."*

Repeat after me, "Qǐng chuán shòu wǒ wú wéi."

Nythan repeated the phrase, butchering the pronunciation.

The monk nodded, then stood and uttered words Nythan didn't understand. The rest of the monks rose and began making their way out of the dragon-mirror hall. They smiled and gestured for Nythan to follow.

"What did you tell them?" Nythan whispered.

I told them to teach you wú wéi.

Chapter 77

WÚ WÉI

Nythan spent a great deal of time shifting from room to room and monk to monk, being shown stances and movements that reminded him of what he had learned in India. The Sanhe monks still declined to speak to him. They'd only smile and nod politely whenever he asked them a question.

At these times, Nythan would lose his patience faster than an ice cube melts in the heat of summer. *What do I say to them?*

I'm not sure what would help in this situation. They're trying to show you wú wéi.

Well then how come I'm not getting it? Nythan thought, clenching his teeth.

You're not paying attention, that's why. You don't need words to understand wú wéi. See how they're letting their hands roam? It's like water. Be like them.

I'm trying, Nythan whined. He kept messing up their movements, having to correct himself every few seconds.

Stop trying to mimic them. Move how you naturally feel.

That makes no sense. The point is for them to show me this thing. Why would I just randomly move my arms?

Because that's the exact point. Nature. Being natural. Similar to how your heart beats. How you breathe and blink your eyes. You don't know how you do it, you just do. So do it.

Nythan stared ahead with the blankest of expressions.

Do it.

He began weaving his arms from left to right, then right to left. *This's stupid.*

Shut up. Close your eyes and clear your mind.

Nythan's thoughts steadied as he kept his hands flowing in front of him. After what seemed like an hour, he dropped his hands and opened his eyes. The monks all still performed their movements, but they didn't synchronize with each other any longer.

At what point do I learn wú wéi? Nythan thought.

It just comes.

It's not coming.

You're in a rush. Slow down.

We are *in a rush, remember? You're the one who told me that.*

Bane started laughing. *You got me there. This is important enough to slow down.*

Tell me again what wú wéi means?

It means non-action. *Another way to say it is* non-forcing. *It's knowledge of the tide's pattern. Sailing, rather than rowing. Your heart beating is wú wéi. Your unconscious breathing is sailing. When you intentionally breathe, you're rowing.*

Why's this important?

Because receiving a gift from thousands of people is much *different than hundreds.*

Nythan's body froze. Bane waited him out. *What do I say to that?*

Remember when we were walking down that underground tunnel while following the monk? We felt the presence of all those people far above.

Yeah, Nythan acknowledged.

To handle a mass of people like that, you need to be able to ignore them and focus on the environment. It's almost like throwing a net into the water. You're going for the fish, but you're using the sinking net to get the fish.

Uh, okay.

Let's try it this way. Remember when we took the souls of the Worshipful Master and his lackey back in Europe? There were two other souls that we grabbed from the guys hiding underneath the table. You didn't mean to take those two crouched below, but they were a part of the same environment you used to get the Worshipful Master.

Like an area of effect? Nythan thought.

Yes, like an area effect.

What does this have to do with wú wéi?

Wú wéi is calming your mind enough to handle such a vast environment. This environment has too many variables. Your brain will get overwhelmed in an instant.

Fine. What do I do next?

First, we get the concept down. Then, we practice.

CHAPTER 78

BABY STEPS

Nythan got out of an old beat-up car and stretched his sore back. He found himself standing in a small village with a breathtaking view across a forested mountainside.

Wherever they were, it had taken them four days of non-stop driving. Palaou and the Prey had returned to Hong Kong, where Nythan ordered them to stay put until he came back. Three Sanhe monks traveled with him; they had dropped one off a half an hour ago in the previous town. The two remaining monks listened and did whatever Nythan asked, but they never verbally responded or made conversation.

They certainly have their own way of doing things, Nythan thought. He sorted through all the minute sounds of many hundreds of people busying themselves about their day.

The driver bowed and gestured toward a massive, white structure that looked like a fortress, sitting atop a hill. Nythan glanced over his shoulder at the other monk, arching his eyebrow.

"Am I supposed to..." Nythan said, letting out a frustrated sigh. "Are we going up there?"

Bane offered the translation.

One monk wobbled his head and arms, which Nythan assumed meant the monk agreed. Shrugging, Nythan proceeded along a steep, uneven path. He passed a group who were obviously tourists. Nythan, to Sanhe's credit, was dressed to fit in with a knee-length, robe-like cloth and a white scarf wrapped around his neck.

They entered the castle, and Nythan let himself be guided by the monks, who gently took hold of either side of him. As they advanced through the building, Nythan noticed an assortment of artifacts on display: statues, spears, clothing.

He came to a brief stop at an information placard. "Druk Desi, Tenzin Rabgye," Nythan read aloud.

Tenzin Rabgye was an ancient Bhutan ruler. Druk Desi was his title as ruler.

Did you know him? Nythan thought.

No, we were never acquainted. Bhutan is a country between China and India, where people are known for their archery skill. We must have left China and crossed into neighboring Bhutan.

Why did we come here?

Probably to avoid drawing attention.

Nythan continued walking forward as his Sanhe attendants nudged him left or right. They walked to the end of a hallway and into a dusty rectangular chamber with its exterior wall missing that overlooked the village. The monks broke away from Nythan and seated themselves, assuming a meditative posture.

Nythan stood still, looking across the village and forested hills below. *Now what?*

Need you even ask? You know what's about to happen.

Nythan shivered.

Don't get scared on me now. Everything has been building up to this.

I thought I had more time, Nythan protested.

So did I.

Nythan laid down. *How does this work?*

Bane expanded within him as if stretching. *We're going to incorporate the things we learned about wú wéi. Receiving souls like we're about to do is less about searching and closer to casting a wide net. You're going to throw that net and draw in what you can. Then repeat the process.*

Okay, how do I cast a net if I don't know what I'm searching for?

You do *know what you're searching for. When you were standing in front of the Unas, there wasn't a question about what you were after. If you had closed your eyes, you could still have done it. What we're here to do is cast that net so that it catches everything in the nooks and crannies of this town.*

Alright, what's first?

It's perspective. Keep that in mind. Souls travel the airway, which is to say they move through nonsolids, primarily empty space. That's all you need to make your withdrawal.

So, I don't need to see them.

Correct. That's only training wheels.

Nythan shut his eyes. *Yeah, so how do I grab someone far away?*

You need to relax and remember how your environment works. Your teacher at the ashram taught you how to calm yourself, and wú wéi showed you how your surroundings flow together. You already have the senses needed to reach far away.

So, when do I begin?

Begin now.

Just start doing it?

Yes. Sit up and face the opening. Open your eyes.

Nythan did so. He gazed across the landscape, seeing through the light fog to the forest floor. His enhanced vision perceived various wildlife: deer, squirrels, sheep, rabbits, wolves. Then he examined the scattered houses down below where people went about their lives.

Think about everything you see as one organism. One process.

Nythan quieted his mind, then recalled what the Sanhe monks had shown him.

"One organism," Nythan repeated aloud.

Now begin.

Nythan expanded his mouth, inhaling. Two souls rewarded his effort; the monks beside him slumped forward. Nythan sucked in until he about burst before pushing all the air back out.

"Oops," Nythan said, looking on either side of him to the motionless monks.

You're trying too hard. Don't be obtrusive to the process. You want to become *the process. It's like pouring water into a flowing stream and scooping some back out. Take advantage of what is already there.*

Nythan drew his eyebrows together. He closed his eyes, sensing for the breath of everything around the castle. The more still he became, the further his senses reached. The life of hundreds things from the village below started to reveal themselves. The small things, like bugs and rodents, he couldn't zero in on. He followed larger things like people and livestock more easily.

There's more, dig deeper.

Nythan relaxed further still, embracing a state of mindfulness. He let go of everything his brain thought it knew and pictured himself teetering on the edge of a cliff. The flicker of a larger life swirled into his consciousness. It took him a moment to realize that this flicker also blew into his face, traveled through his lungs, and gave him life. The things it made contact with—the trees, mountains, and buildings—exposed the life it contained.

Nythan felt a sudden wave of intense heat grow until it overwhelmed him, and he cradled himself in agony. The surge left as quickly as it came, leaving him breathless.

"What...was that?" Nythan gasped, blinking rapidly as if the sunset blinded him.

That was samadhi.

"It burns," Nythan said, unsure if *burn* described the assault he had just endured. He had definitely stumbled upon *something*, but words escaped him. "I don't understand what just happened."

You first saw wú wéi—the flow of life—which was what you detected in the animals and the wind. Then your senses attuned themselves to see samadhi. It's the awareness that everything has life, which you felt as a burning sensation.

But it felt like souls. As if the wind has a soul. The trees too, Nythan thought.

What makes you think they don't? They're a part of this world, same as you.

Nythan stared off into space. *Why couldn't I sense that before?*

Because you weren't listening.

So can I...take a tree's soul? It sounded like a ridiculous proposition.

No. It would be like trying to drink sand.

But I thought it was all a part of the same flow?

It's…complicated, Nythan. You can go outside and try to consume a tree's soul, or you can take my word for it that it doesn't work.

Okay, okay. What next? He thought, eyes widening.

You need to tap into that same flow of life again and act before samadhi comes for you. That's your time limit, every time.

But it—

Burns? Yes. What you felt was the essence of what creates life. Its border is nowhere and its center is everywhere. That's why you felt an intense wave you couldn't describe. It was literally everything *coming for you. No living thing survives an experience like that.*

"It looked white. It got to be so big I couldn't see anything else," Nythan protested.

That's because the essence is so powerful that it consumes all and leaves nothing. You only see what you see right now because your human senses aren't strong enough to survive perceiving what's really there instead. Some call it God, others call it samadhi. It has many different names.

You're saying it's God? Nythan thought.

I think so, although I've never heard it speak to me. I only know that it's there and is responsible for existence.

Why couldn't you've just told me that?

Because you wouldn't have understood it. It's like teaching a four-year-old how to do calculus.

Whatever. So, I have to do wú wéi, then I have to run before samadhi gets me. Sounds easy enough, Nythan thought.

We'll see.

Nythan relaxed as he had before. The familiar sensation of countless life-filled creatures returned as they existed in the flow of life. With his eyes closed, he *saw* a world of souls reveal itself as whitish silver shapes with bright centers. It took an ungodly amount of concentration for Nythan's *eye* to trace the general outline of each shape. He made out humans, animals, trees, even buckets.

Now draw them in. Breathe.

Nythan inhaled. He *saw* the souls leave their physical forms. As samadhi rushed toward him, Bane wrenched him back.

Whoa, Nythan thought. *What am I feeling?*

There's no way to explain it. Do it again.

Nythan's whole body shook with excitement. He struggled to still his mind once more. When he sensed the flow of life, he breathed three more times before samadhi came.

Again.

He did it again, and again, and again. He *saw* the hundreds of human souls journeying closer to him.

Again.

Nythan repeated the process once more and opened his eyes. He saw a silver stream wafting through the rectangular opening.

Go to it.

He shuffled to the edge and lapped at the soul in front of him. His eyes widened as he surveyed a dense silver mass covering the countryside, reminding him of the surging gray waves of the Atlantic Ocean.

Nythan scooted back, eager to resume his task. He found it difficult to concentrate, his mind too overwhelmed by the pilgrimage of souls outside.

Focus. Concentrate. Still your mind.

Nythan calmed himself enough to feel for the flow of life. He wasted no time drawing in souls as fast as he could manage before Bane pulled him from samadhi's wrath. Life began entering his body en masse. Nythan peeked once more and gaped at the haze of souls obscuring his vision. He couldn't make out anything beyond the floor he sat on.

Nythan again drew in all the souls he could find until, at last, the only life left in the sleepy town were trees and the wind.

CHAPTER 79

COMING OF AGE

Because he had accidentally taken the lives of his Sanhe attendants and didn't know what to do next, Nythan waited outside the castle next to the car until the third Sanhe made his way from the previous village and found Nythan. Without comment, the attendant drove him through the night.

This is ridiculous, why won't they talk to me? Nythan thought. He burped, blowing out silver mist.

I'm not a hundred percent sure. I do know that they aren't all monks. The ones you met are likely a symbolic gesture. I'm sure the others are watching closely.

Nythan stared out the front windshield of the old car as they sped toward a city with lots of buildings. The moonlight exposed the flat dry plains where the metropolis sat between two forested mountain ranges. They stopped at the end of a line of cars and finally inched up to a guard shack. The monk handed the guard two documents. The official inspected Nythan and his attendant, then gave the papers back and impatiently waved them through.

They drove for fifteen more minutes, deep into the heart of a crowded city. To Nythan, it resembled pictures of 1980s San Francisco.

What're we doing here?

You must first learn tactics before strategy. This is where you'll learn how to handle a big one.

A big one, as in lots of people?

Yes. Many thousands of souls. This time, we're going to do it faster.

They came to a stop along the curb in front of what looked like a strip mall hugging the street.

Nythan gestured at it. *Is this it?*

I don't know where we're going.

Nythan laughed. He regarded his Sanhe friend, who imitated him. Nythan jerked his thumb toward the strip mall.

"Is this it?" he asked the monk.

Translate, Nythan thought. Nythan spoke Bane's translation.

The monk grinned and nodded.

Nythan got out of the car. He made an *after-you* gesture toward the mall, letting the monk take the lead. They entered a gift shop full of wooden toys and gadgets. The man inside, who Nythan assumed owned the store, came to greet them. The proprietor exchanged pleasantries with the monk while stealing occasional glances at Nythan.

They then bowed toward one another, and the monk beckoned to Nythan as he went into the back of the shop. Nythan followed and immediately came to a staircase. He climbed not one, not two, but five flights of stairs and found himself in a glass greenhouse on the top floor of the strip mall. A full moon shone through the crystal-clear panels.

This is it. Sit down and let's begin.

Nythan seated himself, calming his mind enough to enter the flow of life. Instead of finding hundreds of living things like last time, he found *thousands.*

Take it easy. It'll be much easier to draw in life this time. There's less to get in the way. The problem will be the intake tube. Your capacity. There are at least twenty thousand souls here.

Nythan's mouth twitched. *Twenty?*

Take a deep breath and go.

Nythan settled in and felt for the flow of life. He began inhaling, but no souls heeded his call. Bane pulled him out as samadhi came.

Why didn't they come? Nythan asked.

Something is blocking you. Open your eyes.

Nythan surveyed the area.

The glass. It's fully enclosed, blocking your attempt to interact with anything on the other side. We need to either open the glass panels or get outside of it.

Is it just a glass thing?

No. Anything strong enough to restrict the airway can keep you from taking a soul.

Wait, Nythan thought. He recalled the battle in Prague when he took the souls of the Ordo Solis. *I thought it was because I focused on getting the souls of those Ordo Solis guards.*

No, remember when you unintentionally took the two souls hiding beneath the table?

But the Raptors didn't die!

The Prey have specially designed masks that keep you from taking their souls.

Nythan gave an involuntary twitch. *And* why *didn't you tell me before?* Nythan thought, narrowing his eyes. *How did everyone else not get taken in every other scenario?*

Until Prague, in every instance where you gathered someone's soul you unconsciously applied minimal force. When you consumed the Unas and the Ordo Solis, the colossal power you had accumulated couldn't be curbed in any way.

Why didn't Wrath get taken?

His mask had something that protected him.

How? It didn't look like it protected much.

Well, it evidently had something. *Otherwise, he'd be dead like the rest.*

Nythan stood and walked a few steps after he noticed a stand with two buttons. He pressed the top one, and gears shifted as the top of the glass structure opened outward.

Bane swelled. *Begin.*

Nythan sat down, entered the flow of life, and began drawing souls toward him. After half a dozen breaths, a tsunami of vaporous silver threatened to spill over the top of the open glass. He couldn't see past the wave of souls coating the entire outside of the greenhouse. In one fluid inhale, the silver avalanche tumbled through the top and down to Nythan.

He kept gulping, ingesting as much as possible. It took him half an hour to reach the furthest soul in the city. He stopped periodically to give Bane a chance to make himself ready for more souls. Bane strained to deal with the immense reception. Nythan grew so warm that he took his sweaty shirt off.

Nythan devoured almost all life as far as he could *see*. His mind's eye noticed several random souls that wouldn't budge no matter how hard he tried to draw them in.

I think they're in cars or some other enclosure. We don't have the time to get them all. It's time for us to run.

Nythan wiped his perspiration-soaked forehead. His skin burned as he pulled his hand away.

Where do we run? We killed the only Sanhe left, Nythan thought.

We'll figure it out on the way. Hurry downstairs and get back into the car.

Bane returned to digesting the souls.

Nythan descended the stairwell as fast as possible, wincing from the pain starting to build in his abdomen. Sweating bullets, Nythan moved through the back room but came to a stop at the threshold to the store. There, in front of him, stood the Sanhe monk, hands knuckled together. He bowed as Nythan approached.

Nythan noticed no mask on or near him. "How did you…?" Nythan trailed off, covering his left eye as he grimaced in pain. "Never mind."

The monk beamed, extending an open palm toward the door.

Nythan proceeded out of the strip mall and onto the dusty street. The stillness of bodies amid idling cars unnerved him. A cacophony of music still emanated from shops and car windows. Some people lay sprawled on the ground while others at outdoor cafes slumped over plates of unfinished food. Cars and trucks had crashed or skidded off the roadways; crushed and broken bodies lay within the smoldering vehicles.

Nythan walked forward and winced as his discomfort made way for a massive headache. He looked to the nearest car with a man slumped over its hood and saw a little pair of brown eyes peering at him through the window. He figured she was no more than five years old.

"Don't ask me to," Nythan said aloud. He suppressed a pang of guilt when his mind made the connection that the slumped man was probably her dad.

I won't.

Nythan waved. Her little fingers wiggled back. He bit his lip to distract himself from the ache hurting all over.

"How's she still alive?"

The windows are up. The car is on. The air conditioner is probably set to recirculate. I'd guess that the others are in a similar circumstance. You could reach them if you really wanted to.

The monk coughed, standing next to the car. Nythan got in and they drove away, weaving through motionless traffic. The swaying back and forth distracted him from the city of bodies they left behind.

CHAPTER 80

SQUARE ONE

They came to a stop on a vacant side street following a long drive. After much debate with Bane, Nythan had settled on going back to Quánzhōu to connect with the more aristocratic Sanhe. Nythan suggested they keep going to the final stage of their plan; Bane didn't agree.

You could barely handle twenty thousand souls, Nythan. I struggled to keep your body from being overwhelmed. It was too much for you.

I thought all this stuff I'm learning was supposed to prevent that, Nythan challenged.

It was. But it isn't doing the job. So we need to take additional steps to get there.

Then what's next? Everyone's bound to notice what we did this time.

That's true. Whatever time we had left just evaporated. That was a large Bhutan city. The world will notice the loss of all those people.

Why couldn't I take that much?

Your body temperature skyrocketed after you finished, and I think you went into mild shock from too much internal activity.

You're saying I reached my limit?

Yes. But that's no surprise. Remember how your body reacted when you took the soul of that elderly lady at the Grand Coven? Under normal circum-

stances, I'd tell you to give it a little while longer. You build tolerance like you build muscle. But like I said, we're on borrowed time.

So, what're our options?

Talk to Sanhe. The actual *Sanhe. See what they say about how we can discreetly build your tolerance.*

I'm not sure what we can do, Nythan mused. *At this point, it's volume. Gotta do volume to get volume, yeah?*

Yes.

Nythan got out of the car and followed the monk, continuing his conversation with Bane.

What's the backup plan? Nythan asked.

Better left unsaid for now.

Nah. I just killed twenty thousand people, Bane. Stop being vague and spill it.

It'll involve us lowering your body temperature and stopping all non-vital organs.

Can't you do that already?

Not without consequences to your health.

If you were to do it, would it help?

I don't know. I've never been in this situation before.

You've never had to take this number of people?

I've been in hosts who have taken multitudes more people than you have, but not this fast. Not with this kind of population density. I hid for hundreds of years. Populations have changed since then.

Nythan was led through a marketplace until they went inside a shop of scented candles. As the shopkeeper cashed out the last person, Nythan and the Sanhe monk stepped behind the register. The shopkeeper moved aside as the monk rolled the floor mat up, revealing a trap door underneath. The two of them climbed down into the familiar underground route with all the ladders. They proceeded until the monk pointed for him to climb up one such ladder, whereupon he found himself in the same small wooden closet that led down to the dragon-mirror hall. Nythan advanced down the hallway, past the small rooms with decorated curtains. He sensed numerous souls in each room this time. Nythan stepped down into the assembly hall. As an infinite number of him walked under the disco balls, Nythan's mind touched on the show that Bane had put on for the monks.

For you, as well.

Nythan approached the Hydra and saw a single monk sitting with his or her back to him. He wanted to ask the monk to take him to the one in charge. Nythan repeated Bane's translation.

"There is no one in charge here, *Shénlóng*," the monk spoke in English.

Nythan walked around to get a good look at the monk's face; it was the same woman he had met in the triangular garden.

"You're back," Nythan said. "I haven't seen you since you brought us here."

"I never left, *Shénlóng*."

She's toying with us again.

"Where're the ones I came with?"

"They are with the others."

"Show me."

The monk arose and walked toward the hallway. As they passed by the curtained rooms, she abruptly took a turn into one of them. The monk went to the far wall and pushed. A panel of the wall gave way and slid sideways to reveal another hidden corridor. Nythan stepped into the space and closed the access panel behind him. His enhanced vision cut straight through the resulting darkness; he only needed to contend with a slight shadowy haze that meandered through the short passageway. He followed the monk, who stretched out her arms and stumbled toward a door at the end of the corridor. Nythan extended his senses and felt a cluster of souls in the distance. When the monk reached the door, she peered through a tiny peephole before opening it.

She ushered him into a spacious closet crowded with sets of clothes on hangers. She closed the door as soon as she stepped through after him. They exited the closet and walked into a large hotel bedroom. Nythan saw Palaou in the kitchen through the open bedchamber door.

Nythan left the monk behind in the bedroom. He entered a living room of about two dozen Prey. Cards were being played at the dining table, some Prey huddled around the TV, others slept on the couches or cooked in the kitchen. They quickly took note of Nythan's arrival, giving him their full attention. None spoke a word. Palaou nudged his way through and bowed to Nythan.

"My Lord."

Nythan spied Devin in the crowd. "Devin," Nythan said. "I need that white lotus flower."

I thought you had forgotten about that.

Devin hurried out of the hotel room.

"Palaou, it's good to see you," Nythan fibbed.

"My Lord," Palaou repeated. "Was your trip successful?"

"Very," Nythan said. He surveyed the Prey. "You all have shown your-selves to be remarkably talented. We're nearly at the end of our struggle. It'll require every ounce of discipline and skill you have to see it through. The world will soon know who I am."

No one spoke a word.

"I'll need you to be ready," Nythan continued. "Things are going to get rough. Soon, you won't need to hide who you are."

The potent vigor emanating from the Prey intoxicated him. From the look of them, each had found a way to keep their zeal caged, but they clearly longed for some action.

I sense pure resolve from each of them. They're true believers.

Devin returned and gave Nythan a see-through plastic container. He took the white, multi-petaled flower out and handed the box to Palaou.

Is it go time?

Nythan turned and made his way through the Prey to the master bed-room. The monk waited, smiling as he approached.

"Tell me," Nythan said, coming to a stop in front of her. She regarded him with an even bigger smile. "How long have you been Sanhe?"

"I've been all my life."

"How long?" Nythan pressed.

"About three years, plus or minus," she said, winking.

"Do you like what you do?"

"I attend to an essential part of life," she replied. Nythan confirmed her emotions aligned with her words, sensing no malice or deceit.

"I need to get in touch with the leaders of Sanhe," he said, handing her the lotus flower. She peered down into its yellow heart.

Just like in the movies.

A grin spread across Nythan's face. The Sanhe monk bowed and half-turned toward the closet, saying, "I trust you can find your way back." The monk turned without waiting for a response and entered the disguised passageway.

Nythan raised an eyebrow.

"My Lord," Palaou whispered behind him.

"Yes, Palaou," Nythan answered, eyes still locked on the subtle outline of the door the monk just left through.

"May I assist you with something?"

Nythan's mind began racing, finally coming to rest on a single decision. *Ah, so you decided to rid us of him after all. It's about time.*

"Actually, yes," Nythan said, turning toward Palaou. "I need you to send Devin and Ahgo on a mission for me."

CHAPTER 81

RITE OF PASSAGE

Nythan waited an hour before the female Sanhe returned. She took him back to the dragon-mirror hall with the closets, and then they went down into the long underground tunnel. They marched for what seemed like half an hour, passing countless ladders along the way. Finally, she stopped at one.

"This is where my journey ends," she said, gesturing to the horizontal rungs next to her. "I will leave two small lights next to the appropriate ladder to guide your return."

"Thanks." He grunted as he took hold of the ladder and climbed, ascending a tight cylindrical tube. The climb itself lasted much longer than Nythan anticipated. At last, Nythan got to the top of the ladder and stepped onto a minuscule ledge. He figured he was at least four floors above ground. He grasped an overhead handle for balance and inspected the door in front of his face. He peeked through its peephole, as he had watched the monk do earlier, before opening the door.

This time he entered a room stuffed with shelves of neckties; he wandered through until he stumbled upon another door. Nythan slowly pushed it ajar and saw a tailor measuring something at a large table.

Nythan coughed. The tailor turned, scouting for the disturbance. When he spotted Nythan, he motioned *come here* with a brisk wave of his hand. Nythan went to the tailor, who wasted no time in taking his measurements. He said something Nythan didn't understand before getting up and scurrying through another nearby door. Nythan examined his surroundings. All around the circular room was sewing equipment, cloth trimmings, hanging suits, and rolls of fabric. Nine other doors spaced evenly along the wall around the room.

They're so secretive, he thought.

They live in an invasive society. Secrecy is currency.

The tailor came back, put a jacket down, and went into another room. He returned again, set down a shirt, then headed to a third room. He came and went until he had gathered an entire outfit.

The tailor spoke to him.

Translate, Nythan prodded Bane.

I can't. He's speaking a dialect I don't understand.

"Dress," the tailor said, tapping the jacket.

Nythan took the outfit in his arms, spinning around and eyeing the assortment of doors. "Where's the dressing room?"

The tailor shook his head, prying the articles of clothing out of his hands. "Dress!"

Just do it already. No one cares how small your wee wee is.

Nythan laughed aloud as he undressed and donned the outfit. The tailor went to work hemming the trousers and sleeves by hand, muttering the whole time. When he finished, the tailor walked to one of the nine doors, tapping it for Nythan to see.

"Six zero," the tailor mumbled, then returned to the task of measuring at the large table. When it became clear the tailor didn't intend to talk further, Nythan walked through the indicated exit. A short corridor dead-ended at an elevator, which he stepped inside.

"He told us the floor," Nythan mumbled with a smirk as he pressed the button for the sixtieth floor. As the lift climbed, Nythan inspected his black jacket and white shirt, shaking the lapel rolls to make it fit snug to his body. He liked his tie the most; it incorporated an array of bright green and dark teal patterns that weaved into a long slithering dragon. Nythan imagined that the tie represented *Shénron,* the dragon from the anime television series *Dragon Ball Z.*

Nythan stepped out of the elevator and noted an oblong table up against a window overlooking the city. At it sat six middle-aged people working on their laptops or reading books. They set aside their items as Nythan approached the table.

"Nǐ hǎo," Nythan recited.

Some smiled; others scrutinized Nythan. They were all dressed impeccably.

"Nythan," one of them said in accented English. "You wished to see us?"

Nythan expected he would need to confirm his identity. He looked left and right, trying to guess who among them would be his sacrificial lamb.

They don't have time to waste. So don't.

Nythan shrugged. "We encountered a problem. I need a way to increase my tolerance quickly." He looked at each of them in turn. "The end is near," he said, wanting to cringe from uttering the unavoidable cliché.

The man who greeted him looked to a woman on his left. "What do you propose?" she queried.

"I was hoping you had an idea of where I could discreetly get access to at least a hundred thousand people."

The group met him with silence.

"We do not have access to a hundred thousand discreet souls," the woman answered, after looking to her colleagues.

"I'm about out of ideas then. There isn't much time left. What happened the last few days will certainly motivate the Ordo Solis and the people they convinced to help them find me."

"We believe our strategy to be working as intended. Bhutan is a small and remote country. It will take time for the enemy to understand and mobilize."

"Okay, can we do more of that? Or speed it up?"

"Of course," the woman said. "But we advise a more deliberate pace."

"Why's that?" Nythan asked.

"It was inevitable the enemy would detect your return. If you command us to act rashly, it will hasten the enemy's resistance."

"What do you propose?"

"Trust," the woman asserted. "We will look after your well-being and are sensitive to the movements of others."

That's when Nythan surmised they were meeting with him only out of politeness. "Ooookay."

Nythan felt Bane laugh.

What's so funny? Nythan thought.

Feel them out, they're annoyed. They feel disrespected that you don't trust them to manage this.

Nythan felt out their emotions and confirmed Bane's assessment.

"I trust your leadership and expertise," Nythan said, gesturing to the members of the table.

Now what? Nythan thought.

You could try apologizing.

"I wanted to make sure that the silent monks I saw weren't the only ones running this operation. I'm happy to see that you've created a potent system. You all clearly know what you're doing."

That wasn't much of an apology, but it helped.

Nythan held his head high. *They're here to serve us. I don't need to apologize.*

"We have carefully planned your itinerary to fit your needs," the woman continued, speaking for the group.

"You might not be aware, but the last city was tough to swallow... no pun intended." When none of them laughed, Nythan coughed in embarrassment.

Tough crowd, Nythan thought. "Whatever you can do to speed up the process, I'd appreciate it."

"We will take that into account," the man next to the woman noted.

"Well, okay then," Nythan said, raising his hands from his sides before slapping his hips. "Anything else?" His mind brought him back to a time when his middle school principal had called him into his office for stealing the bus driver's cigarettes. This scene felt like that, except the principal had also told him how stealing made him a criminal.

He ended up being way *more right than he intended,* Nythan mused.

"Actually, there is," the woman added. "Your companions. They have expressed their wish to accompany you. We advised them against this, and they intend to beseech you nonetheless. They will serve a purpose, but we suggest they remain where they are until that time."

Nythan raised his eyebrows. These Sanhe types exhibited a boldness that their Unas and Raptor counterparts hadn't. It surprised him, given what he'd read about Asian culture.

Stereotypes.

"That's fine, where to next?" Nythan asked.

"You will be taken to your next destination."

"Sounds good," Nythan said, giving up. "Thank you for your time. It was great to meet you. Good luck."

The woman rose from her seat. "And you."

The others at the table rose with her. Nythan could only make out her nod to him. He turned around and went back to the elevator, mashing the key for the fourth floor.

How'd I do? Nythan thought.

Not bad. It did confirm one thing. Things haven't changed.

What do you mean?

Bane smiled. *They're still the most powerful of the three.*

I could see the Unas, but...more powerful than the Raptors?

Sanhe sit atop a skyscraper in a major Chinese city.

Nythan rubbed his chin. *Yeah, I guess that makes them pretty powerful.*

CHAPTER 82

THERE ARE ONLY TWO

Palaou and the Prey didn't dare voice their displeasure when Nythan told them he intended to take the advice of Sanhe leadership and continue without them. Palaou understood, but Nythan felt the bitterness coming from the Prey, who yearned to be close to him. He assured his loyal bodyguards that he needed them to fill a special role, and that heeding Sanhe's direction, no matter how obscure, would see that role fulfilled.

He left and worked his way back to the dragon-mirror hall, where several monks led him to a van and accompanied him on yet another lengthy journey. Police stopped them along the way, but a van full of monks apparently bought them ironclad credibility. They navigated to multiple cities, switching vehicles and the color of their robes at each location.

Nythan took all the inhabitants he could find whenever they stopped, with each city proving larger than the last. He managed twenty thousand souls at the first city; the next yielded fifty thousand. At the third city, Nythan's improving rhythm netted a hundred thousand souls with ease. They entered the largest cities on the last two days of the trip, where Nythan first consumed half a million people and then, finally, a million.

After they departed the last city, Bane took a pause while digesting their most recent stop. *A million souls…that's a record, for sure.*

Stop that, Nythan thought. *That's almost two million people dead because of us.*

Oh, come off it. It's a little late for you to reach for your morals.

It's never too late.

Well, whatever you call it, there's no going back now. You're definitely an accomplice.

Devil made me do it!

I am not the Devil. And I didn't make you do anything.

Nythan's shut his eyes and dragged his fingers across his scalp as a wave of guilt washed over him. "What have I done," he whispered.

You did what you had to.

I didn't have to.

You did if you wanted to live. But none of that matters anymore. You made the tough choice to persevere, and we're almost to the end because of that. I'm so close to freedom I can taste *it. The world will understand when the price paid means never having to deal with me again.*

Nythan let the silence between them linger as he struggled to stifle his guilt. After a time, he asked, *What do you mean by freedom, exactly? It's about time for you to spill the beans and tell me what you are and how you got here. You've been hinting at it since I discovered you.*

After I'm done absorbing this last batch, I'll tell you the story.

Fine, Nythan huffed. His body ached all over; his joints groaned at him to lie down.

Nythan stared out the window as they crossed a long bridge that spanned the width of a waterfall on their left and flowing rapids on their right. Toward the end of the bridge, they reached another checkpoint with armed soldiers. An armored personnel carrier sat fifteen yards away.

They halted the van. The soldier nearest them tapped on the window and the driver rolled it down.

"*Zhèngjiàn!*" the soldier said. The driver handed him a stack full of identification sheets.

These soldiers are on edge. There's a whole squad of them in that truck tank thing over there.

"It's an APC," Nythan said. He felt the squad out, sensing the anxiety in them. He turned his face down and put it against the person next to him. Out of the corner of his eye, he saw another soldier walk down the other side of the van.

The soldier tugged on the door, sliding it open. *"Chǔlái."*

The monks got out of the van; Nythan followed suit. The twinkling mist from the waterfall flooded Nythan's nostrils as the squad of soldiers got out of the APC and made their way closer.

"Zài zhèr miàn cháo pù bù pái duì," the soldier said, pointing to the downstream guardrail on the bridge. He and the monks lined up along the side of the bridge, facing downstream.

I don't like this.

The squad of soldiers lined up behind them. Sudden shots rang out across the river valley as the soldiers fired into the monks at close range. Some fell where they stood; others plunged over the guardrail and into the raging waters below. That's when the butt end of a rifle slammed into the back of Nythan's skull, knocking him out cold.

Nythan came to when the vehicle he was in ran over a pothole, but he managed to not make any sudden movement. He opened his eyes a tiny amount and peeked out through the slits to find himself on a cot. Standing over him, a soldier bowed his head while pressing his knuckles into the opposite palm. Another soldier sat to his right, thumbing a syringe dripping with a clear liquid. Nythan noticed a blood spot on the inside of his elbow and unfastened straps laying across his arms and legs.

As Nythan gathered his wits, he determined that he should take the soldier's souls before they realized their mistake.

Whoa, hold on there, cowboy, Bane prodded. *They're with us.*

"Huh?" Nythan said. The soldier next to him eyed Nythan.

Take a closer look.

It took Nythan only a second to understand what Bane meant as he glimpsed half a dozen soldiers piled on the floorboard. He also saw what looked like globs of red spray paint and gray goo around the van's interior.

What happened?

While you were drugged up, these two fellas took out the rest of their team. With your eyes closed, I could only see them as spirits, but I heard what went down. The driver is in on it too. They're taking us to an undisclosed rendezvous.

"Be fine," the soldier next to Nythan said, putting his arm on Nythan's forearm. "Don't go up." The soldier spoke rapidly in another language. The other guy, who'd been bowing to Nythan, replied in the same incomprehensible dialect.

One is asking if you can keep going. Tell them, "Wŏ méishì."

Nythan repeated the words.

The soldier next to him beamed and began chatting away at him.

He thinks it's exciting you speak Mandarin.

Nythan focused on the splattered gray matter. *How did this happen?*

We were ambushed by Chinese special forces. They started following us two cities ago. The Chinese government is aware of your existence now.

Where're we going again?

Not sure, they *seem to know though.*

How much further?

Like I said twice already, I don't know where we're going. They didn't mention how long a drive it is.

Nythan sat up, rubbing the back of his head.

Ouch, Nythan complained.

I'm working on that. It's hard to multi-task. Soul assimilation is more critical than numbing your pain receptors. Though I'm nearly done.

Nythan left Bane alone, letting the soldier continue to talk to him in a language he didn't understand. Nythan nodded and smiled. He then realized how others felt when he spoke a language they didn't know.

Tell him "Bié tíng xià, wŏ méishì. Dài wŏ qù xià ge dìfāng."

Nythan repeated the words. *What am I saying?*

You're telling him that we're fine and to take us to our next destination. Aaaaaand, now I'm done clearing out the souls.

Nythan clapped his hands as he felt a massive relief of pressure leave his chest. A gradual loosening spread throughout the rest of his aching body.

Nythan shook with excitement. "Spill it!" he demanded.

"Shénme?" the soldier next to him said.

Nythan looked at the soldier. "Shhhhhhh," he said, then lowered his eyes.

"Spill it," he whispered. "The elephant. The whatever else you said."

Okay. Okay. My very first life as a human. A regular human.

"What was your name?"

I no longer remember. But I lived in northern Bhārät, what you call India today. I was something of a local guru for the temple there; I dedicated myself to meditation after leaving society as an insignificant maker of something forgetful. Gurus went on regular journeys across the plains. It was a cleansing act. My elephant, Vāyu, was my closest friend and stayed with me wherever I went. One time, Vāyu was taking me on an extraordinarily long trip. I had gotten into the habit of meditating on his back as he stomped across the plains. It became a rhythmic beat from which I could open my aperture. Our ashram used to employ a practice that later became known as maranasati, *although the word we used translated closer to* cold mind. *We'd lie down flat and will ourselves to lose touch with different parts of the body as we contemplated our own deaths. For instance, I'd will my leg to die, and it would grow cold as it was abandoned by my heart.*

That actually works? Nythan raised an eyebrow.

I had a degree of success, yes. It's not as crazy as it sounds. You can mentally influence your body with surprisingly little practice. Try thinking about something sexual. Your heart rate will skyrocket, and your pores will open. This is that, but more practiced.

Mm-kay, what happened next?

Samadhi *happened next. We were all seeking samadhi. Seeking is the wrong way to think about it, but it translates well enough. In any case, I experienced samadhi on that trip on top of Vāyu. I was in a deep state of maranasati, in large part due to the plant I had smoked before setting out. Sometime during that trip, samadhi came. I slowly felt the same intense heat as you did. I knew this feeling was different than all previous meditation, but at the time, I didn't realize what samadhi was about to do. Right before I was to achieve* moksha, *which is kind of like ascension, something must have upset Vāyu, because he stood up on his hind legs and threw me off. I was in such a deep state of meditation that I never noticed Vāyu falling backward on top of me. I was either crushed to death or suffocated. I'm still not sure which. I think that my physical death interrupted everything. When my spirit tried to return to my body, it had nothing to come back to. I was tossed around until I slipped into another human being. When that person passed away, I tumbled out and got sucked into someone else, their soul pulling me like a magnet. For whatever reason, nothing seems to kill me, and this nightmare won't end. It's been going on and on like this for centuries.*

Nythan scratched at his hairline. *Hmm. I expected something with a stone of power, an ancient prophecy, and a magical dragon.*

You watch too many movies.

Yeah, but I...I don't understand how you survived samadhi. There seems to be something missing from that explanation.

I haven't been able to answer that question in three millennia. I should have either ascended to the spiritual world or died a physical death. Instead, I was left somewhere in between.

Oh c'mon, Nythan pressed. *Not even an idea?*

I told you all that I know. Samadhi came, it didn't take me, now I'm here.

There have been millions *of monks like you since then. How's it in all that time, no one else did what you did?* Nythan thought.

I have no idea, Nythan.

Okay, Nythan thought. *When you said that your elephant crushed you and you suffocated, how didn't you just die like a normal person? Like the way you kept me from that heatwave thing—*

Samadhi.

Sure, Nythan continued. *So the way you kept me from samadhi was by grabbing me and bringing me back. Do you think your suffocation brought you back?*

Well. See, I don't exactly *grab you to keep samadhi at bay. I persuaded your soul to move out of harm's way. When we take the souls of others, we are—in a sense—coaxing that soul to come to us. You could say* grabbed *or* pulled, *but a soul isn't something you command. It's something* influenced. *When samadhi comes, it comes for your soul. It's so overwhelmingly powerful that your soul absorbs right into it, like a glass of water poured into the ocean. A soul doesn't have an allegiance to the body. It's only renting out the space. That's why it's easy for us to take a person's spirit.*

So, wait, wait, wait. You said samadhi is like the ocean, and it's so powerful it just sucks everything in. Why doesn't it suck us all in right now? Didn't you say it was like a magnet?

The magnet only pertains to me and souls, not samadhi. In the water glass analogy, your body is the glass vessel, and the water is your soul. Your vessel carries your soul and keeps it afloat in the ocean. But it doesn't have a lid, so it's subject to being knocked over or engulfed by choppy waters. You're young, so your soul is new and lightweight. It keeps afloat. But as you get older, your soul gets heavy with experience until it sinks the glass into the ocean. That's why we got so much more power from that old lady in the Raptor headquarters. Her soul was extremely experienced.

And samadhi is the choppy water?

Samadhi's purpose is to knock over all the vessels in the ocean.

So where do you come into play?

Imagine water discovering it can jump from one glass to another.

Don't people already do that when they fight?

No, your vessel does the fighting.

So, glass jars can fight, but water can't. Yeah?

That's how it looks on the surface. But there's a secret. You see, the ocean moves itself. Thus, water in a vessel can move itself. But most never realize this until the end, right before they sink. Those that do jump out of their vessels without aim or intention. They splash into the ocean and end up in the same place as everyone else.

But that's not what happened to you, Nythan asserted.

You got it. It was supposed to happen, but it didn't. Samadhi's rough waves tried to tip my vessel into the ocean when something set it straight. The only thing I can think of was me suffocating or being crushed, but a physical death shouldn't have trapped me. All it did was make my freedom elusive. No matter how many vessels I'm in that get knocked over, the ocean doesn't take me. As I have said, I never achieved moksha…my freedom. I'm stuck in this never-ending struggle.

It sounds like the ocean is treating your soul like it's oil.

That's an interesting parallel.

What happens when the water jar you're in does tip over?

I get tossed around like a ragdoll until I get sucked into another vessel.

Kind of how oil swishes around when poured on top of water.

Are you suggesting that something caused the ocean to reject me like I'm oil?

That's what I'm hearing.

The vehicle came to an abrupt halt. The driver glanced into the cabin, speaking Mandarin.

Let's continue this later. We're here.

Nythan sprang up as the soldiers readied their rifles, opened the door, and jumped outside. The rich forest overhead blocked the moon. Nythan's enhanced vision pierced the darkness, illuminating everything from the mossy forest floor to the creeping bugs in the tree bark. A conversion van idled some feet away with its sliding door open, ready to receive him.

"In here, *Shénlóng*," a Sanhe man called out from inside the van.

Nythan turned around to say goodbye to his three saviors, who waited behind him. They smiled, motioning him into the van. Nythan jumped in, and his new ally shut the door and switched on the cabin light. Glossy coffins on racks lined the interior.

The man pointed to a coffin on a bottom shelf that was pulled out slightly with its top ajar. "This will be uncomfortable," he spoke in English. "They will not look there."

"Where?" Nythan asked.

"Please, go inside. We are behind and must catch up."

Nythan got inside the casket. The guy handed him a face mask, an oxygen tank, a bottle of water, and a couple of pills.

"Please take, they will help you sleep."

"It won't have any effect on me."

Yes, it will. I won't do anything to prevent it.

"Never mind," Nythan quickly said.

Nythan settled into the coffin bed, snuggling against the welcoming hug of soft linen. His new Sanhe acquaintance closed the casket and slid it back into the rack.

Nythan swallowed his pills, put the face mask on, and fiddled with the oxygen tank valve. It took him time to grow used to breathing in pure oxygen, but he got the hang of it.

Hey Bane.

Yeah?

Tell me about that discussion you had with Thomas Jefferson that ended up in his writings. You never told me what happened.

He and I attended the College of William and Mary. We both had the same professor, William Small. We would frequently get into heated discussions about the nature of force. Jefferson's favorite line was, "The movements of nature are in a never-ending circle." I argued that the author of nature wrote everyone into the world with a right to his own person and will, and that the actions of a person were not patterned after a circle. Jefferson used a version of that argument to justify the rebellion against the British.

That's cool, Nythan thought.

You never know what sort of impact you're going to have.

Nythan waited a long time before he grew drowsy. The practice felt foreign to him. He did a quick calculation and realized he hadn't slept in an entire month. His vision blurred and his mind stilled as he fell asleep, dreaming a dreamless dream.

CHAPTER 83

I CAME, I SAW, I CONSUMED

The casket thudded to the floorboard, ending his moment of rest. Someone pried open the container, and three faces peered at him. Two of the men helped Nythan out of the coffin.

"Easy, easy," Nythan cautioned as he worked the kinks out of his stiff back. He stood erect, rotating his shoulders. "We here?"

One pointed to the door. "Hurry." Nythan heard the whining of turbine engines.

This is an escape. Where are they taking us?

Nythan allowed himself to be guided out of the van toward a private jet about fifty yards away.

"Where am I going?" Nythan asked.

"Please," the Sanhe to his left repeated, gesturing forward.

"Where?"

"Please, please! You must go. Or else you never go!"

Nythan kept moving, stepping up the boarding stairway of the plane. Once inside, he counted four people: two pilots in the cockpit, one person at a table in the cabin facing Nythan, and another seated away from him across the aisle. The one at the table turned when Nythan stepped into the cabin; the guy seemed familiar, but Nythan couldn't place him. Whoever he was, he smiled big, tapped his ear, then made a circular motion with his finger.

Someone else is listening.

He tapped his ear again, pointing to various places around the cabin, then placed a finger on his lips.

Don't speak.

Nythan bit his tongue to prevent an involuntary scoff. *I don't have to speak Mandarin to know what that means.*

The person pointed to the seat across his table, then began chatting with his companion. Nythan went to his place, taking care to avoid making noise. His sensitive ears listened intently for anything out of the ordinary. He didn't hear much other than the two gentlemen talking, the pilots clicking buttons, and the humming of electricity. The intensity of the whirling of jet engines took some time for Nythan to drown out.

The aircraft door closed and the plane began moving.

Nythan listened to the conversation, which lasted the majority of the three-hour flight. Bane didn't tell him anything exciting. The gentleman's name across the table was *Heng*; apparently, he was an avid racquetball player and a high-level executive at a car equipment reseller. The other man paid Nythan no attention, and the flight went without incident.

They disembarked the aircraft and stepped straight into an expensive-looking Toyota sedan with dark-tinted windows. Once inside, Nythan made faces at Heng, trying to ask if he could speak. Heng disappointed him by shaking his head and tapping his ear.

They drove for twenty minutes in silence. Then Heng remarked something to the driver.

I don't know what he just said. I think he switched to Japanese.

They pulled into the parking lot of a rest stop with two bulky, multi-colored buses. Undecipherable symbols covered the entire length of each bus, the only readable word being, *Non-Step Bus*. Nythan saw a great many silhouettes through the bus windows, but his vision couldn't penetrate the tinted window panes. Heng opened the car door and got out with his companion, and Nythan followed.

Pay attention, something is about to happen.

Instead of boarding the bus, as Nythan expected, Heng continued into an adjacent building and located a public restroom. Heng took an open urinal. Nythan took the one beside him but didn't need to pee. He suppressed the awkwardness of trying not to stare at Heng the whole time by contemplating what might happen next. As Heng finished, he eyed Nythan and jerked his head toward the exit.

Go.

Nythan left the bathroom by himself. He didn't take two steps outside the restroom door before three touristy-looking individuals he didn't know approached and threw their arms around him, smiling at him and talking at him in Mandarin.

Heng emerged from the bathroom and walked by as if he didn't recognize Nythan.

One guy kept his arm around Nythan, and the three men escorted him back toward the car. But at the last minute, they ushered Nythan into the first bus full of people. The person behind Nythan gently stopped him next to an empty seat before continuing down the aisle. He recognized the faces of several Prey, dressed as tourists, scattered throughout the bus.

This is it.

What's it? Nythan thought with confusion.

All these people are loyalists. Every one of them, even those on the second bus. Wherever we're going, it's going to be the big one.

Nythan looked down at the other person in his row and stifled his discontent when he recognized Palaou's bald head facing out the window. He seated himself and kept quiet.

The door closed, and the bus lurched forward a few seconds later.

It's not his fault, Nythan reminded himself, but this thought did nothing to abate the urge to make Palaou the target of his ire.

We already established that it was yours. Your plan. Your failure.

It took Palaou a moment to realize who occupied the seat beside him.

"My Lord!" Palaou exclaimed.

Nythan forced a smile. "Good to see you, Palaou."

"My Lord, the country is in crisis. The news has said that the people of China and Bhutan are at war with an enemy. Many cities have been attacked."

"I know, I was there. Where're we going?" Nythan asked.

"I am unsure, my Lord. They will not say." Palaou leaned over, then whispered, "I believe we're in Japan."

Palaou sat back, resuming a conversational tone. "I am uncomfortable with this, My Lord."

"I know Palaou, but this is the end," Nythan said. "It'll be over soon. We've all come together to see it through."

"I suspected!" Palaou hissed. "None of them will confirm who they are!"

"They're very secretive," Nythan said. He paused, then turned to Palaou. "Do you mind if I ask you a personal question?"

Palaou's eyes widened. "My Lord, of course!"

"Why do you serve?"

Palaou expressed his delight as he responded. "My Lord, *you* are our savior. In you, I see our deliverance from the suffering of this world." Nythan saw tears forming in Palaou's eyes. "All the pain, all the hurt. *You* will take it away."

Nythan turned his head and stared into the back of the seat in front of him. He contemplated Palaou's words with a tinge of regret. Part of him felt mortified at how much all these people worshipped a nineteen-year-old kid, barely out of high school. They had made him the leader in a war that started long before he became a twinkle in his father's eye. He knew so little about how to lead these people or live up to their idea of him.

You don't. You just go on living, doing your best. People have this perception of a leader being like Superman or Wonder Woman, who always knows what to do. That's not leadership. It's the blind leading the blind. The leaders are slightly less blind than everyone else.

We have a saying in the military, Nythan mused. *Perception is reality.*

It's much more accurate to say that perception confuses reality.

Reality certainly is confusing.

Leadership is looking at that confusion and convincing others that you've figured it out.

What if you don't have it figured out?

Then your failure brings others down with you.

The bus traveled for almost an hour before, at last, everything came together all at once. Ahead, a giant billboard overstretched the highway. On it was written one word, in huge, bold letters...

TOKYO.

CHAPTER 84

...MUST COME TO AN END

The buses turned into a circular driveway and stopped in front of The Peninsula, a posh-looking hotel. Sanhe jumped off the bus, grabbing luggage out of the side compartments after they opened.

"What do we do?" Nythan asked.

"My Lord, all we were instructed to do was take a piece of luggage and follow," Palaou said, waiting for Nythan to get up.

"What luggage?

"My Lord, I am unsure."

Nythan got off the bus, seized a suitcase, and followed the group into the lobby of the hotel. Nythan and his companions gathered in front of the receptionist, who was busy checking them in.

"There must be eighty people here," Nythan said with amazement.

When he got to the front of the line, he received his key without having to speak. Palaou elected to stay with him, as did a number of Prey and Sanhe. When he walked into his room, he found Sanhe already inside, waiting for him. Nythan set his clunky suitcase on the ground and looked at them for a clue about what would come next.

"*Shénlóng,*" one of them said, bowing. "My name is Heng."

"That's funny," Nythan said. "The last guy's name was Heng, too. What're we doing here?"

"This is for you, *Shénlóng*," Heng gestured all around. "We have booked the entire floor for our party so that we will not be disturbed. We have reserved Peter, the hotel's restaurant on the twenty-fourth floor, exclusively for tonight's banquet." Heng bowed low. "The feast will be held in your honor."

"Okay," Nythan sighed. "So, I have some hours to kill. No problem." Nythan paced the room. "What's in the suitcases?"

"They contain clothing and items that will be of benefit. Your companions from the west will find it acceptable."

One of the Prey unzipped the nearest suitcase and slung it open. He threw out light green and dark teal clothing, revealing a submachine gun and a handgun underneath. Another suitcase contained dark business attire, Prey masks, and grenades. Nythan felt the Prey's approval.

They brought an entire arsenal in those suitcases.

As the Prey left to go hunting for more luggage, Nythan peered out his window across the vast city. He entered the flow of life, withdrawing instantly as the sheer magnitude of souls assaulted him.

I can't even begin to count them. There are many *millions.*

Nythan went back toward the living room and turned on the television. Other Prey who had found adequate gear out of the suitcases sat nearby. Nythan watched them don their signature dark masks featuring twisted faces of agony, horror, and rage, then he looked at their Sanhe counterparts.

Those are some strange colorful bathrobes they have there, Nythan thought.

They're kimonos, not bathrobes.

Ohhh. Nythan smirked. *Well* excuse *me.*

He asked one of the Prey for a knife and sliced his mother's initials into the armrest while flipping the television channels. Several clicks later, he came across an English-language news broadcast. The headline scrolling across the bottom of the screen said it all. *China Militarizes, Calls Martial Law Amid Highly Contagious Disease Outbreak.* The news anchor told a story about how China was engaged in a struggle with an enemy attacking its cities. The Chinese government wouldn't identify the perpetrator or state how the disease connected to the attack. Already reports were circulating about a phantom menace eradicating the entire populations of cities. The news anchor reported on the outbreak bearing a striking resemblance to the two in Bhutan. The broadcast then switched over to the United Nations, where the Press Secretary spoke. Nythan didn't pay much attention until the spokesperson mentioned his nickname.

"The Security Council's rapid approval of this measure makes it the first peacekeeping mission with authority to investigate the Soulstealer…" the Secretary droned.

Bane sighed. *It doesn't matter now. By the time they figure themselves out, this city will be ours, and I'll be rid of the chains that bind me.*

Nythan nodded his agreement, switching off the television. He meditated with Bane until he was roused by Palaou for the banquet. Palaou insisted that Nythan wear a tuxedo, convinced it was the most important occasion of Nythan's life. He complied, feeling it pointless to resist.

Palaou inspected every inch of the jacket and pants, removing frayed strands of fabric and blemishes that his inner OCD demanded be fixed. Nythan dressed and scrutinized himself in the mirror, feeling proud of how well he cleaned up.

It's time.

"It's time, my Lord," Palaou said. A smile crept across Nythan's face. As he walked outside his room, the hallway lights shut off; the only lighting came from the red emergency exit signs. Sanhe and Raptors lined both sides of the hall, stretching all the way to the elevator. Bane made no comment about the ceremony.

The Prey had outfitted themselves with choice handguns, submachine guns, and grenade pouches. Each masked Raptor wore a black suit. Sanhe had chosen more exotic clothing and accouterments. Their sophisticated kimonos came in a three-piece robe. The combo of a white-collared shirt, cardigan-like blouse, chained half coat, and kilt reminded him of long skirt pajamas. They too wore masks—V-shaped dragon faces with horns at the chin, ears, and head, running down the middle of the forehead to the nose. Each costume had a scaly dark green-blue texture. They toted an assortment of shotguns and swords.

Nythan ascended the elevator to the twenty-fourth floor in the company of as many Prey and Sanhe as the elevator could hold. When they stepped from the elevator, he observed a hallway to the right lined with people. A wall of guards blocked the path to the left. Nythan proceeded down the hall, which led him to a high-ceilinged restaurant with a flood of windows on the far side that offered a panoramic view of the city. A centerpiece table rested on a raised platform with built-in liquor bars on the left and right. Nythan noticed restaurant staff and bartenders scattered about the room, each chaperoned by Sanhe or Prey. He didn't need to sense the staff's emotions to know they weren't there because they wanted to be.

They look just as scared as I did when I first encountered you, Nythan mused as he wandered to the windows.

He looked out and saw with delight the night sky above the bright city lights. His mind's eye conjured the peaceful image of his teacher from the Watwa monastery meditating with him on the wooden floor, and he recalled the words she spoke to explain the part he would play.

A wet streak drizzled down his cheek as he recalled images of dead bodies strewn across the streets of cities whose names he didn't know. He wiped away the tear on his tuxedo sleeve.

If I don't do this, it'll never stop. Nythan nodded his head vigorously. *One more time...just one more time. Then he's gone and it's over. Everyone gets peace.*

Something glittered far below. Nythan looked down, and his enhanced vision saw flashing lights near the base of the hotel. Japanese police barricaded and stood watch at the entry points to the hotel driveway. Nythan scrutinized the streets beneath him, seeing more flashing lights a few miles out, making their way toward him.

They know we're here.

They know something's wrong, he thought. *They probably don't know it's us yet.*

It won't stay that way for long.

Nythan turned and walked to the center table. A mass of Sanhe and Prey waited at the entrance. He gestured at them and they poured in, spacing themselves throughout the room. Palaou slid a chair out and seated Nythan.

Nythan gazed up at Palaou, relieved at the absence of anger toward his loyal servant. "This may be the last time we see each other, Palaou." He felt bleak acceptance emanating from his friend.

"Yes, my Lord. I knew this day would come," he said, smiling through tears. "But it is for the better."

Palaou reached behind his coat jacket, pulled out a Raptor mask, and affixed it to his face. Nythan gave Palaou a sad smile, finding it fitting that his loyal friend had chosen a somber-faced Raptor mask for the occasion.

Once you start, take your time. It won't matter what they do down below.

"Open the windows," Nythan commanded. Sanhe and Prey attempted to pry open the glass, but something held them in place. One of the Prey grunted loudly with frustration. He stepped back and shot a window with a burst from his weapon. It fell away in pieces down the side of the building.

"Well, I guess that's—" Nythan began before the sound of gunfire and breaking windows drowned his voice out.

Better hurry. They'll be charging up those stairs in no time.

Nythan observed what remained of the glass wall with satisfaction as the cold wind pricked his face.

He closed his eyes and entered the flow surrounding him, braving the intensity that immediately assaulted his senses. It took time for him to grow numb to the feeling; Bane promptly pulled him out.

What's wrong?

There're so many souls, Nythan thought. *I can barely think. I'll get used to it, though.*

Nythan reentered the peculiar state, facing the assault once more. As he again grew numb to the extreme sensation, he inhaled, ushering the souls of the restaurant staff to him. He then concentrated on drawing out the life of the city, but he soon felt an intense heat engulfing him. Bane yanked him back to reality.

That was too close.

What do you mean? Nythan thought, gasping.

Whatever you're feeling is affecting me as well. I didn't feel samadhi come until it was already on you. I'm surprised you survived that.

How come I was able to last so long?

I'm not sure. I think it's because of the sheer volume of life there is here. Samadhi came much sooner than usual, that's for sure.

Nythan returned to the flow, drawing more of the city to him. He periodically glanced through the shattered windows and saw a tsunami of souls just starting to form above the skyscrapers. About ten minutes later, Nythan got out of his chair, walked to the building's edge, and looked over the streets below.

"My Lord, is something wrong?" Palaou called through his voice filter while fidgeting with his mask.

Nythan didn't respond; he remained fixated on the tsunami a mile from him that was charging over the body of rivers and forest separating the hotel from downtown Tokyo. An ethereal silver mist coated everything in sight. Nythan looked down, staring into the souls of the police hovering a few feet away. He could see their still bodies lying on the ground far below. One stared straight up at Nythan, wide-eyed with frozen surprise.

Nythan slurped up the departed souls. He peered to his right and left and felt the admiration his servants had for his work.

We're almost there, Nythan thought. He returned to the center table.

After half an hour of taking in a steady stream of souls, the bulk of the city arrived en masse. Nythan helped himself to the foul feast, inhaling as much as he could. After some time, his skin grew hot and pressure built in his chest. Nythan wiped his damp brow.

I'm having a hard time. Slow down.

How slow is slow? Nythan thought.

As slow as I tell you. Just hold on.

Nythan opened his eyes again. The silvery mist was packed so densely that he couldn't find his hands, nor could he distinguish anything more than an arm's length away. He exhaled, creating a small air pocket around his face. The souls edged back toward him in slow motion.

Nythan's ears perked up as he distinguished the *chop-chop-chop* of a rotor blade.

What's that? Nythan thought.

It sounds like a helicopter.

He reached out but was only able to detect a subtle disturbance somewhere off in the distance. The sound grew in intensity, and Nythan eventually sensed the overlap of at least three inbound helicopters.

Why're they able to come here? Nythan thought, unable to keep his hands from shaking.

Dunno. They might have come from outside the city. Draw the life out of them.

Nythan resumed drawing souls toward him. He ingested a massive amount of souls as he tried to kill the people in the helicopters, but he only heard the aircrafts growing closer. His chest starting throbbing, and his body tingled from a scalding sensation on his skin. Nythan clutched himself, wincing.

It's not working. They must have something that keeps us from reaching them.

Nythan still couldn't see anything, but he figured the uninvited guests couldn't see him either.

We're both blind. Use that to your advantage.

How on earth can I use that to my advantage? Nythan pointed into the cloud. *They're in a helicopter.*

Maybe now's a good time to use the army you brought with you.

"Palaou!" Nythan shouted over the increasing sound of the propeller blades.

"My Lord!" Palaou answered.

"They're coming. Multiple helicopters. Don't let them get close!"

Although he couldn't see them, Nythan clearly perceived the helicopters making their way to him. He guessed they'd reach him in less than a minute. Tiny gusts of wind sliced through the ethereal cloud next to his face. It appeared as though someone had taken a finger and skimmed it along the surface of a pool of water. The mist parted; Nythan heard the *rata tata tat* of submachine gun fire and hoped his people knew where to shoot. He barely saw the flashes emanating from their guns.

This can't be good for us. Try again!

It's starting to hurt, Nythan protested. He felt like someone had dumped molten lava all over his body.

No time! I'll manage. Do it!

Nythan again drew the mass of souls toward him, trying to capture the helicopter's occupants. Despite this effort, he detected no change in the helicopter's course. His attempt did, however, have an undesirable impact on his level of pain. He doubled over on top of the table, gritting his teeth. It felt as though he had overgorged himself with food. Which, Nythan figured, was literally true.

Bane rummaged within him.

What's wrong? Nythan thought, massaging his abdomen.

You're not taking this well.

Naw, ya think?

Sit tight, I'm going to—

Before Bane finished, two machine guns started firing in the distance. Nythan's hands clamped down on his ears as the thunderous sound punished his enhanced hearing. Fragments of furniture began dancing all around him. He threw himself to the ground and crawled in the direction he thought would lead him to cover. Agony visited various parts of his body as shrapnel struck him.

Something raked his leg, causing Nythan to cry out. He rolled over to his left and dragged himself across the step-down. His head knocked against the base of the raised platform, but it provided him a shield from the assault.

Uh oh.

Nythan couldn't think straight enough to comprehend what Bane meant. He didn't feel any more pain in his leg, but he instinctively grabbed at it and was horrified to find nothing below the knee.

"Wha...WHAT?" Nythan heard himself scream.

I stemmed the pain. Nythan, you need to focus. Get me to where I need to go. More souls!

"WHAT HAPPENED?"

Nythan. Focus. Your leg is gone.

"GROW IT BACK!"

I can't fix something that doesn't exist anymore.

"MAKE IT COME BACK!"

Stop screaming! You want your leg back? GET ME MORE SOULS SO I CAN HELP YOU!

Nythan settled himself and quickly began sucking in more souls. A painful expansion within reminded him of his limits.

I'm...ugh.

Bullets flew everywhere, whizzing by his face and chewing up the furniture and fixtures throughout the restaurant. Raptors and Sanhe rushed into the room to join the fray. They blindly fired in the direction of the destructive guns that could be heard but not seen.

I…ackkkk!

Nythan cried out in torment at each inhale and curled into the fetal position. Someone tripped over him and crashed onto the raised platform. Nythan opened his mouth loosely, gasping for the souls around him.

I'm losing control.

Someone started shooting directly over Nythan. The sound devastated his already deafened ears. Nythan could make out the colorful kimono of a Sanhe soldier. Blood spattered all over as the soldier shook and crumpled to the floor.

Stop.

He kept inhaling, siphoning the dense cloud.

Nythan, STOP!

Nythan couldn't comprehend what was transpiring around him. Sounds muted, and his vision blurred. He opened his mouth for another scoop of souls.

I can't, it's too much…

In one last moment of clarity, time slowed as Balin's rendition of Moonlight Sonata played in Nythan's ears and his eyes followed a bullet sailing over his nose. As it struck a wall, his vision fled. Nythan blinked, trying to see, but he could no longer recognize the ground he laid across. Instead, he *saw* a dark brown background with a turquoise luminescence take form. It changed to green, then to bright blue with flecks of yellow. Squashed geometric shapes and squiggles flashed before him. He opened and shut his eyelids, but doing so didn't change the vision.

Nythan flailed about. "Huh?" His senses were so overwhelmed with pain that he didn't know if he was still alive. Something in his stomach burst with a sickening crunch, and he began to thrash in a complete frenzy.

This wasn't supposed to hap—

"HELP!" Nythan howled.

There's nothing I can—

"HELP!" Nythan cried out again.

*F*** it. Nythan. If you can hear me, keep drawing in souls. There's noth-*

ing I can do to save you, but I can keep you alive long enough to give me the power I need.

Nythan wildly bucked and choked as his body tried to die. He drew in souls at random, his mind as blank as a sheet of paper.

We're almost there. Push, Nythan, PUUUUUUSH!

The thundering guns continued their bombardment, but there was notably less resistance.

C'mon, Nythan. Don't you quit on me now. You've gotten further than anyone else. Keep going!

Blood oozed from Nythan's ears and nose. He foamed at the mouth.

Few weapons fired back at their enemy. The helicopter guns kept pounding away, finally silencing the last of the opposition in the restaurant.

Nythan was motionless, save for the occasional involuntary twitch. Palaou crawled next to Nythan and clutched his shoulder. "My Lord," he said over the sound of the helicopters, shaking Nythan. "My Lord, can you hear me?"

He can't hear you.

"My Lord," Palaou said, continuing to shake Nythan.

He's gone, Palaou.

Bane roamed Nythan's body, imbuing him with enough life to keep him from dying a physical death.

I'm so close. It's right there. Keep going, you son of a b****.

"Don't worry, My Lord, I'll get you to safety." He stood and dragged Nythan into the hallway, wading through the haze of souls. A dozen Raptors and Sanhe lined the corridor. A Prey muscled a smaller Sanhe man out of the way and tossed Nythan over his shoulder.

"We must leave," Palaou said, throwing a concerned look down the hall to where Sanhe battled an unseen foe. "What's happening? Who's there?"

The Prey touched his earpiece, saying, "Owl to roost, owl to roost, bait the worm."

He turned and led Palaou, four other Prey, and several Sanhe around a corner to two elevators. As they approached, the far elevator dinged open. Their group immediately retreated as a squad of heavily armed people in helmets with polycarbonate face shields ran out and engaged them. Both sides suffered casualties, but Bane's side lost more by getting caught in the open. The doors of the nearest elevator slid open as one of the Raptors pulled the pin on a grenade and hurled it toward the furthest elevator. The enemy squad dove in every direction before a deafening blast reverberated through the hall. A second squad of soldiers spilled out of the nearest elevator and joined the fight, followed by the survivors of the first squad.

Sanhe and Raptors backpedaled in full retreat, taking as many twists and turns as possible to slow their pursuers. They made it halfway down a long corridor when a team of soldiers rounded the corner at the far end. The Sanhe fighter in front pivoted and threw his shoulder into a nearby swinging door. One of the Prey chucked another grenade as the enemy tried to push on their position. Bane's faction barged into a laundry room with row upon row of washers and dryers. They searched in vain to find another way out.

A split second later, the double-swinging traffic doors crashed open, and the attack squads charged into the room. Nythan's savior threw him behind a row of dryers as the two forces engaged in a merciless fight. A grenade exploded close to the door, blowing twisted metal and sheetrock everywhere. But the shootout didn't last long. Their enemy surrounded and eliminated all remaining opposition, leaving Palaou and Nythan unprotected.

Palaou crouched over, hands in the air, trembling uncontrollably. His white shirt was drenched in red. As a dozen muzzles trained on Palaou, he backed up against a washer and slowly slid to the ground, whispering with his last breath, "Be at peace, my Lord."

Nythan's body lay unresponsive, both physically and mentally. Bane kept him alive, squeezing out as many inhalations as possible.

C'MON, I'M THIS *CLOSE! AHHHHHHHHHHHHHH!*

A third team came rushing into the laundry room, scurrying across the debris. "Is it him?" someone exclaimed. Bane recognized the voice but couldn't view through Nythan's eyes anymore.

"Move!" the voice demanded, "I want to see him." Without a dense cloud of souls obstructing his sight, Bane could only detect the outline of the robust entity that approached.

Bane felt the man touch Nythan's neck with his fingers. "The pipsqueak's still alive." A few seconds later, the man said, "Smile, b****, you're on camera! Yeah, I know it can't be easy for you right now, but tough s***." Bane sensed intense bitterness emanating from the person. "Take a good look, boys. This is the face of your enemy," the guy said, cocking his gun. "This is for the Ordo Solis…and all those you made suffer."

Bane finally realized who spoke.

Steven, you fat bastard!

"For Raeleigh."

A loud *BANG* echoed throughout the room, marking the final end of Nythan.

CHAPTER 85

FROM THE ASHES

Bane raged at Nythan. *You're a failure. I was* this *close to my freedom!*

Bane felt Steven jump on top of Nythan and attempt to put a glass jar over his lips. Not only did the rigid bottle fail to fit the contours of Nythan's jaw, but it also didn't cover Nythan's nostrils. Bane tumbled out in the wake of Nythan's last breath and entered the world of what Nythan had always referred to as the breathing state. He perceived impressions of things in the room as the gray and white flowed against and around them. Bane attempted to merge with Steven while he stared down at Nythan's mangled corpse, but instead he bounced off the gray outline of Steven's face shield. The air-handling system in the laundry room created currents that threw Bane about like a ragdoll.

Motherfu—AHHHHH!

Bane slipped through filaments of white that stretched all around the room before ricocheting off one of the dryers. He bounced about the room, trying and failing to grab hold of anyone within reach, but the forward momentum proved too fierce to navigate. Bane wished for the nightmare to end. With any luck, he would be able to merge with another soul before being sucked out of the room. As if right on cue, the traffic door swung open.

Aw, c'mon!

A fresh draft spearheaded its way in while muscling the stale air out. He felt intense dismay as it drew him closer to the exit.

Of all the things that could happen, Bane hated this the most.

He crossed the threshold and entered what felt like a Herculean tornado as new and old air engaged in a fight that took no prisoners. The vortices spun him so fast he thought he would rip in two, shooting him out of the tornado and slapping him against a hallway window.

Damn, I can't stand those things.

Bane slithered along the hall with enough control to surf the wind waves flowing through the corridor. He attempted to attach himself to each person that he flew by but couldn't impact the flow's directional force.

All this power and I still can't navigate this worthless plane of existence.

Bane was slung into the restaurant and dragged out of the shattered windows far above the streets. Bane saw an enormous number of souls drifting aimlessly, no longer responding to Nythan's siren call.

Bane ascended at the mercy of the air currents. A jet stream hooked Bane and whipped him along at high speed. Bane was battered senseless, unable to tell if the winds held him for minutes or months. He was blinded to everything except for the white swirls of air passing him by.

At long last, Bane could feel himself floating back toward the earth. He fell between a cluster of skyscrapers before getting swept through the streets by the turbulence of zooming cars. He whizzed past men and women going about their day. Bane tried and failed miserably to grab hold of them. Following a series of bumps and turns, he was sucked into a building where the flow of air became more regulated.

The strength that Bane had accumulated in Nythan gave him the capability to exert a minute amount of directional force. Bane glided into a large room and watched as the currents of air pressed against and flowed around the gray outlines of countertop gadgets, allowing him to make out a beaker, a microwave, and a Bunsen burner. He looked around at the silver wraiths of eight people going about their work. He zeroed in on two of them, the first seated on a lab stool and the second towering over him.

"Have the toxicology results for the *Nature* paper submission completed for our private meeting tomorrow," the second said to the first in a British accent.

The soul of the underling seemed to wither. "Of course, you're right…and the final studies aren't scheduled to complete until—"

"I don't want excuses," the boss cut in. "Just get it done. And make sure they're reproducible."

Bane focused his attention on the boss. *You're the one.*

Bane moved toward the boss's face. When Bane saw white threads of air slip into the man's nostrils, he nudged himself forward before grey exhaled breath could blow him backward. Bane latched onto the boss's nose, causing the man's nostrils to twitch.

Bane waited for the grey exhalation, then cartwheeled downward as white strands carried him straight into the man's airway. Bane felt the familiar tug from the man's soul as he surfed down the boss's windpipe and into his lungs. The man bent over, put his hands on his knees, and started panting.

"Are you okay?" the underling said.

The boss squeezed his eyes shut and touched his temples. "Stop talking."

The underling tilted back on his stool.

The immense gravity of the boss's soul pulled Bane through his lungs and clamped Bane firmly against his soul. The boss stood upright and leaned against a bulky piece of equipment for support. His head jerked as he gasped for breath, and a silver stream erupted from the subordinate's mouth and slipped through the boss's lips. The subordinate's body teetered for a moment then collapsed to the ground.

Mmmmmmmm, I made it once again.

The boss flailed his arms, knocking a Bunsen burner off the countertop. It clattered to the floor, raising the attention of the other scientists and lab techs. The boss screamed in agony as something struck his lungs, causing him to convulse as he coughed.

His eyes darted around the room. "I—I do…I don't…I don't know what—" The boss pointed to the subordinate. "Help him!"

A few of the scientists rushed forward, two stood frozen in place, and one ran for the exit.

The boss's fingers dug into his own chest as his lungs were squeezed. He wheezed, and the silver souls of the men in the room left their bodies.

The last sound the boss heard was a thud as the tech running for the exit stumbled headfirst into the lab door.

The boss stood, wide-eyed, his whole body shaking uncontrollably.

"Oh my God," he whispered.

God had nothing to do with it, wretch.

Epilogue

You persevered. You listened. The hardest part is over. Now you get to judge me, scold me, and tell me what a horrible monster *I am. I accept your criticism as the lion accepts the gazelle's cry. For those of you who see it different, I offer you a chance to join me. Embrace...a larger view of the world, one that sees it delivered...from* me.

Enlightenment carries with it a heavy burden—awareness of the evil *inside you, influencing your every move. With it comes the knowledge that, should you be where I am, you would have done what I did. My freedom comes at a terrible price, and I have no choice but to pay it.*

What's that? Too much for you? Are you unable to cope with the choices that must be made? There's no shame in that. But, expect to be moved aside by those who can.

Like I said in the beginning...you shouldn't have come.

But I'm glad you did.

You reached the end! I hope you enjoyed reading *Soulstealer* as much as I enjoyed writing it.

I ask that you please **rate and review** wherever you bought the book, especially if it's Amazon. I'd also appreciate a review on Goodreads. **It's so helpful to me as a self-publishing author.**

Your review will let others know that this is a book worth reading, and your rating will move *Soulstealer* to the **top of the list**! Thank you so much for your support!

☺

Scan the QR codes below or type the link into your browser.

bit.ly/SoulstlrAmznRvw

bit.ly/SoulstlrGR

GET CONNECTED!

SoulstealerBook.com

@SoulstealerBook

fb.me/SoulstealerBook

bit.ly/SoulstlrCmnity

discord.gg/upzZnZQ

bit.ly/SoulstlrYT

@SoulstealerBook

/r/SoulstealerBook

ACKNOWLEDGMENTS

This five-year labor of love wouldn't have happened
without the help of so many others.

**There's a long list of extraordinary people
who made this story what it is today.**

I kept track as best I could as time passed. I apologize if I missed you!

A huge thank you, in no particular order, to:

My family	Trisolaran5151	Greg H.
Kelhi D.	maisels	Dr. Hal T.
Sydny M.	SuperCarbideBros	Andrew J.
Pamela C.	Uqbari	Grace J.
Cassy B.	Rks1157	Jenna C.
David S.	Vignaraja	Zella B.
Amy T.	national_sanskrit	Damonza
Ashlesha G.	Hunt B.	Michelle C.
Myrka & Ra'ef	Xiaobo G.	Leo R.
Steven, USPS Hanscom	Kimberly Q.	Sharon N.
Phantagor	Class 18C SOS, C36	Maggie M.
Jake A.	Donsun N.	Jeremiah H.
Allorria H.	Lauren F.	Alexandra G.
Oscar S.	Dr. Mary H.	Vince B.

THE AUTHOR

SHANE BOULWARE is an unconventional idealist from Orlando, Florida. *Naturally*, he commissioned as a Contracting Officer in the United States Air Force in 2012, where he promptly got tased, was hit with pepper spray, participated in a mock riot, jumped out of an airplane, and lived in a combat zone. These experiences tempered his creative instinct and led him to publish two music albums, found an innovation company, break a Guinness World Record, and learn over sixteen dance styles.

Having grown up a huge fan of *Dune*, Star Wars, Stargate SG-1, Warhammer 40K, Harry Potter, *Avatar: The Last Airbender*, and *The Lord of the Rings*, Shane always wanted to create and share a world of his own. His imagination set him on a path to write the supernatural thriller, *Soulstealer*, and its sequel, *Ordo Solis*.

When he's not negotiating contracts or salsa dancing the night away, you can find Shane taking his creative passion out on an unsuspecting keyboard. If you want to know when his next book will be available, visit his website at ShaneBoulware.com, where you can sign up to receive release updates and join a community of savants, swashbucklers, and nerds.

Made in the USA
Las Vegas, NV
08 September 2021